SQUAD KILL

ALSO BY JACK CAMPBELL

The Lost Fleet:
Dauntless
Fearless
Courageous
Valiant
Relentless
Victorious

The Lost Fleet: Beyond the Frontier:
Dreadnaught
Invincible
Guardian
Steadfast
Leviathan

The Lost Stars:
Tarnished Knight
Perilous Shield
Imperfect Sword
Shattered Spear

The Genesis Fleet:
Vanguard
Ascendant
Triumphant

Outlands:
Boundless
Resolute
Implacable

The Pillars of Reality:

The Dragons of Dorcastle

The Hidden Masters of Marandur

The Assassins of Altis

The Pirates of Pacta Servanda

The Servants of the Storm

The Wrath of the Great Guilds

The Legacy of Dragons:

Daughter of Dragons

Blood of Dragons

Destiny of Dragons

Empress of the Endless Sea:

Pirate of the Prophecy

Explorer of the Endless Sea

Fate of the Free Lands

The Doomed Earth:

In Our Stars

Destiny's Way

Other:

The Last Full Measure

The Sister Paradox

SQUAD KILL

JACK
CAMPBELL

SQUAD KILL
Published by Vault
In association with Aethon Books

ISBN 978-1-63849-348-8 (hardcover)

First AETHON: Vault Edition: Summer 2026

Printed in the United States of America.
1st Printing.

Aethon Books
www.aethonbooks.com

Vault Storyworks
www.vaultstoryworks.com

Cover art by Filip Dudek. Cover typography by Steve Beaulieu.
Print formatting by Kevin G. Summers, Adam Cahoon, and Rikki Midnight.

To

Every ensign and second lieutenant who got tossed into the deep end of the pool while wearing lead boots, but somehow managed to survive while also learning a bit along the way.

And to every enlisted man and woman who saved the butts of those ensigns and second lieutenants when mistakes were made or were about to be made.

For S, as always.

SQUAD KILL

ONE

"WHAT the hell are you doing aboard my ship, Ensign Osiris Aquino?"

Aquino, standing before the desk of Captain Carmen Jardyce, wondered once again whether he should salute. But Captain Jardyce was a civilian in command of a civilian ship, so, probably not. Jardyce had a nicer, bigger office than a Navy captain on a warship would have, and had clearly remained in command long enough to have populated the office with personal memorabilia. Along with an imposing wooden desk that she now sat at, glaring at Aquino as she awaited his response. "I've been assigned to command the Marine detachment aboard this ship, Captain."

"What?" Captain Jardyce squinted at the orders Aquino presented. "You're not a Marine."

"I'm an ensign," Aquino said, trying to hide how little he wanted this job, and how little he liked the way the Navy bureaucracy had shoveled him into it. Captain Jardyce wouldn't care about any of that, and was unlikely to be impressed by a junior officer whining about his fate. "That naval rank is equivalent to that of a Marine second lieutenant, and naval officers and Marine officers are equivalent in terms of organizational alignment. Since there's a shortage of Marine second lieutenants, I was given this assignment."

Captain Jardyce made a disgusted noise, flinging out one hand in irritation. "That's just like the military. Something needs done but they don't have the right means to do it, so instead, they offer up something that technically meets the requirement without actually doing so. How much do you actually know about being a Marine, Ensign Aquino?"

"Very little, Captain."

That honesty earned him a brief, thin smile before Jardyce turned serious and aggravated again. "Listen, Ensign. The *Darwin* is a civilian space research and exploration vessel. Because our mission requires us to visit new planets, the rules require us to have a detachment of Marines aboard. I follow the rules, Ensign Aquino. But that doesn't mean I like them. My job is to transport and care for the scientists who use the *Darwin* as their home base. As far as I am concerned, and as far as those scientists are concerned, you and your Marines are useless, disruptive cargo. In an emergency, you have some authority on this ship, but if you declare an emergency, I'm telling you now that you'd better have the best damned reason for it in the history of the entire universe or I will personally boot your ass out of an airlock even if we're a long ways from anywhere. Barring such an emergency, you are under my authority. Understand?"

"I understand," Aquino said, trying not to let any feeling into his voice or expression. He had looked into the regulations on the way here and knew there were some exceptions to Jardyce's authority under even normal conditions, but this didn't seem like a good time to debate the issue.

Captain Jardyce leaned back in her chair. "I always let my officers know my expectations for them. For you, Ensign Aquino, my expectations are that you leave this office and do nothing to remind me of your presence aboard this ship until the day you check out and depart for the last time. Oh, and that you keep a tight rein on those damned Marines. No more incidents, understand?"

Should he ask about previous incidents? Probably not a good time for that, either. "I understand," Aquino repeated.

"Then we're done here." Captain Jardyce waved him away. "And, uh, welcome aboard."

"Thank you, Captain." Aquino did a neat, military pivot and walked out of the captain's office.

This job was going to suck even worse than he'd thought it would.

The *Darwin* was a big spaceship, so it took a little while to reach his new combined living area and office. Being a civilian spaceship, the passageways and rooms he passed were much nicer in appearance than on a Navy warship. The guts and nervous system of the ship, the conduits, pipes, and vents, were exposed on warships, easily available to repair if needed. A ship like the *Darwin*, not a luxury liner but intended for civilian use, hid those things in most areas behind smooth walls and overheads. Those walls were painted soothing colors and decorated with panels displaying art or landscapes or other pleasant scenes. The deck was cushioned by a sturdy yet slightly spongy material.

Most of the people he passed, who either ignored his unfamiliar-for-the-*Darwin* uniform or gave him a single curious glance, wore the ID badges and office casual attire that marked members of the scientific research team aboard the ship. He hadn't found exact numbers yet, but the research team outnumbered the crew, roughly three hundred scientists and junior researchers as opposed to about two hundred members of the crew. The crew was large for a civilian ship, but since they had to serve the needs of the researchers, that wasn't surprising.

Aquino overheard snippets of conversation as he passed researchers and crew members, most of it speculation as to what new planet they'd be heading for. The companies who ran ships like the *Darwin* bid for the rights to explore (and exploit) new planets, a process in which everything was kept secret right up until the official announcement. In a way, it was comforting that no one else aboard knew any more than he did about where the ship would be going from here.

He went past some of the areas he had already checked in at. Medical, a small but nicely appointed area for seeing to the needs of everyone aboard. Ship's office, a typical-looking sea of desks, where Aquino had been told his room assignment and downloaded assorted necessary apps onto his data pad. The purser and ship's bank. He probably wouldn't have cause to spend much if any money on the ship, but if he needed something, it was there.

As he entered areas meant for the lower ranking crew members, he wasn't surprised that the nice appearance of everything gradually went away. The worker bees never got things as nice as the supervisors. The wall panels still occasionally showed pleasant images, but were just as likely to display safety warnings, announcements for the crew, and lists of activities that were either required or prohibited. The cushioning on the deck disappeared, leaving only easy to clean and very hard to damage bare metal. The fancy wall and overhead coverings also vanished, revealing exposed pipes and ducts and everything else attached to the walls and overhead, all easy to see and access.

In a strange way, he felt far more at home in this part of the ship. This was like one of warships he was used to serving on, functional and basic, with no frills that cost extra money and required extra maintenance.

Pallets of newly-loaded supplies were being moved around the passageways here. They'd come on the same large transport shuttle that had brought Aquino.

He passed the ship's laundry and the ship's maintenance offices.

He passed some storerooms.

He still hadn't reached the rooms assigned to the Marines.

Aquino had already checked the layout of those rooms while waiting for his short and not particularly pleasant interview with the captain. The small area of the *Darwin* reserved for the Marines could be kindly described as out of the way, and wasn't exactly spacious. It consisted of only a few compartments, including individual offices and living areas for the detachment commander and the detachment lead sergeant, and a single communal living and recreation compartment for the rest of the Marines. A small armory for the Marines' weapons was accessed through the shared barracks room.

His room, with a bunk against one wall, lockers against another, the door to a tiny private bathroom/shower, and a desk fixed facing the door, wasn't anyone's idea of luxury. But it was probably at least twice as big as whatever he would have qualified for on a warship. Ensigns, Aquino knew, had to settle for what the most junior of junior officers could get.

Finally reaching his room, Aquino found that his baggage was already delivered, haphazardly piled on the bunk rather than neatly set on the deck. That told him the rest of *Darwin*'s crew shared their captain's opinion of the Marine detachment.

He sat down in the basic chair at the bare desk, surrounded by mostly unadorned steel walls, feeling depressed.

He had enough experience to know that sort of let-down, stressed feeling was natural when reporting to a new assignment. It was definitely magnified when the assignment was one that no one, himself included, wanted. And when it was an assignment he believed himself extremely unqualified to fill.

But he couldn't wallow in those feelings. The two years he would be in this job would be long enough even with a positive attitude. Eventually, he roused himself and used the desk's data unit to send out a call for the detachment sergeant. He'd requested special training before reporting to the *Darwin*, only to be told there wasn't time and there wasn't money, and in any case, not to worry. His detachment sergeant would teach him everything he needed to know.

After a few minutes, a large, imposing figure appeared in the doorway, wearing regulation Marine coveralls and gazing curiously at Aquino. "Who are you?" the sergeant asked.

"The new commander of this detachment," Aquino said, waiting to watch the sergeant's attitude change.

It did, and not for the better. The sergeant grinned and laughed. "They sent us an ensign? Hah!"

Aquino kept his temper. He couldn't afford to alienate the senior enlisted in the detachment. "What's your name?"

"Antaeus," the sergeant said with another smile. "Sergeant Brad Antaeus. I've been running things here."

"I'll look forward to you filling me in on everything." Aquino kept his voice level.

"I can keep handling things," Antaeus said with another smile that approached but stayed just short of being condescending.

"Thanks, but no," Aquino said, letting his voice get a bit colder. "I'm going to run things. I want a full report on the status of the detachment, training underway and completed, and any special circumstances."

Antaeus spread his hands. "I'll put that together for you. Anything else?"

"I need access to the unit records and command system."

"Yeah, I'll send Rowdy by to get you into that."

Aquino wondered whether he should try to assert himself against Antaeus now or hold it until later. Later, he decided, after he'd learned more about the detachment. "You do that, Sergeant."

"Okay." With a negligent half-wave, Antaeus left the office.

Aquino sat, rerunning the conversation in his mind to confirm that the sergeant had never once used the respectful and required "sir" when addressing him.

Sure. He could count on the detachment sergeant for any training and support he needed. The hell he could.

About five minutes later, a corporal stuck her head into the office. "You the new commander?"

"That's right," Aquino said.

"Then we've got to get you in the system, sir," the corporal said cheerfully. "I'm Rodriguez," she added, pointing to the name on her uniform coverall's left breast. "I handle all the IT stuff for the detachment. You run into any problems, let me know."

"I'll do that." Aquino's attitude eased as he took in the corporal's breezy but respectful behavior. He waited as Rodriguez entered data on her pad.

"You've got a log-in screen now, sir. See it? And a prompt for your password. Twelve to twenty letters, two special characters, at least three digits, and a drop of unicorn blood." She paused to look at him. "I'm just kidding about the drop of blood. But there is a second-level biometric you'll have to enter for access."

"Got it," Aquino said. He entered the new password, waiting for confirmation, allowed his data pad to scan his retina, then called up the detachment roster to test his access. "Okay, looks good as far as…" He stared hard at the data. "Six? Aside from the sergeant, the detachment only has six Marines?"

"That's right, sir," Corporal Rodriguez said. "Me, and five privates."

"The detachment is supposed to be a full squad. Twelve Marines, plus the sergeant, plus me."

"Ah, no. Not enough Marines to go around these days. I guess you already know that, though, you being here," Rodriguez added, "instead of a Marine officer."

Aquino sighed, rubbing his eyes. "Thanks, Corporal Rodriguez."

"Sure thing, sir. Call me Rowdy. Everybody else does."

"I'm not everybody else," Aquino said, that barrier he had to maintain between himself and the enlisted slamming down.

Rodriguez didn't take it badly, simply nodding. "No, sir. Good luck, sir."

When she left, Aquino closed his eyes, consoling himself with the thought that it would be easier to ride herd on six Marines than on a dozen.

That consolation vanished as he skimmed through their records.

Rodriguez had been busted twice for disciplinary infractions.

Private Smith was almost kicked out for poor performance, but then apparently saved from that by a requirement that his unit provide a body for this detachment. So, of course, they'd sent Smith rather than anyone they might miss having.

Private Lachman had been facing a court-martial for negligence, but given the chance to "volunteer" for this assignment, had instead jumped at it.

Private Ichikawa attempted to maim her platoon leader using an ingenious trap that only failed due to accident. She'd been given a second chance because the platoon leader really was universally reviled, and because she'd also agreed to volunteer for this detachment.

Private Kenyatta had been caught running a black-market scheme, except the evidence had been disallowed on a technicality. When her unit was tasked to provide a Marine for this detachment, they'd sent her.

Private Obonsawin had once been a corporal, until he was busted for malingering and forgery.

Aquino sat back, thinking this just kept getting better and better.

He wasn't qualified for this job, but apparently, no one else in the detachment was, either.

Except for maybe Sergeant Antaeus.

Aquino called up that record, seeing commendations and glowing fitness reports, but nothing that explained Antaeus being here, in an assignment that clearly even the Marines didn't regard as important. Then he started noticing a pattern in the fitness reports, describing Antaeus as being "extremely self-assured," "absolutely confident," and "certain his answers are the correct ones."

Adding in some reading between the lines and his own brief experience with the sergeant, it appeared Antaeus was the sort of capable person who decided they were in fact perfect. Who decided they didn't need supervisors telling them what should be done. That would explain why this highly rated sergeant would have been transferred as quickly as possible from each previous assignment he'd been in. His superiors all felt Antaeus' abilities didn't compensate enough for his arrogance.

But no one could leave this assignment early. That was probably why Antaeus had finally been shuffled here, where he'd be out of everyone's hair for a couple of years.

Out of the hair of everyone except the poor sap stuck commanding this detachment.

There was probably a good way to handle Antaeus, a way no one else had yet thought of. Aquino was damned if he knew what that might be.

Aquino's gloomy thoughts were interrupted by a series of soft chimes. What the hell did that mean? He checked the time—it was a call to dinner. Not being a military ship, *Darwin* didn't simply make an announcement that meals were being served. It used soft chimes that wouldn't jar any deep thinking scientists.

He might as well get something to eat and get to know more of the people aboard this ship. Aquino got up with a sigh, trying to calm the knot threatening to form in his stomach, as if he were facing another ordeal instead of dinner.

Darwin might be a civilian ship, but it still had its own hierarchies. Most of the crew ate in a separate cafeteria, while the ship's officers and all of the scientists ate in the "executive dining area" that resembled a decent restaurant in the quality of the chairs and tables and their arrangement. But even most of the executive level people got their food from a serving line.

He wasn't a "ship's officer" but he was an officer, so he got to eat with them. For the first time today, Aquino saw something that cheered him. The food looked good. At least as good as anything that would be served on a Navy ship.

Trying to ignore the glances directed his way because of his Navy uniform, Aquino filled a plate and looked for a table with a vacancy.

Spotting a four-seat table with one seat unoccupied, he took it, nodding to the three scientists in the other seats.

They returned him looks of varying curiosity. "Who are you?" one asked.

"Ensign Osiris Aquino," he said. "I just came aboard."

His questioner sighed heavily. "We can *see* your name," he said, pointing at the left breast of Aquino's coverall. "*What* are you? Are you a ship's officer?"

"No. I'm military. With the Marine detachment."

"Oh."

In that moment, Aquino now knew how it would feel to instantly cease to exist. The other three simply ignored him while they finished, then left without another word to him.

The food was good, yet Aquino couldn't taste it.

He was distracted from his moodiness by an inquisitive, "murp?"

Looking down, there was a large Siamese cat looking back at him. Smiling, he reached to let the cat sniff his hand. The cat watched Aquino as it sniffed, sizing him up, then bumped her head against his hand before giving him a cat-smile and walking slowly away.

Apparently, he'd been assessed as non-threatening, Aquino thought, cheered that at least a ship's cat welcomed him aboard.

He pushed the food around his plate until he noticed someone else sitting down at the table. Startled, he looked up to see a young woman nodding to him.

"Hey."

"Hey," Aquino said.

"I'm KT."

"Katy?"

"No. K. T. Katarina Tirgatao."

"Hi," Aquino said. "I'm Oz."

"The great and powerful?" KT grinned at Aquino's reaction. "How many times have you heard that?"

"Probably less than a million."

"So, you're a military guy?"

"I am. I guess that makes me not too popular."

KT smiled again. "Most of the people in here were not part of the cool kid's club growing up. Instead of learning from that, most decided that when they could, they'd form their own cool kid's clubs and exclude other people."

Aquino regarded KT for a moment. "But you're sitting here with me."

"I said most, not all." She nodded to a four-legged shape wandering farther away. "I saw you've made the acquaintance of Lady Macbeth. If she approves of you, you're probably okay."

"That's the cat's name?" Aquino asked. "Lady Macbeth?"

"The other two ship's cats are Macbeth and Judy," KT added.

"Macbeth, Lady Macbeth, and Judy?"

"Don't look at me. The crew named them."

"Sure." Ship's cats were found everywhere. "They tried a lot of other ways of controlling vermin on ships, but nothing has been found to beat cats for keeping ships clean of that kind of invader."

KT nodded, taking a drink. "One of nature's finest predator designs. I'm an eco-system analyst, by the way."

"Oh," Aquino said. "Do you just work on planetary eco-systems or do you also consult on the life support for ships like this?"

She gazed at him with surprise that shaded into a half-smile. "You get that, huh? That big ships like these are also eco-systems?"

"Navy training," Aquino said. "They emphasized that when we're out operating alone in space, we become a closed eco-system and have to keep everything in balance."

"Yes! Someone I can talk shop with! Hey, Hakim, get over here and meet Oz."

A young man came to the table, smiling at Aquino. "The great and powerful?"

"He really needs a new nickname," KT observed.

"That's okay," Hakim said, taking a seat. "I'm Hakim Marvin. Chemistry department. Guess how many times people ask why I have two first names?"

"Or try to guess what ethnicity Tirgateo came from," KT added. "Don't bother guessing, Oz. It's Maeotian."

"May what?"

"Maeotian. Like, around the Sea of Azov."

"Maeotian would have been my second guess," Aquino said.

"Sure," KT said with a laugh. "Have you met the captain of the ship, yet?"

"Briefly," Oz said.

"Everybody says she's really good at her job. See that big table over there? That's where the senior scientists and senior ship's officers sit. *They* get served their meals. Don't go near that table without a good reason." KT pointed to another large, round table with several people seated around it. "There's supposedly a council of the senior scientists to make decisions, but in practice, Dr. Gohara is pretty much in charge."

"What's he like?" Oz asked, glad that no one had asked what he thought Captain Jardyce was like. And, in truth, she probably was very good at what she did, and like almost everyone else, simply didn't want the Marines around.

KT and Hakim glanced at each other. "He's a good scientist," Hakim finally said. "Can I ask you something, Oz? What exactly is it the Marines do?"

He'd been trying to think of a simple answer to that. "They're here in case anything goes wrong and only they can handle it."

"Sort of like firefighters?" KT asked.

Aquino had engaged in some basic firefighting training, so he understood exactly what she meant. He nodded. "Just like firefighters." And, as he gave that answer, he knew what he was going to be doing, what he had to do, if he was going to be in charge of the Marines aboard the *Darwin*. Because even if they were never called on, firefighters had to know what to do, in order to do the jobs they'd been assigned.

Which meant he'd have to somehow learn to really fill the role of a Marine second lieutenant. Not just in terms of authority, but in terms of knowing this job. Even if nobody ever needed him to display such knowledge.

The question was whether he'd have to do that learning on his own.

The next morning, Oz started his first full day by being present for morning quarters, watching six Marines shuffle into line shoulder to shoulder while Sergeant Antaeus waited impatiently. "Rowdy," Antaeus said, "show Smith how to wear a uniform. Again. Ichikawa, wake the hell up. Obonsawin, when's the last time you got a haircut? I've sent you all work assignments for the day. Get it all done right this time. Questions?"

Everyone glanced toward Aquino.

"Oh, yeah. This is *Ensign* Aquino, the new commanding officer," Antaeus said.

Aquino had decided to keep his remarks as brief as possible while he sized up everyone. "We've got an important job to do, and we're going to be ready to do it. After this, I'm going to call each of you in for a one on one. Until then, carry on."

They seemed surprised, and also grateful, at the lack of an extended speech brimming with naïve, gung ho enthusiasm. Aquino wanted to first tackle the meeting he was least looking forward to and turned toward Antaeus. "You first, Sergeant."

Once in his office, he sat down, noting with annoyance that Antaeus had already taken the other chair without being invited. "How's that status report on the detachment coming?" Aquino asked.

"It's being worked," Antaeus said.

"Off the top of your head, what are the major issues we're facing?"

Antaeus waved toward the door. "We're half-strength."

"I saw that," Aquino said. "What else?"

"What we've got are all screwups."

Aquino waited, but Antaeus didn't say anything else. Time to start pushing back. "Are you telling me the detachment is ineffective?"

The sergeant's casual attitude abruptly stiffened. If the detachment wasn't effective, the blame would rest with the senior enlisted who'd been running things, and that was him. "No. I'm not saying that. I can do the job. You don't need to worry about anything."

Aquino gave him a level gaze. "Sergeant Antaeus."

"Yes?"

Aquino said nothing, holding his eyes on Antaeus, waiting.

After several uncomfortable seconds, Antaeus' mouth twitched. "Yes, *sir*?"

"I didn't ask if you could do the job. I asked if the detachment was able to carry out any assigned tasks."

The sergeant hesitated, his eyes on Aquino, plainly rethinking a bit who he was dealing with. "Yes, they can carry out assigned tasks."

"Good," Aquino said. "At morning quarters, your comments implied they couldn't or didn't do their assigned tasks properly."

"That was just, um, motivational," Antaeus said. "You know. Tell them they're doing good and they'll slack off on you. You'll learn that someday."

Should he push back on the put-down implied by that last sentence? Not yet, Aquino thought. It looked like his earlier assessment of the sergeant was depressingly accurate. How much could he trust what Antaeus told him when the sergeant would avoid saying anything that might make himself look bad? And how much would Antaeus push back against Aquino's authority?

And how could he could count on learning important things from someone who clearly wanted to keep as much to himself as possible? "I'll look forward to seeing that report. Thank you. Carry on."

Sergeant Antaeus nodded and left.

Great. A power struggle with the senior enlisted Marine. Just frickin' great.

Aquino called in Private Akira Smith, who saluted stiffly and stood nervously at attention. "Sit down," Aquino told him. "Why did your last command try to process you for discharge?"

Smith sat down awkwardly, making the simple movement appear complicated, before shrugging with an unhappy expression. "Sir, I'm just not a good fit for the Marines."

"Why not?"

"I can't do anything right. I'm pretty much useless. Sir."

What could he say to that? "Listen, you've got a fresh start with me. Show me what you can do. That's not a get out of jail free card. Screw up and I'll be unhappy. Do your best to keep me happy."

"Yes, sir." Smith didn't appear very confident in his ability to keep his boss happy, but at least he didn't argue.

After Smith left, Private Paul Lachman came in, saluting smartly.

"Okay, Lachman," Aquino said. "Negligence. What happened?"

Lachman smiled sheepishly. "My mind wanders a bit."

"What, daydreaming?"

"Yes, sir. Like, I'm somewhere else."

"Uh huh. I'm going to expect you to stay focused."

"Um, I'll, uh, try, sir," Lachman said, not attempting to sound or look very confident.

Was that how Lachman played it? Keeping expectations low so he could avoid being hammered when he messed up? Aquino leaned forward a little. "Do your job, and we'll get on okay. But if you do something, or don't do something you should have, and it injures or endangers or kills anyone else, I swear I'll come down on you like a twenty-kilometer-wide asteroid impacting a planet. They won't even be able to find any ashes from what's left of you. Got it?"

"Y-yes, sir. I got it."

A visibly worried Lachman left, to be replaced by Private Alice Ichikawa. She looked competent, and wary of him.

"Still designing traps?" Aquino asked.

"Yes, sir."

He stared at Ichikawa, surprised by the easy, calm admission. "Why?"

"Just for funs, sir," Ichikawa said. "I like coming up with complex ways of doing simple stuff. Rube-Goldberging it, like that Mousetrap game that's been around forever. But it's just a mind game, you know? I don't build anything."

"So, I have nothing to worry about?" Aquino asked.

"No, sir!"

After Ichikawa's open book personality, Private Estefhany Kenyatta came across like a locked vault, her every thought and feeling carefully concealed. She said all of the right things and acted in all of the right ways, claiming to have put her black-market activity in the past. Still, she said as little as possible. When she left, Aquino wondered if she was running a numbers game or another black market, or both, aboard this ship.

Then came Private Naveen Obonsawin. He was slightly nervous, but respectful.

"Malingering and forgery," Aquino said. "What happened?"

"I got injured during training," Obonsawin explained. "The doc gave me a week of light duty. Uh… I liked light duty. So when the week was almost up, I went back to the doc and asked for more time off, and she said no way I was fine. During training, they always tell us to 'find a way,' so I found a way to hack into the medical records system and make myself another light duty chit."

"You hacked into the medical records system?" He had been told that was, in all practical senses, impossible.

"Yes, sir," Obonsawin admitted. "I don't want to pretend it was easy, sir. It was hard work."

"You did hard work to get out of doing hard work?" Aquino asked.

"Yes, sir." Obonsawin paused as if he'd never thought of it that way before. "I guess that was kind of dumb."

Aquino nodded. "Because they caught you?"

"Not that time," Obonsawin said. "It was after the third time. I'd been on light duty for a month. My sergeant got suspicious and checked with the doc, and… they were pretty unhappy with me."

"I'll bet," Aquino said. "Why weren't you charged with breaking into the system?"

"They told me they'd drop that charge if I showed the IT guys how I'd done it. That way they could stop anyone else from using that method. I don't do that any more, sir. I put in a good day of work, every day."

"I'm glad to hear that," Aquino said. Obonsawin sounded sincere, though time would tell. "Keep it up. Find Corporal Rodriguez and send her in here." None of the Marines he'd interviewed so far appeared to be what he needed, but Rodriguez had seemed promising during their brief encounter yesterday.

She entered the office and gave a casual salute. "Corporal Isabeau Rodriguez reporting as ordered."

"Take a seat." Aquino rubbed his forehead as he studied her record on his read out. "You've made sergeant twice."

Corporal Rodriguez smiled and nodded as she sat down.

"After the first time, you were busted back to corporal for conduct prejudicial to good order."

Another nod.

"You made sergeant again," Aquino said, "and were busted back to private for insubordinate conduct and failure to obey a lawful order."

"Yes, sir."

"And now you're a corporal again." Aquino leaned back in his seat, fixing Rodriquez with a questioning look. "What's the story?"

She shrugged. "I get bored. I do stuff. That's how I got the nickname Rowdy."

Aquino sighed. "Someone once told me the most dangerous thing in the universe is a bored Marine."

The corporal grinned. "They were onto something, sir."

"Why do you get bored?" Aquino asked. "Too much free time?"

"I'm not dumb enough to say yes to that, sir." Rodriguez finally looked serious, and a bit dejected. "I can work my butt off and be happy. If it's a challenge. If I've got to think and test myself, and not just do routine dumb things every routine dumb day."

Aquino snorted. "Corporal, you should've figured out by now that the military is all about routine dumb things every routine dumb day."

"That's true," the corporal said, looking quizzically at Aquino. "I didn't know you'd already figured it out."

"How do I challenge you, Corporal?"

She stared curiously at him. "Seriously?"

"Seriously," Aquino said. "You look like a great Marine—on paper. How do we keep you that in real life? How do we get you back to sergeant and keep you there?"

"You're asking me?" Rodriguez stared harder, as if Aquino had suddenly grown a second head. "You are asking me?" She sat back, looking baffled. "Damn."

"What's the answer?"

"Umm… I don't…" Rodriguez focused on him. "What do you need, sir? I know this set-up sucks. We all do. If you seriously want to challenge me, tell me what you need to fix."

It was Aquino's turn to study her as he thought. Maybe Rodriguez was the Marine he was looking for. "How are you at tactics? Simulations?"

"Pretty good. I ran the sims for my company before the, uh, last incident."

"The incident that made you a private again?"

"Yes, sir."

Aquino nodded. "You may have noticed that I'm a Navy officer, not a Marine officer."

Rodriguez grinned again. "I have noticed that, sir."

"But, if everything goes to hell, I'm supposed to command you guys. To do that, I need to learn a lot of stuff and I need to learn it fast." Aquino pointed at her. "Can you do that?"

Rodriguez raised both eyebrows at him. "Turn a squid into a Marine? That may be a bit too much of a challenge, sir."

"I don't need to be made into a Marine. What I need is to know what commands to make, how to make them, what to do, what tactics to use, that kind of thing," Aquino explained. "I know how to give orders on the bridge of a ship. What I don't know, is how to command a small group fighting inside that ship. Can you help me learn the Marine side of things using the simulations available on this ship?"

She eyed him doubtfully. "I can try, sir. When do you want to start?"

"How soon can we set up a schedule?"

"I'll get one together, sir, if you shoot me a copy of your daily sked."

"Good." Aquino pointed at her again. "Corporal Rodriguez, I'm giving you what you asked for. I need your best."

"You'll get it, sir." She stood up. "This did not go as I expected, sir." Rodriguez rendered him a crisp salute unlike the sloppy one she'd offered when entering. "By your leave, sir."

Aquino stood up and returned the salute. "Carry on, Corporal."

He sat down again after Rodriguez left, wondering if he should reveal his background. The Marines all thought he was a typical, clueless ensign, a newly commissioned officer who thought he knew it all but really knew very little. In fact, he'd been an enlisted sailor for almost three years before gaining admission to the slot reserved for such in the officer training academy. That gave him a bit of a leg up.

Maybe.

He was stuck in this job for the mandatory two years. He could just roll with it, not really trying, because none of the Marine detachments on any of the exploration and research ships had ever been called to action. Just as if they were firefighters who'd never been called on to fight a fire. As a result, people did what people tended to do, deciding that meant the Marines would never really be needed. That was why the Marines sent to this detachment had clearly been people no one else wanted or would take. That was why the captain of the *Darwin* didn't want to waste any time or attention on them.

He couldn't help thinking of the old saying that a pilot might never need a parachute, but if the pilot ever did need a parachute and didn't have one, they would be guaranteed to never need one again.

How could he stay motivated when literally no one else thought this job was important? When even the Marines saw it as a dumping ground for the unwanted?

An opportunity to excel. The old, sarcastic joke fit this situation perfectly.

Movement at the door drew his attention as a female black cat ambled into the room. This obviously wasn't Macbeth, so it must be Judy. "Hi," Aquino said. "How's your job going?"

Judy jumped onto the bunk and settled down, gazing at him.

At least the ship's cats had decent jobs and knew what was expected of them.

He thought about spending the next two years doing whatever he wanted, letting Sergeant Antaeus run the detachment, assuming nothing would ever require the Marines because nothing ever had required the Marines.

Except… parachutes.

He'd been a sailor. He knew how things could happen. Things no one expected to actually happen. If you were prepared, you could get through them. If you'd gone along assuming what you didn't expect would never happen, you were toast.

Maybe he *was* naïve. Or maybe he was experienced enough to know you didn't get second chances when things went to hell in a hand basket. Either way, he was going to give it his best shot. He couldn't do otherwise and live with himself.

He wasn't looking forward to it, though.

TWO

THAT afternoon, he inspected the Marine room labeled as a barracks and common living area. Everything was… acceptable. The bunks were neatly made, belongings stored in lockers, the automated cleaning bots obviously functional and doing their jobs. The room wouldn't have passed the sort of serious inspections they held in boot camp, but it could have been a lot worse.

Aquino couldn't help noticing that half of the bunks were empty though, with no Marines to occupy them.

Conducting the inspection also gave him a chance to further size up each of the Marines he did have. As they stood by their bunks at attention, Aquino noted their uniforms and their attitudes. Corporal Rodriguez, cheerfully confident and competent. Private Smith, his appearance barely acceptable, looking as if he expected a tongue-lashing for something. Private Lachman, projecting confidence even though his appearance and his bunk were done to minimum standards. Private Ichikawa, seeming bored, but her uniform and bunk both well turned out. Private Kenyatta not revealing anything about herself, except that there was nothing wrong with anything that would have caused Aquino to pay more attention to her or her belongings. And Private Obonsawin, slightly nervous, as if expecting special and unwelcome attention, with everything about him otherwise looking at least okay.

Sergeant Antaeus had been "busy" and unavailable to assist in the inspection.

Aquino had Rodriguez open the armory so he could inspect the weapons, too. He gazed at the neatly racked short-barreled carbine rifles, which at least from the outside appeared to be in good shape. "These aren't the latest models, are they?" he asked Rodriguez.

She shook her head. "No, sir. Not even close to being the latest. They're about the oldest models still in service. We need to print out spares if something breaks."

"How well do they work?"

"They work fine, sir. That's the upside of them being old models. No glitches like new stuff has all the time. These are rugged and reliable, and they are kept up, sir. You will not find any problems with any of these weapons."

"How about the capacitors?" Aquino asked. "Those go bad earlier than anything else, right?"

"They do," Rodriguez agreed. "But we've got plenty in stock to power the magnetic rails on the carbines, and just like the guns, they're a proven, reliable design." She gave him a speculative look. "Do you have experience with mag rifles, sir?"

Aquino shrugged. "Just basic firearms familiarization. I qualified on rifle and pistol. That's it."

"That's something, sir," Rodriguez said. "You know what you're talking about, anyway." She appeared inordinately impressed that an ensign would have even basic knowledge about Marine weapons. "You said you qual'd on pistol, too?" Rodriguez pointed to racks holding several side arms. "And then the grenades, in those lockers. I don't imagine you've fired or thrown any of those."

"I fired one during a familiarization session," Aquino said. "I didn't hit anything."

Rodriguez grinned. "The nice thing about a grenade is you don't have to hit your target. You just have to get it close enough."

"Thanks, Corporal. You can seal the armory again." That part of the inspection provided an unexpected boost for him, because as Rodriguez had said, he did at least have basic familiarity with the weapons the Marines used. And even though no one expected to ever use those weapons, they were being properly maintained. "How often do you practice fire them?"

This time, the corporal grimaced. "Never, sir. There's no room on this ship for a real firing range, so we can only use simulated ones. That's… better than nothing."

"I guess it is," Aquino said. "There's never any opportunity to go to real firing ranges off the ship?"

"No, sir," Rodriguez said. "This ship doesn't go to military bases, and we're not authorized to travel to bases for training."

"Excuse me?" Why hadn't Antaeus mentioned that?

"No off-ship training budget, sir," the corporal said. "No money for that. That's what we've been told."

Not trusting himself to speak, Aquino nodded to acknowledge her words. Why would anyone spend money on training for Marines who were never expected to have to do anything? Wasn't anyone worried about the fact that the Marines were posted to ships like *Darwin* because enough people were convinced they *might be* needed someday? Only, that 'might be' hadn't protected them from budget cutters looking to squeeze some savings out wherever they could.

He couldn't learn this job by running real drills, either. But he could use simulations. They'd have to do.

One nice thing about the Marine field manuals he had access to was that they were written as simply as possible, using lots of illustrations to guide the reader and explain the concepts. To his surprise, Aquino discovered the very basic ways of operating were based on the same principles as his ship training. Maybe he shouldn't have been surprised, though, because the same challenges led to similar solutions.

Warship formations were always led by lighter units scouting for danger. The main body was farther back, surrounded by other units protecting against attacks from the sides or behind. When soldiers or

Marines moved, their scouts were called "point." They used "flankers" to protect the sides, and a rear guard. It was basically the same idea.

What was very different were the environments. Ships in space could see for practically forever and had immense amounts of room to freely maneuver in. Infantry on land had to change formations based on terrain that hindered line of sight and movements. But Marines operating inside ships faced mazes of compartments and passageways, surrounded by walls that blocked sight and sensors. Security cameras could counter that, though attackers were always assumed to knock out such cameras as fast as possible. It was like a deadly game of hide and seek, combat likely to be at very close quarters with little or no warning.

The more Aquino learned, the less confidence he had that he could ever learn enough.

The Marines had a small compartment that was grandly labeled TRAINING AND SIMULATIONS. In a pinch, the maximum number of Marines who were supposed to be assigned to the unit could have fit in there comfortably if they were standing. The sim gear available was several generations old, which meant it could do the job even though any self-respecting gamer would have turned up their nose at it.

The basic simulations Aquino started out on used simple branching tree results. Clear choices were offered, and each choice led to more clear choices, until you either ended up having failed the mission or succeeded. That made it easy to figure out which choices were mistakes and which ones kept you on the path to winning.

He'd played enough games to understand that kind of plot led the player to think there was always one optimal way through the warren of decisions, that the choices would always be easy to see and make, and the opponents or problems would conform to a limited number of possible responses. Aquino had faced enough real-world situations to know none of that was how things worked.

Which was why he wanted Corporal Rodriguez to challenge him inside simulations, pushing him to learn more against a real opponent.

As Corporal Rodriguez pointed out, there was nothing he could do about really firing a rifle or pistol to learn how to use those better. His basic small arms qualification during officer training meant he knew what he was doing. It just wasn't the same as having the ability to hit targets in a tense situation.

After four days of running sims against her, Aquino was painfully aware that none of his learning so far about combat operations on a ship made him a match for someone like Rodriguez.

As he pulled off his virtual helmet after the latest match, angry at himself, Rodriguez gave him an encouraging look. "You're getting better, sir."

"You waxed me three times without breaking a sweat," Aquino said.

"No, sir," Rodriguez protested. "The third time was harder. You're giving your virtual squad the right orders the right way. You just have to be faster and… give different orders sometimes."

The carefully-worded criticism struck him as funny, evaporating his anger. "I'll go over the simulation's critique of my actions. Thanks, Corporal. Until the next time you virtually kill me tomorrow."

"You got it, sir."

Aquino was back in his office, going over the simulation's assessment, and its recommendations to improve his so-far zero win percentage, when Sergeant Antaeus stopped by.

"What's up?" Aquino asked him. So far, Antaeus had pretty much avoided all interactions with him, except what was required.

Antaeus made a face. "People have been noticing that you and Rowdy have been spending a lot of time together."

Oh. So that was the angle Antaeus was going to come at him from. Knock him off balance by implying improper behavior. "Corporal Rodriguez is supervising my simulation-based training," Aquino said in a level voice. "Since you have access to all training records, you should already know that."

Sergeant Antaeus, apparently having expected an anxious, worried, defensive reaction from the junior officer, hesitated. "It still looks bad. You might want to review the regulations on fraternization between officers and enlisted."

"I don't have to, Sergeant. I'm already familiar with them. Speaking of which, I've been forwarded reports from the ship's first officer that some of the women in the ship's crew have complained about your approaches to them." None of those women were willing to press any formal charges, and simply wanted Antaeus to back off, but why not let the sergeant sweat a bit?

"I don't know what that's about," Antaeus protested.

"You might want to review your interactions with the crew, then," Aquino said.

The sergeant hesitated again, scowled, and left.

His attack had been blunted, and he'd been unprepared for Aquino's counter-attack, though that was unlikely to be the end of it. Antaeus probably wasn't above spreading rumors. There was an easy way to fix that, though.

He sent a text to Corporal Rodriguez, telling her to have one of the privates along for the next training simulation run. She'd already told him he needed to practice commanding some real Marines in the sims instead of virtual ones. Starting training with multiple Marines at once should adequately armor him against any suggestions of improper behavior, and further his training.

Corporal Rodriguez brought along an obviously reluctant Private Lachman to the next training session. "Might as well start with a challenge so your learning curve is steep," she advised Aquino.

What she meant became obvious even before the simulation began, with Lachman having trouble donning his equipment even though he must have done it a thousand times before. Aquino knew that game, played by someone who wanted to make supervising them such a pain that the supervisor would stop wasting time trying to get them to do the job well.

Once in the simulation, Lachman went left instead of right, paused when he should have advanced, and managed to get taken out by Rodriguez almost immediately. That meant he didn't have to do anything for the rest of the simulation except sit back and watch.

Aquino kept his temper, running through the rest of the simulation until he lost once again to Rodriguez.

As Aquino pulled off his VR helmet, Lachman grinned sheepishly at him. "Sorry, boss. I guess I didn't understand the orders."

Instead of answering the obviously false explanation, Aquino just stared at Private Lachman, saying nothing. Rodriguez watched them both, obviously waiting to see how Aquino handled it.

After a long minute, Lachman looked down, scowling.

That's when Aquino finally spoke, "Hey, Private Lachman, how good are you at math?"

Lachman looked up, frowning in confusion. "Math? I'm okay at it. I guess."

Aquino leaned in toward him. "Let's run some numbers. Give me your best guess of exactly how many ways I can make your every waking moment miserable for the rest of this tour of duty."

"Sir?" Lachman glanced at Corporal Rodriguez with a worried expression. "How many what?"

"How many ways. Can I make your. Every. Waking. Moment. Miserable. For the rest of this tour of duty? Care to hazard a guess, Private Lachman? Or should we find out by counting the ways as I work at seeing how many I can come up with?"

Lachman swallowed nervously. "Sir… there's no need to… I mean…"

"Or," Aquino said, "you can start understanding orders and give me your best performance in these simulations. Which way do you want to play it?"

"Sir, I can do this!" Private Lachman protested. "I was just out of practice and a little confused, that's all. I can do a lot better."

"Can you?" Aquino leaned back, looking doubtful.

"Yes, sir! You ask Rowdy, there! I know my stuff!"

Rodriguez nodded, her face carefully clear of emotion. "Private Lachman can perform well, sir. When he wants to."

"All right," Aquino said, letting reluctance appear in his voice. "We'll give it a try. Let's run that one again and see how it goes."

Properly motivated, Lachman made what seemed to be real efforts to follow orders and stay "alive." But he was obviously out of practice, fumbling to react rather than showing the quick actions Rodriguez used to once again roll over her opponents.

It confirmed his suspicions that Sergeant Antaeus was focusing on giving the other Marines tasks that presented a good front for inspections, and left Antaeus himself as much free time as possible.

No wonder he'd begun thinking of Rodriguez as the detachment's real senior enlisted. She'd been picking up the slack, despite lacking any guidance doing so.

"Thanks," Aquino told Lachman when the sim was over. "You improved a lot, but you and me both need more practice. We're going to keep at it until we beat the corporal."

"In your dreams, sir." Rodriguez nodded to Lachman. "Let's go. You've got sentry duty and the officer needs to go over his sim results."

Rodriguez started to follow Lachman out, then paused, waiting until he'd left the compartment. "Sir, permission to ask a question?"

"Sure, Corporal," Aquino said.

"Are you really an ensign? That's, like, a second lieutenant, right?"

"I'm really an ensign."

"And you were just commissioned?"

"A little over two months ago," Aquino said.

Rodriguez eyed him skeptically. "Sir, with all due respect, I never yet met a second lieutenant who could've handled Lachman that way. How'd you get so clued in?"

Aquino smiled. "I'm former enlisted. That probably helps."

"Former enlisted?" Rodriguez laughed. "For reals? Were you just yanking me around pretending you need to run these sims?"

"No," Aquino said, shaking his head. "I'm Navy all the way. I know sailor stuff. And… I know how to motivate people who need motivating." He let himself look as serious as he felt. "I'm not yanking you around. One of the most important things I learned as a sailor was that not knowing my job would sooner or later bite me in the butt and maybe get me or other people killed. I don't know this Marine stuff. But I know I have to learn it."

Rodriguez smiled. "Cool. How come the sergeant didn't say anything about you being a former deck squid?"

"The sergeant has never asked," Aquino said. "So, the sergeant doesn't know."

The corporal's smile grew. "That's some interesting tactics, sir. I hope I'm there when he finds out."

"We'll see. Wait," Aquino added before Rodriguez could leave. "Tell me something. Quick and dirty, what did I do wrong in that last sim?"

"You assumed I'd come down the best approach with the best cover," Corporal Rodriguez said. "You also had Lachman watching the second-best approach. I came down the third approach."

"So how do I handle that real-world?"

"You figure the enemy can think as well as you can. Now, maybe they're stupid. But counting on that is… well, also stupid. You figure the enemy knows where you'll most likely put your guns and try to counter whatever he'll do."

Aquino shook his head. "How do I do that? I only had two guns, me and Lachman. There were three approaches."

Rodriguez shrugged. "You want me to tell you some special secret? There ain't one. You go into any fight with limited resources, and you fight it as best you can with what you've got. And, if what you've got isn't enough, you're screwed."

"Unless you can figure out how to make *not enough* do the job of… enough."

"You do that," Rodriguez said, "and I will follow you all the way into hell, sir. But…"

"It's a hell of a lot easier said than done," Aquino added.

"You got it, sir." She grinned. "Former enlisted. Oh, please let me be there when the sergeant finds out!"

"Don't tell anyone," Aquino cautioned her.

"I would not dream of doing so, sir."

It quickly became apparent to Aquino that both the crew of the *Darwin* and the scientific researchers aboard the ship treated the area assigned to the Marines as if it were a plague zone. Aside from Marines, the only occasional visitors to his room/office were the ship's cats. Both Macbeth, a fluffy, dignified sort, and the Siamese Lady Macbeth stopped by every once in a while on their rounds of the ship. Judy was a far more frequent visitor, always taking up a station on the bunk before gazing steadily at Aquino. Either she'd decided he was worth spending time around, or Judy thought Aquino needed more feline supervision than the other humans aboard. Happy for the company, he didn't press Judy on it.

Especially since when he left the Marine area, the rest of the ship's crew took their cues from Captain Jardyce. They didn't ignore him as pointedly as many of the researchers did, but they also didn't seek out or prolong any meetings. Most of his encounters with ship's officers were along the lines of, "How can you not be a Marine? You really are one in a different uniform, aren't you? Why are you hiding it?" Which at least was preferable to the equally common, "What is it you do?"

If not for KT, his social contacts would have been close to non-existent. She seemed to enjoy sharing the table at meals, almost always calling over some other junior scientist or junior ship's officer to meet him. Aquino's social circle wasn't huge, but it existed and was slowly expanding.

Unfortunately, that also increased his exposure to the attitudes of the others toward him and the Marines. At dinner one night, a ship's officer left with an apology about having to get to work, phrasing it in a way that made it clear he didn't expect Aquino to understand that sort of thing.

Afterward, KT glowered at her meal before looking at him. "Sorry, Oz."

"It's no secret how the crew feels about the Marines," he said, trying not to display his own feelings.

"Yes, but… serious question, Oz. Why'd you choose this job?" KT asked. "You don't seem the sort who likes being kicked around or looked down on."

"I'm not, even though I ought to be used to it by now." That applied to a lot longer period than this current assignment, but there was no need to burden KT with that story. "And I didn't exactly choose it," Aquino said. He didn't want to say anything else, but he noticed her watching him, waiting. "Officially, the assignments available when you get commissioned are offered based on class rank which is totally based on merit."

"Totally based on merit? Nothing really works that way," KT said.

"Right. In practice, assignments get reserved for certain people. People who are the sons or daughters of admirals or generals, captains or colonels. People who are related to politicians with enough pull. People who have cultivated the right connections." Aquino made a face, trying not to let anger enter his voice. "So, once all the best assignments have been reserved for all of the right people, what's left is available based on class rank. In theory."

"That gets rigged, too?"

"Yeah." His mind filled with the memory of how he felt when the assignment list finally cycled to him, and there was literally only one job left for him to "choose." "Long story short, I didn't pick this job. It was the only one available to me."

KT sighed. "There are people who study social hierarchies. I don't know how they stand it, because they can look at what's going on around them and see the games being played by other people just like they can when observing animals or birds. I guess neither of your parents is an admiral?"

"Both of my parents were enlisted sailors," Aquino said.

"You're solidly working class," KT said. "No pull and no connections. How'd you get into the academy?"

"My mother," Aquino said. "One time, there was a serious accident on her ship. She saved a lot of people and got a medal, along with a medical discharge because of the hurt she suffered saving them. That medal made her son eligible for a special slot."

"Huh." KT eyed him. "I'm suddenly understanding why you're taking your job so seriously even though everyone thinks it's a waste of time."

"Right," Aquino said, surprised she'd been able to see that so clearly. "I need to be my mother's son. I need to make her proud of me, and do my best. Even if the system tries to sideline me. How did you figure that out?"

KT smiled at him. "You're not too complicated, and it is part of my job to figure out how different things fit into their environments, including someone like you in an environment like this."

He wondered what he should say, worried about pushing too hard in the only solid social relationship he had on this ship. "How do I fit into your environment?"

She smiled again. "I'm still trying to figure that out while gathering data. My research results are promising but far from complete."

"Fair enough. Can I do anything to help your research?"

Another smile. "Continue making yourself available for research opportunities. I'll let you know if I decide to expand my research."

The conversation was interrupted by several loud chimes. The magnified images of Captain Jardyce and Doctor Gohara appeared in the center of the executive dining room, floating midway between deck and ceiling. "I am happy," Captain Jardyce said, "to announce that our next destination has been confirmed."

"Janus Five," Dr. Gohara broke in, as if eager to not let Jardyce steal the whole spotlight. "The robotic scouts exploring the Janus star system found very promising indications of intelligent life on the fifth planet! I want everyone ready to push themselves to the limit while we discover everything Janus Five has to offer!"

"We have clearance to jump tonight and should arrive at Janus Five three days after that," Captain Jardyce said. "That is all."

The twin images vanished.

KT gave him a look combining excitement and regret. "Intelligent life! That'd be huge. It looks like I may be working really long hours once we get close enough to Janus Five. I'll... have to put other research on hold."

"Understood," Aquino said. "Hopefully, I won't have anything special to do after we get there."

"Has that ever happened?"

Aquino shook his head, not trying to conceal the truth. "No. None of the Marine detachments in exploration and research ships have ever had to act."

"If there's intelligent life on Janus Five..." KT began. "Although, using the Marines would mean something went really wrong, wouldn't it?"

"That's right," Aquino said. And what could seven Marines and one ensign accomplish against an entire planet? The most they could do was to try and defend this ship. "Hopefully, the Marines won't be needed, no matter what's on Janus Five."

To his own surprise, Aquino saw the captain again that day.

Captain Jardyce having made her opinion of him clear when he first came aboard, he was understandably concerned when he received a summons to her office.

Jardyce eyed him sourly as he stood before her desk. "Did I not make my expectations clear to you during our last meeting, Ensign Aquino?"

"You made you expectations very clear, Captain," Aquino responded.

"No incidents, I said." Captain Jardyce tapped her data screen. "Ensign Aquino, someone has been raiding the ship's liquor stocks. It's been done very discreetly, very carefully, but the inventory discrepancies finally became clear. My security office has been able to rule out any member of the crew being involved. Who does that leave, Ensign Aquino?"

It obviously left the entire scientific contingent, but it was equally obvious that Jardyce wasn't going to look that way if at all possible. She was a commercial captain, and the scientists aboard were her primary clients.

Aquino wasn't about to point suspicion at his own people even though Captain Jardyce had set him up to do so. And he had enough experience to know that, when in doubt, answering a question with another question could avoid giving a real response. "Is there any evidence pointing in a specific direction, Captain?" he asked, thinking if there were, Jardyce would have already thrown it at him.

The captain glared at him for what felt like almost a minute before speaking, "There is not. But my security office is focusing their efforts. I expect your full cooperation, Ensign Aquino."

"Yes, Captain."

"I do not need distractions while preparing for an interstellar jump and arrival at a newly-discovered planet."

"Yes, Captain."

"That's all."

Aquino went back to his office, took a deep breath, and called in Private Kenyatta.

He spent a moment looking her over, noting that she didn't display the slightest trace of nerves at the unusual summons. "Private Kenyatta, the captain of this ship has informed me that liquor is being diverted from the official inventory."

Kenyatta gave him exactly the sort of look someone would give who had no clue why she was being told this. "Yes, sir?"

"Do you know anything about that, Private Kenyatta?"

"Why would I know about it, sir?"

Clearly, Private Kenyatta also knew the answer a question with another question game. In this case, the fact that she'd avoided giving him a direct *no*, instead replying with her own question, told him that his suspicions were on target. But if he pushed her, she would say no, and then have no option but to keep doubling down on her denials. And he would have no way of proving her wrong without finding the sort of evidence he'd be duty-bound to turn over to the ship's security office.

Aquino leaned back, looking steadily at her. "Private Kenyatta, the captain says her security force has ruled out any of the ship's crew being involved. That means they're going to focus their efforts on finding someone who isn't ship's crew, and on getting the evidence they need against that person."

Kenyatta didn't say anything, still projecting innocent ignorance of the entire matter.

"There are two kinds of smart, Private Kenyatta. One kind is figuring out how to acquire booze from the ship's stocks without leaving any kind of evidence of who did it or even obvious signs that it was being done. The other kind of smart is recognizing that when complacent security wakes up and focuses its efforts in one particular direction, the only wise thing to do is to shut it down. Because, if evidence does develop, the incident cannot be overlooked, and there are worse things than being a Marine on this ship."

Kenyatta managed to project slight skepticism without actually looking skeptical.

"Have you seen the two cells the security force has, Private Kenyatta?" Aquino asked. "They're usually empty, so you can check them out if you want. Small. Uncomfortable. Twenty-four/seven surveillance, even when you're on the toilet. Which is right out in the open. And spending time in a cell doesn't get a prisoner out of work. Prisoners get pulled out long enough to put in a full day, or longer, of the most unpleasant tasks available. That's what the ship's captain can do. Anything the Marines do will be on top of that."

Kenyatta watched him, her eyes calculating.

"But," Aquino continued, "if not one more drop of booze disappears from the ship's inventory, there won't be any way for ship's security to get the evidence they need. I won't have to come down hard on a Marine. Captain Jardyce won't have to come down hard on me and that Marine. Everyone will be happy. The alternative is, that Marine isn't smart, and that Marine, and me, becomes very unhappy. Even though you know nothing about any of this, I want that to be clearly understood. Is it?"

"It is clearly understood, sir," Private Kenyatta said. "I'm sure that any smart Marine would give serious consideration to your… hypothetical scenario."

"Good. Do you have any questions?"

"No, sir."

She left, and he went to work on other matters, hoping Kenyatta really was as smart as she seemed.

Maybe if the captain and crew had been even remotely welcoming, shown any sign of regarding him as part of the same team, he'd feel some loyalty toward them. But his job was different from theirs, and he couldn't afford to have one of only seven total Marines under his command locked up in a ship's cell. Besides, this would give him some critical information about Private Estefhany Kenyatta. Was she simply smart enough to get into trouble? Or was she *smart*, smart, enough so to know when she'd stuck her neck out too far? Knowing the answer to that could be critically important someday.

Something else might also be critically important. He called up some regulations and legal manuals, checking to see what options he had in case this got worse.

Even with the help of automated assistants to explain what legal terms meant, it was a tough slog. He was still at it late in the ship's evening, when the warning chimes sounded.

"All persons aboard *Darwin*," Captain Jardyce announced, "the ship is preparing to jump to the Janus star. Jump is a physically stressful and unique experience. Review the safety precautions posted in every compartment of the ship. If special medical circumstances exist and have not previously been reported, notify the medical office immediately. The ship will jump in exactly one hour from now."

Aquino looked over at the notice on one wall of his office.

JUMP IS A PHYSICALLY STRESSFUL
AND UNIQUE EXPERIENCE
TIME DILATION AND CONFUSION ARE
FREQUENT SIDE EFFECTS
REMAIN CALM
WHEN JUMP ENDS ALL WILL RETURN TO NORMAL

That wasn't too informative, or reassuring. But he had been through jump before and knew how it would feel.

Some people actually looked forward to the sensation of a jump. A couple of those in Aquino's class of officers were among them. Everyone else thought those two were insane.

Civilian jumps were often done during ship's night so anyone wanting to sleep through the experience could take a strong dose of sleep aid and wake up light years from where they'd gone to bed. Aquino, and every sailor he knew, preferred experiencing the stress of a jump awake. "The universe expects us to pay a price for trashing its rules," a chief petty officer once explained to him when he was facing his first jump. "We look the universe in the eye, and we pay that price. It's bad luck to do otherwise. So, suck it up, sailor."

An hour later, as Aquino still struggled with exactly what "what" could mean to lawyers, a series of very soft chimes sounded. Very soft, so as to avoid waking any civilians. Five seconds after that, *Darwin* jumped.

He knew the theory from his officer training, and he knew the equipment, though not as well as trained technicians. None of that helped when jump twisted reality, momentarily altering the probabilities of the ship and everyone and everything within it, so that instead of being *here* they were suddenly at a *there* very far distant.

People debated how it felt. Some said it resembled being turned inside out. Others said it felt as if they'd become a mirror image of themselves. Or that jump folded them like sheets of paper. It took an instant, and felt like much longer.

Aquino gasped a breath as the jump ended, trying to control his heart rate. For him, jump felt as if his eyes turned inward, gazing through his insides as they twisted and spun. *Pay the price.* He'd done that once again.

A soft announcement came, "The ship has arrived at the Janus star. Proceeding toward Janus Five. Expect arrival at the planet in three and a half standard days."

The next morning, a worried Corporal Rodriguez stuck her head into his office. "Ensign Aquino, sir? There's something going down that you ought to know about."

"Show me," he said, getting up quickly and following Rodriguez to the enlisted Marines' barracks.

He found the others standing around, tension filling the air, while Sergeant Antaeus spoke with two officers from the ship's security force.

"What's going on?" Aquino asked in what he thought was a calm, authoritative voice, but which caused every eye to instantly focus on him.

The senior ship's officer cast an equally authoritative eye his way. He wore a big security badge and an attitude even larger than that. "The captain has ordered that these individuals be interrogated regarding a criminal matter. We're here to escort them to the security offices for that purpose."

Aquino tamped down his temper. He couldn't object to the security force asking questions. "The Marines can give you their statements right here. You can use my office to take down individual statements."

The officer, an older man, leaned in toward Aquino. "The captain has ordered that the interrogations be conducted in the security offices."

"Why?"

"I don't have to explain the captain's orders to you!"

Having dealt with higher authority many times before this, Aquino didn't give way. Instead, he met the officer's intimidating stare with his own determined expression. "Yes, you do have to explain those orders. These personnel fall under Marine regulations. I don't surrender control of these Marines without a full and complete explanation of need."

The woman ship's officer spoke up, "The interrogations are to be carried out under full criminal protocols."

It took a moment for Aquino to process that. "Full criminal protocols? Body sensors? Simultaneous brain scans?"

"That's correct. Now, if you will—"

"No, I will not," Aquino interrupted. "Full criminal interrogations are only allowed for individuals reasonably suspected of and formally accused of a crime." He blessed his foresight in looking up those rules last night.

The man shook his head angrily. "*The captain* has ordered that these individuals be fully investigated, which is within her authority as captain of this ship!"

Once again, Aquino stood his ground. "The captain can order such interrogations only in cases in which someone is suspected of actions which pose imminent danger to the safety of the ship and/or anyone aboard the ship. Are you claiming these interrogations involve such a matter? Because I know they don't."

"Are you defying the captain's orders?" the officer nearly shouted.

It never occurred to Aquino to back down in the face of the attempted intimidation. His reply came without any second-thoughts or hesitation, "I'll be happy to obey the captain's *lawful* orders. In *writing*, sir. I insist on orders for these interrogations in writing, signed by the captain, with the captain officially on the record stating that it involves a matter which poses imminent danger to the ship or those aboard it."

A long silence followed, both ship's officers staring at Aquino as if he were something incomprehensible.

The man finally spoke again, his voice a low rumble, "Do you have any idea how unpleasant your life can become if you insist on this?"

"Your threat of retaliation, in front of witnesses, for insisting on my Marines' legal rights, is noted for the record," Aquino said, his own voice also low and totally unyielding. "Don't try this again. Anything you want to do regarding my Marines goes through me."

"Are you out of your mind?" the woman officer demanded.

"I will do my duty," he informed her.

The other ship's officer shook his head again, like an enraged bull unable to charge. "The captain will be informed of your actions."

"I expect nothing less," Aquino said.

The two ship's officers stomped off, leaving silence in their wake.

"There's going to be trouble because of this," Sergeant Antaeus finally said, casting an annoyed glance at Corporal Rodriguez that told Aquino she hadn't been sent to get him, she'd done it on her own.

Aquino rounded on the sergeant, angry that Antaeus had been handling this on his own instead of notifying him, the officer in charge. "If there's trouble, it will come down on me. Understand? Nobody messes with my people. If something needs done, I'll do it. If something like this happens again, I expect to be notified immediately."

Antaeus' expression was that of someone who had finally realized he might have badly misjudged another person. "Yes, sir."

Aquino looked at the other Marines. Rodriguez, Smith, Lachman, Ichikawa, Kenyatta, and Obonsawin were watching him. What were they thinking? "Carry on."

How long would it be before he received another summons to see Captain Jardyce? He had no doubt it would be far more unpleasant than the two previous trips.

But what else could he have done?

An image filled his mind of his mother at her station on her ship, injured, fire gnawing at her protective suit, refusing to leave as she kept trying to restart safety systems.

She had never spoken of that. He learned about it from his father and official accounts. The only thing she ever said to him about her actions that had saved dozens of others at the risk of her own life was, "When people are counting on you, you have to do your job."

He hadn't been consciously thinking of that when he confronted those security officers. Though Aquino had no doubt it was a big part of what drove him in that face off.

When people are counting on you, you have to do your job.

No matter what.

THREE

THE next simulation training session was an hour after the confrontation with the ship's security. Aquino showed up, grimly determined to not let recent events distract him and hoping he wouldn't have to devote too much time to making sure those on his side, this time Private Lachman and Private Ichikawa, did their best. He had no doubt Rodriguez would be at her best, as usual.

To his surprise, both Lachman and Ichikawa put forth extra effort, responding to his commands as quickly as they could. It was a particularly tough scenario, set on a ship even larger than the *Darwin*. Aquino's small force was tasked with hunting down Rodriguez through the labyrinth of passages and rooms. Meanwhile, Rodriguez was hunting them. To further complicate things, there were non-combatant non-player-characters wandering around. Shooting one of them by accident meant an automatic loss. Without a single area to fort up and defend, or a single area to attack, Aquino had to organize a seek and kill search through the unfamiliar and confusing deck layouts.

Against Rodriguez, it was pretty much an impossible challenge.

And, yet, he was surprised that he did okay. The fact that the two privates worked to actively assist him didn't hurt at all.

Aquino pulled off his helmet to survey them approvingly. "Damn good work, you two. We almost beat Corporal Rodriguez."

"Rowdy's days are numbered," Ichikawa announced. "We got time for another run?"

"Yeah," Lachman said. "Let's do it!"

Baffled by their enthusiasm, Aquino agreed. They ran a quick scenario, and came very close to a victory.

"Next time, Rowdy," Ichikawa promised as they left, both her and Lachman pausing to salute Aquino before leaving.

"Hey, Corporal," Aquino said before Rodriguez could leave. "What did you do to get those two so motivated?"

She stared at him. "You think *I* did something? Sir, those two, every one of us, knows after this morning that you've got our backs. That means we've got your back. You don't even have to ask anymore. I think Smith might even turn in a few good days."

"I only did what I should have done," Aquino protested.

Rodriguez snorted. "People doing what they should do isn't nearly common enough. Give yourself credit, sir. You stood up for us. We won't forget that."

He spent the next few hours waiting for the summons to see the captain that never came. When dinner serving time arrived, Aquino headed for the executive dining room, stubbornly deciding not to cower in his office while awaiting his sentence to a metaphorical firing squad.

He hoped it would only be metaphorical.

Darwin felt like a disturbed hornet's nest, frantic activity and tension filling ever nook and cranny of the large ship. His conscience wanted to attribute that to his confrontation with the security officers, but he realized it was because the ship had arrived at Janus and was headed for the fifth planet from the star. Aquino knew what the multi-spectrum sensors on Navy ships could spot even at this distance from a planet. He expected the sensors on a dedicated exploration and research ship would be at least as capable.

Worried that everyone he knew would be too busy to eat at regular hours, Aquino was relieved when he spotted KT at their usual table. "Grabbing a quick bite?"

She smiled briefly at him. "I've got time for a decent meal. So far, what we're spotting on the planet isn't much more than what the robotic probes reported. The atmosphere is a little denser than that of Earth and has a fair amount of moisture in it, so it's blocking a lot of details. We'll have to get a lot closer before we can see the surface really well."

"Are there any more signs of the intelligent life?"

KT sighed. "Not yet. Hi, Hakim."

Hakim Marvin joined them, shaking his head. "It's not looking good, Oz," he said. "There *was* a lot of intelligent life. But is it still there? Like, we can tell the locations of cities. There should be markers in the atmosphere over those cities, the sort of pollutants and other things that large concentrations of people, or aliens, should generate. We're not seeing anything like that, and we should be able to, even at this distance."

"Surely they're not extinct," KT said.

"Hopefully not," Hakim agreed. "But we're not seeing signs of them yet using analysis of the atmosphere."

"Are there any clues as to why the cities would be empty?" Aquino asked.

"Not yet," KT said. "It happens, though. There are places on Earth where civilizations had big cities, a lot of them, and then abandoned them because of environmental causes and wars and what all. That causes a population crash, but it still leaves a lot of people living in much smaller groups."

"But this looks like the whole planet," Hakim said. "Every city we can see. Maybe some kind of solar flare hit them?"

"That would leave a lot of markers in the environment," KT said. "Forests burning worldwide, for example."

"Which would also leave a lot of particulates in the atmosphere," Hakim said, nodding. "Unless it happened a really long time ago."

"Do we have any idea what kind of technology level they had? Have?" Aquino said.

The question was met with shrugs by both scientists. "We know what they don't have," Hakim said. "No artificial satellites, for example. Nothing detected on either of the planet's small moons that would indicate anything had been sent to them. Based on the available evidence, I'd think they're preindustrial."

"Unless they do things a lot differently than we did," KT noted.

"Yeah. There's that. I can't wait to see what we spot when we get closer."

"Maybe one of the ship people can tell us how that's going. Huh," KT said after her attempt to wave over one of the ship's officers was met with a shake of the head. "I didn't think I'd offended the crew. I guess they're really busy, too?"

"They're not steering clear of us because of you," Aquino said.

"Oh?" She fixed him with a demanding look. "What happened?"

Aquino shrugged. "A run-in with security and Captain Jardyce."

Hakim grinned. "One of the Marines?"

"There's no evidence one of the Marines was involved," Aquino said, which as far as he knew, was true, and he wanted to keep it that way. "But they really tried to lean on my guys and treat them all like criminals."

"With no evidence?" KT asked. "So, what happened?"

Aquino made a face. "I said no. No full criminal interrogations of any of my Marines."

"Whoa," Hakim said. "They insisted and you said *no*?"

"What else was I supposed to do?"

Hakim laughed. "Throw your people under the bus to protect yourself! You wouldn't last five minutes in academia, Oz! And now you're expecting trouble from the crew?"

"From the captain," Aquino said.

"That's real heat," Hakim said. "Wait. Was it, uh, Senior Ship's Security Officer Corba?"

"Yes," Aquino said. "Him and another officer named Delvechio."

"Ah." Hakim sat back, looking annoyed. "That guy came after my department. He tried to claim somebody was using our chemicals to generate controlled substances."

"I remember that," KT said. "But they didn't have any proof, right?"

"Right! They'd found some bad stuff on the ship, and since security didn't want to admit someone could've smuggled it aboard, they tried to pin the blame on us." Hakim glanced toward the table where senior ship's officers usually sat, empty now as the *Darwin* approached Janus Five and those officers were fully occupied with their jobs. "Doctor Gohara had to take it up to Captain Jardyce to get the guy to back off. Hey." Hakim gave Aquino a speculative look. "You might not be in as big a trouble as you think, Oz."

"That'd be nice," Aquino said. "Why not?"

"That guy, Corba, was shoving his weight around trying to go through everything in our labs and interrogate everyone, and from what I heard, Captain Jardyce didn't even know about it. Maybe that happened again."

"Maybe," Aquino said cautiously. Corba had seemed like the sort of guy that would take a general instruction and turn it into highly specific actions that might not have been intended at all. "But I know Captain Jardyce was very unhappy about the… uh… thing that Corba was investigating. And even if she didn't approve that specific thing, she might be really unhappy that I defied that guy."

"True." Hakim bent a skeptical look at Aquino. "You didn't think of that?"

"Of course, I thought of that."

"But you didn't throw your guys under the bus? Damn."

Feeling awkward, Aquino made a vague gesture. "That's not who I am." He noticed that KT was smiling at him. "What?"

She smiled wider. "I like data that fits regression analysis projections." Her data pad buzzed urgently. Checking it, she sighed. "They need me to relook at some previous scans of the planet. Like there's going to be something there that wasn't there before. Why not wait for new scans? Later, guys."

Hakim stood up as well. "I need to check in, too. Hang in there, Oz. Even if Captain Jardyce did approve of Corba's actions, with everything going on, it's going to be several days at least before she'll be able to spare time to deal with it. And by then, maybe she'll have cooled off."

"Maybe," Aquino agreed, though he didn't think Captain Jardyce was the sort to cool off in any length of time measured in less than years.

As the next couple of days went by, Aquino tried to focus on his training with the Marines instead of worrying when the hammer would fall on him.

Sergeant Antaeus had stopped any attempts to trip up the new junior officer, now warily watching as he apparently tried to reassess who he was dealing with. The other Marines were on their best behavior, at least when Aquino was dealing with them, but he couldn't help wondering how long that honeymoon would last.

"What's up?" Aquino asked Corporal Rodriguez when she showed up for a training session wearing a glower.

"It's Smith again," she complained. "He messed up something simple."

"Should I come down hard on him?"

Rodriguez considered that before shaking her head wearily. "No, sir. It wouldn't help. Smith isn't screwing up because he doesn't care or he isn't trying. He's screwing up because he's Smith. Nothing's going to fix that."

Aquino made a face. "Everything I hear about Smith says he's a problem."

"Yes, sir, he sure as hell is. But not because he *wants* to be a problem. He's doing his best, which isn't very good. He studies stuff. He takes stuff seriously. And he screws it up anyway."

A well-meaning, well-intentioned screw-up. Keeping him in the Marines hadn't done Smith or the Marines any favors. Though it had let his last command pawn Smith off on this assignment rather than give up someone they wanted. "I'll take a look at the discharge rules to see if we can restart the process for him. An unsuitability discharge can he honorable."

"Don't waste your time, sir," Rodriguez said. "People assigned to these detachments cannot be discharged for anything except the most serious offenses. Believe me, we have all looked into that. They don't want anybody using anything that wouldn't result in serious jail time to get out of serving their full two years in this… situation." She paused, thinking. "Well, I guess a medical discharge might go through, if someone was physically incapable of filling the job. Problem is, we can't make that claim of Smith. And, if we shot him to make a medical discharge possible, people would probably get on our case about that."

"I imagine they would," Aquino said.

"I have been tempted sometimes! Sir, he's not a bad guy. We all like him. We just wouldn't trust him to drink anything without spilling it."

"Got it." Aquino hesitated. "What about Kenyatta? How's she doing?"

Rodriguez gave him a knowing smile. "Do you mean *what* is she doing? Stef keeps her cards real close to her chest, but the rest of us figured it had to be something she did that led those goons to try to treat us all like criminals. She knows we're not happy about it. On top of that, we've let her know that you put yourself on the line for us, and we'd take it very badly if you got hammered because of something she did. She might think she can twist her way out of any official charges, but she knows she can't get away from us. You don't have to worry about Kenyatta, sir. She's going to be a good little Marine, for a while at least."

"I'm glad that's one less thing to worry about," Aquino said.

"Do you know anything about this planet we're heading for? Are we going to have a chance to hit the surface?"

"I don't know much, but I don't think so," Aquino said. "We're still a good distance away, and there are no signs they'll need Marines."

"Same old story," Rodriguez said with a sigh. "I'm not sure why you're working so hard on these sims, sir. Nobody ever needs us. Even the Marines as an organization thinks this job is a waste. Look who they send to do it." She jerked with a sudden realization. "No offense intended, sir."

"That's okay," Aquino said. "None taken. But I have to think it matters. If that makes me crazy, so be it."

"Crazy can help when it comes to getting through the day," Rodriguez said with a grin.

Or getting through two years at this job, Aquino thought.

Over the next couple of days, Aquino found the information available to him was limited because he wasn't a researcher. He was able to find the exploration model that would be used, though. The ship would continue scanning everything it could see as it approached the planet, and once there, would assume what was called a polar orbit, looping continuously around the planet and passing over the north and south poles on each orbit. Since Janus Five rotated much like Earth (though a bit slower, with longer days) that meant each successive orbit by the *Darwin* would cover a different part of the planet, allowing the *Darwin* to scan and map in detail the entire planet.

As soon as it was judged safe, drones under the observation of human researchers would be sent down to closely examine everything they could and take samples of the air. If all went well, more drones would follow, an entire fleet examining the biology and every other aspect of the planet. Only after those drones had done their work, and no significant threats were identified, would humans follow, stepping foot onto the surface of another living world.

He wouldn't be seeing any of whatever the drones and the close-in planetary surveys found.

Exactly why that was had been explained to Aquino by an unusually helpful man, a code monkey who called himself Blitz, at the usually ironically-named help desk in *Darwin*'s Information Technology center. "I have clearances," Aquino had said, having decided to visit the IT center in person.

"Yeah, well, that's why you can't see the information," Blitz had explained. "You have clearances because you are an agent of the government. In fact, I think *the* senior agent of the government on this ship."

"I can't see the information because I have clearances to see information?"

"Right! See, the big corporations that fund the *Darwin* and most of the researchers aboard this ship want to be able to make money off whatever is found. So, the information isn't *classified*. It's *proprietary*. Privately owned. And you don't work for the private companies that own it."

"Isn't this an official exploration mission?"

"It's an officially *approved* exploration mission," Blitz said. "We get some government support. Like you! And those Marine guys. But the government doesn't want to pay for everything so it doesn't get to control anything."

Aquino had sighed. "There's no way for me to request access?"

"Request? No. You can get access if you get a court order."

"Where's the nearest court?"

Blitz pointed down and off to one side. "About thirty light years in that direction. Right, Priscilla?"

A woman looked up from her work, studied the direction he was pointing, and gestured slightly to the right of there. "More like that direction."

Blitz nodded. "Sure. Okay. Is there anything else I can help you with?" he asked Aquino.

"There's no way I can get access to any of that information?" Aquino pressed.

"No. Not even if you turn your unit off and turn it on again." Blitz flashed a smile. "That's a really old IT joke."

"I've heard it," Aquino had said. "Thanks."

Fortunately, unlike detailed research information or analysis, basic planetary scans were available to anyone linked to the *Darwin*'s information systems. Commentary from anyone wanting to talk about the scans was also accessible. Aquino sat watching the scans and reading the comments, the details becoming clearer and clearer as the ship grew closer to Janus Five.

One thing that jumped out from the images of the planet was the lack of mountains. There weren't any Janus Five alps. There weren't even lower mountain chains that had been eroded by time. Aside from occasional ranges of hills, Janus Five had a remarkably undramatic landscape, the most prominent features being large oceans that were fairly shallow as oceans went, and broad, sluggish rivers. Forests covered large areas, but so did open plains that transitioned into inland deserts. The poles seemed to be sheets of ice with few interruptions.

There were definitely cities, though, and a lot of towns.

Every single one showed no signs of those who had built and lived in them.

It was impossible to judge just how long they'd been abandoned without knowing more about the planet's weather and plant growth rates and other factors. But everyone seemed to be in agreement that it had been at least a century as measured in Earth time, possibly longer. The cities were ruins, collapsed buildings here and there, and vegetation growing in every available foothold.

Aquino had searched the images carefully for any signs that the cities had been abandoned because of war. But even though defensive walls existed outside or inside many of them, there were no indications that combat had destroyed the cities. No craters, sections of the walls looking like they had gradually crumbled over time rather than having been broken by long-ago attackers. No siege works or trenches could be seen outside any of the walls.

Also, nothing resembling airfields or spaceports, not even train tracks. No signs of oil fields being exploited, or refineries. The comments posted with the images were agreeing that the societies which once produced those cities must all have been preindustrial.

But what had led to their abandonment?

The closer the *Darwin* drew to the planet, the clearer it became that there were no signs of inhabited villages, even small ones, anywhere. Individuals wouldn't have shown up yet. But why wouldn't survivors of whatever killed the cities have gathered to build new towns?

If the inhabitants of Janus Five were extinct, what could have killed all of them? An extraordinarily lethal epidemic?

Janus Five was unquestionably a pretty world when seen from space, blue seas and green continents and islands and white clouds. Yet even when a graveyard was bedecked with vines and flowers, it was still a graveyard.

Frustrated by the lack of more information, Aquino kept eating every meal in the executive dining room, which had far fewer customers for each meal these days. Most of those were diners racing in to gulp down food and race back to their work. The ship's officers were still avoiding him, but there were some researchers he'd grown friendly with. He hoped someone he knew would stop by.

He missed talking to KT. Was that the sort of data she'd referred to?

While he was getting to know the Marines better as individuals, he couldn't really relax or socialize with them. That sort of familiarity was prohibited between officers and enlisted. He had no doubt if he left an opening to a charge of fraternization, Sergeant Antaeus would jump on it. All of which left Aquino feeling more isolated than ever.

All of which was why he looked up with a smile when Hakim dropped by his table during one lunch, taking time to say "hi" while wolfing down a sandwich.

"How's it going, Oz?"

"I have no idea," Aquino said. "I don't have access to any of the research information, and I don't want to bother guys like you."

"Oh, sure." Hakim paused to take a long drink. "Man, this exploration stuff is cool, but exhausting. What do you want to know? Janus Five has the same elements as Earth, of course, but some of the molecules are *interesting*."

"What about the environment?" Aquino asked. "The planets and animals?"

"That's not my area," Hakim said, "but I've seen the results so far. The life on Janus Five is sort of like us. I mean, they use oxygen like we do. Which just makes sense, because oxygen is a great fuel source. But their genetics and bodily functions work differently from us. Like, our bodies would be toxic to Janusian germs. Janusian insects wouldn't be attracted to us, and if they bit us, it'd probably either kill them or give them a really bad taste in their mouths."

"Would they poison us, though?"

"Good question! Probably not." Hakim cast his eyes upward as he thought. "Almost certainly not. They're getting ready to sample some of them, bring them up to the isolation labs and run tests."

Aquino gazed at Hakim in alarm. "They're going to bring living things from the planet to this ship?"

Hakim held up a calming hand. "To isolation labs. No danger. Anything else? I gotta run."

"Have the drones spotted any signs of the intelligent inhabitants?"

"Signs. Yeah." Hakim made a face. "Lots and lots of skeletons, in various states of decay depending on where they are. Inside or outside, what the climate in that part of the planet is, that kind of thing. All very, very dead for a long time." He pulled out his data pad.

"This is the current rough image of what we think they looked like, based on the skeletons and surviving fragments of wall paintings."

"Kangaroos?" Aquino studied the image. Sort of like a kangaroo, only with a wider upper body, and long, spindly arms. Insectile-like eyes set wide apart were on either side of the short, broad face. "First contact with those would've been…"

"Interesting," Hakim finished. "Yeah. But that's not going to be a problem or an opportunity. There hasn't been a single sign of living ones anywhere, and they all seem to have died within a relatively short time, maybe a few years, a few decades at the most." He tapped his data pad. "See this?"

Aquino looked again, the image seeming to be based on a squirrel. Fluffy fur covered it. The legs were powerful, and the arms were long and muscular, bringing to mind the arms of a monkey. The face was also flatter than that of a squirrel, with a very strong jaw that protruded a bit. Pointed ears rose above the head. Insectile eyes gazed straight at the viewer, making Aquino feel vaguely uneasy even though the entirety of the creature seemed… cute. "What is it?"

"Something that's everywhere the Janusians were," Hakim said, putting away his pad. "Packs of them roaming the ruins. Some skeletons of these guys have been found mixed in with the skeletons of Janusians. Best guess at the moment is they were pets and working animals, like dogs."

"Dogs?" Aquino thought about the image. "That's possible. Places humans have abandoned usually have packs of wild dogs."

"Yeah. The owners have gone but the dogs remain. They've got an official scientific name but everyone is calling them squonks, from a combination of squirrel and monkey. Adorable, aren't they? You just want to reach out and pet them."

"How big are they?"

"One of the adults sitting down like that is a bit more than a meter tall. They can stand on their hind legs, and then they're close to human height."

Big dogs, then. "Are they predators?" Aquino asked.

"Omnivore predators, yes, the kind who eat just about anything." Hakim shrugged. "They haven't acted aggressively toward any of the drones. Just watching them. So, they're probably not dangerous to anything but their usual prey."

"You can't assume that," Aquino warned.

Hakim laughed. "Oh, yes. The military has to worry about that, huh? Don't worry, Oz. We're being careful. Science!" He got up. "Sorry to eat and run."

"Thanks for filling me in," Aquino said. He sat for a few minutes after Hakim left, thinking about an intelligent species that had died out for still unknown reasons. And thinking about the undeniably cute squonk, its glittery eyes watching. Did the squonks roam the ruins of the cities because they missed their former owners? Recalling those eyes, Aquino wondered if that was the reason.

The next few days were more frustration, watching and feeling the excitement aboard *Darwin*, while remaining a bystander to everything.

And dealing with the absurdity of knowing that he and the Marines had a responsibility to protect those aboard *Darwin* from as much as possible, while they were only allowed to know as little as possible.

Two days after speaking with Hakim Marvin, Aquino felt a slight tremor as one of *Darwin*'s two big landing shuttles undocked to leave the ship, taking people down to the surface of Janus Five for the first time. The shuttles were big, the equivalent of Navy Large Landing Shuttles that could carry more than two hundred passengers. He wondered how many researchers and crew members were aboard for the historic landing.

Of course, neither he nor any of the Marines were invited along.

The shuttle made several trips to and from the surface over the next day and half.

Driven by an odd compulsion, or maybe just seeking a distraction from feeling superfluous, Aquino dove even harder into training simulations. Even Corporal Rodriguez's enthusiasm flagged a bit after the last few. "Sir, is there anything planned that we don't know about?"

"No," Aquino said. "This is just preparation. Like every other sim we've run."

He wasn't sure if she believed him.

Three days after that, as Aquino made another futile search for more information before heading for bed, he was startled by a knock on his door frame.

He was even more startled when he looked up.

"KT?"

"Hi, Oz." She looked tired as she gazed about his office and living area. "Boy, they don't give you guys luxurious rooms, do they?"

"If I was on a warship, I'd probably have half this much space. Maybe less," Aquino said. "So, to me, this *is* luxury. What's up? Not that I'm not glad to see you."

She smiled briefly, walking in and sitting down on the bunk next to Judy. "The cats like you, don't they?"

"Judy does. She's spent more time than usual here the last few days."

"Really?" KT seemed to consider that information to be disconcerting. "Oz, there's something I need to talk about. It's building up inside me, and if I don't let it out, I'll explode."

"Go ahead," he said, now worried himself.

KT reached down to pet Judy, who permitted the display of affection with a smug cat-smile. "How much do you know about the squonks?"

"They're… cute," Aquino said.

"Yeah." She sighed. "Two of them are aboard *Darwin*."

"*What?*"

"For a few days now." She carefully removed her hand from stroking Judy's fur before clenching it into a fist. "In the biggest isolation enclosure in a lab room, being studied, even though no one's really been able to study them much because we haven't figured out how to sedate a squonk without killing it and they're not engaging in any behaviors."

"What are they doing?" Aquino asked.

"I'll show you." She brought out her data pad, opening a video.

On the screen were the two squonks, sitting in a big enclosure that was completely sealed except for filtered air exchangers. The squonks didn't move at all, except for their eyes. Even though the eyes resembled those of insects, they weren't fixed. The eyes shifted, tracking something. As the view pulled out a little, Aquino could tell the squonks were watching every movement and every action by the humans in the lab. "We're studying them?" he said. "It looks to me like they're studying us."

KT gave a gasp of relief. "I knew you'd see it! I keep getting told that I'm overreacting and imagining things, projecting my own worries. But you can see it, too! Oz, I objected to bringing the squonks aboard. And nothing I've seen since has made me feel any better about it."

"What is it you don't like about the squonks?"

She made an angry gesture. "I can't make them fit! Every creature has an environmental niche. Something they evolved to fit. The squonks are obviously apex predators even though they're omnivores. There is nothing else on Janus Five that is anywhere as numerous as they are. And they are *everywhere* on the planet. Every climate, every piece of land that was once occupied by the Janusians."

"I heard they were thought to be pets or working animals," Aquino said. "That the Janusians had brought them everywhere."

"That's what everyone is saying, but it doesn't feel right, Oz. I look at the squonks and they don't fit."

"Do you think they're dangerous?" he asked, remembering the way he felt looking at the eyes of the squonks.

"Yes," KT said. "You've noticed their jaws, right? The teeth are numerous and big and sharp."

"Like dogs," Aquino said.

"Yes, yes, like dogs! And I know dogs are pets. Look at the forepaws, though." KT brought up another image on her pad. "It looks like a paw, right? Except there's something folded inward on the bottom. We can't tell what, yet. I don't think it's just a paw. But we can't examine it more closely until we figure out how to sedate them.

"And the muscles, Oz! Again, we can't really get a good examination of them, but look at those forearms! Do you know how strong a chimpanzee is on Earth? Much stronger than a comparable human."

She sat back, grimacing. "I have a bad feeling about this. Most of the others look at the squonks and say 'cute' and dismiss any worries. But you know what, Oz? Do you see Judy here? Since we brought those squonks aboard, the cats have avoided the areas of the ship near that lab."

"They don't like the smell of squonks?" Aquino said.

"Oz, the squonks are totally isolated. There shouldn't be any smells, there shouldn't be *anything*, coming out of the enclosure they're in. And they're not making any noises. No sounds. And yet the cats are avoiding that area."

He looked at Judy, who returned his gaze with an enigmatic cat expression. "There have been suspicions for a long time that cats might have some sensory abilities beyond anything humans can perceive. And they don't like the squonks. Does that bother anyone else?"

KT made a scoffing noise. "It's not scientific, Oz. I can't explain exactly what's happening, and I can't quantify it. My strong feelings that squonks are an environmental puzzle are also something I haven't been able to establish in scientific terms."

"When experts have hunches, it's almost always a good idea to pay attention to them," Aquino said.

"Hunches are not science." She sagged where she sat. "I'm worried, Oz. And no one is listening to me."

"I am."

"Yeah." She looked at him with a wan smile. "Am I overreacting?"

Aquino didn't hesitate before shaking his head. "Doesn't everyone agree, all the researchers, that there's a lot we don't know about the squonks? Some of the things we don't know could be dangerous. That's common sense."

"You can't quantify common sense, either," KT said.

"But why not wait? Why keep the squonks on board? Why bring them on board in the first place?"

She looked pained. "Oz, they're cute, right? Fluffy? Maybe once pets kept by the Janusians? Absolutely unique?"

"Right."

"Do you have any idea how much money squonks could be worth as exotic pets if only a few are offered for sale? Do you know the going price for a chimera from Epsilon Eridani?"

"No, and no," Aquino said.

"Chimeras are incredibly expensive. Millions, Oz. That's for *one*. If you have to ask how much a breeding trio is worth, you can't afford it. That's what they cost. Prestige pets for the wealthy to show off. Think how much someone could charge for a squonk! Every billionaire from here to Andromeda would be aching to get their hands on one."

"That seems like a really bad reason to be rushing something like research on the squonks," Aquino said. "But… money. I guess I'm not surprised."

"Yeah. I'm sorry to dump this on you, but I needed to talk to someone who wouldn't blow off my worries, and somehow I knew that would be you."

It seemed odd to feel good after everything else she'd said, but that made Aquino smile. "What can we do?"

"Not a damned thing, Oz. And thanks for saying 'we.' All I can do is hope that I'm wrong and vent to a friend who is willing to listen to me and not dismiss my worries."

"That sucks."

"It does." She got up, watching him with a worried expression again. "Oz, if… if something happened, the Marines could handle the squonks, right?"

Should he be honest or reassuring? Looking at KT, he decided he had no choice but honesty. "I don't know. I think so, but as you say, there's a lot we don't know about them. I don't know how hard it would be. But I think we could handle them."

"Thanks, Oz." As he stood up to say goodbye, she surprised him with a quick hug. "You're the best. I better go get some sleep while I can."

"Okay." He watched her go, wishing she had held the hug longer, and fighting that sense of foreboding inside him.

He was getting up early the next morning when his comm panel buzzed loudly with the urgent light blinking.

Aquino activated it, expecting that Captain Jardyce had finally found a few moments to rake him over the coals as a result of the confrontation with the security officers.

And, sure enough, it was a summons to report to the captain's office as soon as possible.

This day was starting off great.

FOUR

CAPTAIN Jardyce, once more seated at her desk, looked like someone who needed at least one more cup of coffee.

She finished up whatever she was doing on her display, then sat back and fixed Aquino with a dagger-like glare. "Ensign Aquino. Tell me something, Ensign Aquino. If I kicked you off this ship at the next port we arrived at, what would you do?"

That answer was both easy and hard. "I would immediately go to the spaceport authority," Aquino said, "and inform them that the *Darwin* was in violation of government sailing regulations, and therefore could not be allowed to leave port until the violation was corrected."

"A by-the-book answer," Captain Jardyce said. "Did you look that up before your confrontation with Senior Security Officer Corba?"

"No, Captain. I looked it up after that."

"Sloppy, Ensign Aquino. If you're going to jump off a cliff, make sure you already know what's at the bottom." Jardyce examined him silently for a moment. "I don't have time for trying to discipline you. Especially since you are something unique, Ensign Aquino. You are the closest thing to an independent observer aboard this ship. I serve the corporations and the researchers. The researchers serve their corporations and labs. Who do you serve, Ensign Aquino?"

That was an unexpectedly difficult question to answer. "I'm supposed to remain alert for and prepare for any danger to the ship or anyone aboard it."

"In other words, when it comes to the safety of this ship and those on it, you have no conflicting loyalties tugging at you." Jardyce made an angry gesture. "How much do you know about Janus Five?"

"I've been able to learn only the basics," Aquino said. "I'm locked out of everything else."

"Have you been able to learn about the mystery, Ensign Aquino?"

Mystery? he thought. "Do you mean the fact that it appears the Janusians are extinct?"

"Yes." Jardyce shook her head irritably. "An intelligent species, extinct. And nothing telling us how that happened. Is it something that vanished when the last Janusian died? Or something still there that is as yet invisible to us? Or something in plain sight we can't see the significance of? Does that worry you, Ensign Aquino?"

For once, that was an easy answer. "Yes, Captain, it does."

"Because *that* is the only priority you have to think about!" Captain Jardyce closed her eyes before fixing Aquino with another glare. "Does your interpretation of your duties extend to reconnaissance and research, Ensign Aquino?"

"I would think it would have to, Captain."

"Good." Jardyce leaned forward. "I can't get you down to the planet. That's because the researchers have every available shuttle seat tied up for weeks. It's also because, to my own great surprise, I find myself unwilling to risk losing you, Ensign Aquino. If you're actually on the surface of Janus Five looking for what the rest of us have missed, and you find it, there's a good chance you wouldn't survive that experience. Believe it or not, I don't want you dead."

"I never assumed you did, Captain," Aquino said, still trying to accept the unexpected direction this meeting had gone.

"Never make assumptions, Ensign Aquino. It's dangerous." Captain Jardyce tapped her console. "I'm giving you full, priority access to the planetary surface simulations created by feeds from the research drones. Go to a sim room, don the gear, stand in the right spot, and you might as well be on the surface of Janus Five. Sights, sounds, smells, everything. Move around in any direction you want. Even the artificial gravity at that spot you're standing will adjust to match that on the planet. I can't order you to do this, but I am *requesting* that you use those simulations to learn as much as you can about the situation on the surface of Janus Five. I want your eyes, your mind, seeing what's there."

Jardyce sat back, sighing. "I'm well aware that you may see nothing everyone else hasn't already. But an entire intelligent species is extinct and no one can tell me how that happened."

Aquino nodded, understanding why that bothered Jardyce. "Captain, how are the researchers taking this? Are they raising any red flags at all?"

"Not a one." The captain made an angry wave in the general direction of Janus Five. "The researchers are using their checklists and their precautions. They say there are no identified obstacles to proceeding with a routine, step-by-step initial exploration of a new, life-supporting planet."

"Data," Aquino said.

"Yes. They want data." Jardyce paused before fixing a demanding look on him again. "Ensign Aquino, you are the only officer on this ship who doesn't care about making me happy, and will not hesitate to make me unhappy if he thinks that is required. That makes you valuable to me, and to the ship. Please see what you can find."

"I will, Captain." He didn't have to, because Jardyce was a civilian, but Aquino brought his hand up to salute her.

She flipped a quick salute in response. "That's all."

As he left, Aquino realized he could finally understand why Jardyce's crew liked her. She was only being a bit nice to him because she needed him, but she was smart enough to know that and not let previous events and attitudes get in the way of protecting her crew.

It was nice to know he was apparently no longer completely useless. At least for now.

The meeting with the captain had been brief enough for Aquino to make it back to the Marine area while morning quarters was still being held.

As Aquino walked up, he noticed Sergeant Antaeus smiling. Oh, of course. Antaeus would have heard that the ensign was summoned to the captain's office, and likely expected Aquino to have had his ears pinned back.

"Anything to report, Sergeant?" Aquino asked in a no-nonsense voice.

"All personnel present and accounted for," Antaeus said, his earlier anticipation shading into disappointment.

"Good. I'm going to be tied up for some time in one of the Class A research simulators. I want to emphasize that if anything comes up that I need to be aware of, I should be notified immediately, even if I'm in there." Aquino let his gaze leave Antaeus and wander across the other Marines, pausing at Corporal Rodriguez. He was sure she'd pick up the message and make sure he was notified if necessary.

Sergeant Antaeus frowned. "Perhaps you haven't been informed, but we're not allowed access to those simulators. They're reserved for the use of researchers."

"I have access, Sergeant," Aquino said. "Priority access. As I said, if I need to be informed of anything, interrupt me."

"Yes… sir."

He shouldn't push this too far. It felt too much like fun to needle Sergeant Antaeus, and he shouldn't be actively undermining the sergeant. "I'm coordinating with Captain Jardyce to check out the surface of the planet. I'll try to get you and the other Marines access. The more eyes on this, the better."

"Eyes on what?" Antaeus asked.

"We'll know the answer to that when we find it, Sergeant."

Aquino found several researchers already waiting for their turns in the simulator rooms. He received looks ranging from curious to annoyed as he logged in for his turn. When a sim room assignment immediately popped up for him, those looks shifted to surprised and outraged.

At least this proved Captain Jardyce had meant it when she said she was giving him priority access. As Aquino headed for his room, he noticed that the time limit that normally restricted how long one person could use a simulator was listed as "indefinite" for him.

After the last few weeks, it was very strange to be getting VIP treatment aboard this ship.

The sim rooms for individuals weren't that large, but the special decks allowed someone standing on them to "move" indefinitely in any direction inside a simulation by walking or running, without actually going anywhere in the sim room. Aquino finished adjusting the sim gear on his head, then the body suit, before tapping the *Begin* command.

The lights in the room dimmed, allowing the glowing virtual menu that appeared before him to stand out clearly. He touched the simulations library menu, and a sub-menu appeared—he touched *Janus Five*.

There were already a lot of different Janus Five surface simulations, assembled from observations made by the scores of drones that had explored the planet, collecting data about every possible aspect of the world. One caught his eye, though. Janus Five Prime. Touching that brought up a description. *Exploration of area near and inside the ruins of one of the largest Janusian cities.* The thumbnail image next to it, an overhead view, showed an expansive area of buildings, one of the broad, slow rivers running along one side. That seemed like as good a spot as any to start getting acquainted with the reality of Janus Five and whatever happened to its former inhabitants.

He touched that again, confirming, then waited.

The world of Janus Five began to gradually come into existence around him, first in dim outlines which slowly grew in sharpness and detail. The light shifted, little by little becoming more intense. Tiny sounds grew in volume step by step. As the surface of Janus Five solidified around him, Aquino also became aware of unusual scents.

Anyone who did modern simulations was used to those slow transitions. Top-end sims had gotten so good that "sim shock" could be a real problem if the sim suddenly leapt to full life around a person, as if they'd instantaneously teleported somewhere else. Teleportation sounded cool in theory, but human minds did not like abrupt changes to the entire environment around them.

Aquino took a moment longer to let himself adjust to Janus Five. The air was heavy, a bit denser than what humans were comfortable with. At this place on Janus Five, it was also humid enough to cause sweat to start beading on his skin. The gravity had adjusted as well, pulling down on him with 1.15 times that of Earth. That extra .15 might not seem like much, until you were trying to hold yourself up against it and walk in it. He'd need to move carefully to avoid any missteps that might produce no results in Earth gravity but could sprain an ankle in the higher gravity of Janus Five.

He could direct the sim to shift the gravity back to Earth standard, making movement simpler and safer, but decided not to, wanting to experience the reality of Janus Five as much as any simulation could.

Looking about, Aquino saw vegetation ranging from tangled grasses to knee-high weeds. He was on what might be the verge of a forest, to one side scattered tree-like plants increasing in numbers until they merged into a mass with gloom under the many branches.

Were those "trees" ferns? Or something like ferns, though the branches grew out in corkscrew clusters of six.

In the other direction were mostly open fields choked with lots of lower lying plants, and beyond them, the walls of a city that had once been the home of a great many Janusians. The river should be visible from here if he were a bit higher.

He used the sim controls to raise his point of view as if he were rising into the sky, spotting the river making its sluggish way toward the nearest sea. A tiny forest of bare poles rising above the water showed where a few boats and maybe ships had sunk, possibly at piers that eroded away since the city had died. Wouldn't a city of that size have boasted a larger fleet of boats? Maybe those who could fled in most of the boats in the face of whatever disaster had struck.

Aquino brought his perspective back to ground level and started walking toward the city, trying to take in the sounds and smells. Some sort of very low clacking noise kept zooming in and out nearby. He caught glimpses of tiny bodies and guessed these were Janusian insects, their wings creating sharper noises than the buzzing of Earth insects.

There were a lot of scents. He recognized the smell of raw dirt. Something had been digging. Various scents were slightly spicy, and slightly off-putting. He couldn't tell whether he was smelling plants or animals or both.

Harsh, loud sounds caused Aquino to spin in that direction, seeing things about the size of an Earth rabbit leaping into the air with net-like mouths extended to catch dozens of insects.

Every step was more difficult than a step in Earth gravity. The sun was too intense, the air too thick. What he'd seen so far held a strange sort of beauty, but he didn't believe humans would be flocking to Janus Five to settle this world. This area, at least. Maybe other climates were easier to bear.

He suddenly realized that the field of overgrown vegetation he was walking through had once been farm land. Many of the plants seemed similar to his eye, bearing heavy pods of seed. The sim, recorded by drones flying above the surface, couldn't match the effort it would really require to walk through this field, but Aquino thought it would be a tough struggle. Some of what might be weeds bore wicked spikes. It made sense that plants here would have developed the same sort of defensive armaments that plants on other worlds had.

A small, partially collapsed wooden shed came into view to his left. He angled that way, wondering why he had yet to see any large creatures. If humanity had been exterminated, even if that same calamity wiped out every cow and horse, wild creatures such as deer and pigs and even elephants would have made fields like these their grazing grounds. Where were those sorts of beasts on Janus Five?

The decaying shed had little to offer, except for the sad sense of abandonment that such structures always wore like a garment of mourning. The door had fallen from an entry wider than what humans would usually have used. Remembering the images he had seen of the Janusians, those wide kangaroo-like lower bodies and legs, that wasn't surprising.

The sim didn't allow him all of the way inside the shed, but there was a pile of decomposing hardwood sticks that might once have been the shafts of tools. He didn't see any signs of rust from decayed hinges or tools, so perhaps the Janusians used wood or leather in many places where humans usually employed metal. There were fragments of something on the floor of the shed, though. Zooming in on them, Aquino noted pieces of ceramic or pottery scattered about, as well as a few stones shaped into what looked like hammers or edged tools. Some of the ceramic pieces had sharp edges as well.

It looked like the Janusians had been a very metal-poor civilization, making do with what other materials were available.

Aquino, already a bit weary from fighting the gravity and the air, headed toward the city walls.

A flock of things moving very fast shot past overhead, flying almost silently, except for the tiny snaps of their wings. Birds? Or something that filled that niche in the ecology. He'd have to try to get a better look at them.

In a denser atmosphere, birds could be larger than on Earth, right? But they'd also be dealing with the higher gravity. He'd have to ask KT about whether birds could be significantly bigger here.

As he drew closer to the city, details of the wall around it became more easily seen. Only about four meters high, it wasn't made of bricks or stone, neither cut and fitted stones, nor dry stone carefully piled to take advantage of the natural shapes. Instead, the wall seemed to be some kind of rammed earth or mudcrete that had not stood up well against the elements since the last Janusian died. Sections had collapsed, while other portions were still crumbling in place.

He had the impression of a wall hastily thrown up by defenders who hadn't the time to build something stronger. That implied a serious threat had emerged, but no matter how closely he searched, Aquino found no sign of damage from any attacks.

Spotting a cluster of holes near the top of one section of the wall that had remained intact, Aquino searched the area under it, eventually finding sharpened wooden stakes decaying in the vegetation. The Janusians could not manufacture barbed wire or razor wire, so they resorted to larger versions of the same sort of spikes that weeds used to defend themselves.

Clearly, these Janusians had felt a sudden need for a wall topped with spikes. But who was that wall a defense against? Other Janusians? Were there any other candidates at this point?

His attention on the wall, Aquino had been paying less thought to what was at the foot of the wall. Coming around a high pile formed when a large section of the wall had fallen down and outward, he found himself almost on top of a fair-sized group of squonks.

They all looked at him.

He froze, his heart in his throat.

The squonks didn't move, just watching him. He couldn't read the expressions on their fairly flat squirrel-monkey faces. He could tell they didn't seem to be bracing themselves to leap, but how long would it take them to do so?

He had just about decided to begin slowly backing away when the gaze of the squonks shifted, focusing on something over his head.

Oh.

Hell.

Idiot.

These squonks hadn't been looking at him. They'd been looking at the drone that collected all of this information days ago. The immersion was just so well done, Aquino had felt he must be the target of those gazes.

No wonder they hadn't reacted. Nothing he had seen indicated the Janusians could have made anything like one of the human drones. Nothing in the experience of the squonks could provide them with any clue as to what the drone could be, because the squonks never could have encountered something like this.

He paused to calm himself, watching the squonks and becoming aware of a scent coming off of them. It wasn't a bad scent, sort of musty. An image appeared in Aquino's mind as he recalled the last time he'd smelled something similar. An old barn, carrying the scents of rotting feed and seed, decaying wood, dried manure, and long-ago discarded hair from cows or horses or llamas or whatever. The squonks smelled like that.

And… they really didn't feel threatening. Not here, in their native environment.

Many of the squonks were grazing on the wild-growing former food crops, crunching the seed pods. A couple of adults near the wall were using their powerful back legs to unearth a buried colony of something too big to be ants and not big enough to be rats, the adults and juveniles snapping up the ant-mice with their mouths as the ant-mice scrambled to escape.

A small group of squonks were facing each other, speaking in chirps that sounded like cartoon chipmunks, their mouths forming smiles that resembled those of humans. Their long, fluffy fur rippled in the gentle breeze, waves of light and dark chasing across it. High, pointy ears flicked around in response to sounds.

The cute was so intense it almost burned.

For the first time, Aquino understood why the great majority of the researchers weren't worried about the squonks. It wasn't just their adorable appearance. In this pack, he saw no aggressive behaviors.

Aquino scanned what he could make out of the city ruins from here, spotting more packs of squonks and occasional flocks of sorta-birds. But no other ground animals of significant size.

That didn't make any sense. How did an apparently non-aggressive animal like the squonks dominate an area like this? Where were other, larger animals competing for the same resources?

No wonder the squonks puzzled KT.

He continued on past the squonks still watching where a drone had been. Getting beyond the squonk pack, the stripped remains of what might have been one of the insect-eating rabbits lay on what had once been a road into the city. A horde of the clack bugs had descended on the carcass, rapidly removing every trace of meat or cartilage. Even though this wasn't the sort of thing Aquino liked to watch, he came closer to observe them.

The clack bugs were not only removing every trace from the bones, they were gnawing on the bones themselves.

No wonder the skeletons on this world were in such bad shape.

He took a moment to feel the too intense sun beating on him and the too strong gravity pulling at him. He was tempted to order the sim to put the gravity at Earth normal, but again decided not to. For some reason, he believed it was important to continue to experience Janus Five as it was.

Finally moving again, he "walked" into the city over the broken, decaying gate, where a large open area beyond that was bordered on the other three sides by buildings ranging from one to three stories. A large fountain in the center must be fed by a spring, because water had never stopped flowing. As vegetation growing wild filled the fountain, the water had spilled out to turn most of the courtyard into a swamp. Fetid, stale water rested over thin layers of dirt and scattered plants fighting to survive.

Oddly, several very large, flat stones lay haphazardly just inside the gate, as if they'd fallen or been dropped there long ago. They didn't form any kind of defensive wall. Perhaps the defenders had been bringing them to reinforce the gate?

Under his feet, Aquino saw bones. A lot of Janusians died here. The bones were a jumble, and had clearly been worked over by the clack bugs and probably other scavengers. He couldn't tell anything about how these Janusians died.

This was depressing in a way nothing had ever hit him before. He had seen ancient abandoned cities, the traces of lost empires. But he'd known others lived on, founding new cities. Not here. This dead city marked not the fall of a city-state, but the extinction of the species which built it. There was something profoundly sad about that.

He noticed mixed in with the bones were fragments of what seemed like very old leather that had deteriorated badly due to mold and exposure to the sun. The larger pieces might have once been rectangles as tall as his hand was long. Clothing? Aquino could see that some of the leather pieces had once been thick enough to make moving in them difficult. Had this been some sort of armor? The damage to the leather made it hard to judge.

Wanting to get out of the sun and see more of Janusian life, Aquino walked toward one of the buildings lining the courtyard, this one still mostly intact. The wide door lay broken in the doorway. Had it fallen when the hinges gave way, or had it been broken when disaster overtook this city? There was no way of telling. As he passed the fallen door, he studied it, noting tiny creatures crawling over the old wood, portions of it already reduced to dust.

Janus Five seemed to like keeping the secrets of its past.

The floor showed signs of having been flooded at various times in the past. Mostly dry now, it was covered with a sort of mold that stank, and partially concealed the bones on the floor.

What sort of building had this been? What purpose did it once serve? There was nothing remaining to offer a clue. The downstairs was one big room, broken only by a couple of pillars that supported the roof. Empty windows faced the courtyard.

Here and there on the walls were fragments of pictures that had been painted directly on them. Aside from occasional bits of images of plants, they mainly showed pieces of paintings of Janusians, too little of the pictures surviving to give a clue as to whether the Janusians had been painted posing or engaging in activities.

A ramp rose along the back wall. Perhaps because of the higher gravity, perhaps because of the way their legs were built, the Janusians may have preferred ramps to stairs.

He dragged himself up the ramp, thinking that maybe he'd explored enough. But really, he'd seen so little.

The upstairs was also one large room, a doorway leading out in front to where a balcony must have once rested.

No bones here. That was a relief.

A pile of broken wood in front of what seemed to be a small alcove drew his attention. Had something once concealed whatever was in there?

The drone hadn't gone into the alcove, but it had come to the entrance and examined what was inside.

A jumble of Janusian bones. Some of the decaying remnants appeared large enough to be those of adults, while others, including a large fragment of a skull, looked like those of children.

What brought them there? Had they been hiding, concealed by whatever piece of furniture the wood scraps had once been, hoping they would remain undetected?

Something about the pathetic clutter of bones reminded Aquino of virtual tours he had taken of the ancient Roman cities of Herculaneum and Pompeii. The bones in Herculaneum where families had huddled together before the heat and gases from the volcanic eruption slew everyone. The body casts of the victims in Pompeii, revealing even the expressions of those who died lying next to each other.

Toxic gases? Could that explain at least some of this?

"Is there a volcano near here?" Aquino asked the sim AI.

"There are no volcanoes in this region. Only one volcano has been mapped on this world. The planet, Janus Five, is exceptionally geologically stable."

Not that kind of natural disaster, then. What had these Janusians seen coming and tried to hide from? It could be almost anything. Invaders from another city. Someone enforcing quarantine during a plague. And this might not even mark an event in what had exterminated the Janusians, but just a side tragedy. If the Janusians had been anything like humans, when societies collapsed there would be riots and looting and murders.

How had a society like the Janusians, with their limited technology, been completely wiped out?

"Have mass graves been discovered?" Aquino asked the sim AI.

"Define mass graves."

"Large numbers of bodies piled into pits or fields without normal burial processes."

"There are remains of Janusians all over every abandoned city and town."

Aquino blew out an exasperated breath. Dealing with AIs could still be frustrating. "Are there places with an exceptional number of such remains in a small area?"

"None have been found."

"What appear to have been the usual burial procedures for the Janusians?"

"From what has been learned so far," the AI said, "it appears that the Janusians universally practiced cremation of remains of the dead."

Which would have left very little in the way of remains to examine.

Aquino walked to the opening leading out to where the balcony had been, gazing out on the swamp that was once a courtyard to greet new arrivals to this city. "Has anything been found which leads people to believe a plague was responsible for the deaths of the Janusians?"

"No," the AI said. "All evidence to date is ambiguous. None of the markers we would expect to see from a plague have been detected. Those remains found in the best state of preservation are still too badly deteriorated to permit identification of a virulence that might have exterminated the Janusians."

That seemed wrong. An entire intelligent species dead, and no sign of what caused it. Shouldn't such a species have an epitaph? We were here, we tried to do these things, we looked up at the stars and wondered, and then…

As he turned to head back down the ramp, Aquino paused at the alcove again. He breathed a brief prayer for the spirits of these Janusians, a few among so many who must have died in a fairly short span of time. In truth, he wished those specters would appear before him to tell him how and why they'd come to die here. Because their bones alone told him nothing.

As he moved down the ramp to the first floor again, Aquino spotted something white that didn't appear to be bone. Moving toward it, he found what was unmistakably a fragment of pottery. Looking carefully at the floor, there were numerous pieces of broken pottery. Just like in the shed. "Have many intact examples of Janusian pottery been found?"

"No intact examples of Janusian pottery have been found."

That was weird. Wouldn't at least a few pieces have survived? Except there didn't seem to be even large fragments anywhere that Aquino could see.

One piece caught his eye. He knelt to look at the broken piece of ceramic in which one side was intact, displaying a knife edge.

This had clearly been part of a ceramic knife. Or possibly a ceramic weapon instead of a multi-use tool like a knife. Broken along with everything else. Humans looking for remnants of metal weapons could easily overlook those.

He took another look at the piles of decaying wood. "Have any intact examples of Janusian furniture been found?"

"No intact examples of Janusian furniture have been found."

Not only had all of the Janusians died, all of their belongings seemed to have been destroyed, too.

A death cult? Capturing city after city, town after town, destroying everything and killing everyone?

On an entire planet? No survivors, anywhere?

"Are there estimates of when different cities and towns died?"

"Clarify question."

"Can you show me which cities and towns died first, and which died later?"

A pause. "Only rough estimates can be provided."

"Display."

A globe appeared before him with cities and towns glowing in various colors. Looked at from this perspective, there wasn't any pattern at all, no apparent wave rolling over town after town, city after city. Instead, it looked random. Various cities in various places had been wiped out, the devastation possibly spreading out from different locations that formed a patchwork with no obvious pattern.

And the city wall, decayed and eroded as it was, showed no signs of having been breached in a battle.

"Show me ceramic fragments in this courtyard."

Hundreds of pieces in the courtyard were highlighted.

"Can you tell which ceramic pieces were constructed with sharp edges?" Aquino asked.

Many of the highlighted fragments vanished, while many remained.

Had there been a battle here? And then the victors smashed everything and left? Or killed themselves?

None of this made sense.

The land beyond the walls of the city smelled different but not bad, a mix of Janusian creatures and vegetation. Inside the city, it stank of swampy, shallow ponds and decaying plants. As Aquino stood there, thinking, another group of squonks moved at a leisurely pace through the courtyard and into various buildings they passed.

It all made the theory that these were once pets seem reasonable. That, or former working animals, still roaming the cities and towns in an endless, futile search for their vanished masters.

How did an intelligent species with the low level of technology that the Janusians possessed get wiped out? Humanity had come close to annihilating themselves more than once, but only *after* developing the technology to do it. Before that, even the worst plagues left enough survivors to rebuild.

He didn't have any conclusions to report to Captain Jardyce, just the same frustration she must feel.

Tired from fighting the gravity and hot from the bright sun, Aquino stubbornly chose another sim destination.

The world around him swirled, fading and then regrowing in strength as it transitioned from one location to the next.

He was in what he'd call a town square, with roads running outward. From the low position of the sun, these recordings had been made either early in the morning or late in the afternoon.

No walls protected this town.

The flatness of Janus Five's terrain was emphasized here without the "trees" to interrupt the view. Nearly level ground ran all the way to the horizon.

This town had been a farming community, he guessed, located in a drier, hotter area than the previous city. The town square was littered with bones, but the well in the center had dried out. The entire town felt as dry as death, the wind carrying dust as well as faint scents from the parched fields all around. Had the fields once been irrigated?

A pack of squonks lay in the sun in one corner of the town square. One yawned. The others dozed, young ones cuddled against older squonks, the cuteness of the squonks forming a bizarre contrast with the death-haunted ruins of the town.

A pile of broken wood on one side of the square revealed the arc of a wheel. Aquino went closer, seeing what had once been a wagon. A wagon implied the presence of draft animals to pull it. Sure enough, not far away, a substantially complete skull rested among the dust. It didn't look like the skull of anything Aquino had ever seen or ever wanted to see, but anything with a head that size had certainly been big enough to haul a wagon.

"How many of these draft animals have been found alive?"

"None of the creatures matching that skull have been found alive."

Aquino paused to take that in. "Have the skulls been found in more than one location?"

"The skulls have been found in many places once occupied by the Janusians."

The draft animals were also wiped out. That explained why he hadn't seen herds of these beasts grazing in the fields of abandoned farms. "Are there any indications how they died?"

"The remains are too badly deteriorated and damaged to draw conclusions as to cause of death."

"Were many remains found in enclosures or barns?" Had most of the draft animals slowly died after their owners were no longer around to feed and water them?

"Some remains were found inside the wreckage of such structures. Other remains were found outside them."

So much for that idea.

Aquino went inside one of the larger buildings fronting the square. Sunlight lanced in, illuminating dust motes dancing in the dry air. The floor was covered with bones, causing him to expect them to crackle as he walked on them and broke them. But, of course the drone that recorded this hadn't damaged the bones as it slowly flew through here.

He didn't feel like climbing the ramps this time. "Third floor."

Reality swirled, reforming into a room much like the first floor, except that instead of a door it had wide windows looking out on the town square. And, of course, bones.

To his surprise, another ramp led up to the roof. He took that, seeing near the top, large, wide stones, and broken, rotting wood beneath them. A barricade or wall that had been destroyed? Or simply roof structures to keep out rain and other weather that subsequently collapsed? The stones looked too heavy for roofing, though.

There were, of course, bones up here as well, though only a few. Aquino approached the edge of the roof and looked down, spotting other bones on the ground. Were those the remains of Janusians who'd been pushed or fell or jumped from here? Perhaps simply Janusians who died on the ground?

He looked out over the dead town, thinking that the entire planet was like this.

Before he ended the simulation, Aquino spent a few more moments watching the squonks in one corner of the town square. The attention of the squonks was fixed on something, probably one of the drones which had recorded this. They didn't move, just watched.

Calling up the virtual menu, he punched the "end simulation" command and Janus Five slowly faded out of existence.

Walking in normal gravity again, without the hot sun of Janus Five beating down on him, Aquino felt ten times better by the time he reached his room.

He was still beat, both physically and in his spirit that was weighed down by the scenes of ancient mass death. When Corporal Rodriguez stopped by, he shook his head. "No combat sims today. I'm worn out from hiking around Janus Five."

Rodriguez looked envious. "What's it like?"

"It sucks." Aquino rubbed his eyes, trying to smear away the memories. "Too heavy, too hot, some seriously carnivorous bugs, and death everywhere. They should have named this star after Hades, not Janus, because Janus Five is a boneyard."

"That bad?"

"Worse. Believe me." He leaned back, grimacing. "And not a single clear sign of what killed them all. An entire intelligent species wiped out, and we can't tell what did it. Do you know why that bothers me, Corporal Rodriguez?"

She nodded. "If we don't know what killed them, how do we know whether or not it's still there?"

"You nailed it the first time. See you tomorrow, Corporal."

He had missed regular meal times during his extended period in the sim, but was able to grab some food from the evening work stations in the dining room.

Once back in his room, he paused before getting ready for bed, finally punching in a number he hadn't felt comfortable using.

KT answered, gazing at him in surprise. "Hi, Oz! What's up?"

"I spent most of the day in surface simulations," he said.

"What did you think?"

"I hated it."

"It's freaky, right? So much death." She hesitated. "Did you see anything you think others might have overlooked?"

"I don't know. Are you aware of the broken pottery?"

"Yeah?"

"I think some of that was weapons with ceramic blades."

"Really?" KT gave him an appraising look. "That's been a big question. Where are the weapons? Because even if they'd rusted, there should be residue in the surface soil. Some people have been arguing the Janusians didn't have weapons, that they were peaceful by nature."

"They had defensive walls," Aquino pointed out.

"Those could have been to keep out animals. Let me check… okay. The edged ceramics have been evaluated as kitchen tools."

"They had a whole lot of kitchen tools, then."

"Yeah. I'm going to have the system run an evaluation to estimate total 'knives' from the fragments found. That'll take a while. But something killed all of those Janusians."

"It sure didn't look like a plague," Aquino said. "I did see the squonks."

"And?"

He shrugged. "It's a lot easier to understand why people are gaga over them. But… I don't get it. Say the squonks were dogs for the Janusians. Why did every other animal associated with the Janusians also die out?"

"You mean like the draft animals?" KT said. "Does it bother you? That the squonks seem to be so peaceful and non-territorial, yet anything that could challenge them is dead along with the Janusians?"

"Yes. But… their visible behaviors don't match that kind of dangerous animal scenario! Why not?"

"That's the question we need the answer to," KT said.

"KT, there was something else I noticed, but it's something I *didn't* see."

"What's that, Oz?"

He took a beat to order the words properly. "My mother has a cat. A little cat. I think it's a little monster. But Mom loves it. There are pictures of that cat everywhere in her and Dad's home."

"Yeah, cat people, dog people, horse people," KT said. "Anyone who's into a particular animal tends to put up pictures of it."

"I didn't see any pictures of squonks. After I ended the sim, I asked the AI if any paintings including squonks had been found, and it said no."

"That's interesting. Though the observation is also based on human practice. If the Janusians never made pictures of squonks, it might have been for reasons that made perfect sense to the Janusians."

"I didn't see any pet beds," Aquino added. "Okay, any food or water dishes would have been pottery and smashed along with all the rest, but no beds, no toys, no signs in those buildings that squonks had ever lived there."

"Again, Oz, we're dealing with aliens. Maybe they wouldn't keep pets or working animals in their homes."

"Maybe not."

"But, yes, that's odd from a human perspective." KT sighed. "You didn't see any smoking guns?"

"No. Just that vague sense that things weren't adding up. Same as you. I'm going to sleep on it and see if my subconscious keys on anything by the time I wake up." He smiled. "Good night, KT."

"Thanks for giving it a look, Oz. And for taking my concerns seriously."

"Always," he said, wondering why that single word seemed to startle KT in a good way.

For the second morning in a row, he was brought fully awake by the urgent buzz of his comm panel. Except, this time, it wasn't Captain Jardyce.

Instead, Aquino was surprised to see Doctor Gohara looking back at him. Why would the senior researcher aboard the ship be contacting him directly? And this early in the morning? "What's the matter, sir?"

Gohara grimaced unhappily. "We may have a problem that requires your assistance."

"A problem?"

"The, um… there has been… an incident. Involving… two specimens."

"An incident?" Aquino checked the room number the call was coming from.

The largest isolation lab on the *Darwin*.

"Does this involve the squonks?" Aquino asked.

"Squonks." Another grimace. "Yes. The, uh, squonks we had isolated in this lab are, uh..."

"*Had* isolated?" Aquino asked, a chill of concern growing. Why was Gohara using the past tense?

"Had isolated," Gohara repeated. "They have, um, temporarily evaded safeguards and are... currently... unlocated."

"Unlocated? Do you mean they escaped?"

"That's not a completely accurate term, but fine. Escaped. They're somewhere on the ship, and we, er, request your assistance to reacquire them."

"I'll be right there," Aquino said. He hesitated before pulling on his uniform, visions of the death fields on Janus Five running through his head. Deciding, he hit the button that would alert Sergeant Antaeus. "There's a problem in one of the labs. I need our Marines up and ready. I'll notify you when I have more details."

FIVE

AQUINO walked briskly down the passageways of the ship, encountering few people this early in the ship's "morning." It seemed to take forever to reach the lab. He kept fighting down an urge to run, knowing that might alarm anyone who saw him.

The door to the lab was open. Inside, Dr. Gohara and several other researchers were standing around as if waiting for something or someone to jar them into motion.

"What happened?" Aquino asked, taking in the wide-open door to the isolation enclosure. The lab looked as he expected one to look, with counters laden with equipment, shades of white on every surface, and everything neatly organized. Except for one counter with a jumble of knocked-around equipment, above it the broken bracket of a high-end surveillance camera that had been disabled the hard way.

"I told you," Gohara almost snapped. He seemed to be trying to project calm, but the chief researcher couldn't conceal his tension. "The specimens evaded their safeguards and are currently unlocated."

"How did they evade their safeguards?"

"Why does *how* matter?"

Apparently, senior scientists were like senior Navy officers and needed to have things explained to them in ways that sounded respectful. What argument would work best with a scientist? "Sir, I need to know as much as possible about what I'm dealing with."

As he hoped, none of the scientists objected to the idea that someone needed access to all available data. A woman gestured to the enclosure. "They… let me show you the footage." She tapped some controls, bringing one of the large screens to life.

The two squonks were sitting in the enclosure, just as they had in the video KT showed him. The time indicator confirmed the video had been recorded in the early morning hours. Suddenly, the squonks moved, heading toward a small, sealed pass-through intended to allow very limited access to the enclosure. Each squonk raised their forepaws, the bottom padding unfurling into three finger-like digits and an opposable thumb. Grasping the inner door, they pulled and twisted, arm muscles bulging, popping the door open.

That left the outer door, secured by a mechanical latch.

One of the squonks reached in two, thick, wicked-looking claws extending from between the three fingers. Inserting one claw into the latch, the squonk applied pressure.

The latch snapped.

Pushing open the outer door, the squonk extended its long arm to reach the electronic lock to the main entrance of the enclosure. The controls for the lock were conveniently located near the pass-through. The squonk tapped quickly, creating a string of musical tones.

Nothing happened.

The squonk tapped again, producing a slightly different set of tones.

Again, nothing.

The squonk made a third try, the notes close to but not identical to the first two tries.

The main door opened.

The squonks hurled themselves out of the cage, but instead of bolting out of the lab, ran toward the camera.

The camera went dead.

Aquino took a deep breath. Fingers. Claws. KT had been right about something being hidden or protected inside those front paws. "They killed the camera?"

Dr. Gohara said nothing, but one of the men spoke up, "We've watched replays of them on these screens. If they were observing us do that, they'd have been able to tell where the cameras were that were watching them."

And they were smarter than anyone had accounted for. Aquino looked at the keypad for the electronic lock. "How did they know the combination for that close enough to get it on the third try?"

"We can only guess, but of course we entered the combination when we locked the enclosure after bringing the squonks up here," the researcher explained. "They were awake and alert, because we couldn't safely sedate them. They must have heard the musical tones and remembered them well enough to reproduce them after three tries."

"That's part of a popular song, isn't it?" Aquino said.

"That's right. It's a user-friendly feature to allow people to remember the combinations as a tune. That… may have aided the squonks as well in remembering the tune."

"User-friendly," Aquino said. Should he mention that making locks "user-friendly" for those who wanted to open them sounded like a contradiction? And having the lock combination panel set so close to the access? That would have made it more convenient for users as well. "Do you have any idea where they might have gone?"

"They didn't go left out of that door," the woman said, pointing at the entry to the lab. "Some of us were approaching the lab from that direction. We couldn't see the door when the, um, squonks departed, but they would have run into us very quickly if they'd gone left."

"Then they went right out of here," Aquino said, gazing at the door. "Heading aft. Aren't the engineering compartments in that direction?"

"I think so. That's the next set of compartments anyone would encounter going toward the back of the ship from here."

Engineering. Full of equipment large and small, with lots and lots of places things the size of the squonks could hide. "Okay. They're strong, they're smart, they've got claws. I'll get my Marines and… what?"

The woman hesitated, looking toward Dr. Gohara, who scowled but said nothing. "We, uh, already sent three people looking for the specimens."

"You sent three people? Who?" Aquino asked, a now-familiar knot forming in his gut.

"Graduate students," the woman explained. "Junior researchers. We sent one out, and when we didn't hear from him, we sent two more."

"And you haven't heard back from any of them?" Aquino demanded. "How long ago was this?"

"The last pair went out about half an hour ago, now."

Oh, crap. "Did they have any special equipment?"

"Sampler nets," Dr. Gohara said. "We couldn't use any incapacitation gases or sprays because those could have harmed the specimens."

Sampler nets. Three people sent out unarmed against the strong, smart, squonks. "Thank you for that information. I guess I'll also be looking for those three graduate students. I'll prepare my Marines and we'll search aft from here." How much should he prepare them, though? Body armor seemed smart. Marines on ships couldn't use massive power armor because of the limited space to move about, but their body armor would protect some against those claws and teeth on the squonks. What weapons should he have them carry, though?

Aquino turned to rush back to the Marine compartments, but paused as another thought struck. "What is the captain doing about this?" Captain Jardyce must be mad as hell. Had she deployed the ship's security force? That was only eight people strong, including the officious Senior Officer Corba. Aquino didn't want to work at cross purposes to other teams that might already be conducting searches.

Dr. Gohara answered, his voice stiff, "There hasn't been any need to bother Captain Jardyce about this. If we can resolve this situation quickly, I can notify her afterwards at her convenience. I appreciate your discretion on this matter."

Aquino, momentarily lost for words, didn't trust himself to speak. He nodded at Gohara, a gesture that could mean almost anything at this point, and left the lab.

He stopped at the first communications panel he encountered in the passageway and made a call to the ship's bridge.

The screen shifted to show a ship's officer who Aquino vaguely recognized. "Duty Officer. What do you require?" the officer asked in a rote way.

"This is Ensign Aquino. I need to speak to the captain."

The duty officer squinted at Aquino. "Oh. You're that guy. The captain isn't available right now."

"Sir, I need to speak with her right now. This is very important."

"Very important? Are you sure? She's not going to like being interrupted."

"I'm sure," Aquino said. "This concerns a matter she's discussed with me and wanted to hear back from me on."

"Okay. It's on you if she blows up. I'll page her." The officer tapped a command, waiting.

Seconds ticked by, Aquino acutely aware of each moment wasted.

The duty officer frowned. "No answer. How important is this?"

"I think it qualifies as an emergency," Aquino said. "Potential danger to human life."

The duty officer gave him a skeptical look. "Okay," he repeated. "I'll give her an emergency page. The captain will answer that no matter what she's doing. I'm warning you that this had better be the real deal."

He tapped another command.

They waited.

The duty officer's frown grew deeper, matched with uncertainty. "That's… weird. I'll try paging the chief engineer."

"Why the chief engineer?" Aquino asked.

"Captain Jardyce is with him."

Another pause, the duty officer looking about him as if seeking an answer. “Are there any problems with internal comms?” he called out to someone else. “No?”

“Where are they?” Aquino asked. “I can go there.”

“They went to engineering.”

“What?” Aquino tried to calm his voice. “Engineering?”

“Yes. Engineering.” Clearly worried, the duty officer was getting short with Aquino.

“Where in engineering?”

“I don’t know!”

“Don’t the cameras in engineering cover all of the compartments?”

The duty officer shook his head. “That’s what they went back to engineering to investigate! The cameras went out! What the hell is—”

“Listen!” Aquino snapped. “Have you heard anything from the engineering watch team? You’ve got people on watch there, right? Have they contacted you recently?”

“No. We haven’t been able to get an answer from them. That’s another reason the captain and chief engineer went to check on things.”

“Damn.” Aquino took a deep breath. “Who’s the second in command on the ship?”

“First Officer Christina Lopez. Do you have some idea of what’s going on?”

“I’m afraid that I do,” Aquino said. “The researchers brought two squonks aboard the ship, and I’ve just been informed that those squonks escaped early this morning.”

“Squonks? Why would—”

“They’re believed to have headed toward engineering!” Aquino broke in. “After they disabled the cameras in the lab!”

The duty officer stared at Aquino, his mouth hanging open in almost comical shock.

“The researchers have already lost contact with three people they sent looking for the squonks,” Aquino continued. “I’m activating my

Marines. We're going after the squonks. But if they're dangerous, and you've lost contact with the captain and the chief engineer…"

"Oh, man. Oh, man. Are you serious?" the duty officer demanded, regaining his ability to speak.

"I am serious. You need to notify the second in command immediately. I'm going to get my Marines."

"Right. Okay. Damn! Okay." The duty officer cut off the call, doubtless to contact First Officer Lopez.

Aquino broke into a run back to the Marines, this time not caring who he might alarm.

He found the Marines standing around in the common room, dressed in working uniform coveralls, but otherwise unprepared for anything other than routine tasks. Tamping down his temper, Aquino turned to Sergeant Antaeus. "Get everyone into full combat gear. Complete body armor. And…" This was the tough call. But numerous people weren't answering pages they should have been responding to. "Open the armory. I want everyone carrying a weapon. With ammunition."

Instead of relaying the order to the other Marines, Antaeus looked skeptical. "Full combat gear? Loaded weapons? With all due respect, sir, giving these clowns loaded weapons is asking for trouble."

"I did not ask for your opinion, Sergeant! Get these Marines moving!"

Antaeus paused just long enough to be insolent but not long enough for Aquino to repeat the order. "You heard the man," he told the Marines. "Start getting ready. Full battle rattle. Rowdy, open the armory."

"Yes, Sarge," Corporal Rodriguez said, running to the back of the compartment where an armored door blocked access to the Marines' rifles, pistols, and grenades.

Aquino caught his breath, knowing he had to let the Marines know what was happening, and he needed to sound calm and controlled while doing that. "Here's the deal. The researchers brought two of the squonks aboard this ship. The squonks have escaped from the isolation enclosure they were held in and are loose on the ship, probably in engineering somewhere."

"What do the engineers say?" Antaeus asked. He hadn't yet moved to start putting on his own body armor.

"Engineering is out of contact," Aquino said. "Security cameras and communications are both down. The squonks—"

"That kind of junk happens all the time on civilian ships," Antaeus said. "They don't keep up their equipment well enough. Squonks? Those dogs?"

"They're not just dogs, Sergeant," Aquino said, trying to keep his temper from exploding at Antaeus. "They're strong. They've got claws."

"Dogs," Antaeus said. "Overreacting just risks an incident with the crew."

"Sergeant—"

"With all due respect, sir, you seem to be on the verge of panic. I can handle this."

Aquino was momentarily shocked into speechlessness, aware that the other Marines had ceased all activity and were watching him and the sergeant.

Antaeus started walking toward the door.

"Sergeant!" Aquino snarled. "Get back here!"

"I'll handle this," Antaeus tossed back over his shoulder as he reached the door. "A couple of dogs aren't that big a deal."

"Sergeant, you will return here now!"

Antaeus went out as if he hadn't heard a thing.

The fool was going to look for the squonks without any body armor or weapons. Always confident. Always sure he knew the answers.

Probably happy to have a way to openly undermine Ensign Aquino.

Aquino turned to the six other Marines, who were waiting to see how he reacted. Carefully controlling his voice to sound once more in command, Aquino pointed roughly at them, "Finish getting ready. Full body armor. Rodriguez, get that armory open and issue weapons and ammunition."

"Shouldn't we go after the sergeant?" Smith asked. "What if he gets into trouble?"

The temptation to charge after Antaeus was strong, but that might mean all of the Marines facing dangerous creatures without any protection. "We need to be ready before we go. See how fast you can do that."

It wasn't fast enough, Aquino thought as he struggled with his own body armor. He'd only tried it on a few times, unfamiliar with the equipment intended for the Marine officer commanding the detachment.

Rodriguez came up as Aquino struggled with a clasp. "Here, sir." She snapped the clasp closed, checking over the rest of his armor. "You look good otherwise."

Aquino saw the other Marines checking each other out, ensuring each had their armor and other equipment on right. "Weapons."

"Sir," Rodriguez said in a careful voice, "are you sure about that?"

"Yes," Aquino said. Inside himself, he wasn't so sure. But numerous people were missing, out of communication. And those squonks had looked not cute but deadly when they broke out of that enclosure. "I want weapons loaded and kept on safe until I order otherwise."

"Understood, sir." Rodriquez handed out the weapons to each Marine in turn. Blunt carbines with loaded ammunition magazines. Pistols. She hesitated over the grenades, looking toward Aquino.

Grenades? That seemed like overkill. "No grenades."

Rodriguez closed the armory and brought Aquino a holstered pistol. "Here's your sidearm, sir."

"Thanks, Corporal." He strapped on the pistol, then looked over the Marines, appearing alien in their battle gear and helmets, holding their weapons.

This was the real thing. He'd run simulation after simulation, but this was real. They were looking to him for orders.

"We're going to treat this like a threat situation," Aquino said, trying to sound as if he were giving a routine lecture. "At least five people are out of communication after going where the squonks probably are. The squonks are fast and strong. They have very tough claws as well as their teeth. I don't know if they'll attack once spotted. We're going out there to find them."

"Do you hear that?" Corporal Rodriguez shouted. "You apes do this right! Anybody who screws around will find my boot up their ass! Stay sharp!"

Aquino swallowed before speaking again, "Corporal, you take point along with Lachman. Obonsawin, you take the rear. Everybody else, with me. Do not take your weapons off safe or fire unless I order it. Any questions?"

No one said anything.

"Let's go," Aquino said.

The Marines left their room and started down the passageway, bulkier than usual, their firearms pointed upwards or down at the deck for safety.

His helmet felt odd, heavy, restricting his vision a bit above and to the sides. He felt more than a little ridiculous, like a kid playing at army. He kept the helmet on, regardless. The Marines were watching him, trying to see how seriously he was taking this.

There weren't as many people as usual in these passageways. Had First Officer Lopez already reacted to the problem? Those crew members and researchers the Marines did encounter gawked at them in disbelief, crowding against the walls to let the battle-ready Marines pass.

A security officer rushed up to them. "What the hell are you doing?"

"We're doing our job," Ensign Aquino told him. "Contact First Officer Lopez."

"You can't—"

What little patience he still possessed frayed and snapped, "Get the hell out of our way. NOW!"

The security officer faded back, clawing at the communications device at her belt.

They passed the lab the squonks escaped from, a few researchers still inside gazing out with worried expressions. "Try not to hurt them!" one of the researchers called.

Private Ichikawa laughed.

"Shouldn't we be seeing the sergeant soon?" Private Kenyatta asked.

Wouldn't that be supremely embarrassing? If they encountered Antaeus coming back, the big man holding a subdued squonk by the neck in each hand? It would destroy any respect he'd managed to generate with the other Marines.

Which was probably what Sergeant Antaeus intended.

Aquino opened his mouth to reply.

A bellow of anger sounded ahead of them, shifting from surprise to rage to pain before being abruptly cut off.

The Marines came to a halt, staring down the passageway toward the open door to engineering that had just come into view.

"That sounded like the sergeant," Private Smith gasped.

Rodriguez looked back at Aquino.

This was it, then. "Let's go!" Aquino called out. He hesitated for just a moment before giving the next order, knowing the potential for disaster in it. But that yell from Antaeus had sounded really bad. And the sergeant wasn't making any sounds now. "Take your weapons off safe! Be ready to fire on my order!"

Corporal Rodriguez broke into a fast trot, her rifle now level, pointing before her as she moved into engineering. The others followed, Aquino feeling like he should be leading Hollywood-style. However, based on the sims he'd run, sound tactics meant him staying in the center, able to evaluate the situation and give the others whatever orders were needed.

Engineering was filled with the hum of working equipment, and a sharp scent in the air, something coppery that made the hairs stand up on Aquino's arms.

He saw what seemed like recent damage to the exteriors of some of the equipment as they passed it.

Corporal Rodriguez came to an abrupt halt, her weapon questing around for targets. "Sir, I found the sergeant."

Aquino pushed forward, seeing Antaeus lying face down flat on the deck. Deep slashes were visible on his neck and back, blood pooling around him. *Oh, damn.* Not this. He'd wanted the sergeant to get taken down a notch, but not in the form of a fatal lesson.

Stay in charge. Stay in control of yourself. Keep your voice calm, Aquino told himself before saying anything, "Kenyatta… check him. Everybody else, watch for trouble."

Appearing unfazed by the situation, Kenyatta knelt by Antaeus, checking his vitals. "He's not cold yet, but he's dead, sir. Maybe blood loss, but it looks like this slash might've severed his spine."

Now, what? Aquino looked about him, not really seeing the machinery and equipment surrounding them, acutely aware he'd just lost the senior enlisted who was supposed to be his primary support when dealing with the Marines, and that the squonks were not just theoretically dangerous, but extremely dangerous.

What should he do? What did he *need* to do?

One thought pushed forward. There might be more people down here, still alive.

"Hello!" Aquino shouted. "Can anybody hear me?"

The words echoed through the compartment.

No one answered.

"We can protect you and escort you out of here! Anybody in engineering, respond!"

Nothing.

"Captain Jardyce! This is Ensign Aquino! Can you hear me?"

The only response was the hum of the equipment around them.

Were the others dead? Should he push on, try to find them, just in case?

The Marines were nervously scanning their surroundings, while darting anxious glances at him. They needed him to tell them what to do next.

He wished he could be certain what he should do next.

Lachman edged one foot back toward the door. That gave Aquino something to be certain of. "Hold your positions!" Aquino called out in a harsh voice.

"You heard the man!" Rodriguez added in a voice as hard as the steel deck they were standing on. "Wait for orders!"

Orders. He had to give them. But, what? Hunt the squonks now? This wasn't the only way into and out of engineering. While the Marines were searching here, the squonks might head out into the rest of the ship. If he'd had twice as many Marines, he could have left half here to search while the rest defended the remainder of the ship. But he only had six. And there was no way he could leave only two or three Marines here against two deadly enemies.

You fight with what you've got. And, if that isn't enough, you're screwed.

No. He could still warn everyone. That cleared his head, offering a course of action that felt right. If everyone in engineering was dead, his primary responsibility now was to ensure the ship's remaining crew was alerted. Wasn't that right? To do that, he needed to get out of engineering.

And, maybe, Antaeus could still be revived.

"I want Kenyatta and Smith to pick up Antaeus," Aquino said, speaking more slowly than usual to keep his words from sounding rushed. "If they need help, I want Ichikawa and Lachman to assist. Corporal Rodriguez, you're now rear guard. Obonsawin, you're point. We will… fall back from engineering and get the sergeant to medical. From there, I will alert the crew to the danger and we will… develop a new course of action."

A chorus of, "Yes, sir," answered him, the Marines springing into action now that they had clear tasks laid out for them.

Backing out of engineering seemed to take forever.

Rodriguez closed and sealed the door behind them, but after watching the squonks figure out how to escape their enclosure, Aquino didn't think that would slow them down.

"Dammit, Smith," Kenyatta grumbled. "Can't you even carry something right? Get in here and help him, Lachman."

Lachman moved in, taking some of Antaeus's weight. "Good thing Ant-man is dead. He'd be yelling at us for doing this wrong."

"Damn straight," Kenyatta agreed.

Aquino didn't say anything. He'd wondered what the other Marines thought of their sergeant. The shock they clearly felt over Sergeant Antaeus's death wasn't matched by grief, though. That told him everything he needed to know.

Backing down the corridor, they reached the isolation lab. "Hold," Aquino called, moving to look inside. Several worried researchers looked back at him, startled by his appearance in battle gear, a pistol still in hand. "Get out of here," he said. "Right now. It isn't safe this close to engineering."

"Why isn't it safe?" one demanded.

Then they caught sight of Antaeus' body, dripping blood onto the deck.

"Get out of here," Aquino repeated. "The squonks are deadly. Tell Dr. Gohara. Go!"

They ran. Maybe they were more afraid of him than they were of the squonks, but at the moment, he didn't care so long as they ran.

"Keep moving," Aquino told the Marines. "Head for medical."

"That's down this way," Private Obonsawin called.

They moved faster, Rodriguez still covering against any pursuit by the squonks, encountering occasional crew members or researchers who were all warned to clear any area near engineering.

Aquino had only been to the medical rooms once while checking in aboard *Darwin*. It was as he remembered, with wide windows looking out into the passageway and soft lights intended to offer a calming, inviting, non-threatening environment.

Looking at those wide windows now, Aquino could only wonder whether they'd provide warning that the squonks were near or simply offer easy entry for them.

As the Marines shoved their way into medical past a couple of people waiting in line, the receptionist looked up with an annoyed expression that quickly changed to alarm. "What happened?"

"He's dead," Aquino said. "Maybe he can still be revived."

"Oh-gawd-why-on-my-shift." The receptionist hit a place on her screen. "All doctors, code green in entry area. Clear surgery room one!"

Two women and one man rushed out of side rooms, racing to where the Marines were still straining to hold up Antaeus' body. "Room one!" one commanded, pointing.

"What kind of accident was it?" another doctor demanded of Aquino as Antaeus was carried into the surgery room.

"It wasn't an accident," he said, suddenly feeling very tired. "Two squonks are loose on the ship. One or both of them did that. Haven't you been alerted?"

"No!" The doctor ran toward the room where Antaeus was being taken.

"I need your comm panel," Aquino told the receptionist.

Eyeing him in his battle gear, she slid back and gestured toward it.

He called the bridge.

This time, a woman answered, "First Officer Lopez. Who— You're that Marine guy."

"Ensign Aquino," he said. "We've just been in engineering."

"Have you regained control of the specimens?" Lopez asked. "What are Captain Jardyce's instructions?"

He had to take a breath before answering, "No. The squonks are still loose. They've killed Sergeant Antaeus and—"

"Killed? Did you say *killed*?"

"Yes," Aquino said. "They have deadly claws. They're very strong. They—"

"Where is Captain Jardyce?"

How to answer that? "Captain Jardyce is very likely dead, along with everyone else who was in engineering."

Lopez's mouth hung open but no words came out. "No," she finally said.

He knew how she felt. "I called out multiple times. No one answered. First Officer Lopez, you have to assume you are in command of this ship. There is a deadly threat in engineering."

"Then why aren't you in there?" Lopez demanded, shock giving way to anger.

"Because I had to get my injured man out and make sure you knew how serious things were!" Aquino gestured aft. "We're going to go back in. But you need to clear people from the area near engineering. I don't have enough Marines to hunt the squonks *and* set up any security in case the squonks leave engineering."

Lopez had closed her eyes, breathing slowly. When she reopened them, her eyes were clear and determined. "Clear the area. Yes. I'll activate the entire ship's security force. You're going back into engineering? When?"

He wanted to rest. He wanted to rest more than he'd ever wanted anything. "Right now," Aquino said.

"Please hurry. We're getting readings of cascading damage to equipment in engineering. A team was going to head down there but I told them to wait until we heard from you. Keep me informed."

"Yes… Captain," Aquino said.

Cascading damage in engineering. He remembered the buildings on Janus Five, their floors covered with broken pottery and furniture. Why were the squonks so destructive as well as deadly?

Ending the call, he turned to the six Marines waiting for their next orders. Kenyatta, Smith, and Lachman had Sergeant Antaeus's blood smeared on their body armor and uniforms.

Before he could speak, one of the doctors came out of room one, shaking her head. "He was too badly hurt. Revival is impossible. What cut his spine?"

"The claws on a squonk," Aquino said.

"A squonk? Those cute things?"

"Yeah. Those cute things. Captain Lopez should have orders for you, telling you what to do."

"Captain Lopez? Where's Captain Jardyce?"

The same question he'd gotten from Lopez, but he needed to give a different answer here. Panic might break out otherwise. "We're going back to engineering to try to find her. Contact Lopez."

Turning again to the Marines, he saw Lachman looking toward room one with a baffled expression. "Sir? The sergeant is dead? For good?"

"Yes," Aquino said. "Revival is impossible."

"But… but… sir, we need a sergeant."

Someone to help hold the detachment together. He could understand that need. He wanted a sergeant, too.

Aquino pointed to Rodriguez. "We've got one. Rodriguez, you are hereby field promoted to sergeant using my authority as senior officer present."

"Congratulations, Rowdy," Ichikawa muttered sarcastically.

"Maybe third time is the charm," Obonsawin added.

They were nervous, Aquino knew, and trying to vent those worries using dark humor.

Rodriguez nodded, licking her lips nervously. She clearly felt the weight of the responsibilities that had just fallen on her. "Understood, sir."

"Then let's go," Aquino said. "Sergeant Rodriguez, you're point again. Take us back to engineering."

"We're seriously going back?" Kenyatta asked, as unflappable as ever.

"Yes, we're going back," Aquino said.

"But…" Private Lachman looked at the others. "What if…"

"Hey, Lachman," Obonsawin said in an almost-friendly voice. "We do the job, right? And, if you screw around, and the squonks don't kill you, I will. Okay?"

Lachman stared at Obonsawin. "Okay."

"Move out," Aquino said.

Within moments of leaving the medical rooms, the ship's general announcing system emitted a loud warning tone. "All crew and passengers aboard the *Darwin*, this is First Officer Lopez. There is a hazardous situation near the engineering compartments. Everyone is to maintain a safe distance away from any of the entrances or exits to engineering. Follow any instructions you are given by the ship's security officers. Or by the Marines, who are seeking to contain the threat. Everyone is to remain calm. The Marines are handling the hazard."

"Hey, Sergeant Rowdy," Ichikawa called. "What's a safe distance from engineering?"

Rodriguez glanced back for just a moment. "Whatever Ensign Aquino says it is. Now shut up, straighten up, and be sharp."

They were almost to engineering when two figures approached from a side passage. Aquino saw rifles in the hands of nervous Marines swing toward the newcomers, suddenly remembering he'd never told them to safe their weapons, and hastily shouted, "Hold fire!"

The two were Senior Security Officer Corba and one of his other officers. "We've been sent out by First Officer Lopez. What's going on?"

Aquino nodded toward engineering, impressed that despite their earlier confrontation, Corba was being totally professional during a crisis. "Two squonks brought onto the ship are loose inside engineering. We're going in there."

"And these squonks are dangerous?"

This time, Aquino gestured to where drops of Antaeus's blood lay on the deck. "They killed Sergeant Antaeus. And probably several other people. No one in engineering is answering."

Corba wiped his mouth, looking at the Marines' weapons. "We have orders to assist you. I can send in backup."

Aquino shook his head. "I think your people may be overmatched by this. Or underequipped. I don't doubt their courage. But I think your people are better employed keeping crew and researchers away from any entrances to engineering."

"Are those things likely to come out if you're chasing them in there?"

"I have no idea," Aquino said. "I only know, per First Officer Lopez, I mean, Captain Lopez, that I can't have the squonks in engineering continuing to damage equipment. And there may be some people still alive in there."

"Yeah. Right. I understand." Corba turned to his assistant, pointing to a device. "Give me your comm relay. Here," he said, handing it to Aquino, "in case we need to speak."

"Thanks. What kind of weapons do your people have?" Aquino asked.

"Stun rods," the other officer said, hefting a baton-like device.

"I don't think those will do much good against the squonks," Aquino said. "If they come out, I'd recommending avoiding them."

"If they come out of engineering," Corba said, "and threaten anyone on this ship, we will fight them."

Aquino, knowing arguing would be useless, and respecting the security officer's determination, simply nodded. "Let's go, Rodriguez."

They paused at the entrance to engineering as Rodriguez unsealed the door. The wait gave Aquino a moment to wonder what the hell he was doing here. An ensign, leading a few Marines into a dangerous situation. With so many people depending on him not screwing this up.

One of those people being KT.

Hopefully, she was nowhere near engineering.

They went inside, Rodriguez on point again, everyone's weapons searching for targets.

His pistol, though much smaller than the carbines carried by the Marines, felt heavy and awkward in his hand. He worried that if he fired it, he would hit one of the Marines rather than one of the squonks. The body armor and helmet weighed him down, constraining his movements and vision. The coppery scent of blood still filled the air. Was it just the blood of Sergeant Antaeus? Or also the blood of several others?

He was scared, recalling the deep slashes that had killed Antaeus, his heart pounding loudly in his ears. He worked to control his breathing. Nothing in his life, or his training before coming to *Darwin*, had prepared him for this. Worse, the lives of these six Marines were riding on his decisions. Antaeus had killed himself through arrogance. But if any of these others died, it would be because they were following the orders of Ensign Osiris Aquino. He wanted to be anywhere but here, doing anything but this.

They were counting on him.

He had to do his job.

Aquino kept walking, kept searching every direction for danger, kept trying to be the leader these Marines needed. That every person aboard *Darwin* needed.

Engineering, like every engineering compartment, was full of equipment, some big, some smaller, sometimes with only narrow accesses between them. It sprawled across more than one level. There were countless places for someone, something, to lie in wait to ambush anyone passing by.

Rodriguez irritably tapped the visor of her helmet. "Our warning sensors don't work worth a damn on ships. Too much interference, too many obstacles. They're useless."

Which meant they had to depend on human senses for warning.

They'd gone another three meters past where Sergeant Antaeus had been found when Rodriguez made the hand signal to halt, her weapon pointed down a side path. She advanced cautiously, Aquino bringing the others behind her.

Once at the junction with the path, he could see Rodriguez kneeling by another body, this one in civilian clothing rather than one of the crew uniforms. "Dead," Rodriguez reported in a low voice. "Any idea who this is, sir?"

"Probably one of the graduate students the researchers sent out after the squonks," Aquino said.

"I wish those researchers had to look at this," Rodriguez said, glancing around. "There's another one. Was there a pair of them?"

"Yes," Aquino said. "The second set of searchers was a pair."

"We found them." Rodriguez straightened and continued on, the others following, placing their feet carefully as they passed the dead researchers, trying to avoid stepping in the blood pooled around them.

"Where the hell are those things?" Kenyatta muttered.

Rodriguez stopped abruptly, then moved again, crouching.

Aquino moved to cover her, seeing that she was by someone sitting against a piece of equipment.

No. Not sitting. They'd fallen that way, blood soaking the front of their uniform.

"Isn't this the captain?" Rodriquez asked.

Aquino forced himself to look into the lifeless eyes of Captain Jardyce. "Yes."

"I can't wait to get a clean shot at those things," Obonsawin said, searching their surroundings.

A scream sounded, faint with distance or obstacles blocking the sound.

"That wasn't in here," Ichikawa said, pointing. "It came through that ventilation duct. Where does it lead?"

Aquino looked, his naval training allowing him to decipher the letters and numbers providing information on the duct. "Outside," he said, hearing the despair in his voice. "Outside of engineering. While we were searching for them in here, they avoided us and went into another part of the ship. Those damn things are out there killing people."

SIX

AT least in this moment, Aquino didn't feel totally out of his depth. Thanks to his naval training, he knew about where that ventilation duct should come out. "Come on!" he told the Marines, breaking into a run.

They followed, Rodriguez racing to shoulder him aside with a cross look and take point again. Right. He shouldn't be literally leading these Marines.

They raced down several short passages between equipment, passing the slashed body of someone in ship's crew uniform who'd probably been part of the engineering watch team.

Rodriguez slammed through the door into a passageway outside engineering, her weapon seeking targets.

As Aquino and the others came up behind her, they found the bodies of two security officers, both with death grips on their useless stun batons.

Where to go? Aquino wondered. Where would the squonks be now? "Rodriguez, that way. There should be another entrance to engineering about ten meters down and around that corner."

Remembering the security force comm link, he pulled it out. "Officer Corba. Can you hear me? Officer Corba!"

He didn't answer. Aquino hoped that was because he wasn't using the comm link right.

They rounded the corner and found Officer Corba.

He and his assistant both lay on the deck surrounded by their own blood. Aquino stared at the bodies, remembering Hakim Marvin's assurance that humans would be toxic to life from Janus Five. If human blood was toxic to the squonks, it wasn't strong enough to stop their killing spree.

Pointing again, Aquino led the Marines toward where the next access to engineering should be. He keyed the security force comm link again. "Anyone on this circuit. This is Ensign Aquino. Fall back. Get away from engineering."

"Who is this?" a woman replied. "You have no authority to give us orders!"

"This is Ensign Aquino! Withdraw! Now!"

"We—"

The voice cut off abruptly, just as Aquino heard a shout around the next corner.

They rounded it in time to see the woman officer, the same one who accompanied Corba on the attempt to arrest the Marines, hit one wall, blood flying. The other officer was already down, a squonk hitting him again.

"Light 'em up!" Rodriguez shouted. She opened fire, the other Marines joining in. The mag rifles only made a loud hum when they accelerated a round out of the barrel, but as the bullets themselves tore through the air at supersonic velocity, they created sharp reports, the sound of each shot echoing loudly.

Aquino held his pistol, watching the squonks move with amazing speed and agility, launching themselves back into engineering.

They acted nothing like the squonks he had seen in the surface simulations. Instead of peaceful, gentle appearing creatures, these were predators operating at the peak of their killing ability.

It was the difference between a cat slumbering in the sun, and the same cat if a mouse appeared.

Why hadn't the squonks shown those behaviors on the surface?

The Marines ran to the door the squonks had escaped through, aiming inside. "Where are they?" Ichikawa gasped.

"Already gone," Rodriguez said. She looked around. "I don't see any alien blood. Just human. We didn't score any hits."

"They're so damned fast," Obonsawin said. "At least they're back in engineering."

"Until we go back in there hunting them again," Kenyatta said. For the first time in Aquino's experience, even Kenyatta looked nervous, though her voice was steady enough. "What are we going to do, sir?"

It was back on him again, and he had no ideas.

Aquino heard the security comm link he was carrying squawk. "Ensign Aquino, are you still on this?"

He raised the comm link. "Yes."

"This is Lopez. What's happened?"

"We went into engineering. The squonks avoided us, came out, and killed six security officers. We just chased them back into engineering." As Aquino spoke, the Marines watched in all directions, the aim of their weapons twitching from one point to another.

After Aquino was done, there was a long moment of silence. "We need to have a council to make some decisions," Lopez finally said. "I need you on the bridge."

"What about my Marines?"

"Can they keep the squonks inside engineering?"

Aquino sighed, feeling very tired again. "No. There aren't enough of them. But, based on what's happened so far, as long as we don't go in, the squonks may stay inside."

"Leave the Marines on guard, then, and get up to the bridge as fast as possible."

He was reluctant to follow that order, and in this kind of situation, he didn't have to defer to the civilian ship's officers, but he really didn't have any alternatives. His Marines were tired, too, though. "Sergeant Rodriguez."

"Sir."

"We're going to maintain a guard in this area. Keep everyone here while I report in. Get as much rest as you can, but keep two Marines on sentry the whole time in case the squonks come back."

"Yes, sir. I'll rotate the sentries so everyone gets some time off their feet."

"I'll be back as quickly as I can," Aquino promised.

He began trotting down the passageway, feeling strange again in the body armor, his helmet thumping on his head a bit with each step. Realizing he was still tightly grasping the pistol, he holstered it.

The bridge. This way. The Marines were counting on him for answers. He didn't have any. Maybe someone on the bridge would have some.

The atmosphere on the bridge was hushed and nervous in that way that would cause anyone to walk on eggshells. Almost everyone was watching Doctor Gohara and First Officer Lopez, *Captain* Lopez, who were engaged in a low-volume but obviously very intense discussion.

Lopez noticed him as soon as he entered. "Aquino! Get over here!"

He hastened to join them, still panting a bit from his fast trip.

"How many dead did you personally see?" Lopez demanded with an angry glance at Doctor Gohara.

Aquino paused to think. "Four… five in engineering. No, six counting Sergeant Antaeus. And six security officers just outside engineering, including Senior Officer Corba."

"This does not make sense," Gohara insisted. "Predators do not kill indiscriminately and keep on killing!"

"These are!" Lopez replied hotly.

"The, uh, squonks on the surface of the planet are not doing anything like that! Something on this ship must have driven them into a frenzy."

"Something on this ship?" Lopez demanded. "Are you blaming the ship for this?"

"I'm trying to understand what's going on!" Gohara said.

Lopez gritted her teeth. "Ensign Aquino, did you find any trace of Captain Jardyce? Until we know for a certainty that she's dead, my ability to command is constrained."

Aquino nodded. "We found Captain Jardyce." He hated to see the flare of hope in Lopez's eyes that vanished with his next words, "Her body. She's dead."

Lopez sagged for just a moment before straightening and speaking in a loud, firm voice that carried across the bridge, "It has been confirmed that Captain Jardyce is dead. I am assuming full command of the *Darwin*." She looked at Aquino and spoke again in a much lower voice, "What do we do?"

I don't know. He couldn't say that, as true as it was. He could describe the problem, though. Aquino gestured aft. "I don't have enough Marines to hunt the squonks in engineering and protect the rest of the ship. Either the squonks know that or they're acting on some instinct."

"They can't *know* that," Doctor Gohara said with an eyeroll.

"Sir," Aquino said, "I am not going to underestimate the intelligence of the squonks until I know with a certainty what they're *not* capable of."

"Don't you have gas that can sedate specimens, Doctor Gohara?" Lopez demanded.

"Yes," Gohara said. "Sedation gas designed to deal with life forms with similar biology to ours. We have no idea how it will work on something from Janus Five. There is a slight chance it might sedate them or kill them. More likely it won't have any impact on them."

"Doesn't that slight chance make it worth trying? We should be able to seal off the ventilation to engineering and release the gas into it. How long does it take to dissipate?"

"About five minutes," Gohara said. "It's deliberately designed to break down quickly so it will only affect the targeted specimen."

"We could do that, then. Ensign Aquino, what do you think?"

"I think it puts us in the same position, facing the same dilemma," Aquino said. "To find out if the gas worked, my Marines will have to go into engineering. If it killed the squonks, great. But, if it doesn't, they'll avoid us again, going outside engineering to kill any other people they find."

Lopez sighed. "The same problem. There has to be another solution."

An idea born of the sims he had run against Rodriguez jumped into Aquino's mind. "Maybe we can… Captain Lopez, is there any way to seal off a large enough portion of the ship for everyone to retreat into while the Marines hunt the squonks? I don't mean just closing off to make air tight. I mean strong enough closures that the squonks can't break through them."

"I don't know," Lopez said. "The *Darwin* wasn't built for that. Second Officer Pearce! Get over here!"

Pearce ran up to them. "Yes… Captain?"

"We need to seal off a large portion of the ship. Seal it off strongly enough to stop any break in. Is that possible?"

"How much time do we have?" Pearce asked.

"Almost every minute those squonks are in engineering we're getting alerts of more equipment damage," Lopez said. "We need to do this fast."

"Fast. Okay. Maybe. I need to check schematics."

Doctor Gohara was frowning furiously at the deck. "The abandoned Janusian cities and towns show a lot of damage inside buildings, damage to artifacts. We've been unsuccessfully trying to work backwards to date their extinction from that. But if the squonks can be so destructive, maybe that's why our calculations keep running into problems. The damage to the former civilization of the Janusians may not just be attributable to time and climate and vegetation."

"Why would the squonks destroy things?" Captain Lopez demanded.

"I have no idea," Gohara replied. "Perhaps when they enter the killing frenzy state, they can't help also destroying anything around them. But that is just a guess."

"Captain?" Second Officer Pearce was staring hard at his data pad. "I'm getting an alert from the power system. The main power supply is initiating a total shutdown due to damage to external controls and safety equipment."

"Total shutdown?" Lopez gasped. "Halt that shutdown!"

"I can't! The system is designed for safety reasons to—"

The lights went out, followed by the slowly descending hum of fans in the life support system and other systems as they powered down. Ships always had fans running, circulating the air through every room and compartment to bring in fresh oxygen and remove carbon dioxide. The absence of that familiar background noise, so common on ships that people no more noticed it than they did the feel of their own pulse or the sound of their own breathing, felt especially unnerving.

Emergency lighting running on batteries sprang to life, offering partial illumination. But the strange, unnatural silence of a ship with dead life support stayed.

"The ship's wireless network has crashed." Second Officer Pearce plugged his data pad into a nearby console, waiting a second as it reconnected. "All life support systems are down," Pearce said, his voice carrying far in the strange silence.

Captain Lopez sounded remarkably calm considering what was happening, "Where is the back-up power?"

Second Officer Pearce was frantically tapping at his data pad, his face illuminated by it. "They're not activating. The squonks must have damaged their controls, too. All we have access to are other systems with secondary battery backups located outside of engineering."

A soothing and authoritative voice filled the weird quiet as the general announcing system, one of those with backup battery power, made an automated announcement, "There has been a temporary loss of power aboard the ship. Everyone is requested to remain in their current locations while the ship's engineers carry out corrective action. Power will be restored as soon as possible."

The silence afterwards felt even more oppressive.

"How long do we have with all life support out?" Lopez asked.

Pearce hesitated. "I'd have to run numbers. But with everyone aboard, it won't be long before oxygen depletion and carbon dioxide build up reach danger levels."

"What about the gravity?" Doctor Gohara said, staring about him frantically. "Why is the gravity still working?"

Aquino answered, "The artificial gravity fields induced in the decks will persist on their own for about a week after power cut off."

"Right," Pearce said. "You're Navy, aren't you? You know what we're facing here." He turned back to Lopez. "Captain, emergency procedures call for us to evacuate the ship if at all possible to reduce demand on the internal environment and give those aboard time to fix the problem."

"You know what that means!" Lopez snapped at him.

"Yes. I do. But what's the alternative?"

"Why are we delaying?" Doctor Gohara demanded. "If we should evacuate to the planet, let's do so. There's no danger down there."

"You mean except for countless numbers of the same squonks who are destroying this ship and killing those aboard it?" Lopez asked.

"The squonks on the planet are not acting hostile! They have made no threatening moves against any of our exploration parties! Why not evacuate? Don't you agree, Ensign Aquino?"

Aquino didn't answer right away, wondering why an ensign like him, the most junior of junior officers, was being asked to weigh in on such critical decisions.

Lopez spoke before he could, though.

"This is outside of Ensign Aquino's area. He is unaware of many of the factors involved."

Gohara frowned, the partial illumination causing the expression to form odd shadows on his face. "I am co-leader of this expedition, with equal authority to make all decisions. Equal to Captain Jardyce."

"Captain Jardyce is dead," Aquino said.

"Yes! Which makes me the one in charge!"

"That's wrong," Lopez insisted. "Regulations clearly state that when a ship's captain is dead or incapacitated the second in command assumes full authority as commanding officer."

"That's not what the agreement regarding this expedition says!" Gohara replied. "That states I am co-leader with *Captain Jardyce*, no one else. That means I now have sole authority regarding decisions impacting the expedition!"

Captain Lopez, momentarily unable to muster more arguments, shifted her gaze to Aquino as if asking him to refute the doctor's claim.

But Aquino could only spread his hands helplessly. "I haven't been allowed to see any of that. I have no idea what the expedition agreement says." What could he legally do if there was a power struggle between the ship's captain and the expedition leader?

Doctor Gohara already had the answer to that, too. He waved a dismissive hand toward Aquino. "The Marines cannot act in this matter. It concerns civilian legal agreements. They are prohibited from doing anything. Isn't that correct?" he demanded of Aquino.

He hated having to agree. "To the best of my knowledge, yes."

"Doctor," Lopez said, her expression and voice fierce, "you must be aware of what evacuating the ship means."

"I have to think of the greatest good for the greatest number," Gohara said. "Are you prepared to take responsibility for more deaths as we debate this issue? Everyone on this ship could die. The Marines need time to deal with the escaped specimens. This is the only way to give it to them. Do you know of any other?"

Lopez, newly thrown into her position, hesitated.

Even Aquino couldn't think of a good argument to refute Doctor Gohara's plan. It made a great deal of sense to evacuate the crew and the scientists, not only to reduce the use of oxygen, but also so the Marines could go after the squonks without worrying about protecting anyone else. Why was Lopez so reluctant to go ahead with an evacuation?

Gohara plugged his pad in as well, then began tapping through menus. He paused when he reached the one he wanted, looking around to see if anyone else would object, then with careful deliberation, tapped a command followed by a confirmation.

An urgent squawk came from the general announcing system, followed by once more commanding words, "Attention, everyone. The ship is being evacuated for safety reasons. Everyone should proceed calmly and quickly to their assigned emergency evacuation stations aboard Landing Shuttle One or Landing Shuttle Two. In the event you cannot remember your assigned station, go to the emergencies application on your data pad, open the menu for actions, and tap on the *my station* icon. That will provide you the station and directions to it."

The announcement began to repeat, "Attention, everyone. The ship is being evacuated for safety reasons." But the strong voice was getting weaker, the volume dropping as the batteries drained under the load of so many speakers being activated. "Everyone should… proceed… calmly… and…"

It cut off.

In the ensuing quiet, Aquino heard shouts outside the bridge accompanied by the sound of running feet.

Doctor Gohara, despite his earlier certainty looking worried if he had done the right thing, nodded abruptly to Lopez and left the bridge.

Captain Lopez gestured to everyone else on the bridge. "Get to the emergency evacuation stations. Help maintain order and get everyone aboard their assigned shuttles. Go!"

All of the watch standers stood up and raced for the exit from the bridge.

Aquino turned to do the same, thinking he needed to fill in his Marines on what was happening, when he was stopped.

"Ensign Aquino!" Captain Lopez grabbed Aquino's shoulders, staring into his eyes. "Listen to me. We can't completely evacuate the ship with the two landing shuttles."

"Huh?" Aquino shook his head in bafflement. "That's impossible. Regulations require enough shuttle capacity to carry everyone aboard a ship."

"I know what regulations require! The *Darwin* has been repeatedly modified, the size of the crew and the research staff we can carry being increased each time. We've exceeded what the landing shuttles can carry. Captain Jardyce has sent repeated requests for an upgrade to the shuttle docking stations so we can carry an additional shuttle, but it's *expensive*. The company keeps putting it off."

"How can you be authorized to operate like that?" Aquino demanded, aghast.

"Waivers, Ensign Aquino! Waiver after waiver! Because big companies and big research organizations have a lot of pull when they don't want to shell out money for safety!" She paused to regain control. "After those who have died, there should be… thirty to fifty who won't fit in the shuttles even if we pack people in. I won't know exactly until we see how many we can carry."

"You can send one of the shuttles back up to get them," Aquino pointed out.

"No, I can't! We're going to be on that planet, surrounded by squonks, and who knows what other as yet undetected dangers. If I send a shuttle back up, that will mean leaving all of the passengers who rode it down outside and unprotected. And when the shuttle returns, thirty to fifty people would have to stay outside." Lopez's face clearly revealed the strain upon her. "The shuttles can't stay sealed with everyone aboard as it is. Their life support won't manage it indefinitely. Adding more people would be… irresponsible. Ensign Aquino, I can't fix this now. All I can do is ask you to do what you can. You need to protect the people I have to leave behind. Protect them from the squonks."

Aquino shook his head. "That's going to be difficult."

"Find a way," Lopez pleaded. "I can't stay on the ship. My responsibilities require me to be with the great majority of the crew and the researchers. I'll be the only person with sufficient authority to serve as a check on whatever Doctor Gohara does next. I have to be on the planet's surface. Please, Ensign Aquino. Find a way to protect those I can't protect."

"I'll do my best." What else could he say?

Captain Lopez ran off the bridge, leaving him alone.

Aquino checked his data pad, confirming that he had also lost his link when the ship's wireless network went down. Another check confirmed the security comm relay he'd been given was also dead.

He looked around the empty bridge, dim, with unfamiliar shadows created by the emergency lighting, the powered-down consoles silent. It felt eerie, as if he were on the bridge of one of the ghost ships out of legend, crewed only by the spirits of those who had once sailed on it.

It should have spooked him, but instead, a resolve formed.

Darwin would not become a ghost ship crewed only by the dead.

He ran off the bridge, heading back through the partially lit passageways, weaving between crew members and researchers heading with varying degrees of composure or panic toward their evacuation stations.

His Marines needed him.

When Aquino got close to where he left the Marines, he called out to avoid being mistaken for a squonk on the attack. It seemed a wise precaution when dealing with nervous people carrying loaded weapons.

All of the Marines were on their feet when he rejoined them. "What's going on, sir?" Rodriguez asked. "Our data links are down."

Aquino took a moment to catch his breath. "The wireless system went out along with the power. You heard that the ship is being evacuated, right?"

"Yes, sir. Two of the ship security officers, I guess the only two left alive, had joined up with us, but when the evacuation was announced, they said they had to go help with that. We don't seem to have assigned evacuation stations, though." Rodriguez held up her data pad. "When we tap that 'my station' icon it just says 'not applicable.'"

"We're not leaving the ship," Aquino said. "We're staying so we can kill those squonks." The run back had given him time to think through what needed to be done. He hadn't tried to make any longer-term plans, just what was needed right now. "Before that, we have to help the others get off the ship without panic and without the squonks realizing what's happening and coming out to hunt everyone."

"Six of us?" Lachman asked.

"Yes, six of you," Aquino said. "Here's what we have to do. First, assist and guard the evacuation. Then we have to take charge of those left after the shuttles fill up."

"What?" Obonsawin said incredulously. "I thought the shuttles took everyone."

"They can't hold everyone," Aquino said. "Long story. We're going to be left with anywhere from thirty to fifty random crew members and researchers. We need to get them somewhere we can fort up in to protect them while we hunt squonks."

"Somewhere big enough to hold that many for a while?" Ichikawa said. "How about the auditorium?"

"Yeah," Rodriguez agreed. "That should be big enough."

"The auditorium?" Aquino asked.

"It's some kind of cargo expansion room," Kenyatta said. "In case they had to carry more stuff. It's used for other things, though, since it's mostly empty and people can gather in there."

Aquino scrolled rapidly through the ship diagram on his pad. "Is this it? Secondary cargo and secure storage. Okay. That looks good. There are only two entries, and those are heavy cargo hatches instead of doors. So, we bring everyone left aboard to that compartment. But that means finding them all. And protecting the others until they've gotten off the ship safely." Having laid out what they had to do, he wondered how one small group of Marines could manage that many responsibilities?

"We should break down into fire teams," Rodriguez suggested. "Two Marines in each. That'll give us three fire teams and allow us to cover a lot more ground. There's still way too few of us, but it's the best option, I think."

Breaking their small group into smaller groups made sense. Two Marines might not be enough to get the job done at various points. But three fire teams could protect a lot more people than one group of Marines, especially since the squonks had already shown that they'd avoid a strong group and target much weaker ones instead.

Still, he hesitated, wondering if agreeing would create the appearance that he was letting Rodriguez decide this. That could make him look weak at a time when it was critically important that all of them understand he was firmly in charge.

He could make the obvious compromise and split them into two groups instead. But that wouldn't allow as much protection for the crew as three groups. And it felt like the sort of compromise solution someone would propose simply to avoid going with another solution.

Looking back on his own experience working for various officers, he had definitely preferred the ones who listened to their enlisted. Looking strong and in charge was one thing. Looking strong and in charge and stupid was another.

Paying attention to Rodriguez's advice wouldn't make him look weak. It would make him look smart. And it was probably the best out of the few bad options available to them at this moment.

"Good idea, Sergeant," Aquino said. "We'll do that. Assign the teams."

Rodriguez looked over her companions. "Smith, you're with me. Ichikawa and Lachman. Obonsawin and Kenyatta."

"What about our ensign?" Lachman asked, pointing at Aquino.

It was very odd to feel good at that "our" ensign thing, given how everything was going to hell, but it did feel good. "I'll be fine," Aquino said.

"Sir," Rodriguez said, her face set in stubborn lines, "with all due respect, no way. You are not replaceable, sir. I *strongly* recommend that you accompany one of the fire teams."

He almost denied the need to do that, almost said again that he'd be fine alone. But before Aquino said those words, he looked at the Marines, how they were watching him as if he was their anchor against the storms sweeping this ship, and realized once again that even former-enlisted ensigns still needed to listen to their people. "Okay."

Rodriguez smiled with relief. "Which team, sir?"

He looked them over. Sergeant Rodriguez would be watching over Private Smith and didn't need to be worrying about an ensign's safety as well. Ichikawa had Lachman to partner with, and while Lachman was a lot more capable than Smith, he also could be a distraction. That left the team with two solid privates on it. "Obonsawin and Kenyatta."

But exactly what should those three teams do? Using his experience with the sims again, his options were limited, and therefore easy to decide. He gestured to the Marines to emphasize his words. "I'll take Obonsawin and Kenyatta toward evacuation station one. Ichikawa, take your team toward evacuation station two. Sergeant, I want you to roam and go wherever you think you're needed. Respond to whatever develops."

"Understood, sir." Rodriguez gestured to her fellow Marines. "All right, you apes. Are you clear on the mission?"

"Find and help everyone evacuating the ship," Kenyatta said.

"Guard 'em against the squonks," Lachman said.

"Then escort any left aboard to the auditorium," Ichikawa said.

"Um… and stick with our, uh, fireteam," Smith added.

"Still guarding against squonks," Obonsawin finished.

"Let's do this, then!" Rodriguez called. "Get going, and make your mommas proud, Marines!"

"Oorah!" all six Marines shouted, the sound carrying defiantly through the hushed passageways. Even Smith, Lachman, and Kenyatta seemed fired up.

Maybe, Aquino thought, they had a chance of surviving this.

"Come on, Smith!" Rodriguez set off at a run, Smith miraculously keeping pace with her.

"Move it," Ichikawa told Lachman. He followed as she headed off in a different direction.

Kenyatta and Obonsawin watched him, waiting to follow his orders and his lead.

The last thing he wanted to do was run somewhere. Not after everything else that had happened today. Not after running to the bridge and then back from the bridge just now. While the Marines had been able to get some rest.

This relatively easier life of an officer thing wasn't working out the way it was supposed to.

Aquino nodded to his fire team. "Okay. Let's go." He started at a trot down the passageway, hearing Kenyatta and Obonsawin following close behind him.

Not entirely sure of the best route to evacuation station one, Aquino hauled out his data pad to check. And discovered he'd been assigned that station.

His Marines had no evacuation assignments. But their officer did.

The officer was expected to leave their people behind, while seeking safety for themselves.

He couldn't even count how many ways that sucked.

At least him not going would open up a place for someone else who would otherwise be left behind.

The empty, dimly lit passageways near engineering were still spooky, but having the two Marines with him meant that wasn't as unnerving. As they headed forward, they started to encounter individuals or small groups who were taking their time getting to their evacuation stations, apparently treating this as only a drill or not worrying about the shuttles having room for them.

How many aboard the *Darwin* knew the shuttles couldn't carry everyone?

Aquino urged everyone they met into faster motion.

Coming across a group of three researchers who were simply standing around, debating whether to go back and pick up a few things from their rooms, or maybe stop for coffee at an automated kiosk that might still have power, Aquino lost all patience. "Get the hell to your evacuation stations, you idiots!"

The researchers looked minded to debate the matter. But after one glance at the two Marines with Aquino, both hefting their rifles in a threatening manner, the scientists took off toward the shuttles.

His fire team had made it more than halfway to evacuation station one when Aquino heard a scream and shouts down a side passageway.

Obonsawin took the lead, dashing ahead, his rifle leveled. Aquino and Kenyatta followed right behind him.

More screams. More shouts.

Pounding feet provided brief warning of several crew members, fear written all over their faces, stampeding down the passageway toward the Marines.

Private Obonsawin didn't slow down, weaving between the fleeing crew members, his rifle now up to his shoulder, aiming and ready to fire.

Clearing a corner, Obonsawin came to a sudden stop. His rifle hummed, bullets tearing through the air, as he fired several carefully aimed shots.

Kenyatta ran past him, not yet slowing.

"Just one! It went left!" Obonsawin shouted.

Aquino followed, seeing Kenyatta pausing at the opening to a narrow maintenance alley and firing a series of quick shots down it.

As he caught up with her, Kenyatta cursed. "It dodged into another cross-passage. Should we go after it?"

Should they? Aquino tried to catch his breath and make another decision.

Chasing the squonk sounded like a good idea, until he remembered how fast they moved, and how they could circle around and hit more crew members or researchers while he and the Marines stumbled through a maze of passages. "No. We stay focused on finding and protecting crew members and scientists." Aquino looked around, seeing two crew members who were unquestionably dead, and a third bleeding profusely from the arm he had raised to protect himself.

"What happened?" someone called as two more crew members ran up, staring in disbelief at the carnage.

Obonsawin gestured to one's jacket. "Take that off and wrap it tightly around his arm to stop the bleeding."

Kenyatta was checking the two dead. She raised the fist one of them had their hand locked in. "Fur torn loose. This girl went down fighting."

"Didn't do her much good," Obonsawin grumbled angrily. "I missed. Again. Those damned things move so fast."

"I missed, too," Kenyatta said. "Or I just grazed it without hurting it. I bet those things have really tough skin. We need to score a clean hit to hurt them."

Aquino didn't say anything, thinking of what Rodriguez had told him early on, that the Marines never got to actually practice fire their weapons on actual firing ranges, having to make do with simulated fire on simulated ranges. How much had that cost-cutting measure impacted the ability of the Marines to hit real targets that would be very difficult for even the most experienced shooters? "The squonks evolved on Janus Five in 1.15 Earth gravity," he said. "Their strength and reflexes were designed to fight that heavier pull. Now they're in only one gravity."

"That's great for them," Obonsawin said. "Why are they trying to kill everybody?"

"I don't know," Aquino said. "The researchers couldn't understand it." Whatever the reason, there wasn't any doubt now that the squonks had taken advantage of the loss of ship's power to start going after victims outside of engineering.

Somewhere on this ship, KT would be heading for her evacuation shuttle.

Don't think about that. Focus on the need to protect everyone.

The two new crew members had finished wrapping the arm of their injured colleague. "Get him to one of the shuttles," Aquino ordered. "Keep moving until you get to the evacuation station."

"What happened?" one asked, eyes wide with fear. "What did this?"

"Squonks," Aquino said. "We'll get them. You guys get to your shuttle as fast as you can. Come on," he said to the Marines as the three crew members hurried off, the two healthy ones supporting their injured comrade between them. "Let's keep moving and try to stop any more attacks like this."

"Can we?" Obonsawin said, gazing at the two dead crew members near them.

"We have to," Aquino said, knowing he couldn't reveal his own doubts. "So we will."

SEVEN

THE only way to keep herding people toward the evacuation stations and protect them from the squonks was to keep moving, weaving through passageways, going down a deck, constantly scanning their surroundings for any sign of the squonks, listening for any nearby attacks, weaving, up a deck, weaving…

Aquino stopped, leaning one shoulder against the nearest wall. This would have been exhausting even if he wasn't carrying the extra weight of body armor, helmet, and sidearm. As it was, he had started wondering if he could keep going. How long had he been at this?

"How ya doing, sir?" Obonsawin asked, coming around to peer at his face.

"Catching… my… breath," Aquino said.

"Give it a couple minutes, sir. You can't stop those squonks if you're passed out. Hey, Stef, remember those endurance marches in boot camp?"

Kenyatta made a disgusted noise. "I hated those."

"Everybody hated those." Obonsawin sighed, looking around them. "This feels like that."

"We're trying to cover a lot of ground," Kenyatta said. "Can't be helped."

"Next time we run into one of those things, I'm going to lead it a whole lot with my shots. Like shooting at a fast drone, you know?"

"Might work," Kenyatta said. "Not much room in these halls to lead them, though."

"Nah." Obonsawin looked at Aquino again. "How do the squonks attack on the surface, sir? Did you see any of that?"

"They didn't," Aquino said, still trying to catch his breath. "No attacks against… anything except these… little ant-mice. They just laze around a lot."

"Those things don't even hunt?" Kenyatta demanded. "They're damned good at fighting for something that lays around a lot."

"Yeah," Aquino said. "If they were bots, I'd say… someone had thrown a switch. But they're definitely organic." That metaphor hung in his brain. The squonks on the surface of Janus Five couldn't be matched to the smashed pottery and furniture and dead Janusians. But the squonks up here were exactly the sort of creatures who could have done those things, in fact *were* doing those things. What caused such sudden, extreme changes in living creatures?

"If they're organic, we can kill 'em," Obonsawin said. "How are you doing, sir? You ready to move out?"

"Yeah." Aquino levered himself away from the wall, realizing that Obonsawin and Kenyatta had been chatting to give him time to recover. "Thanks."

"How much further until we reach the evacuation point?"

"It's one deck down, about twenty meters on," Aquino said. "Not far."

"Twenty meters?" Kenyatta said. "Piece of cake."

"Right." Aquino started walking again.

Coming down to the next deck, they almost immediately ran into groups of crew members and researchers converging on the evacuation station. Aquino got another chance to rest as they took up positions guarding the newcomers and urging them on.

Had the squonks given up and returned to engineering rather than face the Marines? Or were they holding back now that there weren't isolated groups of humans moving through the passageways?

How many other people had the squonks killed, perhaps individuals traveling alone who hadn't had any chance to scream for help?

As what seemed to be the last humans went past on their way to the evacuation station, Aquino led the two Marines behind them, protecting the rear. If the squonks were still out there, they still didn't show.

He and the Marines finally reached the point where the crowd heading for shuttle one was backed up, waiting to board. The column of people moved with agonizing slowness, inching down the passageway toward the hatch accessing the shuttle.

Aquino kept looking ahead, trying to judge how many people were left waiting to board. There had definitely been more deaths. Maybe enough to mean these people would all be able to get aboard the shuttle? It seemed a very odd thing to hope for.

"Do they know, sir?" Private Kenyatta asked. "About how much space is available on the shuttle?"

"I don't think so," Aquino said.

Where was KT? Hopefully already aboard one of the shuttles. He couldn't afford to distract himself with worries about her, but he couldn't stop.

The moment he'd been dreading and expecting finally came. There were roughly twenty people remaining in the hall before him when Aquino heard a chorus of shouts combining outrage and fear from the front of the line.

Followed by the thunk of a heavy hatch sealing.

He had to act fast, before panic broke out. "You're not abandoned!" Aquino called, putting as much volume and authority into his voice as he could. "We're right behind you!"

People spun about, staring at him. After feeling ridiculous this morning in his helmet and body armor, Aquino breathed thanks for it, as the sight of him and the two Marines with him looking ready for anything calmed the building terror in the people left behind by the shuttle.

"They left us!" someone shouted.

"That's right," Aquino yelled back. "They left me and the Marines, too. Which means we are here with you. We're not going anywhere.

But we need to get all of you somewhere you can be safe, somewhere we can protect you. I want to know who's in charge of you, though. Are there any ship's officers among you?"

A stirring started in the center of the group as a man came forward reluctantly, urged along by the others. "I'm a ship's officer."

"Great!" Aquino said as if someone special had just appeared. "What department?"

"Pursers."

Pursers? "You're a banker?"

"An accountant," the man said. "Fifth Officer Russell Craig."

"An accountant. Okay." What mattered was that this person could serve as a familiar command presence for the ship's crew members. "You're in charge of all the crew members. Help me get them where we need to go." He raised his voice again, "How about researchers? Is there anyone senior among you?"

A woman came forward, one with obvious age resting on her, yet walking as if she were young and vigorous. "I'm Doctor Trinh. What do you need, young man?"

"Please take charge of any researchers here," Aquino said. He took a deep breath before speaking loudly again, "Here's the deal. We're going to a large compartment that can hold all of you, somewhere you'll be safe. You may know it as the auditorium." He showed his data pad to Fifth Officer Craig and Doctor Trinh. "This is where we're going."

"Oh," Craig said. "There was an awards ceremony there a few weeks ago. I know where that is."

"Good. Do you see Private Kenyatta, there? She's going to lead the column. We need to keep everyone right behind her. The other Marine, Private Obonsawin, is going to follow along behind to make sure no one falls behind. I'm going to be moving along the column, making sure everyone is all right. Are there any questions?"

"Why did they leave us?" a plaintive voice called.

How should he answer that? Aquino decided on the truth. "The ship doesn't have enough shuttle capacity to evacuate everyone aboard. That's why. I can't do anything about that. But these Marines and me will protect you. I promise."

The moment the words left his mouth, Aquino felt as if a heavy weight had fallen on his shoulders. Could he keep that promise?

All he could do at the moment was the next necessary thing. And he already knew what that was. Aquino looked at Craig and Trinh. "Ready?"

They nodded.

"Kenyatta, head out. Obonsawin, take the rear. I'll roam along the column. Sound off if you see anything."

"Yes, sir," Kenyatta and Obonsawin chorused.

Kenyatta started walking, and Trinh followed, the other researchers present following her like ducklings chasing after a mother hen. Craig, looking determined but out of his depth, tried getting all of the crew members to follow closely. Aquino helped get them moving.

Kenyatta held her pace to a walk so no one would have trouble keeping up. Aquino, grateful for having had a little while to rest (even if the "resting" had been on his feet while constantly searching for danger), walked along the column of people, back and forth, trying to make sure no one wandered off and nothing grabbed anyone.

The passageways, now deserted and silent except for this group and the slight noises they made, felt even more haunted than before. And, as in a haunted house, Aquino had to fight the sense that he was being watched by malign things ready to pounce when his back was turned. The critical difference being that in this case, the "ghosts" were all-too-real creatures who had already killed at least a dozen people.

His pistol felt like a leaden weight in his hand, as if its mass had at least tripled since this morning. Aquino was tempted to holster it, to give his weary arm muscles a break. But that would really slow down his reaction if a squonk did show up, so he kept holding the side arm, ensuring the barrel was pointed either down at the deck or up at the overhead so an accidental shot wouldn't hit anyone.

Because he did that, because he was standing still for a moment watching the crew members and researchers filing past, Aquino spotted a flicker of motion near a side passageway the group was walking past. Without thinking, he brought the pistol up, lining up to aim it, his free hand grasping his weapon hand to steady it just as he'd been taught during weapons familiarization.

A paw covered with fur, wicked claws extended, darted out toward one of the crew members close to the side passage.

Aquino fired three shots in quick succession, seeing the bullets hit the wall near that paw, and the paw jerk back before striking its target.

The crew member jumped away from the spots the bullets had hit, staring about wildly, as Aquino ran to the side passage, part of his mind wondering why the hell he was doing something so crazy. Reaching it, his heart thundering in his ears from much more than just the sudden exertion, Aquino swung to point his pistol down the side passage.

Empty. The squonk had already darted into another side passage.

"What's going down back there?" Private Kenyatta called from the front of the column.

"One of the squonks is trying to hit our flank," Aquino called back. "I stopped it, but I doubt it's going away. Pick up the pace a little, Kenyatta."

"Understood, sir. Picking up the pace. You heard the man, let's move a little quicker," Kenyatta called to the crew members and researchers.

The crew member who had been the object of the squonk's attempted strike, was frozen with fear. Aquino grabbed his shoulder. "Keep moving. Okay? You'll be fine. Move."

The man stumbled into motion while Aquino waited, watching down the side passage, as the others pushed past him until the end of the column and Private Obonsawin reached him. "Have you seen anything of the squonks?" Aquino asked.

Obonsawin made a face. "Maybe. Like, instants of what was that? Nothing I could identify or get a shot off at, though."

"One was definitely here. Let's keep moving."

Just a couple of minutes later, they heard the sound of bullets booming through the air and impacting on walls coming from somewhere off to their left. "Rodriguez!" Aquino called. "Ichikawa!"

Two more shots, then a pause.

"Ensign Aquino?" Rodriguez called, her voice carrying along the passageway. "I've joined up with the other fire team. We've got the left behinds from evacuation station two."

"We'll wait here for you," Aquino called. "Wait up, Kenyatta. Sergeant! Are the squonks trying to get at you?"

"At least one, yes, sir!" Rodriguez was clearly drawing closer.

"We've had one hanging around us, too," Aquino called.

Rodriguez and Private Smith came into sight, leading a column of fearful looking crew members and researchers.

"How are Ichikawa and Lachman?" Aquino called.

"Covering the rear, sir." Rodriguez paused when she reached them, grinning, a streak of sweat running down the side of her face. "Don't take this wrong, sir, but you are a sight for sore eyes."

"Likewise," Aquino said. "Let's merge the columns, keeping you, me, and Smith in the middle. Obonsawin! Come on up and join Kenyatta on point!"

The join up took a minute to work through before Aquino started following the back of his column again, the front of Rodriguez's column right behind him. "Did you lose anyone?" he asked Rodriguez.

"No, sir. But one researcher did get slashed. Not too serious." She looked about them, fingering her weapon. "I can't wait to go after those things again."

Finally reaching the heavy cargo door leading into the auditorium, Aquino almost ordered everyone to start entering. Before he could do that, Rodriguez called forward to Obonsawin and Kenyatta. "Get in there and check out that space. Make sure nothing's waiting for us in there."

What if Rodriguez wasn't with them? What if she'd been afraid to speak up? He would have led all of these people into what could have been a death trap if the squonks were waiting inside.

He had so much more to learn, and very little time to learn it.

The two privates entered with weapons at ready.

After what felt like a long time, Kenyatta returned to the big hatch. "All clear."

"Everybody in," Aquino ordered.

The group got stuck more than once as too many people tried to cram in as fast as possible. Eventually, Aquino stood with Rodriguez, Lachman, Ichikawa, and Smith, gazing out at the silent, empty passageway leading here. They backed inside, the others holding their weapons ready while Ichikawa and Lachman sealed the hatch.

The auditorium felt large after the confined spaces elsewhere on the ship, its apparent size magnified by the inadequate emergency lighting that left partial shadows in some areas.

"We should check out the other hatch, sir," Rodriguez told Aquino. "So we know exactly where it is and know it's sealed well."

"Good idea." He walked with the sergeant past the rescued left behinds, who were sitting down on the bare deck, looking as forlorn as they surely felt. "Did your group have any ship's officers in it?"

"Yes, sir. Third Officer Ergenian and Fourth Officer Nijmeh."

"That'll be a great relief to Fifth Officer Craig," Aquino said. "How about the researchers? Any leaders among them?"

"Oz!"

He stared as one of the researchers jumped up and ran to him. "KT?"

She grabbed him, holding on tight, while Rodriguez pretended not to be looking. "You're okay. You are okay, aren't you?"

"I'm okay." He wasn't sure whether to be relieved or upset. "I thought you'd be on one of the shuttles."

"I knew you'd be staying," KT said. "When word went around that the shuttles couldn't hold everyone, I decided to stay, too. So did Hakim." She gestured to where Hakim Marvin had stood up and walked more slowly toward them.

"Hey, Oz," Hakim said. "This is kind of bad, right?"

"This is bad," Aquino said.

KT realized that she was still holding him and stepped back, looking embarrassed. "Anyway, we're here to help."

"My group had a Doctor Trinh," Aquino said. "Do you know her?"

"Doctor Trinh?" KT said, astonished. "*The* Doctor Trinh?"

"I... guess?"

"That would be correct," Doctor Trinh said, also walking up. "You are?" she asked KT in a polite voice.

"Katarina Tirgatao, Doctor Trinh. Environmental analysis."

Hakim also spoke up, "Hakim Marvin. Chemistry."

Trinh turned her gaze to Aquino. "I know you are Ensign Aquino. This lady is?"

It took Aquino a moment to realize who Doctor Trinh was referring to. "This is Sergeant Rodriguez. If you have problems and can't find me, Rodriguez is my second in command."

"I see. What is needed of us?"

"The immediate need is to keep the other researchers under control and make sure their needs are met, if we can," Aquino said.

"Almost all of them are graduate students," Trinh said. "Junior enough to be left off the evacuation lists. But they can do good work."

Good work. What could these researchers do? Aquino remembered Doctor Gohara's assertions, and questions, about the squonks. "If you can figure out anything about the squonks, it could be very important. KT told me that the squonks didn't fit right in the environments on Janus Five. And what I've seen of them up here since they escaped their enclosure does not match what's been seen on the surface. It's like they're totally different creatures. I need any possible insights into what they're doing and why they're doing it and what they might do next."

"And how to kill them," Rodriguez added.

"Yes," Aquino said. "As Sergeant Rodriguez pointed out, we need to know how to kill those things."

"Summarize their behaviors aboard the ship," Trinh said.

"They closely observed the humans observing them," Aquino said, glancing at KT for confirmation that he was describing it properly. "Then they broke out of their enclosure by defeating the safeguards using strength, their claws, and… ingenuity. Since then, they've indiscriminately murdered humans, not just those who stumbled across them, but humans they've gone out hunting. They also continued to destroy equipment in engineering. I can't help thinking of the broken pottery and furniture in the dead cities and towns."

"Hmmm." Trinh considered that for a moment. "Such behaviors aren't totally unique. We're familiar with creatures who can act in such ways. Dogs, for example. It's not unheard of for a dog to break into a chicken coop and kill every chicken, not for food but simply in a frenzy. Dogs also destroy items such as furniture, but that behavior is usually related to boredom. To see such traits occurring at the same time is… thought provoking."

KT spoke up, "Especially since the squonks on the surface still haven't displayed that kind of behavior at all."

"I don't know how much we can help regarding the squonks," Doctor Trinh said. "We'll try to come up with some theories. There's a massive amount of data recovered from Janus Five loaded onto my data pad, including reconstructions of many Janusian documents."

"Documents?" Hakim said, startled. "I hadn't heard about those."

"Yes. Written and painted on material derived from plants. These were in a stone vault fashioned from a natural cave within one of the dead cities. Horribly deteriorated despite their protection, of course, but we have the technology to reconstruct them, page by page, and many are already available. The junior researchers will be invaluable for going through those as quickly as we can. I will let you know immediately if we learn anything, Ensign Aquino."

"Thank you, Doctor," Aquino said. "KT, I need to—"

"Do your job. Of course." She paused. "Oz… be careful."

"Sure." He realized that extreme exhaustion probably made his smile look a little lopsided.

Continuing on, he and Rodriguez checked the second hatch, confirming it was securely sealed and locked. Aquino leaned his back against it, looking out across the compartment. "How many were in your group?"

"Twenty-two," Rodriguez said.

"And nineteen in mine. So, forty-one. Plus us. And no functioning life support. I'd appreciate some advice, Sergeant."

"We're all wiped out, sir." She nodded back toward the other hatch. "I recommend posting a sentry and the rest of us crashing for a few hours."

"Who gets stuck with sentry?"

"I'll work out a rotation, sir."

"Sergeant…" Aquino shook his head. "Can we afford to waste a few hours?"

"Sir, with all due respect—"

"Stop saying that, Sergeant. I know what it means. I'm former enlisted, remember?" 'With all due respect' sounded respectful, but everyone knew it actually meant variations on 'how stupid are you?'

"Understood, sir." Rodriguez rubbed her eyes, clearly very tired as well. "Sir, without rest we're going to be zombies. And zombies aren't going to be able to do anything right. We'll just be snacks for those squonks to snap up."

It took him several seconds to process her words, which confirmed she was right. If his brain had that much trouble grasping a simple statement, it was time to give it a rest. "Okay. Five hours sleep. You get the sentry rotation set up while I tell the ship's officers and Doctor Trinh that we're going to recharge our personal batteries because we're all blinking on the verge of shutdown."

The two ship's officers with the other group were Third Officer Marcus Ergenian and Fourth Officer Joan Nijmeh. Both appeared dazed by recent developments rather than exhausted.

"I need to know where the emergency supplies are," Aquino told them.

"Emergency supplies?" Ergenian asked, looking baffled at the question.

"Food," Aquino said. "Medical kits, maybe individual oxygen masks. Whatever has been stockpiled for you guys to use after you were left by the shuttles."

Ergenian gave Nijmeh a helpless look. "I'm in supply," he said. "I've never heard of anything like that."

"I'm operations," Nijmeh said. "Nobody ever told me about emergency supplies." She gasped a brief, bitter laugh. "But then, nobody ever told me some of us weren't going to be evacuated."

"There's nothing in my app about emergency supplies," Ergenian said, tapping his data pad. "How about you, Joan?"

"Nothing," she said.

Aquino could only stare at them as he tried to gather thoughts, confused by not only extreme tiredness but also the lack of preparations. "Didn't they tell you anything? You guys are the senior ship's officers left aboard."

"Hurray for us," Nijmeh said. "Look, um, Ensign Aquino, I didn't know this would happen. A bunch of the crew being left behind. A friend of mine was told he'd have to stay, and he's married with a kid back home, so I told him to take my spot. But apparently, he hadn't been told anything, either."

"Pretty much the same story for me," Ergenian said.

"I don't get it," Aquino said. "Captain Jardyce struck me as highly capable. Everyone said she was on top of everything. Why wouldn't she have made preparations for this?"

"Captain Jardyce *is* very competent," Fourth Officer Nijmeh said. "I have no idea why things are like this. If we can establish communications with the shuttles we can ask her about emergency supplies."

Aquino sighed, not happy to be passing on bad news again. "You'll have to talk to Captain Lopez. Captain Jardyce is dead."

"What? *Dead?* How?"

"The squonks," Aquino said. "How soon can you talk to the shuttles?"

Ergenian shook his head unhappily. "We don't know. We've already tried, plugging our pads into those physical links over there, but the communications channels we need are down somewhere. Are you in charge now?"

"On this ship, yes," Aquino said. This certainly qualified as the sort of emergency that gave him that authority. "We need two things. One, comms with the shuttles. Please do everything you can to get those working. Second, how long do we have with life support down? We've got more than forty people breathing the available oxygen."

"It's not our area," Ergenian said, once more exchanging a worried look with Nijmeh, "but we'll see what we can do."

"See that researcher?" Aquino said, pointing to KT. "She might be able to help. KT is an eco-system analyst."

"Yeah. Thanks." Nijmeh waved toward the rest of the crew members, who were sitting around looking dejected. "What do we tell the others? They're scared."

Aquino nodded. "Sure they are. Uh, tell them we're here. I mean, me and Marines. We're going to handle this, and then the shuttles can come back."

"Okay," Third Officer Ergenian said, smiling with relief. "Yeah. You guys can take care of those squonks. Those Marines look tough. I don't think we've ever seen them in all that battle equipment and carrying their weapons before. That's… reassuring."

"You look tough, too," Nijmeh added to Aquino. "We're not, umm, combat people, but we'll do what we can to back you up."

"Thank you," Aquino said. What a difference twenty-four hours had made. He had no doubt that if he'd encountered either Ergenian or Nijmeh before that, they would have ignored him.

Dwelling on it wouldn't kill any squonks, though.

"Let me know if you make any progress on either priority," Aquino told. "Right now, the Marines and me have been running hard for a long time. We need a few hours to recharge."

Neither of the ship's officers looked disappointed or surprised to hear that. Watching them, Aquino could see the weariness in them as well. "Make sure you guys get the rest you need. Have you linked up with Fifth Officer Craig, yet? He can help manage your other crew members." With a final nod, Aquino walked to where a piece of deck not far from the Marines looked a bit more comfortable.

He lay flat, and almost immediately passed out while still wondering how well he'd be able to sleep on the hard surface.

Five hours later, Sergeant Rodriguez shook him awake. "Reveille, sir. Per your orders."

"Thanks." Aquino sat up, blinking, wishing he'd told her six hours. But he had no idea how long they had before the environment on the ship deteriorated to dangerous levels.

And, his conscience reminded him with a guilty nudge, the Marines had each had an hour less sleep than himself as they rotated through sentry watch to ensure everyone remained safe.

He took a moment to look around the "auditorium" again. About ten meters long and maybe six meters wide, bare metal walls, the only distinguishable features the heavy cargo hatches at either end, a couple of boxes allowing physical links of data pads to the ship's systems, and a water station on one wall. That last was lucky. Without it, water might have become a critical need. As long as that particular system held any pressure, they could at least get drinking water.

Thinking of water made him think of food, and the gaping emptiness inside him. Where could they locate food for everyone here?

Aside from the Marines and the left behinds, the only other things in the compartment were several large crates securely tied down against the far wall. The content labels on them said they were full of various large spare parts and materials.

He had a limited amount of time to kill a couple of creatures that had proven remarkably hard to kill. Preferably without losing any more of his own Marines or any more crew members or researchers.

"What do we do first?" he murmured.

Sergeant Rodriguez heard him. "Our first priority should be getting more ammo and capacitors. And spare weapons. And anything else we need from the armory and our rooms."

"How about food?"

"There are emergency field rations. Guaranteed awful, but they're food."

"That's good," Aquino said. "How many rations are there? Because we need to worry about feeding all of them as well," he added with a sweep of his arm including all of the crew members and researchers.

"They don't have food?" Rodriguez said. "Somebody really didn't think this stuff through, did they? We've got a lot of the rations, because they're intended for at least a few weeks for fourteen Marines. So… we can probably stretch that for several days to cover everyone here."

"Okay," Aquino said. That gave him a clear course of action. "Some of us need to go get the weapons and food and other things while the rest guard this space and the people in it." Who should do what? "I think I should lead the group going to get the weapons and other supplies, while you lead the guard force inside this room." It would have been easy to pawn off the expedition on Sergeant Rodriguez, but he didn't want to rely on her for everything. He couldn't learn if he didn't push himself.

Rodriguez didn't argue. "I've already keyed your biometrics into the armory lock, sir, and you've got the combo. Bring everything you can. I recommend you take along Ichikawa, Lachman, Kenyatta, and Obonsawin. Smith and me will hold the fort here."

Meaning she'd be holding the fort pretty much alone. "How is Smith doing?"

Sergeant Rodriguez sighed. "He hasn't wandered off, but he didn't use any ammo, yet."

"How could he have not used any ammo?"

"Because every time we encountered those squonks he froze," Rodriguez explained. "Not cowardice, I'm sure. Just a 'what-do-I-do, what-do-I-do' panic that kept him from doing anything. For what it's worth, from the way he's moping around, Smith is even less happy about that then you and me are."

"Okay." What else could he say and do at this point? "Let's get the expedition organized, get that stuff, and plan our next steps after that."

"These guys aren't going to be of any help," Rodriguez added, casting a judgmental eye on the huddled left behinds. "Useless, I guess."

"Sergeant," Aquino said, and something in the way he said it drew Rodriguez's immediate attention. "That's how you and the other Marines, and me, have been described. Useless. Are we useless? Hell, no.

"Earlier, I talked briefly with some of those left behind." He pointed around the room. "That older woman, Doctor Trinh, I've learned she's something of a legend. She gave up her seat on a shuttle to a young researcher, saying she already had a long life behind her and he still had a long life ahead of him. Dr. Tirgatao and Dr. Marvin I'm sure did the same, even though they've both got a lot of life ahead of them if we can survive this.

"And the ship's crew. All three ship's officers chose to stay. They don't have special skills suited to being left behind. They just couldn't go and leave others here."

Rodriguez sighed and nodded. "I've been properly chewed out. If nothing else, the ones who could've left and chose to stay have the right spirit, don't they?"

"Maybe they also have skills that can help them and the others judged worthless. We have to make use of every available skill and resource to win this. So don't write off anybody or anything." Aquino paused, trying to decide what else he could confide to Rodriguez. "We're going to have our hands full dealing with these squonks, I think."

She nodded again. "They're a lot worse than dogs, that's for sure. When you get to the armory, I'd advise getting the grenades, too."

"Hell, yeah, I'm getting the grenades," Aquino said. Those no longer felt like overkill.

The other Marines looked as strung out as Aquino felt, grumpy from lack of enough sleep and twitchy from the earlier encounters with the squonks. Ichikawa in particular looked ready to bite the head off of anyone who spoke to her, but after a low-volume, nose to nose, and obviously intense conversation with Rodriguez, adopted a begrudgingly less hostile attitude.

Aquino looked over the bedraggled Marines lined up before him and decided to skip any motivational speeches. "We're not squonk hunting this time. We're going to the barracks, getting everything we need, and coming back here. Food, ammo, anything we can carry that we ought to have. Any questions?"

"What if the squonks show up?" Lachman asked.

"Then we do our best to kill them," Aquino said. "Anything else?"

"Is it okay to pick up some personal stuff?" Kenyatta said.

"As long as it doesn't overburden you," Aquino said. "The priority has to be what's needed, not what's wanted. Let's get this done."

Aquino checked his pistol as the hatch was opened, then couldn't help looking back to where KT was sleeping among the other left behinds. She, all of them, were counting on him. So were all of the people on the two shuttles that had landed on the planet by now.

That should have landed on the planet by now, anyway. But where had they touched down? Surely not near the ruins of any Janusian city or town, because those ruins were also where many more squonks could be found. He had no way of knowing, and, he couldn't waste time worrying about the shuttles. Not when the squonks were still alive and running loose on this ship.

Captain Lopez had the responsibility for those on the shuttles. Whereas he had to keep his mind focused on here, aboard this ship, and this problem. "Do you have any last-minute advice, Sergeant?"

Rodriguez shrugged. "Just keep your head, sir. You know what to do. You didn't do anything stupid yesterday."

"That's good to know." Not doing anything stupid seemed a pretty low bar to clear even for an ensign, but maybe that would be enough.

Aquino took one more glance back as he led the four Marines out of the auditorium. Rodriguez and Smith were standing in full battle gear, making it clear they'd be on guard. Most of the left behinds were still trying to sleep, except for a few junior researchers working bleary-eyed on their data pads. From what he could see of their expressions, they might be composing final letters to their families in case the worst happened.

As Rodriguez and Smith sealed the hatch, Aquino paused again, looking down the passageways leading away from this compartment, the too-weak illumination rendering the hallways dim. How close were the squonks? As Rodriguez had complained about earlier, the warning sensors built into the Marine helmets couldn't be counted on to spot anything in a ship's environment. With most of the ship deserted, would the squonks continue to hole up in engineering most of the time, or would they roam about in search of human targets, or would they lurk about this area of the ship in hopes of getting chances to attack the humans remaining aboard?

Sooner or later, he would learn the answer.

"Let's go," Aquino said, his voice low. "Ichikawa, point. Obonsawin, rear. Lachman and Kenyatta, with me."

Much of the time before being evacuated, the darkened passageways had carried traces of life in them because of the sounds of at least a few other people moving and talking within earshot. Not now. The air felt heavy without fans moving it around. Every corner held menace lurking around it. Once again, his protective body armor grew heavy, his movements awkward. Aquino thought about drawing his pistol, but decided with the four Marines all ready to fire he didn't need his own weapon ready.

So far, he had managed to avoid accidentally putting a bullet into the deck or the overhead, or into one of the Marines. He shouldn't push his luck, especially since the Marines all seemed to be a bit more nervous whenever they saw the pistol in his hand.

But his hand twitched toward his holster as Ichikawa in front suddenly stopped, her carbine to her shoulder, aiming. She didn't shoot, though, slowly lowering the weapon again.

"What'd you see?" Aquino asked.

"Maybe nothing," Ichikawa said. "I never knew how spooky this ship could be."

Five minutes later, they reached the Marine rooms, Ichikawa making sure nothing was lurking inside before Aquino led the rest into the common room. He went to open the armory while the Marines started hauling out a surprising number of empty duffles and other bags. "Every time something got delivered," Lachman commented, "we were supposed to hold onto the bags they came in until we could turn all of it in. But you can only turn in empty bags at a base, and the ship never goes to military bases. So, we've got a lot of bags."

While Obonsawin kept watch at the door, Lachman dumped field ration cartons and a pair of first aid kits into some of the bags. The armory open, Ichikawa and Kenyatta began pulling weapons off their racks.

There were only five extra rifles, which didn't make sense to Aquino. "Why aren't there seven or eight? There are supposed to be thirteen Marines assigned to this detachment, plus the Marine officer."

"Some broke too bad to fix," Kenyatta said without any clue to her feelings about it. "We cannibalized them. No replacements received. They've been on order for a long time."

Why did this sort of thing still surprise him?

"Grenades?" Ichikawa asked.

"Yes," Aquino said. "Bring them, and all the spare capacitors. Do we have portable chargers?"

"On order," Kenyatta said.

They couldn't bring the wall mounted chargers, so he'd have to hope the charged capacitors they had would do the job.

The six remaining pistols also went into weapons bags.

"What's that?" Aquino asked as Kenyatta hefted another bag that wasn't too large, this one with CAUTION EXPLOSIVES stenciled on the side in large letters.

"Explosives," Kenyatta said.

"I see that," Aquino said. "What kind of explosives?"

"Slabs of Q-7. Very stable, can be molded, beautiful Absolute Weight Strength and Velocity of Detonation."

"Which means?"

"A little of bit of Q-7 makes a big boom," Private Kenyatta explained. "We also have multi-function detonators. Time delay, proximity, contact, whatever we need."

Aquino nodded. "Hopefully we won't require that, but it might come in handy. I take it you're trained on using it?"

"Yes, sir." Kenyatta hesitated. "It's not in my record. But I'm qualified on it."

Why hadn't Kenyatta made sure such a sub-specialty was in her record? Aquino wondered if he wanted to know the answer to that, and decided it could wait. "Okay. I'm going to see how the others are doing."

Aquino checked on Lachman, seeing him with a pile of duffles. “That’s everything?”

“Yes, sir,” Lachman said. “We had to destroy some of the emergency field rations last year because a message identified those lots as tainted. We ordered new ones right away, but they haven’t come in yet.”

Another important thing “on order.” Aquino didn’t trust himself to reply to that. Assuming he survived this, his after-action and lessons-learned report would be very easy to write.

As Ichikawa and Kenyatta came out of the armory loaded with weapons bags, Obonsawin came in to help heft some of the duffles Lachman had filled. “Ready to go, sir,” Ichikawa said.

The Marines were bedecked with bags over their shoulders, on their backs, and in their hands. They’d have to drop some bags to shoot if the squonks attacked, Aquino thought. He couldn’t afford to hesitate if danger seemed close. He also couldn’t jump at shadows, causing the Marines to literally drop everything for no reason.

As they started back, Aquino paused at the door to his room. “I think there might be some emergency supplies in one of my lockers. Hold on while I check.”

He entered his room cautiously.

And saw glowing eyes gazing at him from his bunk.

His heart leaping, Aquino grabbed at his pistol.

As he tried to yank the pistol free of its holster, Aquino realized there were three pairs of eyes. If these were the squonks, there should only be two pairs of eyes at most, and they should be set farther apart.

He clicked on his helmet light, seeing Macbeth, Lady Macbeth, and Judy huddled together on his bunk, all three ship’s cats gazing accusingly at him as if all of this trouble on the ship was his fault.

“Something wrong, sir?” Ichikawa asked, sticking her head inside the door. “Oh. Man. We can’t leave them here. What if the squonks find them?”

"We won't leave them," Aquino said, settling his pistol back in the holster and trying to calm his pounding heart. "How do we get them back to the auditorium, though?"

"Hey, Lachman," Ichikawa said. "There was still an empty duffle back in the barracks, right?"

"There's six or seven of them," Lachman replied.

"Where?" Aquino asked.

"In the middle of the barracks."

"Hang on," Aquino said. He moved quickly back to the barracks, finding the pile of duffles. One of them was more like a tote and seemed well-sized for three cats.

Back in his room, Aquino sat the open duffle down next to the bunk. "Come on, you guys," he urged the cats. "Nice, safe duffle."

After a moment, Lady Macbeth got up and dove into the bag. Macbeth followed.

But Judy sat on the bunk, gazing stubbornly at Aquino.

He cautiously reached toward Judy, thinking he could nudge her toward the duffle. Instead, Judy leapt onto his extended arm, clinging tightly, some of her claws finding their way past chinks in the body armor.

Aquino grunted with pain, looking at Judy. "Was that necessary?"

"Looks like she wants you as her ride," Ichikawa said. "Can you lift the duffle, sir?"

"Hold on." He carefully tried to shift Judy to his other arm. She let go enough to accomplish that, Aquino now cradling Judy next to his chest. He picked up the duffle holding the other two cats with his free hand. "Oh, hell. I forgot to check the locker."

Putting down the tote, he opened the locker with official supplies in it, finding as he had remembered a bag labeled *Expeditionary*. Judy wasn't going anywhere, so he got the bag open with one hand. "There's a battery powered mobile hotspot. We can use that for wireless links to the ship's systems that still have their own battery power."

Once again, they started back, but now Aquino himself was burdened with the tote and the expeditionary bag in one hand and Judy in the other. Three cats. If the squonks suddenly appeared he'd have three panicking cats on his hands. The squonks might not have a chance to kill him before the ship's cats shredded him.

But all three cats remained quiet, Judy resting calmly against his chest, as they made their way along the deserted halls. If the squonks were watching, they couldn't tell how the burdened group would have had trouble responding to a sudden attack.

It had felt like a long walk from the auditorium to the barracks even though it hadn't been that far. Getting back, it felt even longer. Aquino could see the tension in the Marines as they walked under the burden of their loads, and feel it in himself as he looked constantly about in search of danger.

As they finally neared the auditorium, Aquino started to relax.

A moment later, Judy stiffened, growing tense in Aquino's grasp, gazing fixedly down one of the silent passageways. "Oh, hell."

Ichikawa glanced back and saw where Judy was looking. Her arms full of bags, she gazed down the passageway as the others moved past to the hatch into the auditorium.

Aquino sat down the cat duffle long enough to hit the hatch a couple of times. "Open up fast! We've got squonks not far off."

Rodriguez and Smith must have been waiting right inside. Aquino heard the hatch locks releasing and picked up the cat duffle again.

"Let's get inside fast," Aquino told the Marines as the hatch opened.

Rodriguez came out, her weapon sweeping around as she searched for targets, covering the others as they stumbled heavily laden into the auditorium. Once they were inside, the sergeant backed in, not lowering her carbine until the hatch was closed and locked again.

"See anything?" Ichikawa asked the sergeant.

"Nah. Maybe it was nothing."

"Judy thought something was there," Aquino said. He sat down the duffle again. Both cats inside it leaped out immediately, Macbeth and Lady Macbeth heading to the crates, where they jumped up to settle down on top of the highest and gazed out on the humans.

He squatted to put down Judy, who instead of following the other two cats, walked a couple of meters away before sitting down and resuming her close observation of him.

"I think she considers herself part of the unit," Ichikawa said.

"Anything happen while we were gone?" Aquino asked Rodriguez.

"Not much." She turned to gesture to someone. "I found out one of the crew members here is extra valuable. This is Nurse Sastrinata."

"Nurse?" Aquino said. "Extra valuable is right."

Sastrinata, a middle-aged woman with tired eyes, shrugged. "When the medical staff found out some people were being left, we thought one of us should stay with them. I volunteered."

"Thanks," Aquino said. "Hopefully, there won't be much need of your services besides that one guy with the injured arm."

"Good. Because I haven't got any equipment. That's what happens when decisions are made on the spur of the moment."

"You don't have any portable medical kits?"

"Those went on the shuttles," Sastrinata said. "I could put together something from what's in medical, but it'd take a while with power out. I understand that'd be sort of dangerous."

"Yes," Aquino said. No food and no emergency medical kits available for those who didn't fit on the shuttle. Why?

"I saw what happened to that other Marine," Nurse Sastrinata said. "I'm not interested in having that happen to me."

She must be referring to Sergeant Antaeus. Aquino didn't blame her. He didn't want anything like that to happen to him, either. "We brought back a couple of Marine first aid packs."

"Good." Sastrinata eyed him. "Are you guys going out again? Hunting those things?"

"Yes," Aquino said. "We have to."

"Good luck." The nurse hesitated as if unsure what to say next, finally just nodding as she headed back to the other left behinds.

"Also," Rodriguez said, pointing, "those two ship's officers said they had something really important to talk to you about."

"Okay. I'll go speak to them." He offered her the expedition bag. "There's a portable battery powered hotspot in this. We need to get it set up and linked to any ship's systems that are still working."

"I'll get Obonsawin on that," Sergeant Rodriguez said.

"Thanks." Aquino walked over to the two ship's officers, who were talking to each other in low voices.

They looked up as he approached, scrambling to their feet.

"What's up?" Aquino asked.

"It's what's down," Third Officer Marcus Ergenian said. "As you asked, we've been trying to estimate how long we can hold out with all life support not working given how large this group is."

"It's pretty rough going," Fourth Officer Joan Nijmeh said. "We told you I'm from operations, and Ergenian is from supply, right?"

"Fifth Officer Craig is from accounting," Ergenian added. "Which actually turned out to be really useful, because he knows spreadsheets really well. But, still, none of us have dealt directly with life support. And, because we're not part of engineering, we don't have access to the data systems that are still working using battery backup, so we can't get the information they have. We're trying to access those, but so far, no luck."

"That researcher, Doctor KT, helped a lot," Nijmeh said. "With everything we know and can estimate, our best, very rough estimate is four days. But that's a wild ass guess at this point."

"A *scientific* wild ass guess," Ergenian said. "We're doing our best to work it out given too little data and not enough expertise."

"What do the people on the ground think?" Aquino asked. "Have you been able to talk to the shuttles yet?"

Nijmeh shook her head. "No. We've made several more attempts, but we can't talk to them. The communications links are out due to power loss and some other factors we haven't been able to work out."

"Can you give me any kind of estimate on when we might get communications with the shuttles?" Why did he keep asking questions when the answers were so unpleasant?

"No. We're trying to figure out exactly why we don't have comms, and until we know why, we don't know how long it'll take to fix it." Nijmeh waved toward where most of the left behind crew members were sitting or lying. "There's not a lot of expertise up here. All of those people are food service workers or room upkeep or stylists. Crew who were really low on the priority lists for evacuation. Marc and I have access to parts of the ship's control systems that are still running on battery power, but only parts. We're trying to hack our way into other parts, but hacking isn't one of our official job skills."

"Okay," Aquino said, not knowing what else to say, but there was one more critical issue. "What about the cameras on the ship? Can you access their feeds if they're still working?" Getting access to the information provided by those cameras would make tracking the squonks a lot easier.

"The cameras? No," Ergenian said. "That's an internal security equipment access required system. We can try to hack into them, but no promises."

"Okay," Aquino said again. How many cameras were still working? Those in engineering were definitely out. "I think your priority should be establishing communication with the shuttles. I brought back a mobile hot spot that's being set up. That should let you access things better. Do we have any other crew members in here with specialized skills, like Nurse Sastrinata?"

"As noted, we've got one accountant," Ergenian said wearily. "Fifth Officer Craig."

If he'd had any doubts before about what criteria had been used to decide who was left behind, it was clear enough now. No one with any useful skills in a life-threatening situation, just those who would be missed the least if they were gone. And apparently, nothing had been prepared, no food or anything else, to look out for them once they'd been abandoned. He was trying to save people whose own employers didn't care whether they lived or died. That didn't change his obligations, but it did make him wonder how such employers could look at themselves in a mirror.

Four days. That didn't leave any room for wasting time. And the available time might be even less than four days, because that was just a wild ass guess by ship's officers working outside their normal areas.

Aquino fought down a feeling that the air in here was already going bad, with too little oxygen and too much carbon dioxide. It couldn't be that bad, yet.

But it would get that way. In four days or less.

EIGHT

HE'D better not count on getting much sleep over the next four days, Aquino thought.

Sleep. Why did that tease at his memory? Not because of the recent too-short sleep. Because sleep was related to…

Sedation.

"Thank you," Aquino said to Nijmeh and Ergenian. "Please let me know if you get a better estimate. And keep me informed of how your people are doing. And try to get in communication with the shuttles as quickly as possible."

"Will do," Third Officer Ergenian said.

Aquino hastened off, looking for Doctor Trinh.

He found her sitting with her back propped against a wall, frowning down at her data pad. "Doctor?"

She looked up. "Ensign Aquino."

"Dr. Gohara mentioned that the ship carried special gas that could be used to sedate specimens. Do any of the researchers still aboard have any knowledge of that gas?"

Trinh frowned in thought. "Researcher Salinas!" she called.

A young woman got up and raced the short distance to them. "Yes, Doctor Trinh?"

"Didn't you say you worked in the specimen labs? Ensign Aquino needs to know about the sedation gas."

"The gas? What about it?"

"Where is it?" Aquino asked.

"The canisters are in a locked wall cabinet in the largest lab," Salinas said, her eyes gazing outward in the odd way people did when looking inward at their memories. "There's a lock and an alarm. The canisters have tops you pop open, then you throw them and stay away from the gas. It shows as light gray so people can see it and avoid it. After four minutes, the gas begins to break down, and by five minutes after release, all gas should have dissolved into harmless elements." She looked anxiously at Aquino. "That's about all I know."

"That's a lot. Doctor Gohara said he thought the gas would likely not work on the squonks," Aquino said. "But if it did work, there was a small chance, he said, that it would either knock out the squonks or kill them. Do you know anything about that?"

Salinas hesitated, thinking. "We talked about using the gas to capture specimens on the surface, but everyone seemed to think there were too many unknowns until we learned a lot more about the biology of creatures native to Janus Five. Because, yes, there is that chance it will be lethal. It's not a big chance, but it's there." She fidgeted with her fingernails. "We can't even quantify the chance at this point, because we don't know enough about how Janusian biology reacts to things. We just know the chance of a lethal reaction must exist."

Doctor Trinh nodded. "I would agree with that assessment. I assume, Ensign Aquino, that the chance of killing the two squonks would not deter you from using that gas?"

"No, it would not. They're too deadly to try to capture. We're going to do our best to kill the two aboard this ship. It's not like these are the last two squonks in the universe."

That earned him another nod from Trinh. "There are so many on the surface. Doctor Tirgatao is right. Something about their numbers, their clinging to the ruins, their observed behaviors, and their design as living creatures is not adding up. I am trying to understand just how they evolved into their current state. And how creatures who behaved one way on the surface could change their behavior so drastically after a few days aboard this ship."

"I would be happy to listen to anything you come up with. Thank you," he told both Trinh and Salinas.

The next course of action was pretty clear. He went back to Sergeant Rodriguez, sitting down next to her. "There's a sedation gas in that large lab near one entrance to engineering. Odds are it won't work, but there's a small chance. We're going to get the gas, release it into engineering, then go in and either kill the squonks if they've been knocked out, make sure they're dead if they seem dead, or hunt them down if the gas was ineffective."

Rodriguez considered his words before nodding. "Yes, sir."

"Do you have any suggestions?"

"No, sir. Not as long as you keep saying 'kill' and 'dead' when talking about the squonks."

Aquino gasped something that he thought might have been a laugh. "Good. How many Marines should be in on this? I want you and me both on hand when we go into engineering again."

"All of them, sir," Rodriguez said. "I don't want to leave any Marines behind."

"What about guarding these people? Maybe the squonks can't get in here, but we could leave Smith to make the civilians feel safe."

"No, sir," Sergeant Rodriguez said, her expression gone dead serious. "We should not do that. Smith knows he's screwed up big time against these squonks. Look at him over there. He's very down. Leave him here while the rest of us go hunt squonks and two things will happen. One, the left behinds will look to Smith for leadership, which will totally overwhelm him. And, two, Smith will know he's been judged unfit to even walk along with the rest of us, which will confirm for him how useless he is." She gestured to the carbine near Smith. "You'll have a seriously overwhelmed and seriously depressed Marine with a loaded carbine. You can guess what will happen."

Aquino studied Smith, thinking that surely he wouldn't suicide. But Smith's spirits looked just as low as Rodriguez said. And she certainly knew Smith better than he did. "All right. How do we protect the civilians here, or at least help them feel safe, if we all go out after the squonks? And make sure none of the civilians mess around with anything we leave behind, like some of the grenades?"

"We've got extra carbines. Maybe some of the civilians know how to use one and are reliable enough to be trusted with one," Rodriguez suggested. "Form a little guard force to protect them and to protect our stuff."

That wasn't a very good option, but none of their options could be characterized as *good*. And it would free up all of the Marines for the attempts to kill the squonks as quickly as possible. "I'll check with the left behinds and see if any have shooting experience. You notify the other Marines, *all* of the other Marines, that we're going to be headed out again real soon."

"You should eat something first, sir. We all should."

The moment Rodriguez said that, Aquino realized just how empty his stomach was and just how much he needed some nutrients. "We've got a limited amount of food. But it only needs to last about four days."

"What happens after four days?"

"If we haven't killed the squonks by then and gotten life support restarted, not enough oxygen left to sustain human life."

"That's… good news, I guess," Rodriguez said. "The food only has to last four days maximum. I'll get to work dividing up what we've got so it'll go that far. We'll all be on thin rations." She hesitated. "I'm about to point out something you won't like."

"Everything I hear these days seems to be something I don't like. What now?"

"The Marines, and you, need food more than just about all of the left behinds." She held up a calming hand before Aquino could speak. "I'm not saying we keep all of the food for us. But I think we need to prioritize the people who are going out to fight the squonks. I think we should give them more than the left behinds. Equal portions sounds really fair, but we're burning a lot more calories, and we have to keep being able to do that."

"Yeah." One more thing he really didn't want to decide. "How slim is slim?"

"Nobody's going to starve to death, but nobody is going to feel like they've eaten near enough."

"Okay. The Marines get double what the others do."

"Understood," Rodriguez said. "You and the Marines."

"No," Aquino said. "I can—"

"Dammit, sir! With all due respect—"

"Stop." She was right. He knew she was. He had known it as soon as the words left his mouth. "Okay."

"Okay meaning you are getting double as well, sir," Rodriguez said, making it a statement instead of a question.

"Fine. If any of the others notice and complain, send them to me."

"We'll try to keep the extra food on the down low," Rodriguez said. "Have you ever had Marine emergency field rations, sir?"

"I can't say that I've had the pleasure."

"Congratulations on your good fortune up until now. One word of warning, they suck."

Aquino sighed. "Are the rations expired, too?"

"No, sir. But that's because unless they spoil for other reasons, emergency field rations are literally good for about a century, 'good' referring only to safe to eat."

It didn't take Rodriguez long to divide up the rations. Aquino could see the partial rations being parceled out among the left behinds by Lachman and Ichikawa. Some of the left behinds were clearly unhappy about the small quantity of food. None of them seemed ready to raise a fuss about it, though. At least, not yet.

The small carton that Sergeant Rodriguez brought him after passing out food to the other Marines seemed to be filled with some sort of brown casserole. Was that shiny, gooey stuff supposed to be gelatin or gravy of some kind? Aquino used the spork that came with the ration to stab something that looked a bit like meat. It tasted… unusual, with an even more unusual consistency. As he swallowed, Aquino thought it was best described as what chewing on animal meat would be like if the animal was mostly made up of some kind of starchy vegetable.

The "vegetables" weren't any better. Maybe those were also meat.

Kenyatta had been going around to the other Marines, and now walked up to Aquino. She held up a squeeze bottle. "Hot sauce, sir?"

"Where did you get… Never mind," Aquino said. "Yes, please."

Private Kenyatta squeezed a couple of large dollops of hot sauce onto the field ration before heading back to sit with the other Marines and eat.

The hot sauce helped, just not enough. Despite his hunger, Aquino had to choke down the ration. It was strange to feel guilty for having to force down twice as much of the stuff as the left behinds were getting.

It did fill him, though. Just having the food inside him made him feel a lot better. And it was supposedly packed with nutrition.

Looking around, everyone was done eating. With everyone as hungry as they were, no one had turned up their noses at the rations.

Getting up, Aquino walked to the center of the room and called out, "Does anyone here besides the Marines know how to use a rifle?"

To his surprise, Hakim Marvin stood up. "I used to sport shoot in college."

One of the researcher grad students stood as well. It was Salinas. "I was on my high school competition shooting team."

And one of the crew members, an older man. "I've hunted back home. I know how to handle a weapon."

Three. Much better than none. He knew Hakim was solid, and the other two seemed steady enough. "Hakim, you are now in charge of the, uh, enhanced security force onboard. I'm going to give all three of you carbines with loaded magazines and charged capacitors. The Marines will familiarize you with these specific weapons. The Marines and me are going to head out after the squonks. While we're gone, you make sure no one else messes with any of the other weapons."

"And if those squonks show up?" the older crew member asked.

"They shouldn't be able to get through those hatches if the hatches are sealed and locked. If it somehow looks like they are, be ready to spray them with bullets the instant they break in. Don't pause to aim. They're too fast. Fill the air with bullets so even they can't dodge them."

"I've always aimed careful before," the crew member said. "But I understand. Those things are pretty tough, right?"

"Right. Don't give them a chance."

"We're ready to go," Sergeant Rodriguez told Aquino.

"Give these three a quick run down on the carbines, first." He did not want to go back out into those haunted passageways. But they didn't have time to delay.

Aquino caught KT looking his way, her worry clear. He forced a smile and waved to her. "See you when I get back."

She came close, watching him as if ready to say something. Finally, KT looked away. "Doctor Trinh is brilliant. We're making some progress, I think, on figuring out more about the squonks."

"I can't wait to hear it," Aquino said, not having to fake sincerity. He hoped this plan would work, but if it didn't, anything else learned about the squonks would be welcome.

KT nodded, her gaze still averted. "Thanks for getting that food. It was… different. How could they make something taste raw and over-cooked at the same time?"

"I can't help you with that," Aquino said, smiling, and realizing she was trying to cheer him up. He probably looked as gloomy and grim as he felt.

"Oz." She finally looked back at him. "I like you. Please be careful. Make sure you *do* come back."

What should he say? Knowing that his duty might mean he didn't come back? "I'll do my best. I… everyone is counting on us."

"Yeah. I know."

Rodriguez strolled up. "Carbine familiarization completed, sir."

"What's your impression of their skill level?" Aquino asked.

"Umm… good enough they're not more dangerous to the others in here than the squonks would be."

"Fine. Let's get this done." He forced a smile for KT. "Later."

As the Marines left, Aquino's last sight inside the auditorium was of Hakim standing holding a carbine, his usually relaxed expression as tense as anyone could ask for. The other two members of the "enhanced security force" had already started to close the hatch. Somehow, watching that brought forcefully home to Aquino that he was not the same as those still inside the auditorium. They were forced to depend on him, while he was once again the only one who could lead these Marines into danger, no matter how badly unprepared he was to do that.

The hatch sealed, and Aquino ordered the Marines to start toward the big lab, moving once again through the eerily empty corridors.

He had assigned Rodriguez to point again, and Obonsawin to the rear. After the squonk attacks on the flanks of the columns heading for the auditorium, Aquino rationalized he needed to have a strong central force. Smith and Ichikawa walked just ahead of him, with Lachman and Kenyatta just behind.

Aquino felt ridiculously like the "high value unit," which in Navy formations would be escorted by other warships whose job was to protect it. He didn't consider himself particularly high value. He was an ensign, after all. On the other hand, none of the Marines were questioning or balking at doing anything he ordered them to do. So at least he hadn't screwed up too badly. Yet.

Everyone kept alert, scanning their surroundings constantly for any sign of the squonks.

A lot of people had died on this ship recently. Many of them not far from where the Marines were. Even the steadiest nerves couldn't help wondering if the shadows held vengeful spirits.

Private Lachman finally voiced what they were all feeling, "Do you think there might be ghosts out here now?"

"If there are," Obonsawin called from the back, "they're going to be really mad at the squonks. Maybe they'll help us out."

As they approached the lab, Aquino's tension rose even more. This area of the ship should have felt familiar by now. They'd gone through this passageway repeatedly before and after Sergeant Antaeus's death. But with only emergency lighting, the air not moving, and no sign of any other life, it'd become unfamiliar and menacing.

Dark spots on the deck marked where Sergeant Antaeus's blood still lay.

"Why haven't the cleaning bots taken care of the blood?" Lachman complained.

Aquino answered, "The cleaning bots automatically returned to their charging docks when ship's power was lost. They go into a conserve energy state."

"Sort of like you, Lachman," Obonsawin called with a laugh.

"Screw you, Naveen!"

"That's enough," Sergeant Rodriguez said. "If it hasn't gotten through to you apes yet, this is the real deal. That's Ant-man's blood, remember?"

Whether chastened by her reprimand or sobered by the reminder that one of the Marines had already died, the others fell back into a gloomy silence.

The entrance to the lab loomed ahead of them, the entry darkened. How long ago had it been when he'd been summoned here by Doctor Gohara? Aquino wondered. How long ago had those three doomed graduate students been sent out to die? It felt like forever, in a different place from this dim, deserted passageway. But it was probably only a single day, if that.

They went into the lab as if it were occupied by enemy soldiers, not knowing whether one or both of the squonks had returned to the room which held their former enclosure. The lab proved to be as empty and silent as the passageway outside.

"We need to find a locked, wall mounted cabinet," Aquino said.

"Any idea what it looks like?" Ichikawa asked as she and the others looked around.

"No, aside from the fact that it's more than likely locked and mounted on the wall."

"How about this one that says *Caution* and *Gas* on it?" Smith asked.

"That's probably it." Aquino examined the cabinet, which was neither high nor deep. "And it's locked."

"I'll get it." Private Kenyatta had a small packet in one hand from which she was pulling out thin tools.

"Are those lock picks?" Aquino asked her.

"Maybe," Kenyatta replied.

"Okay." This wasn't the time to worry about regulations regarding prohibited personal items. He watched as she worked for a short time before giving a grunt of satisfaction.

"It's open." Kenyatta swung down the door, revealing a rank of what appeared to be old-fashioned cans for foodstuffs that were tightly secured with brackets. The tops of the cans had pull tabs, and each was emblazoned with *Warning*, *Gas*, and *Use Only as Directed*.

"Here are directions. 'Pull tab, throw immediately, avoid area of gas cloud for five minutes.' That looks pretty easy," Rodriguez said, pulling out a can and looking it over.

"How do we know what the area of the gas cloud is?" Lachman demanded.

"The gas is gray," Aquino said. "We're going to toss them as far we can into engineering and then seal the doors for five minutes."

They emptied the cabinet of all eight cans. "How are we going to do this, sir?" Obonsawin asked.

He'd been trying to think that through all the way here. Only one course of action offered the best chances. "Split into two groups and each toss in all the gas cans they've got at the same time," Aquino said.

"Then what, sir?" Sergeant Rodriguez asked. "We all go in? If they're not killed by this stuff, they might just evade us again."

"We could post someone at one of the exits and maybe get lucky," Ichikawa said.

At that, Aquino focused on Rodriguez. "I'm thinking four of us should go in. That's hopefully enough to handle the squonks if they jump us. The remaining three can take up station at one of the exits that has a view of at least one other exit. If the squonks run, that blocking force might be able to nail them."

"Who goes in?" she asked him.

He took a deep breath before answering, "Me, Kenyatta, Lachman, and Ichikawa. You command the blocking force with you, Smith, and Obonsawin."

She gave him a level gaze, then nodded. "That sounds like a plan, sir."

"If you have comments, I want to hear them."

Rodriguez shook her head. "It's a solid plan, sir. And a good distribution of our assets. Splitting into two groups is risky against these things, but it's our only chance to catch them if they try to evade us. I would not recommend splitting into three groups again." She leaned in close, speaking in a murmur, "I believe you are up to this, sir. I wouldn't have said that a couple of days ago."

"Thanks." He raised his voice so everyone could hear, "Let's go. My force will take up position at the entrance to engineering nearest us."

"That fourth exit," Rodriguez said, "where the last two security officers survived. I think that's where my force should toss in our gas and set up a block."

"Why the fourth exit?" Aquino asked. "Wouldn't they go for the first exit again?"

"I don't think so. They seemed to know where the security officers were," Rodriguez said. "The squonks knew they were at those other three exits. But they never had a chance to kill the ones at the fourth exit because we showed up. I have a feeling the squonks will want to take care of unfinished business. Just a hunch."

He considered that. "Maybe you're right. With what little we know, it's as good a reason as any for choosing a place. And… the location should be a good one for tossing gas in to give us full coverage of engineering." Aquino felt a momentary sense of calm following that statement. While facing so many things he felt unqualified to deal with, any time he encountered something he knew well (like the deck plan and compartment layouts on a ship) it was like entering a safe harbor.

Unfortunately, there were far too few things like that.

"Let's go," Aquino said, hoping his voice didn't reveal his building anxiety. Hoping it didn't reflect any of the worries filling his mind, the inner voices telling him he was dangerously out of his depth.

You don't know how to do this. You're going to get everyone killed. And then everyone else on the surface of the planet will die, too.

Shut up.

Rodriguez led the way outside the lab, into the now-depressingly familiar passageway, the deck on the way toward engineering bearing more blood spots left by Sergeant Antaeus as they'd hauled his remains to medical.

Aquino had shied away from admitting he was grateful he wasn't having to deal with Antaeus. Not simply power struggles with the sergeant, but the constant temptation to delegate his responsibility and sit out making the hard decisions. Especially since Sergeant

Antaeus would have pushed to make all of the decisions, certain he knew all of the right answers. It would have been so easy to stop arguing, to let Antaeus lead the Marines into engineering, so easy to let blame fall on Antaeus for any failures.

But the blame would have been his, all the same.

What if Antaeus could have been revived?

From what Aquino knew, revival left the injured person in a very fragile medical state, dependent for some time on various devices monitoring their health.

Meaning, Antaeus would have died again when the ship lost power.

Was everything he was trying to do futile?

When people are counting on you, you have to do your job.

That voice was his mother's. Aquino took a deep breath, determined to listen only to that voice, and not to all of the voices urging him to give up.

He looked around again, not just in search of any sign of the squonks, but also to try to assess the Marines. What voices were each of them hearing? He could only get partial glimpses of each individual's face due to the directions they were looking and the helmets and body armor, but everyone looked nervous as well as determined. All except Private Kenyatta, who was revealing nothing of her inner thoughts, as usual.

The voice he needed them to be hearing was his. A voice encouraging them, not feeding fears.

As Rodriguez, in the lead, reached the door into engineering, Aquino spoke up.

"We're going to split up now. Before we do, I want to ensure that all of you understand something. I'm very glad that you are with me, facing this danger. I believe you guys can handle whatever the squonks throw at us. If I didn't believe that, I wouldn't be going in there with you, would I? I'd find a way to stay outside. But I *am* going in with you. We *are* going to deal with this threat. If this try doesn't work, we'll try something else. And keep trying. I will never stop trying, and I know you'll be with me every step of the way." He paused to take a breath, wondering how each Marine was taking this speech.

"Sergeant Rodriguez, proceed as ordered. We will throw the canisters at..." Aquino checked his data pad, which no longer had any links active but could at least still tell time. "Ten after. Exactly ten after."

"Got it, sir," Rodriguez said. She saluted him. "Good hunting, sir."

He returned the salute. "Same."

They watched the sergeant, Smith, and Obonsawin go, until Aquino abruptly realized they needed to be looking in all directions for trouble. "Let's get against that wall facing the hatch. Keep your eyes out. Who are our best throwers?"

Surprisingly, Lachman raised his hand.

"*You're* volunteering?" Ichikawa said incredulously.

"Yeah, I'm volunteering," Lachman said, looking defensive. "I'm a good thrower."

Kenyatta half raised her hand. "I've got a good arm."

"Okay," Aquino said. "Lachman and Kenyatta are our throwers. Ichikawa and me will cover you. A minute before time to toss, we'll open the door, you guys step just inside, and when I give the word, throw those canisters as deep into engineering as you can. Then you step outside engineering, and we seal the door and wait five minutes."

"The gas might kill 'em?" Lachman asked.

"Small chance of that, but it's worth trying. Once the gas breaks down, we'll all go in and... see what we can find."

"We want them dead, right?" Kenyatta asked. "There's no backup plan to try to capture them if they've been knocked out?"

The others watched him worriedly, waiting for the answer.

Why would they trust the same chain of command that had left them out here with half the numbers they were supposed to have and outdated equipment? A chain of command that hadn't even sent a Marine to command them?

Aquino shook his head. "There is no backup plan. I don't have any secret orders regarding the squonks. We do not want them alive. If you see one or both, do your best to kill them. I'm going to be doing the same, though frankly I'm not as good a shot as any of you."

He noticed Ichikawa and Lachman glancing at Kenyatta. She nodded in acceptance of his words, and then the other two did as well.

That was odd. Nothing he'd seen prior to this had indicated that Kenyatta held or wanted any sort of leadership role among the other Marines. He would have to keep a closer eye out for any more signs of that.

And, then… it was time to wait.

"How much longer?" Ichikawa asked.

"Three more minutes," Aquino said. "We needed to allow plenty of time for Rodriguez to reach that other entry."

"Same old Marines," Lachman said with a nervous grin. "Make us show up for an assault early and then wait."

"We're lucky Ensign Aquino didn't make us wait an hour," Ichikawa said. "Remember that last formal inspection we had?"

"Yeah," Lachman said. "Stand around for more than an hour, then come to attention for thirty seconds while that colonel walked past us and out the door again."

"That was an inspection?" Aquino asked.

"Once a year," Kenyatta said. "Required. The colonel walked on the ship and never stopped walking until he left it again. I think he was aboard for twenty minutes total."

"They're not supposed to find problems," Ichikawa said. "If they found problems, they'd have to fix them. So, no one looks."

"If I survive this," Aquino said, "my after-action report is going to make a lot of people unhappy. I promise you that."

He checked the time. "Okay, we're about a minute to go. Let's get into position near the entrance. Kenyatta and Lachman, open the door, step inside and slightly to either side. Ichikawa and I will cover you through the gap left in the center. I'll tell you when to throw."

"Yes, sir," the three Marines chorused.

"Open it up," Aquino said, gripping his pistol tightly and hoping his nervousness couldn't be heard in his voice.

Kenyatta and Lachman stepped just inside the door, while Aquino and Ichikawa aimed past them in case the squonks were near.

That put all four of them right in the path of the stench filling engineering.

"What's that smell?" Lachman muttered.

"Blood," Aquino said.

"No, not that coppery smell. This is… sweet but not good. Like… rotting meat."

"That's what it is," Kenyatta said dispassionately. "We've got bodies down here. How many? We've seen four."

"At least four more," Aquino said. "The chief engineer, two more crew members who were on watch when the squonks escaped, and the first graduate student sent out after the squonks."

"Eight," Kenyatta said. "They're starting to rot."

"How do you know how dead bodies smell, Stef?" Lachman asked, staring about him in search of the squonks.

"Stuff happens," she said, clearly not intending to say any more.

Aquino's pad showed ten minutes after the hour. "Toss them," Aquino ordered.

Moving swiftly, Kenyatta and Lachman pulled tabs on two gas canisters and hurled them in different directions. Each grabbed their second canister, pulled the tabs, and once again threw them as far as they could.

Aquino could see gray gas fountaining out of the canisters as they flew through the air before falling between equipment. "Back out. Let's get this door closed."

Rodriguez, Smith, and Obonsawin would have also tossed their gas in. Enough gas to saturate the air in engineering.

Five minutes. Maybe they'd be really, really lucky and the gas would kill the squonks.

Everybody leaned their backs against the wall facing the sealed door, weapons not pointed, but ready.

It was funny how long five minutes could be.

"Do you think there's ghosts in there now?" Private Lachman asked.

Ichikawa gave a brief laugh. "If there are, Ant-man's ghost is waiting right inside that hatch."

"What do you think Ant-man's ghost would say to us?"

"That's easy," Ichikawa said. "He'd tell us everything he did was perfect and the only reason he's dead is because we screwed up."

"Yeah," Private Kenyatta said.

"Sir?" Lachman said. "It seemed like you and the sergeant never got along."

"We didn't," Aquino said. "That wouldn't have mattered if he'd done his job right." He wasn't feeling in any mood to say nice things about the late Sergeant Antaeus.

"Him walking into a death trap was the best thing he could've done for us," Private Ichikawa commented. "If he'd been in charge, he would've walked all of us into that."

"Yeah," Lachman agreed. "Rowdy knows her stuff. She wouldn't do that."

"Can I ask you something, sir?" Private Kenyatta said. "We're all here because no one wanted us."

"It's a dumping ground," Ichikawa agreed.

"What are you asking me?" Aquino said.

"Were you dumped here?" Kenyatta said.

How should he answer that? With the truth. "Yes."

"But you're a new officer, right?" Lachman said. "How come you got dumped?"

"No special reason," Aquino said, not wanting to get into the whole story. "I guess I wasn't considered special."

"And now you're stuck with us."

It was obvious that Sergeant Antaeus had rubbed in their discarded status to these Marines. But, really, how badly had they performed for him? "That's what I thought when I first got here," he finally said. "But then I got to know you, as people, not just as your service histories. And then this all happened. And you've all stepped up, and you've been steady. I admit I wish I had about twenty more Marines. Or maybe a hundred. Two hundred. But you guys are doing your best. I'm happy to have you."

None of them seemed entirely convinced of his sincerity, but none of them openly questioned his statement. That would have to do for now.

"Time's up," Aquino said, feeling his stomach knot with apprehension. "Let's go."

NINE

THE Marines stood away from the wall, checking their carbines. "If you get a shot at them," Kenyatta said, "don't fire a couple and then pause to see if you got a hit. Just keep throwing rounds at them until they stop moving."

"And give them a really long lead," Ichikawa added. "They're really fast."

"What if one's coming straight at me?" Lachman asked, his nervousness apparent.

"Hell, Lachman, that's the easiest shot you can get! Zero deflection! Just aim at the center of body mass and keep shooting."

"Yeah," Private Lachman said, nodding a bit too fast. "Keep shooting."

"Okay," Aquino said. Had he already said that? He needed to be careful not to sound as nervous as he felt. "Ichikawa on point, Kenyatta covers the rear, Lachman with me."

They all nodded, Lachman looking unhappy.

"What's the matter, Private Lachman?"

He shrugged. "Nothing, sir. I understand why you wouldn't want me on point or watching the rear."

How to reinforce Lachman's confidence? Because they needed every edge they could get. "Private Lachman," Aquino said, "I want you beside me so I can focus on oversight, knowing nothing will get through to me."

Lachman startled, then grinned. “Yes, sir! Nothing’s gonna get through to you!”

He noticed Kenyatta giving him a brief, wry look. Apparently, she could tell that last hadn’t been the truest thing he’d ever said. But she didn’t say anything to the others.

As Aquino stepped through the door, the warm, moist air inside engineering wrapped about him as if an unholy, invisible creature was embracing him. He didn’t want to breathe that air, but that was one more thing he had to do whether he liked it or not.

He took a breath, trying not to shudder as the smells hit him full strength.

“We’re clear to fire, right?” Ichikawa said at a whisper.

“Yes,” Aquino said.

“Any chance of anybody left alive in there?” Lachman wondered.

“No.” He didn’t *know* that, but it was impossible to see any way anyone could have remained in engineering and still be alive. So lay that out. Make it clear this wasn’t a rescue mission. It was about making sure more didn’t die. “If you see anything moving, it’s a squonk.”

“And it dies,” Kenyatta muttered.

Their route held a depressing familiarity. The large pool of blood, cracked and drying, where Sergeant Antaeus had discovered the difference between self-confidence and capability. Beyond that a little way, the side passage where the two dead grad students still lay. There wasn’t any sign the squonks had disturbed the bodies.

Rather than continue on down the route that led to where the body of Captain Jardyce lay, Aquino directed Ichikawa to move left, wending across the width of engineering.

Aside from the inadequate lighting, growing dimmer as batteries drained, and the horrible smell that filled the air, the other unnerving thing about engineering was how silent it was. Engineering was supposed to be full of noises, as many pieces of equipment hummed or buzzed or rumbled. With power out and the backup power not working either, there wasn’t a single sound, except for the soft noises made as Aquino and the Marines carefully placed their boots on the deck after each step.

"Maybe they're dead," Lachman whispered, the faint noise of his words seeming to echo.

"Quiet," Aquino said.

Around another corner.

He had thought this would be easier than last time. But his heart pounded, his mouth was dry, and every shadow threatened to hold a deadly foe. Even without the heat inside engineering, he would have been sweating. His helmet and body armor were more like confinement than protection, restricting his vision and movement, and weighing him down, and the pistol in his hand once again felt heavy and awkward.

What would happen when they found the squonks? Would he freeze in panic? Would he fire wildly, maybe hitting one of his Marines? He wouldn't run. No. That wouldn't happen—but what would?

Kenyatta, Ichikawa, and Lachman were all counting on him to give the right orders while they hunted the squonks and when they caught the squonks.

Oddly, though, none of them seemed worried about him. They all kept searching for danger around the small group. None spared any searching glances for their officer.

He took deep, slow breaths. He tried to ignore the warning voices inside and instead focus on this task. This step. Then that one. Look there. Now there. Feel the weight of the pistol in his hand. Heavy, yes. But also encouraging, wasn't it? A pistol could lead someone into folly if it made them overconfident. But no one could accuse him of being overconfident. No, this was his means of defending himself against an imminent threat.

And he had three Marines with him. Not the best Marines who had ever been, but even Lachman knew his job.

As Ichikawa came around another corner, whatever was beyond blocked from Aquino's sight by large pieces of equipment, she halted, throwing up a warning hand. After a moment, Ichikawa advanced again, moving more cautiously.

As the path beyond came into his view, Aquino saw a watch station, the controls damaged, many of them showing dents and cracks inflicted by something with considerable strength.

On the deck in front of the watch station were two more bodies in the uniforms of ship's crew. Beyond them was a third, wearing officer insignia.

He must have been the chief engineer, Aquino thought. While the other two had fallen face down, the chief engineer was on his back, wide eyes frozen in shock.

He'd been dead for going on a couple of days now.

Aquino looked away, bile rising in his throat. The stench of death was particularly strong here, making it even harder to fight the urge to throw up.

Ichikawa had knelt to conduct a brief examination of each body before standing again. "Is that everyone who was down here?"

Aquino took care as he spoke so his voice didn't quiver, "No. There's still one junior researcher unaccounted for."

Shaking her head, Ichikawa led the way again.

This was taking a long time. If the gas had just knocked out the squonks, would they be reviving soon?

Please let them be dead.

Ichikawa, looking down a short, narrow side passage that ended against a bulkhead, froze, her carbine pointed down it.

After a moment, Ichikawa lowered her weapon, grimacing, and gestured the others forward.

Against the wall was a mess of wiring and fiber optic cable that had been ripped out of the equipment. The coils had been formed into what looked like a big nest.

"We found where they've been sleeping," Ichikawa said, her expression sour. "And they're not here."

"Damn." Aquino wanted to slam his fist into the nearest equipment. But that would make a lot of noise. "Can we booby trap it?"

"All we've got is grenades," Kenyatta said, glancing at Ichikawa.

Ichikawa made a face. "None of that stuff is heavy enough to hold down a grenade's lever after the pin is pulled and the grenade is armed. I'd have to find something heavy to use, something that would stand out in that nest like a priest at a hooker convention. There's no way the squonks wouldn't see it."

"Poison?" Lachman suggested.

"The gas didn't work," Kenyatta pointed out. "Now what, sir?"

It took Aquino a moment to realize the question had been directed to him. If there had been any spot in engineering where they were likely to find the squonks, it was here at their nest. Now what?

Did it make sense to keep weaving through engineering? When awake and alert, the squonks could easily avoid contact, watching for when one Marine was tired enough and distracted enough to be picked off.

Stopping the search would look bad, though. It would be admitting his plan failed.

His experience as an enlisted sailor came back to slap him. How many times had they kept plugging away at something, not because it was working, but because someone in the chain of command didn't want to admit it wasn't working? Not wanting to admit Plan A had failed was the dumbest possible reason to stick with Plan A.

Aquino looked about them before pointing up and to their right. "This plan was unsuccessful. Let's work our way up and toward where the others are guarding that different exit. Maybe we'll get lucky and run into the squonks watching for a chance to hit the sergeant and her companions."

"And if we don't?" Kenyatta asked.

"We link up with Rodriguez and withdraw back to the auditorium so we can work up a new plan."

The Marines didn't bother trying to hide their relief at an unexpectedly sensible decision.

"Stay alert," Aquino cautioned.

This was the right thing to do, wasn't it? Walking in circles while the squonks simply avoided contact would waste time as well as energy. And time was a critical element here. The stench in engineering was an ugly reminder that with life support not working, there would come a point where the air inside the ship could not sustain human life. Even if the squonks also died at that point, it couldn't be considered a victory.

They went around another corner and down a passage between banks of equipment. A ladder leading up loomed ahead. They took it as carefully as possible, the treads nonetheless making small noises as their weight came on the stairs.

Ichikawa, still on point, began pausing again and again, looking about before moving a bit, and then pausing once more.

Was she seeing something? Or just getting spooked?

Should he try to jar her out of whatever was causing the hesitation? Or would such a distraction be the exact opposite of what was needed if Ichikawa's instincts were alerting her to something that couldn't be consciously pointed to?

It wasn't far to the exit now. Ten meters, maybe. Six meters to the next turn, then four to the exit.

The boom of the exit door ahead slamming open shocked all of them into a second of frozen surprise.

Ichikawa broke into a run toward the door, the others following, as the sound of carbine bullets tearing through the air echoed ahead of them. She went around the corner without pause, her weapon seeking targets, Aquino and Lachman just behind.

Searching ahead, seeing the open door looming, Aquino had completely forgotten about protecting the flanks and rear.

He heard the unexpected snap of bullets being fired behind him. Abruptly realizing his foolishness, he spun to face the back while pushing Lachman to continue after Ichikawa.

Kenyatta had paused at the junction of passages, her carbine to her shoulder as she aimed down one of them.

"What happened?" Aquino yelled, no longer worried about quiet.

"One came behind us," Kenyatta called back. "It was waiting to hit us in the rear."

The sound of shots outside engineering had ceased.

"Is there any sign of it now?" Aquino asked.

"No, sir," Kenyatta said. "It faded fast when I took some shots at it."

"Damn good job," Aquino said, trying not to think about what would have happened if Kenyatta hadn't kept watching for danger from the rear while the rest of them were charging forward.

She spared the briefest moment to give him a dispassionate glance. "I'm on rear guard, sir. It's my job."

"Let's back out of here," Aquino told her. "Sergeant!"

"Here!" Rodriguez sounded okay, but mad as hell.

"Status!"

"One injured. No enemy currently in sight."

Aquino backed through the door, waiting until Kenyatta had as well. He sealed the door again before turning to the others.

Rodriguez, still furious, was swiveling her head as she looked both ways for more danger. Lachman and Smith were bending over Obonsawin, who was lying against one wall, his upper leg bent at a very wrong angle, in a place legs weren't supposed to bend.

Ichikawa and Kenyatta took up positions guarding against another attack from the door or either direction down the passageway.

"What happened?" Aquino asked Rodriguez.

She took a deep breath before speaking, "The damned thing came at us so fast. I hit it, sir. I'm sure I did. But it hit Obonsawin, and then I couldn't fire again without risking hitting him. Then it broke contact and was gone. I tried to hit it again."

Lachman gestured to the deck, where a single drop of something very dark rested. "Looks like you did hit it, Rowdy."

"One drop of blood?" Rodriguez growled. "How tough to kill are these things?"

A moment of deep silence was broken by Private Ichikawa, "Well, that didn't work. This was supposed to be us ambushing them." Ichikawa's weapon and her attention were both pointed down the hallway. "Instead, they ambushed us."

Sergeant Rodriguez seemed ready to snap at Ichikawa, but controlled herself.

Aquino tried to center his thoughts—Ichikawa was right. While the Marines had been trying to find the squonks, the squonks had set up a trap that injured one Marine and could have resulted in worse casualties if Kenyatta hadn't been alert.

What now? He had to make another decision. Long-term thinking was one thing. But, at the moment, only one course of action made sense. "We need to get Obonsawin back to the auditorium where the nurse can look at that leg."

"Shouldn't we chase 'em, sir?" Lachman asked.

"No," Aquino said. "Not while Obonsawin is injured. We get him back, we get him treated, and we figure out a new plan." He knelt by the injured Marine. "Is it just the leg?"

"Pretty sure," Obonsawin gasped. "If the armor hadn't stopped it, those claws might've taken my leg off."

Aquino looked over deep gashes in the body armor protecting Obonsawin's upper leg.

What had led the squonks to develop claws that strong? What on the surface of Janus Five had been either prey with very strong, natural armor, or competition with the squonks as predators?

Rodriguez had regained her composure, gesturing to two of the other Marines. "Kenyatta, Lachman, you're going to do a seat carry of Obonsawin. Smith, you will do all you can to immobilize Obonsawin's leg. Keep it from flopping around while the others carry him."

Kenyatta and Lachman squatted on either side of Obonsawin, threading their arms under him and linking up to form a seat carry position. "Up," Kenyatta said, followed by a grunt of exertion as she and Lachman straightened their legs to raise Obonsawin.

"How are you doing, Marine?" Rodriguez asked Obonsawin.

Even though his face was drawn with pain, Obonsawin tried to grin. "Living the dream, Rowdy. I don't have to walk back."

"I figured we'd end up carrying you," Kenyatta grunted.

"You guys okay?" Rodriguez asked her and Lachman. "Ready to go, sir."

Aquino looked around, trying to ensure he was thinking of everything. "Sergeant, you're on point. Ichikawa, cover the rear. Our goal is to get back to the auditorium without any wasted steps or time. Let's go."

They headed out, Aquino hoping the squonks wouldn't try another attack soon.

This plan had been a total failure, and he was now down one Marine. The next plan would have only five Marines to draw on. Five Marines and one out of his depth ensign.

They were running out of time, and he had no idea what to do next.

The dim and gradually getting dimmer passageways of the *Darwin* were not growing in any way more familiar with more exposure. They instead felt more haunted with each trip through.

Especially knowing the squonks could be anywhere, just out of sight, preparing to leap…

"How fast are they?" Ichikawa called up to Rodriguez.

"Really fast," Rodriguez called back. "I kept misjudging my aim point because I kept assuming they'd move slower."

"You got a hit, though."

"Yeah, for what good it did."

Aside from that brief conversation, everyone stayed quiet, concentrating on their tasks. The only sounds in the passageways occasional grunts of exertion from the Marines carrying Obonsawin, and occasional gasps of pain from Obonsawin as his leg jiggled, despite every effort by Smith to hold it still.

It seemed to take a very long time to reach the auditorium.

Aquino, Ichikawa, and Rodriguez stayed on guard, searching outwards, as the others banged on the hatch for entry and went inside. Only then did the last three back inside the compartment, watching with ready weapons until the hatch was resealed.

Kenyatta and Lachman carried Obonsawin to where some blankets brought from the barracks had been laid, crouching again to set him carefully on the deck, Obonsawin letting out another involuntary grunt of pain.

Lachman straightened with a groan. "Man, you are one heavy pain in the butt."

Hakim had seen what was happening and turned to call, "Nurse Sastrinata! We've got an injury!"

Sastrinata hastened up, her face already composed in careful lines that wouldn't upset a patient. "What have we got?"

"Broken leg," Kenyatta said.

"Looks like you're right," the nurse commented as she knelt to closely examine Obonsawin. "Legs aren't supposed to do that."

Aquino, watching from a couple of steps away, felt someone coming up beside him and looked to see KT.

For a moment, his sense of helplessness and failure faded. "Hey."

"Hey," KT said. "You're okay? What happened to him?"

Aquino pointed to the upper leg body armor that Nurse Sastrinata had just gently removed. "See those gouges? Squonk claws. If not for that armor, Obonsawin would've lost that leg."

"Squonk claws did that?" KT leaned closer to look, her expression equal parts fascination and repulsion. "How tough is that armor?"

"Very tough," Aquino said. He let some of his frustration boil over. "How does that happen, KT? I understand that creatures evolve features in response to challenges in their environment. But what on Janus Five required the squonks to have claws like that? Is there a big prey with serious natural armor? Or are there other predators the squonks have been forced to face frequently?"

"No. We haven't seen anything like that," KT said, shaking her head with a worried expression. "Not in dominance fights or mating battles, either. There hadn't been any sign of claw use on the surface before the squonks got loose on this ship. Oz, I should tell Doctor Trinh about this."

"Let me know what she says," Oz said, watching her go then moving closer to join the group kneeling around Obonsawin.

Nurse Sastrinata had been carefully feeling Obonsawin's upper leg, her brow furrowed with concentration. "It's a bad break, but you got lucky. One, it's a clean break, and two, the broken bone didn't break skin. This could be a lot worse."

"I'm not feeling real lucky," Obonsawin said.

"You are," Sastrinata said. "I need to set this. That will hurt, but I don't have pain reliever with me. How about you Marines?"

"We've got this," Sergeant Rodriguez said, offering a hypo from the first aid kit. "But it's expired."

"Expired?" Aquino asked, thinking this was another of the sort of thing "perfect" Sergeant Antaeus should have been on top of.

"We've got new kits on order," Rodriguez explained. "They've been on order for a long time."

"Ant-man said we were at the bottom of the priority list," Ichikawa said.

Again. Aquino sighed, nodded, and passed the hypo to the nurse.

Sastrinata checked the hypo, shaking her head. "This stuff isn't just expired. It's been recalled."

"Why?" Aquino asked.

"Because," the nurse said, handling the hypo as if it were dangerous, "they discovered over time it breaks down into two components even when properly stored. Usually, both of those components are simply useless as pain killers. Sometimes, though, it breaks down differently, and one of the components is a lethal compound. This will not help him, and it might kill him. Do you have *anything* else?"

"No," Aquino said.

"Hold on." Kenyatta reached into her pack and pulled out a nondescript bottle.

Aquino took it from her, uncapping it and sniffing cautiously before taking a sip. Whiskey. And not cheap, rot-gut whiskey, but some seriously high-class booze.

He passed the bottle to Obonsawin. "Take a good slug of this."

Obonsawin, his hand shaking a bit, grabbed the bottle and took a large swig. After swallowing, he shuddered and coughed. "Can I have another?" Obonsawin asked in a hoarse voice. Without waiting for permission, he took another big slug. "Whew. Thanks for giving me the good stuff, Stef."

"It's all I had with me," Kenyatta said.

"Well, hell, for a minute there I thought you liked me."

"Nah," Kenyatta said as she watched Aquino take the bottle back from Obonsawin.

Aquino hesitated, glancing at Kenyatta to see if she would reach for the bottle or ask for it, but she stayed silent. Kenyatta knew when to cut her losses.

She'd given up the booze when one of the other Marines needed it. Even knowing it would be the evidence needed to tie her to liquor losses onboard.

"I'd be happy to keep the bottle, sir," Obonsawin gasped.

"It's Private Kenyatta's," Aquino said, making a decision and handing the bottle back to her. "Keep that handy in case Obonsawin needs more."

"Yes, sir."

"I don't want anyone else using it unless I direct, understood?"

"Yes, sir."

Nurse Sastrinata braced herself, her hands on Obonsawin's leg. "You guys help hold him down," she told Smith and Kenyatta. "Are you ready?" she asked Obonsawin.

"Would it matter if I said no?"

"No, it wouldn't."

"Hold on." Rodriguez pulled a tear-off patch from Obonsawin's uniform and placed it between his teeth. "Bite down, Marine."

"Oh-kay," Obonsawin mumbled around the patch.

"I'll set the leg on three, okay?" the nurse said. "One… Two…"

Sastrinata's hands moved with strength and accuracy.

"Uggh!" Obonsawin grunted, his body stiffening. His eyes fixed on the nurse as he spat out the patch. "What the hell happened to three?"

"You would've tensed up on three," she said. "Relax. It's set. The worst is over."

"I'm a little suspicious of anything you're telling me!"

Sastrinata smiled. "Honest, all I have to do, all I *can* do now, is improvise a cast to hold your upper leg immobile. When we get power back in medical, we can get the bone healing accelerants to work and you'll be walking fine within a couple of weeks. But until then, you'll have to let mother nature do the healing the slow old-fashioned way. Hang on now. There's going to be a little pain, as I have to get wrappings under your leg. But nothing like earlier."

Obonsawin watched suspiciously, occasionally grimacing with pain, as the nurse used some empty duffles to wrap his upper leg as securely as possible.

"That's the best I can do," Nurse Sastrinata said, sitting back and wiping sweat from her brow. "It's not good enough. Try to limit your movement as much as you can."

Obonsawin grinned, his lips stretched tightly across his teeth. "Too bad this didn't happen to Lachman. He's an expert at doing as little as he can."

"Thanks, man. I love you, too," Lachman grumbled.

"Just kiddin', man," Obonsawin said, raising a fist toward Lachman, both his fist and the arm trembling.

"No problem," Lachman said, reaching his own fist to gently bump Obonsawin's. "You need anything, hero?"

"Not yet." Obonsawin looked at Aquino, his expression grim. "Sorry, sir."

Aquino raised his eyebrows in response. "It's not like you got that leg broken on purpose."

"No, sir, but there's still two of those things out there, and now you've only got five combat capable Marines. I can't do a damn thing now but lie here."

Seeking words to comfort Obonsawin, Aquino looked up toward the ceiling.

And saw a camera.

He remembered what Third Officer Ergenian had told him. Could someone who figured out how to break into the health care system also break into systems on this ship?

"Private Obonsawin, maybe there's still something very important you can do to help me and the other Marines." Aquino pointed. "A lot of cameras on this ship should still be running on batteries, but we can't see what they see because access to the camera feeds is restricted, and no one left aboard the ship has access. Can you break into that? Get me access to those cameras so I can see what they see?"

"Sir?" Obonsawin shook his head. "Sir, I had to sign like a half dozen forms promising I would never do that kind of thing again."

"I understand that," Aquino said. "But this is different. It's an immediate operational need. I am asking, I am *ordering* you, to try to break into the camera feeds and anything else in this ship's systems that we can't currently access."

"You're ordering me to do it?" Obonsawin looked around at the other Marines as if seeking confirmation that he'd heard right.

"I will put that order in writing, Private Obonsawin," Aquino said. "So there is absolutely no doubt you acted in accordance with lawful orders."

"Oh, that's okay, sir," Obonsawin said, gesturing around him. "All the others heard what you said."

"I'll get a ship's data pad from one of the crew so you can work with their ways into the system," Aquino said. "How long should the battery hold out on that mobile hot spot?"

"A week, probably," Obonsawin said. "We don't have to worry about that for a while."

"Good. You lie here and rest, make sure you don't move your leg, but work your ass off getting me that camera access."

Obonsawin grinned. "That sounds like something a Marine officer would say, sir. Looks like we're rubbing off on you."

Aquino paused in the act of straightening up to nod. "I sure as hell hope so."

"Bad news, Oz," KT said.

Aquino had given the Marines a break to rest, and to give himself time to try to figure out a new plan. While he was unsuccessfully working at that, she had approached him, along with Fourth Officer Nijmeh and Third Officer Ergenian. All three of them looked solemn in the manner of people who had very bad news and didn't want to deliver it.

"What happened?" Aquino asked.

"We made a stupid mistake," Ergenian said.

"Very stupid," Nijmeh said, her eyes haunted.

"*I* should have caught it," KT said. "We made a stupid mistake in the initial calculations. We assumed natural circulation would occur, that all of the air on the ship would be uniformly distributed, even as its quality deteriorated. Well, obviously, that's not going to happen because the fans aren't running."

"What does that mean?" Aquino asked.

"To put it as bluntly as possible," Ergenian said, "our earlier estimate of how much time we had before the air got seriously bad was… overly optimistic."

"How overly optimistic?" Aquino asked. "Less than three more days, I'm guessing."

"Twenty-four hours," KT said.

Aquino fought to keep from revealing his feelings, taking a moment to calm himself. "Twenty-four hours? That's how much time we have left?"

"That's our best guess." KT gestured around her. "Have you noticed that the air in here is really musty?"

Aquino inhaled slowly before nodding. "That's because we have only twenty-four hours left?"

"No," she said. "That's the worse news."

"There's *worse* news?"

"Yes," KT said. "And it's so obvious I want to kick myself for missing it."

"We missed it, too," Third Officer Ergenian said, scowling at the deck in embarrassment.

Fourth Officer Nijmeh shook her head. "I'm sorry. This isn't our field of expertise. It's not even close to it."

"It's *mine*," KT said. "But I was looking at the whole system instead of our little piece of it in here. Why is it musty in here, Oz? Because we're *all* in here. The vent fans aren't working, so the air isn't moving. We're all in here breathing what oxygen is in this compartment, and exhaling carbon dioxide that doesn't go anywhere. We're going to have to move to a new location where the air hasn't been used yet if we're going to last another twenty-four hours."

"Maybe we could open both hatches for a while and..." Ergenian shook his head. "That wouldn't help. The air outside isn't moving, either."

Okay, Aquino told himself. *Another problem. Let's tackle it smart. Think through things. Options.* "Can we move everyone? Where else on the ship is this large? We need a big enough compartment for everyone to be in. If we pack everyone in a smaller space, the air will just go bad much faster."

"We could spread out into several different compartments," Nijmeh suggested.

"No," Aquino said. "Unless you want to die real quickly at the hands of the squonks. We need a space we can defend." He needed someone else thinking on this. "Sergeant! We require your input!"

Rodriguez hastened over, looking concerned. "Sir?"

"The air in here isn't moving, so we're using up the oxygen too fast," Aquino explained. "We need to find somewhere else to move everyone."

"There's a lecture hall," Rodriguez said. "We've been in there a couple of times for safety briefings. But I think it just has regular doors that wouldn't slow down the squonks at all."

"That hall has six regular doors," Ergenian confirmed as he checked a deck plan on his data pad. "No reinforcement on them."

"We couldn't protect anyone in there," Aquino said. "We need another option."

"I'm sorry, but the air has to move," Nijmeh said. "We need fans. And without power, we don't have fans."

"That means we *have* to move," Ergenian told Aquino. "Or we suffocate in here before much longer."

Fans. Aquino looked up, seeing vents high up on two walls, one marked as providing air and the other as venting air. Naturally, without the fans running, neither was doing anything.

"Maybe if we had an electronics technician and portable power sources, we could do something," Nijmeh said, her voice dull with despair.

"We do have an electronics technician," Aquino said. "I'm trained as one of those." KT and the two ship's officers stared at him as if he'd suddenly produced a magic lamp. "But unless we have power sources that won't do any good."

"What about the capacitors for the carbines?" Sergeant Rodriguez said. "They can be set to battery mode."

It was Aquino's turn to stare, this time at the sergeant. "That option was removed from firearm capacitors because too many people were using them for unauthorized personal purposes and draining the capacitors."

"That option was removed," Rodriguez agreed, "in newer models. We've got old model carbines, and they use old model capacitors. Old model capacitors that have still got the battery mode built-in."

"You're certain of that?"

"Yes, sir! I know those guns!"

For once, having old equipment might be a life-saver. Aquino looked to the vents again. "Now we need a ladder."

The other Marines had wandered closer after he called over Rodriguez, and heard Aquino's last statement.

"Like that ladder?" Private Smith called, pointing.

Everyone looked, spotting a ladder fastened against one wall, overlooked because its metal blended in with the wall and everyone had been focused on other things.

It occurred to Aquino, that Smith had once again quickly seen something no one else had spotted. He did have an ability that had twice proven useful, though whether that would matter again was an open question.

"Yes," Aquino said. "Just like that. I need that ladder set where I can look into one of those vents," he added, pointing to the intake and outtake vent covers.

Third Officer Ergenian hastily corralled two hefty crew members to move and hold the ladder.

Aquino climbed up, shining his helmet light down the vent duct, and sighing with relief at what he saw. "This fan is accessible through the passageway outside of this compartment. If the other one is, too, we can fix this." And then get back to trying to kill squonks. This would use time they couldn't afford to spend. But if everyone died from lack of oxygen in here, killing the squonks wouldn't matter.

Looking down the second vent confirmed that fan could also be reached. "I need one more miracle, Sergeant. Do we have an electrical repair kit?"

Rodriguez looked offended by the question. "Of course we have electrical repair kits, sir. Regulations call for that for repairs on the carbines. The armory has two. Both got brought here with the weapons."

Even though no one else had cared about these Marines or their mission, the Marines themselves cared enough to keep their gear ready. If they survived this, Aquino thought, he'd have to ensure his report emphasized that attitude had been more important than anything he'd done. "Let me have a look at one of the kits."

It only took a moment to review the neatly stowed contents of the kit, identifying everything he needed. "All right. Listen up," he told the Marines. "We're going out again, right now. We're going to stay in the passageways outside of this compartment. I need this repair kit. I need two, no, make it three, extra capacitors. And…" he faced the two other groups in the compartment, "I need to know if anyone else here has any experience as an electrician," Aquino called.

To his surprise, graduate student Salinas popped up again. "I grew up on a farm. I know the basics."

One of the stewards also stood up. He was a big man, middle-aged, with a hangdog demeanor. "Same here. What do you need?"

"We have to rig some fans," Aquino said. "Sergeant Rodriguez, I want the Marines screening me and these two while we try to get a couple of fans going."

"Yes, sir. Anything else?"

"Yes, I also need the ladder."

"I can get that," the steward said, walking that way. Salinas also headed for the ladder, helping to heft it.

"Uh…" Third Officer Ergenian was gazing about in disbelief. "You can fix this? Really?"

"We have the tools we need and I have the training," Aquino said. "For once, something broke right, huh?"

KT grinned at him. "I think maybe something broke right for us when you got assigned to this ship. Let me know what you need from me, Oz."

"Right now, we just need to get this done. I know we've taken you away from Doctor Trinh."

"Solving the squonk puzzle," KT said, nodding. "I'll get on that."

Now what? He needed to brief everyone who was going out. It helped that he felt on firm ground for the first time in a long while. He'd never been a Marine. But former Electrical Technician Third Class Aquino knew electronics. "What's your name?" Aquino asked the steward.

"Haycock, sir," the steward replied. "Odin Haycock."

"Good. This is Salinas, one of the researchers."

"Still a graduate student," Salinas said. "Hi. Gina Salinas."

"We've got what should be some simple electrical work to do," Aquino told them and the Marines. "I may need help from you two, or just have you check my work. Stay inside the defensive perimeter formed by the Marines. Marines, you will form a defensive perimeter around where I'm working and make sure the squonks don't attack. If the squonks do attack, I want them both dead." This was an unexpected bonus, Aquino realized. If the squonks saw the repair party as possible targets, they might be lured in and taken out. "Any questions?"

"Grenades okay this time?" Kenyatta said.

He didn't have to think very long about that. "Grenades are okay."

"Got it, sir," Rodriguez said. She cast a judgmental eye over the other Marines. "Everyone get a couple of grenades. Smith, this might be a good time to get your act together. Stay sharp. We're ready, sir."

"Try not to get killed!" Private Obonsawin called. "I can watch your pack while you're out, Stef!"

"No, thanks," Kenyatta replied. "I'd hate for anything in it to go missing."

"You get the ensign that camera access, Naveen!" Rodriguez shot back. "Focus on task!"

"Let's go," Aquino said, then turned to Hakim Marvin, who had wandered closer, clearly curious at the activity. "You've got the watch in here again. Obonsawin has to stay immobile, but you can count on him for advice and backup firepower since his carbine is lying near him. We're going to be in the passageways right outside, but keep this hatch sealed until we knock for reentry."

"Got it," Hakim said. "So, what's this about, Oz?"

"Air," Aquino said, wondering what options would exist if this didn't work.

He took a deeper breath, hoping it was his imagination that the air inside the auditorium already didn't seem to have enough oxygen in it.

TEN

RODRIGUEZ led the way out, followed by the other Marines, then Aquino with the repair kit and spare capacitors, and Haycock and Salinas with the ladder.

"Down to that corner," Aquino directed, "then right. About halfway down that passageway before the next junction there should be an air vent duct running along the overhead. That's where we need to go."

"Smith," Sergeant Rodriguez said. "You and Ichikawa with me. Kenyatta, you and Lachman have rear guard."

Aquino followed Rodriguez, Smith, and Ichikawa, Haycock and Salinas staying with him, Kenyatta and Lachman following, their attention focused on anything that might threaten the group from behind.

He felt the absence of Obonsawin, wondering what he'd do if more of the Marines were knocked out of action.

It wasn't far. Aquino stopped at the vent duct, seeing the access panel that would allow him to reach the fan inside the duct.

"Oh, man," Salinas complained. "Those damned so-called easy open access panels."

Aquino glanced at her. "They really are easy to open, if you know exactly the right trick. If you don't know that, they might as well be welded in place."

"I would love to see that trick."

"Set up the ladder, and you will." As soon as the ladder was ready, Aquino went up it to face the access panel.

He twisted the outer clamps to just the right positions, then pushed against the access panel with just the right amount of pressure. It popped off.

Handing the panel down to Haycock, Aquino leaned into the vent to look at the fan. It was within easy reach, its blades almost filling the vent, the power and control line snaking into a sealed junction box set against one lower corner of the duct. "I need a cutting tool, an insulation stripper, and a tube of liquid solder."

The power and control line had a hard outer protective shell, which the cutting tool was designed to deal with. Cutting through the line generated a small bit of professional guilt, but this was no time to follow the rules. At least he didn't have to worry about the line being energized. Sorting out the ground wire and twisting it aside, then doing the same with the fiber optic control line, Aquino stripped a small amount of insulation from the power wires.

Bringing up the capacitor, he checked that the mode was set to battery. Touching one wire to a contact on the capacitor, he let a single drop of liquid solder fall, where it swiftly hardened to securely join the circuit. Bringing the second wire to touch the second contact, he paused as the fan roared to life, fighting an unexpected emotional wave at the once-ever-present and sorely missed sound. Moving carefully, he used another drop of solder to seal that wire to the contact.

Everything looked good. Air flow was in the right direction. It had been almost too simple.

He passed back down the tools, Haycock passed up the access panel, Aquino pushed it into place, and that was that. "One more to do," he said as he came down the ladder. "Left at the corner, down to the next corner, another left, and about halfway down that passageway. Let's go."

Everybody was smiling, as if he'd accomplished a miracle of sorts. When all he'd really done was buy a few more hours of time. "The noise of the fan might attract the squonks," Aquino reminded the Marines.

"I hope so," Private Ichikawa muttered.

They started toward the corner.

"I guess you didn't need me along," Salinas commented.

"We haven't finished the job yet," Aquino said. "You've got a real grab bag of talents. Why were you low on the priority list for evacuation?"

Salinas let out a short, bitter laugh. "The forms you fill out don't ask about things like that. Just your job title and your pay level. When it came to evacuation priority, I was just one more low-level graduate student."

"They always do that," Steward Haycock said. "Stick you into some easy, simple category to try to sum up complicated people. What's the story with you?" he asked Aquino. "You're management, right?"

"Sort of," Aquino said, trying to ignore snickers from the Marines.

"But you're an electrician?"

"It's what I did in my last job," Aquino said. "An electrical technician on Navy ships."

There was surprised silence from the Marines this time. Only Sergeant Rodriguez had known he was former enlisted.

"You've been a working stiff?" Haycock grinned. "Okay, then."

"Why'd you become an officer?" Salinas asked. "That's what you are, right, like one of the ship's officers, but different?"

"Yeah," Aquino said. "I guess I wanted more responsibility."

"Boy, you sure got that."

"Tell me about it."

Finally reaching the second vent duct, Aquino went up the ladder again, popping the access panel, and then leaning inside to look.

And curse.

The fan was more than arm's length down the duct, and the duct was too small for him to fit through even if he removed his body armor.

Aquino looked down at Salinas. "I hope you're small enough to get into this duct."

"There's only one way to find out," she said.

He came down, she went up, and then slowly, carefully, wriggled into the duct. "It's a bit tight," Salinas called. "But I can reach it. Pass me the tools."

"Can you see what to do?" Aquino asked.

"Yeah." Her voice echoed slightly inside the duct. "What do I do with the fiber control line?"

"Leave it loose where it can't get tangled in the fan blades."

"Got it."

The pause that followed seemed long to Aquino, only faint sounds coming from the duct as Salinas worked. He looked around, again wondering if the noise would attract the squonks. All of the Marines were alert, looking each way down the passageway.

Aquino thought about how fast the squonks could move, and about the distance to the nearest corners, and vainly tried to guess what would happen.

"Hell," Salinas said, the word echoing.

"Problem?" Aquino replied.

"Yeah. The battery shows full charge and the connections are fine, but the fan isn't moving," Salinas called. "I can't see any damage to it, and the fan turns fine under a push."

Was the fan burnt out? "Are there any signs of overheating or damage to the fan?"

"No. It looks fine. Have we got a hammer?"

"A hammer?" Of course. A hammer. Aquino looked down at Rodriguez, who offered up a tool from the repair kit. "We've got a fair-sized wrench."

"Pass it to me." Aquino climbed the ladder far enough to be able to shove the wrench forward along her body until Salinas could reach back enough to grasp it and bring it forward. After a moment, a low thud sounded. A moment later, another thud. Aquino heard Salinas muttering something that might be obscenities. Finally, a third thud, louder than the first two.

The fan sputtered, hesitated, then settled into a steady hum.

Steward Haycock grinned. "Percussive maintenance. She knows electronics, all right."

Salinas slowly backed out of the vent, wriggling to slide through the tight quarters until she could reach the ladder, breathing heavily. "That was tight. Are we done?"

"We're done," Aquino said. "Great work. See, we did need you."

"Show me how you got that panel loose."

He did, coming up the ladder to show her the tricks, trying to fight off the sense that Salinas and all of the others would soon be dead, so why bother with this?

When the small group reentered the auditorium, it was to cheers and applause from the bedraggled left behinds. Aquino could feel the air in the room moving. It already smelled fresher.

But that was only a temporary fix.

Instead of giving his spirits a boost, the happiness of the others reinforced his sense of failure. Former Electrical Technician Aquino had been able to buy a few more hours for those in here. But Ensign Aquino had to come up with a way to defeat the squonks, and do it very soon, or none of this would matter.

And he had no ideas at all.

Maybe a Marine second lieutenant would have been able to think of something.

Or this might be one of those situations that Rodriguez had summed up with "you're screwed."

He sat down, feeling depressed and hopeless and hoping it didn't show.

Sergeant Rodriguez came by with a small tray. "Meal time, sir."

"That's all I need." Aquino squinted at the goo. "It looks less dark brown than the last one."

"This is the pescatarian option. Fish."

"How can you tell it's the fish option?"

"It's not as dark brown as the meat version. May I join you, sir?"

"Suit yourself," Aquino said as he tried a bite, grimacing at the taste and not really wanting company, but was unwilling to rebuff Rodriguez.

She sat down next to him. "I figured we should put our heads together, sir."

"It can't hurt."

"Are you okay?"

Aquino considered how much he could confide in even Rodriguez. If the Marines knew how down he felt about their chances… "Um… I was wondering about something. Kenyatta. Is she seen as a leader by the other Marines?"

"Kenyatta?" He'd managed to surprise the sergeant. "Hell, no. Kenyatta doesn't want any leadership responsibilities. I think she'd prefer prison time to becoming a corporal."

"That's odd. When I answered a question, before we went into engineering, both Ichikawa and Lachman looked for her reaction before they acted."

"Really?" Rodriguez considered that. "What was the question?"

"Kenyatta asked me if I had secret orders regarding the squonks, if I'd try to order them to be captured again instead of killed when we got the chance. I said no," Aquino added. "Because that is the truth."

"Oh." Sergeant Rodriguez nodded. "The others didn't look at Kenyatta for leadership, they were looking to see how she reacted to what you said."

"What's the difference?"

Rodriguez blew out a long breath. "I'm not telling you this, sir. I never breathed a word about it. Stef Kenyatta is a human lie detector. She can tell, with what appears to be perfect accuracy, whether someone is lying or telling the truth. That's probably what's kept her from getting caught, except for that one time. She can tell when she's being set up. Ichikawa and Lachman were looking to see if Kenyatta reacted as if you'd lied. When she didn't, they knew you were telling the truth."

So, he wasn't simply a lousy liar. Kenyatta was a very skilled interrogator. "Hell," Aquino said, feeling another level of depression settle over him.

"What's the matter, sir?"

"I'd hoped you Marines trusted me by now. Haven't I been square with you all the way?"

This time, Sergeant Rodriguez sighed. "Sir, you're so clued in on some things that I forget you're still learning the ropes as an officer. You have to remember that you brought a lot of baggage to this hike. Baggage you didn't pick up. Other people, other things, piled it on you."

Aquino studied her face, trying to understand. "What do you mean?"

She waved toward the other Marines. "When you arrived here, you carried with you all of the experiences all of us had already had with other officers. Good experiences, bad experiences, whatever. And you represent the system. So, you carry the baggage of every time each of us got screwed by that system, or just treated badly. Like each of us being assigned here. That was all on you whenever we listened to you or watched you. Is this guy like Colonel SLUF? That's a guy I served under, who was nicknamed SLUF by the *officers* who worked for him."

He'd heard a lot of terms in the Navy, but this was a new one. "SLUF?"

"It's an acronym for Short Little Ugly Fu—"

"I got it." Aquino shook his head. "His own officers called him that? What did the enlisted call him?"

"You really don't want to know, sir. The point is, you show up, and we wonder. Is he going to yank us around so he can feel powerful or tell us to do dumb things because he can?

"Every time since you showed up that you did do something, some of that extra baggage got dropped, and we saw more of who *you* were. Especially when you stood up for us against that ship's security force goon. We were all like, whoa, this is not Colonel SLUF. But we're still watching, still learning. It's going to take a while for all of that unearned baggage you're carrying to get dropped. That's true of every officer when they show up."

"Damn." Aquino felt like an idiot. "Of course. I did the same thing when I was enlisted and a new officer showed up. Yeah, I've still got plenty to learn… Sergeant, here's what really has me down. I'm out of ideas." There wasn't anyone else he could've confided that to.

Rodriguez nodded. "I've been trying to think of some other ways to get those things, and coming up dry. My dad would tell me to think smarter, not harder, but that's a bit hard to do in practice."

"Was your dad a Marine?"

"Yes, sir. Damn good one, too. How about you, sir? Your dad an officer?"

Aquino gave a small laugh. "No. Dad is a gunners mate. He'll have to retire in another couple of years."

"A gunners mate?" Sergeant Rodriguez grinned. "If there is one specialty in the Navy that Marines respect, it's gunners mates. How about your mom? She also enlisted?"

"Yeah. Before she was medically retired, Mom was an Electronics Tech. The Navy calls them Everything Techs, because they get involved in fixing just about everything."

"Medically retired. Injury in the line of duty?"

"Yeah. There was a serious accident on Mom's ship, and… um… she saved a lot of lives, but got pretty beat up doing it."

"Wow." Rodriguez appeared to be genuinely impressed. "Did they give her a medal? Because it sounds like she deserved one."

"Uh huh." Aquino shrugged, trying to avoid the appearance that he was bragging about his mother. "Earth Cross."

"Earth—*Earth Cross*?" Sergeant Rodriguez stared at him, her eyes wide. "Your mom… Damn, sir. That is one hell of a family legacy to live up to."

"I'm trying my best," Aquino said. "Why are you so interested in my family?"

"I'm trying to distract you a bit so your mind has a chance to maybe see something it couldn't while you were focused tightly on our problem."

It was once more his turn to stare. And to realize that Rodriguez's plan had worked. "Dad will sometimes say if you're looking at a problem, and none of the options you see can work, maybe you need to look at the problem from a different angle, and possibly see other options you couldn't before."

Rodriguez considered that. "Okay. So, we're trying to catch and kill the squonks. What's another way of looking at that?"

"We're on the attack," Aquino agreed. "Which means the squonks… which means we're assuming the squonks are on defense."

"They are," Rodriguez said, her eyes scrunching. "But when they evade us, they don't hide somewhere else. They come out to attack somewhere else. They've tried ambushing us more than once. They keep coming out to attack instead of forting up in engineering. The *squonks* are on attack. And we're trying to defend the ship and the people aboard it."

"Which means we need to think of some way of setting up defenses that will stop the squonks dead."

"Mines?"

"Maybe. Do we have any?"

"No. We'd have to improvise some," Rodriguez said. "Can't hide 'em on the deck. Maybe on the overhead or the walls."

"Excuse me."

Aquino looked up to see KT nearby. "Hi," he said, smiling at the sight of her.

"I didn't mean to interrupt, but I was coming back to tell you what Doctor Trinh said about the squonk claws. Can I join in on this, though?" KT asked. "I overheard something just now. You guys are talking about trying to make mines to kill the squonks?"

"Right," Aquino said. "Sit down with us, please."

"Okay." KT sat down on the deck, her expression troubled. "I don't know a lot about mines, but I do know animals. Explosives have a very distinctive scent. Animals can be easily trained to identify it. Now, I know, that's Earth-type biology, but if explosives put off scents easily detectable by animals from Earth, it's reasonable to assume they can also be smelled by something like the squonks."

Rodriguez had been listening with open skepticism that shifted into realization. "The squonks might not know that's explosives, but if it's a strange scent they might avoid it."

"I think that's a real possibility, yes."

"And all the work and time we put into the mines would be wasted." Rodriguez sagged. "Good thing you told us."

"What would work?" Aquino asked.

KT made a helpless gesture. "If you had a giant mousetrap that wouldn't put off any warning scents."

"We're all of out giant mousetraps," Rodriguez said.

A light went on in Aquino's mind. "Giant mousetraps. No. We don't have any. But we have someone who can make some of those."

"Do you mean Ichikawa?" Rodriguez asked. "Those silly diagrams she plays with?"

"Ichikawa actually made one," Aquino said. "That's why she ended up here."

The sergeant gazed at him with an open mouth that shifted to a grin. Turning, she shouted across the room, "Hey, Malice! Get your ass over here!"

Ichikawa came running, frowning at Rodriguez. "Whatever happened, I was not involved."

"Private Ichikawa," Aquino said. "We need giant mousetraps. Traps fast enough, clever enough, and lethal enough to take out squonks. Can you build us some?"

Ichikawa gave him a sidelong look. "Sir, I had to promise not to build that kind of stuff again."

"I am *ordering* you to do it," Aquino said.

"Really?" Ichikawa looked at Rodriguez for confirmation and the sergeant nodded. "Ummm… so what have I got to work with?"

"All of the Marines," Aquino said. "Except for Obonsawin. He's working on something else critical. And any of the crew members or researchers who have the skills or hand eye coordination to assist. That's labor. For material, anything you can find. Anything in those crates over there, anything anywhere else on the ship that we can get to."

"Seriously?" Ichikawa smiled. "I get to loot those crates?"

"Requisition," Aquino said. "We will be requisitioning the contents of those crates, and anything else we can use, in response to an urgent operational necessity."

"I was always told 'requisitioning' is just a fancy way of saying 'looting,'" Ichikawa pointed out.

"Okay," Aquino said. "That's probably true in the Marine dictionary… and the Navy dictionary… and… any military dictionary. But we are using requisition in the legal sense. This is all above the board."

"Cool. How are we going to use these mousetraps?"

Aquino looked at Rodriguez. "What it is called when you are on the defense, and you push forward a bit to a position the enemy has to assault, and then you just sit there and kill them as they come at you?"

"I don't know the technical term," Rodriguez said, "but I know what you mean."

"One other thing," Ichikawa said. "Tools. I need a lot of hand tools. Power hand tools."

"Where can we find those?" Aquino asked.

KT spoke up again, "The custom fabrication shop has a lot of power hand tools."

"The what?"

"Custom fabrication shop," KT explained. "When a researcher needs something new and different, maybe to attract a new kind of animal, they get with the custom shop to work out what's needed. Or if they need something to conceal a surveillance device inside that looks natural. I can show you exactly where the shop is on the deck plan."

"That's the first place we need to go," Ichikawa said. "Tools, and any pieces of metal lying around. I need to know what I can make before I design stuff."

"Let's get ready to go… *borrow* some power tools, then," Aquino said. "Every Marine except Obonsawin. Ichikawa, before we go, check those crates and see if they have anything we can use."

"We're on it, sir!" Rodriguez got up, and sketched a brief salute toward KT. "*Thank you.* Sir, next time we put our heads together, we should make sure your girl is sitting in on it."

As the sergeant hustled toward the other Marines, and Ichikawa beelined for the hitherto-ignored crates, Aquino sat frozen before finally stealing a sidelong glace at KT.

She was watching him with an inquisitive expression.

"I never told them, or anyone, that you were my girl," Aquino said.

"Hakim thinks you're my guy."

"He does?"

KT shook her head. "There's a truism in the field of research that sometimes the answer you're looking for is right in front of a researcher but it takes someone else to see it." She reached to grasp his shoulder, leaning in to kiss him before pulling back a little and eyeing him with a solemn expression. "Oz, if you and me make it out of this…"

"Okay," he said, his lips still tingling from their brief contact with hers. "I'd like that."

She smiled. "Good. Oh, Doctor Trinh. She agrees with you that the claws are an anomaly. There is no reason in the environment of Janus Five for the squonks to have developed claws that strong. We're going to factor that in to our conclusions."

"I'm glad I could help," Aquino said. "Are there any preliminary conclusions you can share?"

KT hesitated. "Not yet. The way we're leaning is… disturbing. We need to check some more things before committing to it. I should get back to helping Doctor Trinh." As KT got up, she looked toward the Marines. "Is there any other help I can give you and your Marines before I go?"

"We need a detection system that can spot the squonks," Aquino said. "If you have any ideas what—" He stopped speaking, staring past her

Ship's cat Judy had been lying nearby, conducting her usual oversight of Aquino, and had come to all fours, her hair stiff. The cat slowly sidled toward Aquino, her attention fixed on a point near the hatch that had been used so far.

He looked over to where Macbeth and Lady Macbeth were sitting on top of the highest crates, seeing that they were both crouching as low as possible, their eyes fixed on the same area that Judy's were. "What the hell?"

KT pointed at Judy. "There's your detection system. I told you the cats seemed to be able to sense where the squonks were, even when they were sealed into an isolation enclosure."

Judy's aim slowly shifted, as if tracking something moving stealthily on the other side of the wall.

At least one squonk, probably looking for a way into the compartment where the remaining humans were. "Why is at least one of them out there now?" Aquino wondered, then answered his own question, "The fans. They can tell two fans are running so they're searching for people in this area. And the cats can tell they're out there."

"You need a way to bring Judy with you," KT said. "How did you get the cats here?"

"Judy rode on my arm, but we can't do that."

"No. How about Macbeth and Lady Macbeth? How did you transport them?"

He looked around, spotting the tote bag. "We used this. It's got a top that can be sealed."

KT looked it over, studying the tote. "It can carry Judy easily, but we need to replace some of the solid fabric on the sides with strong netting so you can see Judy and she can sense squonks. Can you give me a minute?"

"Absolutely." Aquino watched KT run over to where the crew members were gathered together.

"What's up, boss?" Sergeant Rodriguez asked, watching KT.

"I think we've figured out how to get warning when the squonks are near," Aquino said. "One of the cats."

"Judy? She's the one who seems to like you."

"Yeah. KT is modifying that tote into a cat carrier so we can bring Judy along when we go to get those power tools."

Rodriguez grinned. "It sounds like we might have to make that cat an honorary Marine."

"Private Judy?"

"We're short a corporal at the moment."

Aquino sighed. "Sergeant, I need to let you know something critical. The best available estimate of how much longer we have before oxygen goes below critical levels in parts of the ship is about twenty-three hours."

Sergeant Rodriguez inhaled slowly, her expression hard to read. "This is what they call an opportunity to excel, I guess. If Ichikawa's traps work, we can pull it off."

"Yeah. But we can't waste a minute. Those first aid kits have endurance tabs in them, don't they?"

She eyed him before nodding slowly. "They'll keep us going another twenty-three hours without sleep. After that..."

"If we don't get the job done in the next twenty-three hours, it won't matter," Aquino said. "Distribute the endurance tablets to the Marines."

"Including Private Obonsawin?"

"Yes."

"I'll be right back with your tab, sir."

The endurance tablet had kicked in quickly. Aquino felt alert and ready for anything as he led the Marines once more along the haunted corridors of the *Darwin*. One of the side effects of the tablets was, unfortunately, over-confidence, and he worked to damp down that emotion.

Rodriguez once again led the way on point, following instructions from Aquino on where to turn and when to take a ladder up or down to a different deck. Kenyatta was at the rear, while Lachman, Smith, and Ichikawa were with Aquino in the center. Ichikawa had suddenly become a lot more important, so he didn't want to risk her on point or at the rear.

Everyone had empty duffles and packs with them, ready for whatever they could get from the custom shop.

Judy had accepted a place in the tote, which now had mesh-covered openings on both sides. She'd relaxed by the time they left the auditorium, so the squonks must have moved away. But there was no telling how far off that might be. "Anybody know what the effective range of this kind of cat scan is?" Lachman had asked.

"Assume they're really close if Judy alerts," Aquino said.

They moved carefully, but Aquino could still hear the noises they were making. How far did those sounds carry inside the otherwise almost silent ship?

"Custom shop," Rodriguez said, coming to a halt at a door. She pointed to an elaborate sign mounted next to it. "Showing off their work, I guess."

"That's a solid door," Lachman commented, trying the handle. "Locked."

"Kenyatta?" Aquino said.

"On it." Private Kenyatta knelt to examine the lock. "It's electronic with a manual back up. The electronic part opened automatically when power cut off. It's also alarmed, probably on a battery."

The last thing they needed was an alarm blaring to summon the squonks or hide the sound of their approach. "Can you handle all that?"

Kenyatta glanced at Aquino. "Sir, you're going to forget about all of this, right? In the after-action report and everything else?"

He considered the priorities he had to think about, then shrugged. "Forget about what, Private Kenyatta?"

"Okay." Kenyatta went to work while the others waited and watched for squonks, their nervousness impossible to hide.

Judy remained sitting in the tote, displaying no signs of worry.

A loud *click* sounded from the door. Kenyatta eased it open, checking something on the entry. "Alarm is disabled."

"I'll check out the room," Rodriguez said, moving past Kenyatta. She was back almost immediately. "All clear."

"Inside," Aquino ordered, following Lachman and Smith, Ichikawa and then Kenyatta backing in as well. He watched Kenyatta set the manual lock again, then looked about at racks of a wide variety of tools. Ranks of batteries were stacked on one wall, while shelves and bins held an astonishing variety of materials. Two large part printers were also in the room, both silent, useless without ship's power.

"Oh, my," Ichikawa said, grinning as she gazed about. "I am in my own little heaven here, people."

"Stop geeking out and get what you need," Rodriguez ordered.

"Everything I need? This stuff is top of the line expensive."

"Everything," Aquino ordered. "If in doubt, and we can carry it, put it in a duffle."

Ichikawa sprang into motion, grabbing tools and batteries, and passing them to Kenyatta and Lachman. Smith held open the duffles, not always successfully, as the others dumped the equipment into them. Inevitably, that made noise, causing Aquino to gaze worriedly at the door.

After several minutes of frantic effort, Ichikawa slowed down, checking the remaining tools as well as materials in the bins and shelves.

"How much longer?" Sergeant Rodriguez asked.

"Almost got it," Ichikawa said. "Let me do a last check."

"Make it a careful check," Aquino said, despite his own urge to get moving. "We don't want to have to come back here." Knowing they could leave soon, he relaxed a little.

Aquino checked that he could easily reach his holstered pistol, then reached down to pick up the duffle.

And froze, staring at Judy.

The black cat wasn't making any noise, but her back was arched, the hair standing up. She had her gaze locked on the area near the door they'd used to enter this room.

The squonks were here.

ELEVEN

TURNING, Aquino caught the eye of Sergeant Rodriguez and gestured her over, trying to convey the need for both urgency and quiet.

Reaching him, Rodriguez gave Aquino a questioning look. He pointed down at Judy, then at the hatch.

Her eyes following his prompts, Rodriguez's face hardened. She spun about, the motion catching the attention of the other Marines, and brought her straightened forefinger to her lips in the age-old hand signal for silence. The others paused before quietly moving to ready their carbines.

Rodriguez studied Judy carefully before putting her lips close to Aquino's ear so she could speak in a very low voice, "She's shifting her gaze a bit from side to side. I bet the squonks are just outside that door, one on either side, waiting to hit us from two directions again."

He thought of cats waiting patiently outside a mouse hole, knowing their prey would show sooner or later.

Aquino put his lips close to Rodriguez's ear, "Can we turn it on them? Charge out shooting?"

She shook her head. "They can hit us as we come out one by one. Or, if we all try to come out at once, we'll get tangled up in each other and be even easier to kill."

"Grenades?" Aquino suggested. "Open the door and toss out grenades?"

Rodriguez considered that, then made an indecisive gesture. "Maybe. If they're just going to stand there. But if they're planning to charge through the door the moment it opens and get in among us, those grenades won't help."

And they'd already witnessed that. The squonks had always come in fast, trying to close with their opponents so they could disable and kill them as swiftly as possible.

He studied the metal wall on either side of the door, knowing their carbine bullets couldn't penetrate it to hit anything on the other side. If this had been a standard room on the ship, the walls wouldn't have been so strong. But, like the heavy door and its locks, this room had been reinforced to guard against theft, and the Marine carbines had been designed in part to be "safe" for use on ships by ensuring their bullets couldn't shoot through air-tight walls.

They couldn't go out that door, and even opening it would probably lead to a brutal hand to hand fight with the squonks.

Fortunately, that should leave another way out.

"Every room on a ship where people live or work has to have at least two ways in and out," Aquino whispered to Rodriguez. "We need to find the other door."

"Why is it hidden?" the sergeant wondered, her eyes sweeping the walls.

"Probably because no one ever uses it, so stuff has been piled in front of it. That's a blatant safety violation, but people do it all the time."

"Got it." Rodriguez gestured again, using hand signals to tell the other Marines to remain on guard facing the door, before joining Aquino as he tried to quietly search for the other exit.

Aquino moved as silently as possible, wincing when he brushed against something or when his carefully placed feet still made a sound. He used his helmet light to peer behind anything against the walls that wasn't clearly permanently attached, which left a lot of shelving units, boxes, and crates to look behind.

He hadn't told Rodriguez that even though regulations required that second door, it wasn't unheard of for that regulation to be ignored by designers or builders more concerned with fixing complex deck plans. And he'd been told that the *Darwin* had been modified a lot since being built, which was another way in which important safety requirements got "modified" out of existence for convenience and costs.

If there wasn't another way out of here, they'd have to face a couple of bad options.

He had covered the wall opposite the entry door with no luck, moving on to check one of the shorter walls, when he reached a pile of large panels leaning against the wall, kept in place by heavy elastic cords fastened to hooks which looked like they'd been attached after the room was constructed. Leaning in carefully, Aquino shined his light behind the pile.

There it was.

He beckoned to Rodriguez, starting to remove the elastic bands. The sergeant joined him, then gestured to Lachman to help as well.

The panels were unexpectedly heavy and awkward because of their size. It was impossible to move them without making occasional sounds.

Finally, the last panel was moved aside, revealing a door with a large sign on it bearing big, bright-red letters: EMERGENCY EXIT. DO NOT BLOCK.

Aquino heard a muffled noise and saw that Lachman was trying desperately not to laugh.

It was funny, in a way.

Rodriguez gestured to Kenyatta to check the emergency exit door.

Private Kenyatta shook her head, pointing to an alarm, before moving to deactivate it. Then she checked the lock, giving Aquino a thumbs up to indicate they could open it easily from inside.

He looked about. The emergency exit was one wall over from the wall holding the normal entrance. That was far from ideal, but the squonks should be totally unprepared for the Marines to leave from there. A check of Judy showed the cat still focused intently on the main entrance.

Aquino called up the deck plans for this part of the ship, trying to find a way to quickly avoid the squonks or ensure the Marines had good opportunities to shoot them if the squonks attacked.

There. That route would work.

He waved all of the Marines to look at his data pad, showing them the route. Out the door, only two meters beyond that a ladder that would take them up one deck, then a long passageway. If the squonks followed the Marines up the ladder, they'd have to approach along that passageway, giving the Marines plenty of opportunity to kill them. Any other approach would require the squonks to detour, taking so much time, the Marines could get back to the auditorium safely.

Hopefully.

Aquino looked at Rodriguez, a question in his eyes. She nodded in reply, giving him a thumbs up to approve his plan. Turning to the other Marines, Sergeant Rodriguez ran her finger along that passageway before tapping her carbine and one of the grenades she carried.

The Marines nodded, Lachman grinning wolfishly, Smith looking nervous, Ichikawa smiling, and Kenyatta as enigmatic as ever.

Aquino swung one of the loaded duffles on his back before picking up Judy's tote bag. The Marines were carefully loading themselves with duffles and packs, ensuring they could easily bring their carbines into action if necessary.

Drawing his pistol, Aquino went to the emergency exit, breathing slowly. He realized he couldn't hold the pistol, Judy's tote bag, and open the emergency exit. Cursing silently, he holstered the pistol.

Resting one hand on the lock, Aquino looked back at the Marines.

He mouthed numbers.

Three.

Two.

One.

His hand snapped the lock open, then the door handle, jerking the door inward and pausing as Rodriguez went through first.

Aquino followed, pulling out his pistol as he ran after Rodriguez, looking back to see the other Marines charging out of the room, their gazes toward the corner the squonks would have to come around.

Sergeant Rodriguez reached the ladder, pausing to steady her carbine as the others raced up it, burdened by the heavy bags.

Aquino heard the hum of the sergeant's carbine followed by the crack of bullets in flight as Rodriguez fired several shots. Despite knowing he should keep moving, he stopped at the top of the ladder, waiting for her. "Keep going!" he ordered the others.

Rodriguez came up the ladder in a rush, shoving Aquino into motion even as she spun to toss a grenade down.

They ran along the passageway, the *whomp* of the detonating grenade filling the air, Kenyatta dropping back to guard the rear along with Rodriguez.

"One tried to come around the corner," Rodriguez called to Aquino. "I discouraged it. Don't think I got any hits. If they were coming up after me, the grenade might have done some damage."

Lachman laughed, the sound part gasp as he ran. "I was worried those things were smarter than us. But I guess we're still better than them."

"Slow down," Aquino called, thinking that the heavily burdened Marines would exhaust themselves at this rate. "Fast walk. Stay alert. Lachman, take point. I'll tell you where to turn."

"What if they know we're headed back to the auditorium and set up an ambush there?" Kenyatta asked, her voice not sounding as worried as it should have given what she'd just said.

"Judy will let us know if they're close," Aquino said.

He hoped she would, anyway. Judy had jumped inside the tote when the grenade went off. At the moment, she looked very unhappy and was tearing at the sides. Seeing her claws out, Aquino was glad she couldn't get through the tough fabric of the mesh. He'd have to thank KT for how well she'd fixed it up.

Judy's eyes, the pupils huge, fixed on him. She hissed.

No, this cat would not be warning them when the squonks got close.

"Belay that," Aquino said. "The cat warning system is… not available."

"We broke the cat?" Ichikawa gasped. She'd hefted more bags than the others, and now appeared to be having trouble catching her breath as they moved quickly down the passageway.

"It wasn't me," Kenyatta said, her voice as deadpan as usual.

"The cat is broken temporarily," Aquino said, his emotions toggling between worries about their situation and amazement that the Marines could joke at a time such as this. "Keep alert. Our first warning the squonks are close might be them jumping out at us." Was he having trouble breathing as well? Or was he just imagining that the air here was already getting bad?

Sergeant Rodriguez trotted past him to take up point along with Lachman. "They're more likely to hit our front now than our back," she said to Lachman loud enough for Aquino to hear. "Especially as we get closer to the auditorium."

Aquino directed the group through more turns and up another ladder to a different deck, then down another ladder not too far from the auditorium. "See that intersection up ahead? We turn left there, and then it's a straight shot to the auditorium about ten meters further on."

Was it his imagination that the emergency lighting was already starting to dim as the batteries used up their charges? That shouldn't be happening so soon. The batteries should be good for a week, at least.

That was, the batteries should last that long if the batteries weren't old, having been through too many charging cycles. And if they'd been checked and replaced when any started to lose charge too quickly. Replacing and checking batteries cost money, and involved something that was invisible to everyone as long as no emergencies happened. It was exactly the sort of thing that looked like an easy way to cut costs with minimum chances of creating the kind of problems that would make higher ups look bad.

A couple of meters farther on, Aquino found his speculations confirmed. One of the emergency lights had faded into a dull, orange glow, leaving a patch of near-dark around it. That one, at least, had a battery that should have been replaced.

Hopefully, there weren't a lot more like that, he thought, looking about at the inadequately-lit passageways.

As they approached the turn, Aquino listened for any sign of trouble, trying not to let his fears grow. Rodriguez was right. If the squonks were going to hit them again, it would be around here. "Everyone, slow down. Normal walking pace." Had that sounded nervous? Aquino gripped his pistol tightly, seeing that the Marines were all more tense as well.

Glancing downward, he saw that Judy was no longer trying to claw her way out, and was now sitting. Except, she still seemed very much on edge. Was that a warning a squonk was near, or the remnants of her earlier upset?

Approaching the corner…

A loud rattling bang caused every Marine and Aquino to jump, their eyes and their weapons jumping around wildly to find the source of the noise.

"Dammit, Smith!" Rodriguez snarled.

Private Smith had somehow managed to drop one of the duffels he'd been carrying, the power tools loaded inside loudly announcing their impact on the deck.

Smith was making futile efforts to pick up the duffle without dropping anything else he was carrying when Aquino holstered his pistol and grabbed the dropped bag. "I've got it. Let's move." If the squonks hit them now, he wouldn't be able to use his weapon until he dropped the bag. That seemed a lesser price to pay than delaying here any longer than necessary. If the squonks weren't already here, they would have heard that noise and learned where the Marines were.

Rodriguez rounded the corner, followed by Lachman, both pausing to gaze down the passageway beyond.

"What is it?" Aquino said as everyone else halted again.

"Maybe nothing," Sergeant Rodriguez replied.

"Might've seen something," Lachman added, his weapon up and searching for targets. "But if it was there, it ducked out of sight."

Private Smith suddenly darted to the corner, looking in the opposite direction from Lachman and Rodriguez. "Rowdy!"

Before Smith even spoke, Sergeant Rodriguez had already noticed his movement and begun spinning about, her weapon angling to aim, the carbine humming as it accelerated bullets as she fired five shots in quick succession.

Aquino came up beside the others, after checking to be sure Private Kenyatta was still watching the rear. "They tried to hit us from two sides again?" He gazed down the passageway, seeing nothing.

"Yeah," Rodriguez said, sounding angry. "One in front to distract while the other hits from behind. And I almost fell for it."

"Do you think you got any hits?"

"No, sir. They're both gone. Smith!"

"Yes… Sergeant?" Smith asked worriedly.

She grabbed his shoulder with one hand. "Damn good job."

"What the sergeant said," Aquino added. "Damn good job, Private Smith. You've got an eye for what the rest of us are overlooking, don't you?"

"Uh… I guess… maybe… sir," Smith said, looking as if he had no idea how to handle praise.

Given his history as a Marine, maybe he didn't.

"That's all cool, but which way we going?" Lachman asked in a low, tense voice, his weapon still up and ready.

"The way you're facing," Aquino said. "We keep moving until we reach the entry hatch to the auditorium."

With Sergeant Rodriguez and Private Lachman on point leading them, and Ichikawa and Kenyatta watching the rear, the small group began moving again. This time their progress was even slower, the Marines nervously watching for any sign the squonks had returned and were going to make another try at them.

Judy sat stubbornly on the bottom of the tote, refusing to offer either warning or reassurance.

Finally reaching the hatch, Aquino pounded on it. "We're back. Open up!"

It seemed to take longer than usual for the hatch to open, Hakim Marvin gazing at them with concern. "Macbeth and Lady Macbeth were acting as if the squonks were nearby," he explained.

"They were," Aquino said.

He went inside, stopping and turning to watch Smith and Ichikawa come in, followed by Lachman, Kenyatta, and last of all, Sergeant Rodriguez, who kept her weapon up and ready until the hatch had been sealed again.

"How'd it go?" Private Obonsawin called from where he lay, his upper body propped up so he could work more easily on the data pad before him.

Lachman snorted. "You know that 'every day is an adventure' junk they use in recruiting? I'm getting tired of adventure."

Aquino walked toward the pile of crates from the top of which Macbeth and Lady Macbeth were watching him with narrowed-eye suspicion. Setting down the tote, he opened it, jumping back as Judy leapt from it and raced to the crates, not pausing until she reached the top alongside the other two cats.

"What happened to her?" KT asked, surprised, as she walked up to him.

"Judy was fine," Aquino said. "She alerted us to the squonks being near while we were in the custom shop. But after the grenade went off—"

"The *grenade*? You set off a grenade near a cat?"

"Yes," Aquino said, wondering why he felt defensive.

"What did you think would happen when you did that?" KT demanded.

"The effect on the cat was the last thing we were worried about at that moment!"

Judy chose that moment to hiss.

Aquino looked up at her, seeing the cat glaring at him. "What do you think the odds are that she'll come out with us again?"

"That's… really hard to say." KT studied Judy, shaking her head. "How long will it be before you go out again?"

"That depends on how long it takes Ichikawa to put together her giant mousetraps." He looked back toward the rest of the Marines and was dismayed to see them sitting down, resting, after dropping their burdens.

Thankfully, Rodriguez had already reached them and was speaking, her voice too low to hear from where Aquino was, but clearly intense. The other Marines very quickly shifted from relief to annoyance at the sergeant and then to shocked urgency. They scrambled to their feet, everyone emptying out the duffels and other bags so all of the tools and other items were laid out on the deck.

"I guess your sergeant told them about the less than twenty-four hours left," KT commented.

"I guess she did," Aquino said. He nodded to the ship's officers as they walked up as well. This time, Fifth Officer Craig was with Ergenian and Nijmeh. "We've got some urgent work to do," he told them. "Private Ichikawa is going to construct some traps. If she asks for assistance from any of your people, please provide whatever you can. It might just be people to hold things or apply strength. Whatever."

Ergenian looked back at the other members of the crew. "I'll let everyone know. Ensign Aquino, can you level with us? What are our chances?"

Aquino knew he couldn't hesitate in answering that. "I think we have a chance. We've figured out how the squonks are operating, and this should be something they don't expect and aren't watching for. You can see my Marines are working all out. They're not about to give up. Neither am I."

"Okay then," Ergenian said, exchanging relieved smiles with Nijmeh and Craig. "Anything we can do to help, we will."

"Thanks," Aquino said. "I need to talk to Dr. Trinh now."

As he and KT walked the short distance to where Trinh still sat with her back against one wall, KT spoke in a very low voice, "You put up a great show of confidence there. Only someone who knew you really well could have seen how worried you are."

"Someone like you," Aquino said. "Yes, I'm worried. But I'm not giving up, and I do think this idea will work."

"I could see that, too," KT said, giving him a brief smile.

They reached Dr. Trinh, who sighed as she looked up at Aquino. "We should talk," she said. "I have reached some conclusions."

"Okay," Aquino said. "But, first, we're going to be building some traps, and if any of your researchers can assist, I hope you won't mind lending them to us."

"Of course not," Dr. Trinh said. "Dr. Tirgatao, please sit down. You, too, Ensign Aquino. I am certain I know a big part of the riddle of the squonks. There's an equally large part remaining, but this portion may be of use to you. Ensign Aquino, do you know what selective breeding is?"

"Not… really," he said.

KT smiled slightly. "It's a method of modifying plants and animals by selecting seeds, or individuals, with desired traits. By doing that over generations of the animals or plants, you can make the desired traits more prominent and more frequent."

"Is that different from genetic modification?" Aquino asked. "I know what that is."

"Very different. Genetic modification is inserting different genes into a life form to create a change in one generation, and can use genes from totally unrelated life forms," KT explained. "Selective breeding can only be used for plants or animals that are cross-fertile with each other."

Dr. Trinh grimaced. "In this case, I need to emphasize that while genetic modification is a relatively recent development in human history, requiring some complex technology, selective breeding has probably been going on ever since the first humans began planting crops and herding animals. It does not require sophisticated science or equipment. It doesn't even require knowing why it works. It just needs trial and error leading to established practices."

"This is about the Janusians, then," Aquino said. "I saw their old farm fields, and the remains of what must have been herd animals."

"Yes." Trinh looked away, as if reluctant to say more. Finally, she shifted her gaze, focusing on Aquino. "The images the Janusians painted in the records we've been able to reconstruct make it clear they had a very good understanding of selective breeding, and that they applied this knowledge to create the squonks."

"That thing about the claws," KT said. "As you noticed, too big and too strong to be explained by any known reason on Janus Five."

"Any known reason except the Janusians," Dr. Trinh said. "Breeding for larger and stronger claws is exactly what selective breeding can do. From the Janusian pictures, it is clear they bred the squonks for that, and for strength, and speed, and very likely the sort of intelligence useful in…" Trinh hesitated. "In a weapon."

"A weapon?" Aquino said, startled. "Not just guard animals?"

"I don't think so, no." Trinh waved in the general direction of the planet that the *Darwin* was orbiting. "Have you heard that Janus Five is an extremely geologically stable planet? Yes? Only one volcano, earthquakes probably exceptionally rare, and what continental drift there is occurs at an infinitesimal rate compared to a planet such as Earth."

"No mountains," Aquino said, remembering that he hadn't seen any on the surface of Janus Five.

"Yes. Some hills that may over the course of a million years get higher, but no mountains. Those are the product of clashing surface plates, which Janus Five effectively does not have." Trinh paused again. "You noted that the Janusians seemed to have a great many edged ceramic tools. They lacked access to metal. Janus Five has rich deposits of metals, but they're all deeply buried, since no geological processes have forced any deposits closer to the surface. The Janusians couldn't access them. They didn't even know the metals were there."

"How did life develop without access to metals?" Aquino asked.

Both Trinh and KT looked impressed at the question. "There *are* metals in the surface environment," KT said. "Our best guess at this point is that those mostly came from asteroids impacting the planet long ago. When they vaporized on impact, or in the atmosphere, they spread enough metals to help life develop."

"But not enough to allow any metal-based civilization," Dr. Trinh said.

Aquino stared at her as the meaning of what she said sunk in. "The Janusians couldn't build better weapons, stronger weapons, so they *bred* better weapons from the available animals."

"Look at this." Dr. Trinh turned her data pad so Aquino could see the displayed image. "This is one of the restored Janusian pictures. What does it look like to you?"

Aquino studied the image, seeing at either side lines of Janusians, the illustrations stylized in a way that was unusual to human eyes. Between the two lines of Janusians were two large groups of squonks that were rushing toward each other. Both the Janusians and the squonks on each side wore colored bands about their midriffs, light purple on one side and orange-red on the other.

The Janusians also had on some sort of armor made of rectangular plates of what was probably leather fastened to harnesses to protect their upper bodies, the armor also dyed the colors of the bands or sashes. Aquino recognized those oblong leather plates from his simulated trip to Janus Five. His guess back then that the badly deteriorated sheets of leather mixed in with bones might have been some sort of armor had been correct.

Where the squonks from each side had come into contact, blood sprayed in dark red fountains that dominated the painting. "They're emphasizing the blood being spilled. A battle, with the squonks doing the fighting. Or maybe an awful sport, like one of those animal fights."

"Or perhaps both of those things," Dr. Trinh said, sounding angry and sad at the same time. "Something that made sense to the Janusians."

"So, the squonks weren't just guard dogs," Aquino said. "They were weapons. Weapons that turned on their masters?"

KT nodded, also looking upset. "Whatever safeguards the Janusians had to control the squonks must have failed."

"There may be some other critical factor involved," Dr. Trinh said. "I'm not quite ready to say what that is, and in any case, it shouldn't matter to your efforts to eliminate the squonks on this ship."

Aquino looked away from the image on Dr. Trinh's pad, thinking of what he had seen in the dead Janusian city and town. That alcove where some Janusians might have been hiding, until they were found. And then… "Quis custodiet ipsos custodes?" he murmured.

"Excuse me?" Dr. Trinh said.

"It's a very old saying," Aquino explained. "From the days of the Roman Empire. The Romans created this special force to guard their emperors, but after a while, those guards realized they could get rid of emperors they didn't like and install emperors they did like. *Quis custodiet ipsos custodes* means, um, who will guard against the guards? If the Janusians deliberately created the squonks to be deadly weapons, they did so without having any way to protect *themselves* against their own weapons."

"Humans have done similar stupid things," KT pointed out.

"Not on that scale," Aquino said. "I admit we came close more than once to using weapons that could've exterminated ourselves, but we never made weapons we couldn't control. Though… there were people who pushed for artificial intelligence programs to control weapons. That could've done to us what the squonks did to the Janusians. There's something I don't understand in this, though. If the squonks are bred to be weapons, then why have they been so passive and calm on the surface of the planet? And why did the ones we're dealing with on this ship suddenly go from that to deadly killer?"

"I think I know the answer to that," Dr. Trinh said, her voice heavy. "But I'm not ready to commit to that answer. It shouldn't have any bearing on your ability to kill the squonks, I think. It could have major implications for the shuttles on the surface of the planet, though."

"The shuttles we still can't talk to," Aquino said. "Thank you, Doctor Trinh. Your conclusions do help me understand exactly what we're up against." If only such conclusions had been possible before the squonks were brought aboard the Darwin. But that hadn't happened, maybe couldn't have happened, so thinking about that particular what-if would have to wait until he was drafting his after-action lessons-learned report.

Assuming he survived to draft that report.

The comment about the shuttles reminded Aquino of another thing he had to check on. "Thank you, Doctor. Thanks, KT. I need to talk to the ship's officers."

He'd barely taken three steps in that direction when Sergeant Rodriguez came walking quickly up to him. "We need your immediate input, sir."

"On what?"

"Ichikawa needs to know where the traps are going so she can know the dimensions of wherever that is so she can size the traps to fit."

Aquino altered his path in the middle of his next step, hurrying toward where Ichikawa sat, Rodriguez following. By the time he reached Ichikawa, Aquino had the deck plan for the area near the auditorium called up on his data pad. "All right. We know something about how the squonks operate. What's the best location to set up our traps?"

Rodriguez and Ichikawa bent over his data pad, studying the layout. "Not too far from here, right?" the sergeant said.

"Right," Aquino said. "They seem to be lurking in this area. I'll bet they followed us from around here to the custom shop, tracking us somehow while staying out of sight."

"Your girl mentioned the squonks being able to smell," Rodriguez commented. "That's probably how they tracked us."

"Hell, yeah," Ichikawa agreed. "After so long wearing the same outfits and sweating through them? Those squonks could've tracked us from fifty kilometers off."

"They like that tactic of coming at us from opposite sides," Aquino said, trying to get the conversation back on track. "We need a place that invites that kind of attack."

"How about this spot?" Rodriguez said, pointing. "Two big corridors joining with the passageway not far from here, and these smaller routes coming in from each side and behind. The nearest corners to us will be only a few meters away."

"Do we try to cover both of the big corridors?" Aquino asked.

"Yes, sir. Split into two groups of three. We know the squonks will go after a group of three. We'll still be within easy supporting distance of each other." Rodriguez nodded as she studied the deck layout. "Sir, this is the best we're going to find."

"Then I'll put the traps in the smaller passages coming from the back of us," Ichikawa said. "One in each, and the squonks run into them while trying to sneak up on us."

Aquino looked at the deck layout a few seconds longer, trying to spot flaws in the proposal. "It looks good to me. Let's run with that. Do we have what you need for the mousetraps?" he asked Ichikawa.

She grinned. "Yes, sir."

"You know we've got a serious time limitation to work with, but don't hurry things so much the effectiveness of the traps will be compromised. They have to work."

"Got it, sir."

What else should he do to help Ichikawa? His prior experience as a sailor dealing with officers who insisted on micro-managing told him the most helpful thing he could do was probably staying out of the way. "I'm going to let you run with this, Private Ichikawa. Assist her as necessary, Sergeant Rodriguez. If either of you encounter any obstacles, I want to know immediately," Aquino added. "Don't argue with whoever is causing the problem. Get me and I'll straighten them out."

"Is there anybody or anything off limits on this? That we can't use, I mean?" Rodriguez asked.

"Doctor Trinh. And the cats. And Private Obonsawin; he needs to get me access to the ship's cameras." Aquino couldn't think of anything else useful to say, so he gave them a sharp nod. "Get moving."

"Yes, sir," Ichikawa said. "Rowdy… excuse me, *Sergeant Rodriguez*, can you get some people to break open that crate third from the top, the one labeled *struts*? I'm going to need what's in it."

"Sure thing, *Private* Ichikawa." Rodriguez headed not straight for the stack of crates, but for the crew members sitting on the deck. "I need some arms and backs to help us prepare traps for the squonks."

Twelve crew members, including Steward Haycock, scrambled to their feet, following the sergeant toward the crates.

Aquino started to turn away, but looked back at the remaining crew members as he heard angry voices and sobs. The three ship's officers were in among the crew members, from the looks of them unsuccessfully trying to deal with something.

Not his circus, not his monkeys. He could let the ship's officers deal with it.

Oh, hell, the entire circus aboard *Darwin* was his, including all of the monkeys. He couldn't let trouble start now.

Walking up to the edge of where the crew members were sitting, Aquino could clearly hear what some were saying.

"They're just trying to keep us busy!"

"Why haven't they fixed this yet?"

"We're going to die, aren't we? Why not just admit it?"

The talk died down as they noticed he was standing there, heads turning toward him, eyes widening, expressions growing even more uncertain.

That was weird. He'd never considered himself to be visually intimidating.

Then Aquino remembered he was still wearing the body armor, still had the pistol at his side, and after the events of the last couple of days, probably looked like he'd gone through hell and was preparing for another walk past Cerberus.

"What's the problem?" he asked.

"Shouldn't you tell us that?" a woman in a steward outfit demanded. "Why haven't you and those damned useless Marines dealt with those alien things by now?"

Don't lose your temper, Aquino told himself. *Don't lose your temper.*

But he'd been through a lot recently.

Aquino stepped closer to the woman, gazing down at her. "Are you talking about the damned useless Marines who have repeatedly risked their lives to try to save your life? Who will go out there again soon, and risk themselves again, for *you*? *Is that who you're talking about?*"

He realized his voice had risen and throttled it back down as some of the crew members looked away and others stared back defiantly.

"We haven't given up," Aquino told them. "If you want to give up, fine. Go sit in a corner, out of the way of the people who are still trying their best. I fully intend to save everyone here." *Or die trying, but don't say that out loud.*

"And what are we supposed to do?" a man demanded. "Just sit here and wait? Like we've been sitting and waiting?"

Which couldn't have been easy. Swamped with his own responsibilities, he hadn't given thought to those who could do nothing but sit and imagine the worst, for hour after hour. "I'm sorry, but I'm doing all I can. We've asked for volunteers. If you can help with any of the work, please do."

"Useless!" the first woman yelled.

He'd been pushing himself past his limits, running insane risks, and this was the thanks he got? Aquino gave her a cold-eyed glare. "Shut up."

"You can't—"

"Yes, I can." His harsh words cut her off. "This is an emergency situation, I am in command, and if I want to, I can order you bound and gagged and tossed onto a spot next to that wall where you can lie and complain to yourself but not bother anyone else. Am I clear?"

The woman gave a disbelieving look to the ship's officers. "He… he can't…"

Fourth Officer Nijmeh nodded. "Yes, he can."

Third Officer Ergenian slid close to Aquino, speaking in a murmur, "We're trying to deescalate, so maybe you should—"

"I'm leaving," Aquino said. "I have work to do."

He walked away, fuming. His attempt to help there hadn't gone well. It was bad enough that everything he'd done didn't matter to some people, it was also that his attempt to calm things down, to help the ship's officers, had been rebuffed.

Screw all of them. He was still going to save every one of them, even if in some cases, that would only be so he could rub it in their faces afterward.

TWELVE

NOT "helping" Ichikawa was one of the hardest things he had ever done. Standing back, supervising from a distance to keep an eye out for any problems developing, felt wrong, even though he knew it was right. Despite the fact that everyone was working quickly, the traps were coming together, and he could see no reason for being needed, Aquino itched to jump in, to direct things, despite knowing if he did that, it would only slow things down.

He could ask some questions, though.

Aquino walked closer to where some crew members were working on the aluminum alloy T-struts that Ichikawa had "requisitioned" from one of the crates. Using powered hand tools, the crew members, including Steward Haycock, were cutting through the stem of the T-shaped struts, right to the top cross bar, though not cutting into that. "How's it going?" Aquino asked.

Haycock looked up at him and grinned. "You got some smart people. I would've looked at these struts and said 'you can't bend those. Don't waste your time.' But that Marine Ichikawa figured out if we cut through the stem here at frequent intervals, it won't stop us from bending the strut."

"Did she tell you why not to just cut off the stem?" Aquino asked.

"She did!" Haycock's smile grew unpleasant. "See, that stem will be cut up, but it's still on the outside. It'll be like a sword hitting those squonks. We're going to sharpen the outside edge if we have the time."

Clearly, Ichikawa had thought things through. Eight struts were being modified to bend, while other groups were fastening together more struts and pieces brought from the custom shop to form frameworks.

It was both comforting and a bit frustrating that he wasn't needed to keep the trap building on track.

"Oz? Dr. Trinh needs to talk to you." KT had approached him quietly. She seemed oddly subdued, her words coming out almost in a whisper.

Congratulations, Aquino thought. *You're needed again. Happy?* "More bad news?"

"It's…" She shook her head. "It's really important."

He followed her to where Dr. Trinh still sat, her head lowered. As they approached, Trinh raised her gaze, her expression grim.

"I must tell you some important conclusions I have reached," Dr. Trinh said. "They're not certain. They can't be at this point. But I am as close to certain as I can get. Ensign Aquino, you once commented that the squonks altered their behaviors as if they were machines that had a switch pulled. You were more right than any of us suspected."

"What are you saying?" Aquino asked, kneeling beside Trinh. "The squonks are some kind of cyborg?"

"No, not that." Trinh hesitated, as if searching for words. "Do you know what genetic memory is? What used to be called instinct?"

"I've heard of instinct," Aquino said. "It's… innate knowledge, right? Something creatures are born with."

"That's close enough." Dr. Trinh shook her head, seemingly in anger. "Instinct was what it was called when no one knew what it was. Science does that, giving something unknown a name so we can pretend we know what it is and how it works. What we have found is that very complex abilities and knowledge can be passed down to descendants.

"For example, newly-hatched chicks who react to the shadow of a hawk overhead by running under the nearest cover, but don't react to the sight of other birds' shapes. The chicks are born knowing that particular shape means danger and the best defense is hiding under something. We're still trying to understand how that works.

"It probably won't surprise you to know that much of the research is driven not simply by the desire to understand genetic memory, but to figure out exactly how it works so that mechanism can be used to, in effect, program living creatures to have certain inherited patterns of behaviors. It would no longer be necessary to train animals to do certain tasks. They'd be born with the skills, much like herd dogs already are to a great extent."

"That would be highly unethical, though," KT interjected hastily.

"And potentially highly profitable," Trinh said. "Thus far, the ethical questions have only been theoretical."

"What does this have to do with the squonks?" Aquino asked. "Are you saying the way they're acting on this ship is instinct?"

"Worse than that." Dr. Trinh tapped her data pad. " There is only one way I can interpret some of the diagrams and pictures recovered from the Janusian documents. The lack of metals severely limited their ability to develop much of the technology humanity created. But the Janusians seem to have compensated for that by focusing efforts on what they could do, much of which involved manipulating the natural world."

She tapped her data pad again, harder. "The selective breeding that produced the squonks was impressive on its own. But the Janusians went beyond that. I believe they learned how to, for want of a better word, program the genetic memory, the instincts, of the squonks and possibly other creatures, so they would be born ready to carry out the tasks the Janusians intended for them."

Trinh glared across the room as if seeing the Janusians at work. "They didn't simply breed warrior animals, they instilled in them certain reactions and patterns. See this? I'm certain that this shows squonks being implanted with the instinct to attack anyone wearing a sash of that color.

"Now, you could say this depicts the sort of training we're familiar with from working with animals. But there are… anomalies in this image. Perhaps those differences reflect differences in the way Janusian creatures are best trained. But, combined with many other depictions, and taking into account what we have experienced with the squonks on this ship, I believe it indicates not only training the squonks, but also implanting that training in their genetic memory."

Something finally clicked into place in Aquino's mind. "The way the squonks study everything they see. They're looking for… things that would trigger those reactions. If they didn't see them, they did nothing. But if they did, they'd change from placid to all out attack. It's the way human and automated sentries are supposed to act. But… if the Janusians were doing that, implanting patterns of behavior that squonks would have as soon as they were born, they were doing something that couldn't be changed on the fly. They couldn't alter the patterns in less than generations."

"The Janusians must have thought they knew enough about genetic memory to ensure nothing would go wrong," KT said. "But then, something went wrong."

"In that respect, at least," Dr. Trinh added, "the Janusians were like humans."

"Do you have any idea *what* went wrong?" Aquino asked.

Trinh shook her head. "We still don't know enough about how genetic memory works to be able to know what could have gone wrong. Some sort of glitch, perhaps a mutation."

"I had the simulation AI estimate when different cities were wiped out," Aquino said. "The rough data showed it happened at multiple places, before spreading."

"Some new training method," KT suggested. "That wasn't as foolproof as they thought."

"Maybe," Trinh said. "It's all guesswork at this point."

Aquino shook his head. "There have been stories written about humans encountering the remains of ancient civilizations on other worlds, the species long dead but their war machines still fighting in accordance with their programming. I never thought the machines we'd find would be living creatures. Those behaviors of the squonks, to this day, patrolling the ruins of the towns and cities. They're still searching for Janusians to kill, even though they may not be consciously aware of it."

"Yes," KT said with a nod. "And Dr. Trinh's theory would explain the bizarre behavioral differences we've observed. Those differences didn't seem natural, because they're not. The Janusians must have wanted to 'train' their animal weapons to be vicious against threats, but, when not confronted by an enemy they're supposed to attack, placid creatures who would pose no danger to their owners. That's always been a problem with, say, guard dogs, that they might attack someone they shouldn't. The Janusians must have believed they solved that problem."

"Just so," Dr. Trinh agreed. "I am guessing that may be what went wrong. They created an unstable framework by instilling two such dramatically different behaviors in the squonks. If that was the… glitch, or if it was some other flaw in the training, when it broke, the squonks went beyond killing every Janusian instead of only the ones they were supposed to go after. The squonks also seem compelled to destroy anything related to their targets. The furniture, the pottery, the herd animals. On this ship, equipment in engineering and elsewhere. For whatever reason, that glitch didn't include structures, or all we would've found on the planet would be mounds of rubble."

"Then the squonks on this ship went into kill mode when something they saw triggered that state," Aquino said. "Except, what? I guess it doesn't matter at this point."

"It very much matters," Dr. Trinh said, her voice quick and hot. "Because there are two large shuttles carrying hundreds of people on the surface of the planet. And we don't know what about them could trigger the attack and destroy and kill instinct in the squonks."

Aquino stared at her. "We have to—We still don't have comms with the shuttles."

"If we don't get those comms quickly, and warn them, it won't matter whether we manage to deal with the squonks up here." Trinh's eyes were hooded with worry. "Unless it's already too late. Too late for all of us."

Despite an urge to rush off and do… something, Aquino took the time to think. "What kind of protocol would the shuttles be following on the surface?" he asked.

"Protocol?" KT replied.

"I mean, how much would the people down there be allowed out of the shuttles? I know the shuttles couldn't remain sealed because their life support would be strained by the number of people aboard both of them. But they're loaded to capacity, meaning those shuttles will be cramped inside. Would many people be allowed to walk around outside the shuttles?"

KT exchanged a glance with Dr. Trinh. "That's hard to say. I can't think of any specific guidance. It would probably be up to Dr. Gohara."

"And Captain Lopez," Aquino said. He knew what Navy procedures would be in such a case, but even the Navy way of doing things left considerable discretion in the hands of whoever the senior officer present happened to be. "We have to hope they've kept people inside the shuttles as much as possible, and landed somewhere far from anything so the squonks haven't even found them. I'm… going to proceed assuming that they are still alive and can be warned."

Dr. Trinh sighed. "I don't believe there is anything else I can do."

"If… *when* we get in touch with the shuttles," Aquino said, "you need to convince Dr. Gohara that you've figured out how the Janusians were exterminated, and of the danger the squonks pose to everyone on the surface of Janus Five. He probably won't listen to me, but I hope he'll listen to you."

Trinh gave a serious nod. "Oh, he *will* listen to me."

Straightening up, Aquino forced a smile at KT. "I need to…"

"Yeah," she said. "Go do it."

He walked quickly toward where Private Obonsawin still lay. Getting access to the ship's cameras was no longer the first priority when it came to hacking.

As Aquino approached, Obonsawin looked up and smiled. "I was just about to call you, sir! I've got it! Look!"

Aquino studied the data pad, seeing an array of thumbnails for accessing cameras throughout the *Darwin*. A dismaying number of those thumbnails were blank, indicating cameras producing no signal, either because of exhausted batteries or squonk sabotage. Those that remained offered the first real opportunity to see more of the ship and hopefully spot the squonks when they moved. "Great job. Send me the link."

"Sending," Obonsawin said cheerfully. "As long as you're close enough to the mobile hot spot, you'll be able to see what the camera feeds show. Man, I've been going nonstop on that. It's going to be nice to relax a bit."

"It would be nice to relax," Aquino agreed. "But you're not going to be relaxing. We need communications with the shuttles, and we need it five minutes ago."

Obonsawin sighed heavily. "I guess a sleep break is out of the question."

"Good guess."

"Are you sure you're not really a Marine officer, sir?"

"I'm more sure of that every minute." Aquino turned and called out, "Ship's officers! I need you here!"

Only Nijmeh came in response to his hail. "Marcus thought he and Russ should stay with the rest of the crew members there," she said apologetically.

"He'd better be thinking about how to save them and all the rest of the crew," Aquino said. "This is Private Naveen Obonsawin. He just managed to hack into the ship's security cameras. Now he's going to get comms established with the shuttles. I need you to give him everything you've got on that and everything you've already tried."

Fourth Officer Nijmeh hesitated. "There are rules about what we can share with people not in the employ of the company."

Yelling at her wouldn't accomplish anything, Aquino told himself, worried about how hair-trigger his temper was getting. Was that a side effect of the endurance tablets? "I am not exaggerating in the slightest when I tell you that establishing communications as quickly as possible is a matter of life and death for not just everyone still on the *Darwin*, but also everyone on those shuttles," he said, trying to make the words come out slowly instead of in a rush.

Nijmeh stared at him, then nodded. "All right. We'll give him everything we've got, including our access codes. They weren't enough for us to get in, but maybe your guy can use them."

"Thank you," Aquino said. "Obonsawin, tell me the instant you have comms with the shuttles. If I'm out with the others setting the squonk traps, tell Dr. Trinh. That's her over there. She needs to talk to the shuttles."

"Understood, sir," Obonsawin said, his voice sounding slightly distracted, his eyes fixed on his data pad as he worked.

"Tell it back to me," Aquino said.

"Notify you the instant I get comms. If you're not around, get Dr.… Trinh."

"You got it."

Aquino fought off a strong desire to peer over Obonsawin's shoulder to watch his work, something that might drive both him and Obonsawin crazy, instead retreating to a spot where he could watch the traps being built.

Everything was rushing toward a result. Only, he had no idea whether this was a feeling of racing toward a steep cliff with spikes at the bottom, or of finally being about to seize the success that had been eluding them all so far.

"How are you doing?" KT asked as she walked up to him.

"Okay," Aquino said.

"You know that's not true."

He glanced at her, surprised. "You can see that?"

"I can." KT looked around. "I don't think anyone else does. Maybe that sergeant of yours. Oz, we can't afford to have you snap." She centered her gaze on him. "*I* can't afford to have you snap. What do you need?"

For some reason, the question amused him. "A solid night's sleep and no looming disasters."

"Once the disasters are taken care of, you can get that night's sleep." KT shook her head. "I've been trying to put myself in your head, to feel the responsibility that must be tearing at you. Oz, you need to center yourself before you go out there again. You need to be calm and clear when you make decisions."

"That's easier said than done," Aquino commented. But, oddly, this conversation was easing the tension inside him.

"Isn't there anything you can focus on that will help?"

He turned enough to fully face KT, remembering her kissing him. "I think I'm looking at her."

"Oh?" KT smiled. "What are you thinking right now when you look at me?"

Aquino hesitated before answering, "I don't think I should answer that."

"Really?" KT seemed torn between amusement and embarrassment. "Men. That's kind of your default mental state, isn't it?"

"Guilty as charged." Aquino took a slow, deep breath, willing himself to calm as he exhaled. "Thanks. I was working myself up tighter and tighter. Are you sure no one else noticed?"

"Yes."

"I mean," Aquino said, grateful for someone he could talk to about it, "if the Marines see uncertainty in me, it could cause problems."

KT uttered a brief laugh. "Those Marines think the world of you, Oz. They trust you. I can see it every time that sergeant talks to you. It's obvious you care about them, feel a responsibility toward them, and… what's the right word? You *respect* them. They're used to being not respected."

"It's just about treating them right," Aquino said. "It's not like I'm nice to them."

"I don't think they're looking for nice." KT studied the Marines as they worked. "You know, I had a bet with Hakim. He thought you'd gravitate toward the ship's officers, because you were Navy, and you had more in common with the crew than you did with the Marines. But I knew you'd identify with the Marines."

"Really? What made you so sure?"

"I study environments, Oz." She gave him another smile. "And how different things fit into their environments. I didn't realize until recently why the Marines have been such a difficult fit on the *Darwin*. But I finally got it. This civilian ship isn't their natural environment. And they couldn't adapt to this environment because of the rules they have to live by. They've been fish out of water, as the old saying goes. The crew and the researchers looked at them and thought, wow, those fish can't climb trees, what good are they? But, these last few days, the Marines have been in their element. This, dealing with the squonks, is their natural environment, what they're made for."

"I hadn't thought of it that way," Aquino said. "I think you're right."

She grinned. "That's always the right thing to say, by the way. Anyhow, I bet Hakim that you'd stay close to the Marines, because you come from fundamentally the same environment. You're trained to see things in the same ways they do."

"No one but Marines see things the way Marines do," Aquino objected.

"You know what I mean, Oz. You feel at home among them, don't you? You know how you should act, what you should do, how to dress and talk. That's how I knew you'd, um, join their herd rather than trying to force your way in among the crew."

He thought about that as he also watched the Marines. "When I first got to this ship, I was feeling lost, until I was going through personnel files and talking to each of the Marines. I wasn't *happy* with the challenges I was facing, but I understood what I was supposed to do. Which doesn't mean I knew what I was doing, because the job called for a Marine officer, but I felt a lot more at home there than I did among any of the crew."

"All of which," KT said, "is a complex way of telling you that I think you've got this." She sighed, entwining one arm with his and leaning against him. "I'm scared, too. And I don't want to show it. How am I doing?"

"Really well," Aquino said. "Somebody said that being brave isn't not being afraid. It's being afraid and still trying."

"So we're brave."

"Yeah." He leaned his head against hers for a moment. "Thanks. I'm centered. You're… really good for me."

"I'm glad you realize that. Oz… try not to get killed."

He couldn't see her face, but he could feel her body tense as she spoke those words. "I'll do my best," Aquino said.

Anything else KT might have said was cut short by the arrival of Sergeant Rodriguez, looking tired but satisfied. "Private Ichikawa says we're almost done, sir. The traps are in sections we can haul to their sites and put together. Are you okay with about a half dozen willing helpers accompanying us to get that done?"

"We'll have to escort them back here after the traps are finished," Aquino said.

"Yes, sir. That'll take a little time," Rodriguez said. "But if we don't use them, and just use Marines, we can only haul and install one trap at a time, so that process will take at least twice as long."

Could they spare the time for that? As soon as Aquino asked himself that question, he knew the answer. Time wasn't something they could afford to use up. "All right. We'll use the volunteers. Are they all crew?"

"Four crew members and two researchers," Rodriguez said.

"Let's get ready to head out, then," Aquino told her. "KT, I'll see you when we get back."

"Make sure you do," KT said. "Sergeant Rodriguez, could you please keep an eye on this guy for me?"

Rodriguez gave her a solemn nod in reply. "Part of a sergeant's job is to keep an eye on junior officers and make sure they don't screw up."

"Only *junior* officers?" Private Ichikawa asked as she walked up to them.

"I didn't say 'only' junior officers," Rodriguez said. "We ready?"

Ichikawa used the back of her wrist to wipe away sweat on her forehead. "Ready as we can be." She shrugged and smiled crookedly. "I'm staking my life on these traps, after all."

"You're staking all of our lives on them," Rodriguez said.

Ichikawa's attempt at a smile vanished. "Listen, Rowdy, if you don't think I can—"

"That's enough," Aquino said, putting enough force into his voice to make it clear he meant it. "We've all been working our tails off, and we're all tired of the squonks doing what they please. Let's get out there and give the squonks some painful surprises."

He realized that KT had moved away, and turned to wave a quick farewell before rejoining the rest of the Marines and the six volunteers with them. Aquino wasn't surprised to see that two of those volunteers were Steward Odin Haycock and researcher Gina Salinas. With them were one other woman and three other men, two of the men and the woman were members of the crew, and the other man one of the graduate student researchers like Salinas.

Aquino couldn't help contrasting these six, all willing to risk themselves outside of this compartment, with the crew members he'd encountered who were doing nothing except complaining about those who were trying to do something. He wondered if the same sort of attitudes had plagued the Janusians, maybe even as the squonks were massacring their former masters.

He realized that was something that had been bothering him. Because it was far too easy for humans to understand foolish certainty in the face of complexity, far too easy to imagine humans doing the same things the Janusians had. He didn't want to be able to understand how someone could run such risks with such huge potential consequences. Then again, looking at the history of humanity, it wasn't all that hard to understand. Were intelligent species all alike in that way? And had humanity survived its own mistakes thus far, not through some special emotional or intellectual gifts, but only through luck?

Maybe the awful example of the fate of the Janusians would cause people to think twice.

Dr. Trinh had warned that humans had already been trying to figure out how to program genetic memory. And those humans surely were either absolute certain that nothing could go wrong, or weren't even bothering to think about what could go wrong.

"Sir?" Sergeant Rodriguez asked.

Aquino came back to the present, having zoned out. "It's nothing. I was just thinking that we need people like Marines, because other people make mistakes that need to be fixed." Aquino looked around at the others. "All right, we're going to head out there and get these traps installed. I want two Marines doing nothing but providing security while everyone else works on the traps."

"That'll be you and me, Lachman," Rodriguez said.

"Sure," Lachman replied, sounding very determined and very unlike the responsibility-dodging, work-avoiding Private Lachman that Aquino first met.

"Private Ichikawa," Aquino said, "these traps are your baby. You're in charge of getting them set up. Do we have everything we need?"

Ichikawa nodded. "Yes, sir. Ready to roll."

"Not quite," KT said, walking up with the modified tote in her hand. She offered it to Aquino. "Judy relented after I begged her to help you again."

"Our cat is working?" He looked inside, past the mesh, to see Judy sitting on the bottom of the tote, watching him with a look that seemed to convey a message that he should be very grateful she was willing to come along again. "Thanks, KT. I love you."

She grinned. "As you should."

Startled that he'd said that, and surprised that KT had taken the words in stride, Aquino fastened his helmet on before reaching to take the tote. The weight of the helmet had become comforting, reassuring, as well as aggravating. "Let's get going. Hakim! Your guys are in charge of security in here again!"

Aquino looked back as he and the others left, seeing that KT had gone back to sit near Dr. Trinh, while Fourth Officer Nijmeh had returned to the restive group of complaining crew members. But Third Officer Ergenian was now with Private Obonsawin, providing what assistance he could to the task of establishing communications to the shuttles.

If it wasn't already too late.

He tried to banish the images that his imagination too easily supplied, of a horde of squonks overrunning both shuttles, still following instincts implanted long ago, doing to the people and equipment aboard them what their squonk ancestors had done to the Janusians.

As the hatch sealed behind them, Aquino took a deep breath, steadying his thoughts, trying to focus only on the here and now. "Rodriguez on point. Which way first, Ichikawa?"

"This way," Ichikawa said, pointing.

Was it just his perception that the passageways of the *Darwin* were even more dimly lit than before? No, it wasn't. More of the emergency lights were definitely less bright than previously.

Aquino drew his pistol, his head on a swivel in search of trouble, and checked on Judy. The cat seemed nervous, too, but was that due to the squonks being close enough for her to sense, or because of memories of the grenade going off during the last outing with her? Judy wasn't acting as if either of the squonks was nearby, though.

This time, he also had the camera feeds, set to cycle through the views of the cameras nearest to them. Surprisingly, the mobile hot spot was still providing a decent link. But nothing could be seen moving on the working cameras, and there were gaps in the coverage.

Even though the Marines and volunteers carrying the parts of the traps were moving as carefully as possible, the pieces of metal still sometimes clanked together, the sound filling the air.

They reached the main passageway, then the corner to the side passage where the first trap would go. Ichikawa stopped them about six meters down the passage. "Here."

Any doubts Aquino had about Ichikawa's skill vanished as she directed the rapid assembly of the first trap, starting with the frame being securely fastened to the wall using special self-locking bolts she'd picked up at the custom shop.

He edged past the workers to talk to Rodriguez. "How's it look?"

"Same old," the sergeant said. "Feeling like they're out there, just out of sight. What's the cat scan telling us?"

"Judy's on edge, but not in that squonks are really close way."

Moving back the other direction, sliding along the far wall to avoid the trap work, Aquino checked on Lachman. "How are you doing?"

Lachman smiled nervously, keeping his eyes and his carbine pointed down the passage. "I'm ready to finish this, sir."

"Good. Hang in there."

There wasn't much else he could do after that except remain alert, switching his attention between the camera feeds on his data pad, Judy the cat, and looking each way down the passage as the trap came together under Ichikawa's direction.

She called the four struts with frequent notches in the t-stem "hammers," making sure they were set in place, two on each side, staggered as they went up so that the four formed an interlaced barrier starting less than a half meter above the deck and rising to more than a meter high.

He had been wondering how they would tension the hammers, but Ichikawa had prepared for that. Levers were attached to the frame. "One at a time, people," she said. "Work it."

Even with several people straining, getting the hammers bent back as far as the wall took their full weight and strength, Ichikawa carefully setting the clamps that held each ready to release. "Nobody touch these," she cautioned.

The hammers in place, Ichikawa ordered the others to get back before cautiously setting in place a series of ever stronger links that led to a fragile-seeming trip wire stretched across the passage just above the deck. "It's titanium alloy thread," she commented to Aquino.

"Is that what you made to try to get that former boss of yours?" he asked, eyeing the lethal mechanism warily.

"Oh, hell, no, sir," Ichikawa said. "I only wanted to put that… um, person in the hospital for a while to get him off of our backs." She straightened up, eyeing the finished and set trap. "That's it. Hey, Rowdy, come over to this side. Watch out for the trip wire."

"I'm watching," Rodriguez said, eyeing the deck as she stepped high over the trip wire. "It's really hard to see even when you know it's there."

"I know, right?" Ichikawa said cheerfully. "Okay, let's get number two set."

They retreated back to the main passageway and then down it far enough to reach the corner to the other side passage, Ichikawa once again stopping them about six meters down the passage.

The work went even faster this time, since everyone had experience with putting in the first trap. But tensioning the hammers still took time, the heavy breathing of the workers straining at the levers sounding loud enough to worry Aquino that the squonks would hear and somehow guess what was being done.

He looked down, seeing Judy pacing inside the tote. "I think one or both squonks may be getting closer."

"Finishing up now," Ichikawa said from where she was kneeling and setting the trip wire. "It's ready."

Aquino opened his mouth to order the Marines to escort the volunteers back to the auditorium, but stopped when he felt the tote jerk. Looking down, Judy was backed against one side, her eyes fixed on the shadowed passage past the trap. "Just in time. Judy says we have company coming. Back into the main passageway. Volunteers, you'll have to stay with us through this. There's no time to escort you to the auditorium."

To his surprise, none of the crew members or researchers objected.

Steward Haycock smiled. "I don't mind being around when those squonks spring the traps."

"Hell, yeah," Gina Salinas agreed.

Rodriguez led the way back into the main passageway and about halfway between the two side passages. "Sir, I'm thinking we should stay in one group since we have to protect these others."

"Agreed," Aquino said. "You people get over here against this wall. Marines, form a perimeter around them."

"Lachman, Kenyatta," Sergeant Rodriguez said, pointing. "You guys on this side. Smith, you and me on the other. Sir, I suggest you and Ichikawa take a center position, ready to fire in either direction."

"Make sure you fire past us, not through us," Kenyatta told Ichikawa.

"Hey, I am not the one you have to worry about," Ichikawa said.

"I get it," Aquino said. "Sergeant, should we make noise or be as quiet as possible?"

Rodriguez made a face. "We're bait, but we don't want to seem like bait. So, as much noise as we'd make if we were walking, I guess."

"That sounds good," Aquino said. The camera feeds showed nothing moving, but his view of both of the side passages were dim and partial. Neither of the traps could be seen by any cameras. He checked Judy again, seeing the cat had arched her back and was pressed against the side of the tote. Technology had failed him, but feline senses could still be counted on. "Squonks are near."

"Good," Lachman muttered, aiming his carbine down the passageway.

"I want hits this time," Rodriguez told the Marines. "If either squonk makes it past the traps, I want them nailed."

"No problem," Kenyatta said in a low voice.

Aquino glanced at Ichikawa, who was gazing about, clearly anxious. "Those traps looked great," he told her.

She smiled for a moment before her expression went worried again. "I hope so, sir. First time I actually made one that was designed to kill."

Judy hissed.

Everyone tensed.

Aquino heard the sound of hammers being released to their left, the struts making a whipping sound through the air as they slammed closed.

Despite wanting to race and check on the sprung trap, Aquino signaled the others to wait. Only one trap had been tripped.

Seconds crawled by with no other sound.

"Sir," Ichikawa said. "We gotta check it."

"All right," Aquino said. "You, Lachman, and me. Sergeant, hold the others here."

"Yes, sir," Rodriguez said.

Ichikawa led the way in a dash to the corner and around it, her weapon ready.

As Aquino followed, side by side with Lachman, he spotted the sprung trap.

One of the squonks hung unmoving, pinned between the hammers, the t-stems on the hammers embedded in its body, dark blood dripping down to the deck.

Ichikawa came closer to it, studying the unmoving squonk cautiously, stopping about a meter away. "Damn. It worked." She turned to grin at Aquino and Lachman.

The squonk's arm suddenly shot out, reaching for Ichikawa.

Lachman saw the movement, grabbing Ichikawa and pulling her back just in time. Letting go of her, Lachman gripped his carbine with both hands again, aiming at the impaled squonk, which had opened one eye that glared at them with the promise of death.

Lachman fired at the squonk's head from close range, putting several shots into it, then shifted aim to put the rest of the bullets in his magazine into its body.

The light in the squonk's eye went out, the body limp in the grip of the trap.

"Thanks," Ichikawa told Lachman, breathing deeply from the close call.

"No problem," Lachman said, loading a new magazine into his carbine. "That's one down."

"I haven't heard the other trap spring," Aquino said. He checked on Judy, seeing her pacing nervously again, but not in full warning mode. That was odd, since the dead squonk was still hanging nearby. What were the cats sensing when they felt the presence of squonks? "The other squonk isn't near. Did only one try to hit us this time? Let's get back to the others."

Fighting fears that the remaining squonk would attack the rest of the Marines and the volunteers, Aquino was relieved as he rounded the corner to see all of them waiting, alert but unscathed.

"One's dead," Lachman announced as they rejoined the group.

"Have you heard anything from the other trap?" Aquino asked.

Rodriguez shook her head. "I thought maybe I heard something down that passage, but it wasn't anything like hearing that trap sprung. A lot softer."

"We should check it out," Ichikawa suggested.

Looking down at Judy, Aquino saw that she was still not reacting as if a living squonk were near. And the limited camera feeds in this area remained empty of movement. "Okay. You, me, and Lachman again."

They approached the other corner more slowly and more cautiously, Lachman going around it as if expecting to see the last squonk waiting for him.

But the passage stretched empty as far as they could see, none of the shadows from fading emergency lamps deep enough to conceal a squonk.

The trap hadn't been sprung.

"Hell," Lachman growled. "It hasn't been touched."

"I want to check it," Ichikawa insisted. "Rowdy heard something."

They moved carefully closer to the trap, Lachman slightly in the lead.

When they were still about half a meter from where the trip wire should be, Ichikawa suddenly shouted, "Look out!"

Before either Lachman or Aquino could react, Ichikawa launched herself toward Lachman, knocking him aside in the instant the hammers of the trap sprang free.

THIRTEEN

THANKS to being knocked aside by Ichikawa, Lachman was outside the lethal embrace of the hammers. But Ichikawa's lunge to save him left her close enough for the hammers swinging in from one side to slam into her. The force of the blow flung her against the opposite wall, to fall with a loud thud to the deck.

"Malice!" Lachman scrambled to his feet, edging past the sprung hammers to check her. "Come on, Malice! Talk to me!"

Aquino, his pistol out, stared down the passage. Nothing could be seen. Judy, alarmed by the trap's noise, was pacing again with agitation but not in squonk warning mode.

He knelt by Ichikawa and Lachman, fearing the worst.

Ichikawa twitched, a scream of pain caught behind her gritted teeth.

"Arm," Lachman said, pointing.

Aquino looked, seeing both the upper and lower parts of her right arm bent in unnatural ways. At least two breaks, then.

Seeing that her body armor was badly dented on the right torso, Aquino checked gently, seeing Ichikawa twitch and fight back another scream. "Arm and her right side. Maybe broken ribs. Other internal damage. We have to get her back to the auditorium so the nurse can look at her."

"We should reset the trap before we go," Lachman suggested, his face drawn with worry as he gazed at Ichikawa.

"No," Ichikawa said, the word coming out in a gasp of agony. "Squonk… fig… ured… out."

"What are you saying?" Aquino demanded.

"Trip… wire… moved." Ichikawa glared at him, her pain now mixed with anger. "Squonk… moved… wire… fig… ured… out."

Aquino simply stared wordlessly at Ichikawa before he could reply. "The last squonk realized this was a trap and moved the trip wire so it would catch us instead of it?"

"How smart are those damned things?" Lachman said, also aghast.

Shaking off the shock of Ichikawa's near-death, her injuries, and what she had just told them, Aquino gave the trap a long look. How could Ichikawa be right? Except, the trip wire had been moved, just as she said, and that couldn't have happened all by itself. "There's no sense in resetting the trap. The squonk won't fall for it. We need to get Ichikawa back to the auditorium and work out our next steps." He raised his voice to a shout, "Sergeant Rodriguez! Bring everyone here!"

Rodriguez came quickly along with the others. As soon as she laid on eyes on Ichikawa, the sergeant directed the volunteers to carefully hoist Ichikawa so she could be carried back. Despite their care, Ichikawa bit back moans of pain and at least one more scream.

"Let's go," Aquino said. "Do your best to not jostle Ichikawa," he asked the volunteers.

The volunteers, looking stricken, all nodded.

With Kenyatta on rear guard and Lachman on point, Aquino and Rodriguez walked behind the volunteers carrying Ichikawa.

"Damn," Rodriguez whispered when Aquino explained what happened. "That means the second squonk won't fall for that trap at all. How are we going to nail it?"

"I'm… considering our options," Aquino said.

Seeing Sergeant Rodriguez sag with despair hit him harder than anything else. She knew as well as he did that this had been their last, best hope. What was left to try that might have any chance of success?

Rodriguez straightened herself, her face tightening. "We get Ichikawa back to the auditorium," she muttered.

He understood what the sergeant was doing. What's the next step? Maybe you can't see what the long-term solution is, but you can focus on the next step, and the step beyond that.

As Aquino and the Marines and volunteers hastened back through the dimly lit passageways of the *Darwin*, he realized he had no idea what the next step would be after getting Ichikawa to what little safety there was on this ship.

Nurse Sastrinata knelt next to Ichikawa where she lay on the deck, the nurse's hands moving surely and as gently as possible. "Yes. A couple of bone fractures in the arm, and at least two ribs, and very likely internal injury. We have to get this girl to medical." She sighed heavily. "What am I saying? Without power for the equipment, nothing in medical can help."

"There must be something you can do," Aquino said.

"I can set the bones in her arm and try to improvise a cast. That's it. And leave that armor on. It helps protect the broken ribs."

Sastrinata looked down at Ichikawa. "This is going to hurt."

Ichikawa stretched her lips tightly across her teeth in an attempt at a smile. "Al… ready… hurts."

"I bet. Is there any of that, uh, anesthetic left?"

Private Kenyatta brought out her bottle filled with whiskey and raised it with a questioning look at the nurse.

"Good," Sastrinata said. "It'll help with the pain."

"As much as you want," Kenyatta said, raising the bottle to Ichikawa's lips.

Ichikawa swallowed four times before choking and gasping, wincing with the pain her gasps caused to her ribs.

"Dammit, Malice, why'd you do that?" Lachman demanded. He drew his arm across his eyes, roughly rubbing away tears. "I would've been okay."

Ichikawa moved only her eyes to look at him after she swallowed another slug of the whiskey. "Would… have… died… my… fault."

"No. Not your fault!" Lachman sat back, shaking with anger. "If I see that second squonk, I'll…"

The nurse's hands moved, quickly setting the bones in Ichikawa's upper and lower arm, while Ichikawa went rigid with pain, her eyes screwed shut.

As she improvised an inadequate cast, Nurse Sastrinata gave Aquino a grim look. "I don't think any of this will kill her real soon. But she needs proper medical care within the next day or so."

That might have been a looming deadline, Aquino thought, if not for the fact that their oxygen would give out before that. "Thank you."

"Sir?" Lachman said. "What now? How are we going to kill that squonk?"

"I… need to think," Aquino said. "Nurse? We need to discuss some things."

"Sure." Sastrinata stood up. "Thanks for trying, you guys."

After the nurse left, Kenyatta shook her head. "We're down to four Marines and zero ideas," she said.

"We're not giving up," Aquino insisted. He checked the time. Work on the only partly successful traps had eaten up several hours. There was less than half a day left, most likely, before the oxygen levels got too low to sustain human life.

That last squonk was smart enough to have messed with the trap that should have killed it. Another hunt would be a waste of time. It wouldn't be lured in easily, and could avoid them without trouble in the darkening passageways and abandoned compartments of *Darwin*. There were far too few Marines to pen it in or herd it to a place where it could be cornered. What options did that leave?

"How much time have we got?" Private Kenyatta asked, her eyes on Ichikawa. "I mean, with air?"

"We don't know precisely," Aquino said. The Marines' lack of expressions spoke volumes. Didn't he owe them the truth? "Best guess is eight to twelve hours."

"What happens then?" Lachman said.

"People start passing out. From low oxygen and too much carbon dioxide. It's like going to sleep."

"I don't want to die that easy," Private Kenyatta remarked. "Maybe I'll just go out alone and let that thing come at me. It'll go for one person on their own. I might hurt it bad enough for the rest of you to finish it."

"No," Aquino said. "We have too much experience with trying to hit squonks on the move. They're too fast and they position themselves to jump out with little or no warning."

Sergeant Rodriguez nodded wearily. "Ensign Aquino is right, Stef. You'd just be throwing your life away."

"I'm not going to just lie here and die, Rowdy."

"Idea," Ichikawa gasped. "Got… idea."

"What is it, Malice?" Rodriguez asked, her voice gentle.

"Bait. Like… Stef… says. One… per… son."

"What good would that do?" Aquino said. "The odds of hitting that squonk are too low."

"Not… gun," Ichikawa got out. "Ex… plo… siv… vest. Con… tact… det… on… ator."

It took them all a moment to figure out what she was suggesting.

"You're suggesting we rig an explosive vest and send one person out alone?" Rodriguez demanded.

"Yeah," Ichikawa said, her eyes on the sergeant. "One… as… bait… I… can… do… it."

"The hell you can. You can't even walk."

"She's right, though," Kenyatta said. "It should work, and it's all we have time for."

"I don't like that option," Aquino said.

Sergeant Rodriguez sat back, her face lined with unhappiness. "I hate it, too. But… what else are we going to do, sir? What else stands a chance?"

"Ichikawa can't do it," Aquino said. "Who else am I supposed to send on a suicide mission?"

Several seconds of silence followed. "I admit I'd rather not," Kenyatta said. "Going down shooting with a chance to live is one thing. An explosive vest…"

"Yeah," Lachman said. "That's…"

"I should—" Rodriguez began.

"No," Aquino broke in. "We cannot lose you."

"Sir, we have to keep the big picture in mind," the sergeant insisted. "Namely, we're all going to die. Unless one of us goes out to die."

"I cannot order someone to do that," Aquino said.

"Sir?"

Everyone looked in surprise at Private Smith, who rarely spoke up and who seemed oddly calm. "You don't have to order me, sir. I can do it. I mean, I will do it."

Rodriguez glared at him. "Do you know what we're talking about, Akira? Do you understand this?"

"Yeah," Smith said. "I understand it fine. It's a suicide mission. Whoever goes out isn't coming back. Well, I can do that. An explosive vest and contact detonators. All I'd have to do is walk until the squonk comes for me, right? I know I'm pretty damned useless. I always have been. And I know I'm not a real Marine. But I can do that. And then the rest of you will be okay."

"Smith—" Aquino began.

"Sir," Smith interrupted, "pardon me. But you just said we only got a few hours left at best before everyone's dead. And no one's got any other ideas that might work in time. That's why I'm volunteering. No else has to die. Isn't that worth it?"

"I can't order you to do this," Aquino repeated.

"You don't have to, sir. I'm volunteering. Everybody heard me, right?" Smith looked around for confirmation.

"Why, Smith?" Kenyatta asked.

He looked down at the deck and shrugged. "I've… never had many friends. In my last unit, everybody… it wasn't great. But, you guys, I know you get upset when I screw up, but you still treat me okay. You're my friends. I think you're my friends. And… I don't want my friends to die. Not if I can save them. And I'll be doing something right, won't I? There's no way I can screw this up. And you'll all be okay. That's why."

"Oh, hell, Smith," Rodriguez said. "You shouldn't be doing this because you feel like a failure. Right, sir?"

"That's right," Aquino said. Why was he trying to talk Smith out of this when it seemed like their only chance? Maybe because it was the last choice he would have ever wanted to make. Maybe because he hated to see anyone else make that choice.

"It's not only about that, you're my friends," Smith said again. "I don't want you to die. Isn't that reason enough?"

Aquino looked at Smith, thinking about his own mother, staying at her duty station as the flames rose around her. He had asked her once. Just one word. *Why?*

And she had given that question the dignity of a long pause to think, before smiling slightly. *Because.*

I don't understand.

Maybe, someday, you will.

Now, finally, he understood. Smith, of all people, understood.

But *he* had to approve doing this.

No one else could make this decision. He couldn't in good conscience just let it happen while he looked the other way. The responsibility was his.

One life, in exchange for hundreds of others. Those up here, those down on the planet in the shuttles, whose lives might balance on whether they lifted off before the squonks went into kill mode on them. Normally, that was an easy calculation in the military. You did what you had to do.

But this was something beyond that, a planned sacrifice in every sense of the word.

His responsibility, to make the call or not.

He looked down at the screen in his hands, what cameras were working showing dimly lit passageways. So many passageways, so many vents and accesses and compartments. They'd never run that thing to ground. They had to give it a reason to come out. A target too attractive to pass up.

When people are counting on you, you have to do your job.

What right did he have to avoid making this decision when Smith was literally ready to die to save his friends?

Aquino nodded slowly, speaking with careful precision, "All right. I accept your offer to volunteer, Private Smith. I am ordering the rest of you to assist in preparing the vest, so there is no question of personal fault that can be laid against you. If anyone feels they cannot in good conscience assist, I will not attempt to force you to do so."

The Marines gazed back at him, no one saying anything. Smith still appeared strangely calm.

"Sergeant Rodriguez, I need you to supervise rigging a vest with plenty of the explosives we have, tied to detonators set for contact and placed around the vest so the squonk will hit one no matter where it attacks Private Smith."

Rodriguez nodded, standing up. "Who's going to help?" she asked Lachman and Kenyatta.

Lachman stood up as well. "Okay. I mean… yeah."

Kenyatta nodded, both her voice and expression totally impassive. "Okay. I'll get the Q-7 and the detonators."

Ichikawa watched them, her eyes reflecting misery.

Sergeant Rodriguez noticed that, bending to speak to her, "It's not your fault, Malice."

"My… idea," Ichikawa muttered.

"Someone else would've thought of it."

"Hey, Malice," Private Smith, kneeling next to her. "It's fine. You get yourself looked after when the power comes back. Thanks for covering for me that time I messed up the parts inventory."

"Sure," Ichikawa said. "I… no… problem."

"Nobody had ever done something like that for me in my old unit," Smith said. "It meant a lot. It meant you guys thought I was one of you. Please don't feel bad."

"Your traps got one of them, Malice," Rodriguez said. "That means we can take out the other one this way. We have to go… work on this thing. Is that booze hitting you, yet?"

"I… dunno…" Ichikawa said, the words coming out slurred by something other than pain.

"Let yourself pass out if you can, Marine. You earned it."

"I'll keep an eye on her," Aquino said. "Let me know if you need anything."

"Yes, sir." Rodriguez hesitated. "We're going to have to improvise that vest. Is it okay if I talk to your girl about helping with that? She got the tote fixed up to carry the cat."

"It's okay," Aquino said. "But you need to tell her what she's helping with so she can decide if she wants to be part of it."

"Understood. Come on, Private Smith."

Aquino, tired and knowing there was nothing he could do at the moment except watch over Ichikawa, sat and tried not to think about what would soon happen.

Try as he might, he couldn't think of any alternative that had any real chance of working in the time they had left.

He looked up as someone approached, seeing KT, her expression somber.

She probably hated him right now.

KT stopped when she reached him. "How are you doing?"

"Awful," Aquino said.

"Sergeant Rodriguez told me none of you want this to happen, but none of you can come up with anything else."

"I approved it," Aquino said, surprised that she wasn't condemning him.

"Can I sit down?"

"Of course."

KT sat next to him, looking toward Ichikawa. "Is she going to be all right?"

"If we can get power restored to medical within another day," Aquino said.

"The last squonk really figured out the trap?"

"Yeah."

"I need to talk to Dr. Trinh about that. It means the squonks are either intelligent enough to spot traps, or… Am I right that a trip wire type trap was within the capabilities of the Janusians?"

He gazed at her in surprise. "Yes. It's a very basic sort of trap. Do you think recognizing such traps was something the Janusians might have implanted in the squonks?"

"It's possible," KT said. "Wouldn't the Janusians have used traps?"

"They…" Aquino remembered something from his virtual tour of the planet. "The city. There were large stones lying near the gate. Inside it. I couldn't figure out why they were there. But they could have been the remains of deadfall traps. Which can be triggered by snares or trip lines.

"I saw stones like that in the town, too. On a ramp leading up to a roof. Another set of deadfalls. You don't need metal to make a deadfall. Just a big, flat stone, some wood, and something to make the snare or trip line." He nodded in understanding. "That's it. The squonks were implanted with lessons to watch for traps that the Janusians employed as defensive measures. Which would mean the squonks aren't really that intelligent."

"Why do you think one of them failed to spot a trap?" KT asked.

"Probably because what Ichikawa designed, and the trip wire itself, didn't exactly match the sort of things the Janusians used. Like that hawk shape thing you talked about. One squonk was able to, what's the word, generalize its knowledge of traps. The other one wasn't able to do that." He looked to her. "I thought you'd want to say something to me about what we're going to do. I wouldn't blame you for being… unhappy with me about that."

She shook her head, looking at the deck. "My uncle is a doctor. He talks now and then about the decisions he has to make. Even today, with everything we can do, sometimes there aren't any good choices. But people turn to him to decide which bad choice to make. Yes, my first reaction to this was… shock. But your sergeant was very clear how little any of you like this."

"You're okay with it?" Aquino asked, disbelieving.

"Are you okay with it?"

"No."

"Same here." She sighed. "But being unhappy with it isn't the same as saying there are any other choices that can save everyone else. That can save *us*. I admit that I don't want to die in the next several hours. I admit how grateful I am that Private Smith is willing to sacrifice himself for us. And I feel guilty as hell for that."

"Ichikawa wanted to do it, but she can't," Aquino said. "Rodriguez tried to volunteer but I wouldn't let her."

"What if it was only you?" KT said. "If all of the Marines were dead or something? Would you do it?"

He thought about that for a moment. "Yeah. I think so."

"My dad had a favorite story," KT said. "Horatius at the bridge. Have you heard of it?"

"Um… yes," Aquino said. "Ancient Rome. One soldier held a bridge single-handedly to stop the enemy. Why was that your dad's favorite story?"

"He liked to say that was how people should be," KT said. "Hold the bridge and save your friends, the bridge being a metaphor for something that needed defending. He'd say that was why the military was special, because everyone in it was ready to be a Horatius at the bridge."

Aquino grew puzzled. "What military branch did your father serve in?"

"He didn't," KT said. "I guess you could say he admired it from afar."

"Oh." Aquino shook his head. "I guess never having served makes it a lot easier to idealize the military."

"I guess," KT said. "Aren't you an idealist? Because I sure think you are."

"Umm, yeah," Aquino said. "But I think just about everyone who's been in the military recognizes the, uh, flaws and less than ideal aspects of it. I mean, we know the military does important things, but we also know that the military seems to make it as hard as possible to do important things. We do look out for our shipmates, of course. Maybe that's the most important thing we do."

"Shipmates including those Marines?"

"Of course," Aquino said. "They're my responsibility."

"Exactly," KT said. "You guys look out for each other. My dad would be pointing to Smith and saying, 'See, see, he gets it.'" She looked over at Smith, sadness in her eyes. "But it doesn't feel heroic, does it? Not when it's really happening."

"No," Aquino said.

"Are you allowed to do this? I mean, sending Smith out like that?"

"I don't know. I couldn't order him to do it, but letting him volunteer, without any pressure? I don't know if that's legal. I could send him to charge an enemy position and he would have zero chance of surviving, and that would be okay. This, though, is different."

"That's weird."

"That's the military."

"What happens if we survive this and they decide it wasn't legal?"

Aquino shrugged. "When something goes badly wrong, the system always looks for the lowest-ranking person they could possibly blame. Which would be me in this case. Even though they stuck me here without training or enough people or enough resources. Even though they didn't give the Marines better equipment and better training. It'd still be my fault."

"So, why are you doing this? I mean, the whole military thing?"

He shrugged again. "Maybe in a way, I am that idiot on the bridge."

They sat in silence for a while, watching Ichikawa, who was still passed out but occasionally twitching with pain.

Aquino looked up as Rodriguez approached. "We've got the harness done and the blocks of Q-7 attached, sir. I figured you'd want to check it before we set the detonators."

"Yes," Aquino said, standing. "KT, could you get Nurse Sastrinata and ask her to watch Ichikawa for a while?"

"Sure," KT said, getting up and walking to where the crew members were sitting.

"Is she okay with you?" Rodriguez asked as she and Aquino headed toward Smith.

"Yeah," Aquino said.

"Hang onto that one, sir. If you don't mind the advice."

"Thanks. I intend to do my best." Reaching Smith, Aquino tried to close off his emotions as he examined the "vest." It had been made of webbing interlaced and tacked together with fabric glue. Despite looking as if it would fall apart, the vest felt sturdy enough to do the job. "Are we sure it won't fall off? Those straps over the shoulders look a little loose."

"We don't want it too tight," Private Kenyatta said. "And we had a real limited amount of fabric glue to work with. We had to put most of that into making sure the explosives stayed put."

"Okay." The blocks of Q-7, each the same faded red color as the average hot dog, were tied on by crisscrossed straps. Despite knowing the explosives weren't going to explode at anything as mild as a touch, Aquino still had to force himself to reach and tug lightly at one of the blocks. "Yeah. Those are on tight."

Something about the harness and the blocks of explosive on it tugged at his memory. Where had he seen something like that?

Oh, of course. The improvised harness with the rectangular blocks of explosive somewhat resembled the leather armor he had seen the Janusians wearing in the picture that Dr. Trinh had shown him. How strange it was that Smith would be wearing a roughly similar garment. Only, rather than protecting him, it was designed to destroy him.

Detonators were set into many of the blocks of explosives, ready to be activated.

Aquino finally looked at Smith, who had been standing rigidly at attention. "Relax, Marine. Are you still ready to do this?"

Smith licked his lips nervously, nodding. "Yes, sir."

"It looks good," Aquino told Rodriguez.

"Okay." Rodriguez turned to the others. "If anyone wants to give Smith a goodbye hug, do it now before I set the detonators."

Lachman, looking like he was fighting back tears, extended his fist. "Uh, thanks, man. You're, uh, you're… thanks."

Smith grinned, raising his own fist to bump it to Lachman's.

Kenyatta, as impassive as ever, offered her fist as well. "You're a damned good Marine, Smith."

"Thanks," Smith said, bumping her fist with his.

"Ichikawa is still out," Rodriguez said. "You should give Obonsawin a chance to say goodbye."

"Sure." Smith walked over to where Obonsawin was working, bending down awkwardly in the vest to exchange another fist bump, this one wordless as Private Obonsawin struggled to speak.

As Smith returned, Rodriguez offered her fist. "What Stef said, Smith. You're a damned good Marine and a credit to the unit. Go down fighting."

"I will." Smith visibly braced himself. "Okay."

"I'm setting the detonators to contact," Rodriguez said. "Don't lean on any walls or you'll go off early."

"Women don't like it when you do that," Kenyatta added.

"Yeah, I know!" Smith laughed. "Hey, Rowdy, I guess I won't be scheduled for any more extra duty, huh?"

Rodriguez shook her head. "Nope. You finally out-smarted me, Smith. But I did finally break you of leaning on walls, didn't I?"

"You should have tried rigging him with explosives before this," Lachman said, his voice strained despite his attempt to sound casual.

"I might've got in trouble for that," Rodriguez said, squinting as she set another detonator.

"Excuse me," Third Officer Ergenian said as he walked up. "Dr. Tirgatao told me what's… why are you guys joking?"

"People handle things their own way," Aquino said. "No one's taking this lightly."

"But you're making jokes!"

"Sometimes it's what keeps you from screaming," Kenyatta said.

Ergenian stared at her. "I don't get you guys. I don't get you at all."

"No," Rodriguez replied as she set the last detonator. She turned to look at Ergenian. "You don't get us. And you never will. That's why we're Marines, and you're not."

"He's not being disrespectful," Aquino said. "He's trying to understand."

"Do you get it?" Ergenian asked Aquino.

"Yeah. It's like Private Kenyatta said. Sometimes it's how you cope."

"I don't…" Ergenian looked at Smith, who was trying to smile confidently and not quite carrying it off. "I was told you volunteered for this?"

"Yes, sir," Smith said. "For my friends. I'm doing it for them."

After a few seconds, Ergenian nodded. "That I can understand. I… deeply appreciate… I'm sorry, I have no idea what to say."

Smith extended his fist.

Third Officer Ergenian bumped it, briefly holding his gaze. Turning away, he walked slowly back to the rest of the crew members.

"Let's get ready to move," Aquino told the Marines. "Obonsawin, get us those comms with the shuttles!"

"I'm working it, sir!" Obonsawin called back, his voice tense.

Putting on his helmet, Aquino checked his pistol, then his data pad to ensure the link to the cameras was still working.

"We gonna bring the cat?" Lachman asked.

"Not this time," Aquino said. "The squonk won't come after the four of us if Smith is out there alone, and we're going to be far enough from Smith that Judy wouldn't alert before… he's attacked."

"How are we doing this?" Sergeant Rodriguez asked, her voice unnaturally calm.

"Private Smith goes out first. We let him get far enough ahead that we can't see him. He has to be alone." Aquino had to pause to compose his own voice. "We'll follow at a distance. I'll keep track of Private Smith using the camera feeds. Smith, go in the general direction of engineering. Do you know where that is?"

"Uh… roughly, sir."

"That's good enough. You want to act scared and lost, like you've stampeded and now you don't know where the rest of us are."

Smith grinned nervously. "I won't have to *act* scared, sir. That's part's going to be easy. Uh… Rowdy? Is it going to hurt? When all of this goes off?"

Rodriguez took a deep breath before answering, "No, Akira. You shouldn't feel a thing. It'll be too quick."

"Good. I was worried about that." Smith forced another smile. "I'll say hi to Ant-man for you guys when I get there."

Lachman made a rude noise. "You're not going to the same place Ant-man ended up."

"He's right," Kenyatta agreed.

Aquino turned to see Hakim Marvin. "We're heading out. Keep an eye on everything."

"Sure," Hakim said, his eyes avoiding Smith.

"Let's get the hatch open," Aquino told Rodriguez.

They all moved that way, everyone staying well clear of Smith, who was walking with exaggerated care.

"Don't trip, man," Lachman muttered.

The hatch open, Aquino gestured to Smith to step through, then stopped him with a gesture. "Private Smith… um…"

This time Smith smiled awkwardly. "I'm okay, sir. Really. I am. Later I know I'm going to be scared. But, right now I'm okay."

"Listen," Aquino said. "Those things you talked about earlier. About not being a real Marine, about being useless. They're not true. Maybe, up to this moment, people might think that, but not any more. What you're doing, what you are choosing to do, makes you a real Marine. In the finest tradition, and everything else. Just like the others said. Walk out of here knowing that. You're a *Marine*, Smith. I'm proud of you. Your friends are proud of you."

Smith grinned. "Thank you, sir. Wouldn't my dad be surprised to hear that! Can you tell him?"

"I will. I promise. It was an honor to be your commanding officer."

"I never thought I'd hear someone say that! Well… I better get going," Smith said.

"We'll be behind you," Aquino said. "If at all possible…"

"Yeah. But probably not, right?" Smith spread his hands. "Sometimes you just know what you have to do. You take care of the rest of these grunts, sir. I don't want any more of my friends to get hurt."

"I'll look after them." Aquino watched Smith head off into the darkened passageway, moving aft toward the engineering compartments where the last squonk was most likely to be found. If it wasn't already lurking nearby.

Turning away from watching Smith go was one of the hardest things he'd ever done. Aquino saw everyone in the compartment was looking toward him and the hatch, but he ignored all of them except for the remaining Marines. "Hakim, if that thing circles around and hits this place while we're out there, I want you and your helpers to nail it. Keep your carbines ready."

"Yes, sir!" Hakim held his carbine tightly, nodding to Aquino and the two other volunteer guards.

Aquino checked his pad to see if Smith was on any of the cameras. There he was, walking slowly down a passageway, his expression unreadable in the dim light. "We have to keep our distance so the squonk will think it has a clear window to take out Smith. He's not moving very fast, so we need to keep our pace down. Rodriguez, you take point. Kenyatta, rear guard. Lachman with me. I'm going to be putting a lot of attention into watching the camera feeds, so I'll be counting on you to keep that squonk off my back if it hits us. Any questions?"

"We're still free to fire?" Rodriguez asked.

"Weapons free," Aquino confirmed. "We will not let that thing get away this time."

He took a last glance into the auditorium, seeing KT standing back and watching them go.

Aquino nodded to her and went out of the hatch, hearing it seal behind him and the Marines.

FOURTEEN

AQUINO paused a moment longer before starting them after Smith, looking about and listening. The lights were dimmer, making him wonder if the emergency lighting would give out before the oxygen. But it was still bright enough that switching to low-light viewing wasn't necessary.

Smith came into view of a camera as he headed down another passageway, staggering a bit as if tired or scared or both. It was either a very good act or he really was tired and scared.

He should be far enough away.

"Let's go," Aquino said.

Rodriguez moved out first, her carbine ready. Aquino and Lachman followed, Kenyatta bringing up the rear.

Aquino felt his heart beat and breathing quickening. How absurd was it for him to feel frightened when it was Smith facing certain death? But, he realized, his fear was also for Smith. The man he'd sent to die. These moments would surely haunt him for however long the rest of his life happened to be.

The air… felt odd. While the still spinning duct fans had kept the air moving in the auditorium, the rest of the ship was still, motionless in a way that was unnatural. As they walked, sometimes every breath felt like it couldn't get enough air, but at other places, the oxygen level was still high enough for their deep breathing to produce a sudden, dizzying rush.

He kept his pistol holstered, his eyes on his display, trusting to Lachman's protection.

The Marines stayed quiet, their entire focus on their surroundings. The only time anyone spoke was when Aquino called out directions to Rodriguez. "Take a right at this corner." Despite his attempt to keep his voice as low as possible, the sound of his words seemed to echo down the passageways.

He had to keep slowing their pace, fighting against the Marines' instinct to speed up, to catch up with Smith and fight this thing together.

Every time Smith went of sight when he entered a stretch of passageway with a broken or battery-dead camera, Aquino's urge to move faster heightened, sweating out the moments until Smith reached the view of another camera.

The link to the mobile hot spot wavered at times before steadying. At least this one piece of equipment provided to the Marines was more than up to the task it was designed for.

Occasionally, they could hear Smith, his words in a loud voice carrying down the empty passageways through the still air. They were too far back to hear Smith clearly, but sometimes the words came through. "Help! Somebody? I need help. Where the hell am I? Where's everybody else?"

Unlike the calm voice Smith had used when heading out, he now sounded frightened. Aquino didn't think Smith was having any trouble putting that fear into his voice. That produced a new worry, that Smith, alone and facing certain death, would panic, and run, and trip…

Down more passageways, the sound of Smith's voice echoing like ghostly laments ahead of them, the Marines around Aquino watching every shadow in the dim light, their weapons twitching about as they searched for targets.

"Where the hell is that damned thing?" Rodriguez murmured, her rifle questing for any sign of the squonk.

"Get it over with, man," Lachman muttered.

"Heeeeeelp!" Smith's strained voice carried down the passageway and around a couple of corners.

Aquino had his eyes locked on his screen, a strange sense of foreboding building as the tension increased with every step. Smith, once more in a passageway with working cameras, staggered along like someone both tired and scared out of their mind. *Don't trip... don't trip...*

What if this didn't work? What if Smith died and the squonk wasn't stopped? What else could possibly be tried?

The camera images flickered as the link to his data pad failed, reset, failed, reset...

Smith was getting close to another corner, the passageways beyond all having dead cameras. No matter which way he turned, Aquino would lose sight of Smith again.

Smith reached the intersection and started to turn.

It happened so fast, Aquino saw only a blur on his camera view as the squonk lunged at Smith's back from one of the intersecting passages, its claws extended.

Smith tried to twist around to face the squonk, his hands moving as if attempting to raise the carbine he wasn't carrying, but the creature was already on him, claws reaching to slash through the webbing at the back of the vest, rip it loose and hurl it away as if stripping armor from its prey.

In the instant Aquino had to think, he realized that was exactly what had happened. The squonk must have seen the resemblance of the vest to the armor the Janusians had worn, instinct directing it to rip away that armor to allow it to more easily kill the wearer.

But that thought was secondary to the realization that the vest hadn't exploded. Somehow, the squonk missed hitting one of the detonators.

Aquino stared in despair as the next second dragged, everything moving with agonizing slowness, realizing that in another moment, Smith would be dead and the death would have accomplished nothing, the squonk would still be out there and—

The vest thrown by the squonk hit the opposite wall of the passageway and detonated.

His view went blank.

Aquino heard the blast roar ahead of them. He was running before he knew it, and shouting *follow me*, his data pad forgotten in one hand. The Marines were running with him, and they reached the corner and went around it and charged down the passageway. Then around another corner, and there was Smith lying face down. Next to the wall, the squonk was struggling to stand, one arm twisted at an odd angle, dark eyes promising death focusing on the oncoming Marines.

Aquino realized that he had dropped his data pad, that he had his pistol up, aiming and firing as fast he could.

Sergeant Rodriguez shouted and bolted ahead even faster, firing as she ran, her shots hitting the squonk, knocking it back and down. Until she was standing right over it, firing again and again, the squonk's body twitching from the last vestiges of life or simply the impacts of the shots.

Aquino caught up with her and grabbed Rodriguez's shoulder. "Easy there, Marine. Ease up. It's dead."

Sergeant Rodriguez stopped trying to fire her now empty carbine, taking deep breaths and staring down at the squonk. "Is it?"

"You blocked my line of fire," Private Kenyatta told her in a breathless but accusing voice.

"Tough, Stef," Rodriguez. "Is it dead?"

"I'm pretty sure," Aquino said, trying to calm his own heart and breathing.

"Hey!" Lachman called. He was kneeling by Smith. "He's still breathing! He's still alive! How in the hell could he be alive? Why is he even in one piece?"

Aquino froze for a moment in disbelief before dropping down by Lachman and seeing that it was true. Smith was unconscious, one side of his body and armor scarred by the explosion, but his chest was moving.

He looked around, at Smith, and at the squonk's body, and at the wall bearing the damage from where the vest had detonated. "That thing ripped loose the vest and threw the vest behind it. I saw it do that. I think… its body blocked most of the blast from hitting Smith. He still caught some of it. His armor helped protect him, but mostly it was the squonk that saved him."

Lachman gave Aquino a look of stunned realization. "How weird is that? That's so weird. That thing ended up saving Smith?"

"That's not all that's weird," Aquino said. "I think the squonk pulled off the vest because it looked like armor once worn by the Janusians. It was trying to make it easier to kill him, but instead, it injured itself and saved Smith's life."

"He's still hurt bad," Kenyatta remarked, worried enough to let her concern show.

"We've got to get him back to…" Nurse Sastrinata couldn't do anything about the internal injuries and probable brain concussion that Smith had suffered. If only…

The second and last squonk was dead. The ship was safe to move through. "We need to get him to medical," Aquino said. "It's not dangerous any more. No part of the ship is dangerous anymore."

"Come on!" Lachman told Kenyatta. "Let's get him up!"

"Do you know the way to medical?" Aquino asked.

"Yes, sir!" Lachman said. "I've gone there a lot to try to get out of work."

"Then get going," Aquino told him and Kenyatta. "When Rodriguez and I get back to the auditorium, I'll have her escort the nurse to medical."

"Why does the nurse need an escort?" Rodriguez asked, her eyes and weapon still aimed at the body of the squonk and the pool of very dark blood spreading out around it.

"Because right now, no one is going to feel safe on this ship," Aquino said. "Come on!"

Lachman and Kenyatta had already taken off for medical, moving as fast as they could while hauling Smith.

Aquino had taken a half dozen steps before he realized that Rodriguez wasn't yet following. He turned back, ready to shout out another order for her to stay with him.

He saw Rodriguez kneeling by the squonk. She had a grenade in one hand. As Aquino watched, Rodriguez stuffed the grenade into the slack mouth of the squonk before arming it.

Jumping to her feet, Rodriguez ran to Aquino. "We should get out of here, sir."

They were running down the passageway away from the squonk, when the blast of the grenade shattered the silence behind them.

"Was that necessary?" Aquino gasped, wondering why he felt so winded so quickly.

"It was the only way… to be sure," Rodriguez panted, sounding short of breath as well.

"This way," Aquino barely managed to get out as they reached an intersection of passageways.

"Why can't I… catch… breath?" Rodriguez asked, looking baffled.

"The air's… bad," Aquino said. "Not enough… oxygen." How much longer did they have? Had that estimate of the time left to them been too optimistic?

How ironic, and devastating, it would be to finally kill both squonks, and still die as the oxygen in the air gave out.

Despite his sense of urgency, they had to slow down as their lungs labored to extract enough oxygen. Passing through a long patch that still held plenty of oxygen, Aquino hyperventilated at the sudden burst of life-giving air. But within several meters, the air had gone bad again, leaving him and Rodriguez staggering.

The hatch to the auditorium finally came into view. Reaching it, both Aquino and Rodriguez leaned against the wall for a few moments, trying and mostly failing to catch their breaths. Giving up, Aquino pounding on the hatch. "Open up!"

He and Rodriquez went inside, seeing every eye fixed on them, expressions of dread at the sight of only two of them.

What should he say first? Aquino tried to project his voice, something harder to do while breathing was so difficult. "Both squonks… are dead!" He looked at Hakim. "You can leave… the hatch open. It's safe."

Over a chorus of gasps of joy, Hakim stared at Aquino. "Are the others…"

"They're okay," Aquino said. "Smith got… hurt. Nurse!"

Sastrinata came over quickly. "He's only hurt?"

"Long story," Aquino said. "Sergeant Rod… riguez will escort you to… medical. Lachman and Kenyatta took… Smith there."

The nurse's eyes flared with worry. "Both of those things are dead? You're certain?"

Rodriguez grinned like a wolf, showing her canines. "Very, very dead."

"Go," Aquino urged her.

Sastrinata, still a bit dubious, looked over Rodriguez and her weapon before nodding in agreement and following the sergeant out of the hatch.

"Are you okay?" KT asked. She was close by, watching him with alarm.

"Bad air," Aquino said. "Still recovering from running back here."

Before he could react, KT had her arms about him, her hug so tight it almost made it painful for him to draw deep breaths.

But that was okay. At the moment, everything was okay.

Except—

"The shuttles."

KT released her grip, nodding quickly. "We just got through to the shuttles a couple of minutes ago. Dr. Trinh is talking to them. Come on."

Aquino wanted nothing more than to lie down, but he walked quickly with KT to where Obonsawin still lay, grinning triumphantly.

"I did it, sir! I... you said Smith is okay?"

"Banged up bad, but still alive," Aquino said. How badly had that blast hurt Smith? It would be cruel if he had miraculously survived only to die of internal injuries caused by the concussion. "This time you're going to get a medal for your hacking."

"That beats a court-martial any day!"

Third Officer Ergenian and Fourth Officer Nijmeh were standing nearby, watching anxiously. Aquino knelt down next to Dr. Trinh, who was speaking to a split screen showing the image of Dr. Gohara on one side and Captain Lopez on the other.

"Here he is," Trinh said, canting the data pad so that it was pointed at Aquino.

"Both squonks are dead," Aquino repeated.

"You saw them? Both bodies?" Captain Lopez demanded.

"Yes. There's no doubt. It's safe for you to return to the ship."

"Which you should do *immediately*," Dr. Trinh added.

"Take off preparations will take a little while," Captain Lopez said.

"I told you," Dr. Trinh said. "The longer the squonks can observe you the larger the chance that their instincts will activate."

Dr. Gohara looked troubled. "I would not question your conclusions, Dr. Trinh. Not without firm grounds to do so. But we have to proceed according to safe take off procedures."

"Are there squonks near you?" Aquino asked.

"More and more of them," Gohara admitted, looking even more worried. "A few... scouts, I guess you could call them, saw us soon after we landed. Since then, more and more squonks have gathered around us. They've been maintaining their distance, but having them watch us has been... unnerving."

Captain Lopez looked slightly to one side. "Shuttle One and Shuttle Two, begin launch preparations. If anyone is outside, get them inside now. Shuttle Two, report when ready to launch."

"How long?" Dr. Trinh demanded. "How long until you leave the surface?"

"About half an hour," Captain Lopez said.

"Captain," Aquino said, "I don't know how much you've been told about conditions up here, but we're close to running too low on oxygen. We need you back as soon as possible, because if life support isn't running again within a few hours, it'll be too late."

"He's right," Ergenian called. "Our people up here need you."

"I understand," Captain Lopez said. She looked weary and stressed, Aquino realized. What had the intervening time been like for her since the shuttles had left the ship? Not knowing the fate of those left behind, not knowing what would become of those on the shuttles if the *Darwin* was too badly damaged by the squonks? Watching the squonks gathering around the shuttles and wondering when they might also go on a spree of death and destruction? "We'll—"

"Some are moving!" someone called from inside the shuttle holding Dr. Gohara.

Gohara looked far over to one side where another display screen must be. "Yes. Three… four… several more. They're moving toward the shuttles."

"How fast are they moving?" Trinh said anxiously.

"Not too fast. It's like they're sidling toward us. As if…"

"They're preparing to attack! Get those shuttles out of danger! I beg you!"

"A whole bunch more are moving!" someone else shouted.

A second later, Captain Lopez shouted as well, "Both shuttles, initiate emergency launch! I say again, emergency launch! Get off the ground! Everyone, brace yourselves for high acceleration!"

"They're hitting the outside of the shuttles! More and more of them!"

Aquino heard warning alarms blaring for both the launch and external damage to the shuttles.

The images on the data pad flickered, then went out at almost the same time.

"What happened?" Dr. Trinh asked in a horrified voice. "Have the shuttles been…"

"It's the comm antennas on the outside of the shuttles," Aquino said, trying to break the terrified silence with a firm voice. "Just the comm antennas. The shuttles should still be okay."

"Are you sure?" Trinh said, her voice trembling.

"Yes," Aquino said. "The comm antennas protrude in a way that would make them obvious targets for the squonks. And it wouldn't be that hard for the squonks to damage them."

Had he sounded confident enough? He was sure that was true, wasn't he?

But there was no way of knowing if the comm antennas had been the only things the squonks managed to damage. If enough of the squonks swarmed the outside of the shuttles before emergency lift could get them to safety…

Trinh shifted her gaze to Ergenian and Nijmeh. The two ship's officers exchanged helpless looks, before Nijmeh replied, "As far as I know, that should be true. But I haven't worked on shuttle issues much."

"Ensign Aquino is Navy," KT said. "He knows this stuff."

"He knows all of that sailor junk," Private Obonsawin chimed in from where he lay.

Trinh relaxed a bit. "That is good to hear. There is nothing else to do now except to wait, I suppose."

"That's right," Aquino said. "Wait, and minimize physical activity so we use as little oxygen as possible. I don't know what our orbital position is relative to wherever the shuttles had landed, but it might be a few hours before they reach us. So, everyone, stay calm, relax, and think about what you'll have for dinner when they reopen the dining areas."

He stood up, followed by KT. "I'm going to follow my own advice," Aquino said. "Private Obonsawin, get some sleep and do as little as possible."

Obonsawin grinned. "Do as little as possible. Yes, sir. I'll follow those orders to the letter."

Aquino and KT walked back to where Ichikawa lay.

Ichikawa's eyes, clouded with pain but alert, looked a question at him as if dreading the answer. "Smith… alive?"

"Yes," Aquino said.

"Huh." Ichikawa managed to form a small smile. "Just like Smith… even screwed up… suicide mission… and didn't die."

"I guess that finally worked out for him," Aquino said. "How are you feeling, Marine?"

"Hurt… all over."

"Hang in there," Aquino said. "The shuttles are on their way back to the ship. We'll have you in a nice bed in medical before you know it."

Ichikawa managed to give him a skeptical look from where she lay. "They just… give me a pill… tell me… walk it off."

"I won't let them do that," Aquino said.

"Okay." Ichikawa closed her eyes, her face still lined with pain, apparently exhausted by the brief conversation.

He sat down, back against the wall, gazing at Ichikawa and worrying about Smith. They both needed good medical treatment. How long would it take? Too long?

He sat there, thinking of Smith, Kenyatta, Lachman, and Rodriguez in medical, along with Nurse Sastrinata doing whatever she could do without power. Sergeant Antaeus's body was still in there, wasn't it? Hopefully the medical staff had placed the body in a preservation cell before evacuating the ship.

KT sat down next to him, and they leaned into each other's shoulders. "It really is just the antennas on the shuttles, right?" she murmured to him.

"Probably," Aquino said. "It could be something worse."

"High odds? Low odds?"

"Low odds with the shuttles doing emergency lifts. But not impossible."

"That would suck," KT said. "You finally kill the squonks, but the shuttles… No. That won't happen. We're going to sit here together and wait until the shuttles dock and everything gets fixed."

"Sounds like a plan," Aquino said. "Hey, I wanted to say I meant what I said earlier." How long ago had that been?

"When you said what earlier?"

"Um… I love you."

"You don't have to sound embarrassed to say it." She squeezed his arm. "I meant it, too. You said it might be hours?"

"Yeah. Depending on the orbital configuration, it might take that long for the shuttles to reach us."

"Okay."

After days of frantic activity, of feeling the constant lash of diminishing time and the need to somehow kill the squonks, it felt very strange to have nothing left for him to do but wait.

Wait as each breath seemed to become more labored. Wait as the oxygen content of the air lowered and the carbon dioxide rose. Aquino could see the entire auditorium, see everyone else lying down or propped against the walls or the remaining crates. No one was speaking, conserving even that tiny amount of energy.

Even the three cats were curled up, sleeping. Did Macbeth, Lady Macbeth, and Judy somehow know that the two squonks were dead? They certainly seemed to have finally relaxed.

The fans he'd rigged with battery power were slowing down as the carbine capacitors finally lost their charge. That didn't matter any more. The air being brought in no longer brought higher levels of oxygen with it.

KT sat quietly next to him, still leaning against his shoulder, her head drooping and chest swelling with each deep breath that couldn't bring in enough oxygen.

As KT had started to say, how strange to think that he might have killed the squonks, but too late to save everyone. It didn't seem remotely fair.

How much time had gone past?

Was he zoning out or passing out? His thoughts were moving sluggishly.

It had been at least an hour.

Damn, the air was foul. What a weird sensation. Plenty of air to breathe, and yet feeling as if he were slowly suffocating.

The two fans running on batteries had stopped as the charges on the capacitors were exhausted. Maybe he should try to attach new capacitors to those fans…

Aquino blinked himself back to consciousness, wanting to check the time but too tired.

They weren't going to make it, were they?

Mom, I did my best.

Noises near the open hatch drew his attention, even though looking up was nearly beyond his strength.

People wearing oxygen masks rushing in.

Maybe he was delirious.

Why would they have put all of the oxygen masks on the evacuation shuttles?

One more question he'd have to demand the answer to.

Wait. Was he going to live?

A mask slapped against his lower face, cool air suddenly filling his lungs. Air with so much oxygen he grew dizzy.

His mind snapped to alertness, bringing along with it a massive headache.

"Two more breaths," the woman holding this mask said. "Then someone else gets it. We don't have enough to go around."

He sucked in the air greedily before the mask left his face and went onto KT's. "Life… support," Aquino gasped.

"The engineers are on it," the woman with the oxygen mask said.

"Bodies."

"What?"

"In… engine… eering. Dead."

She stared at him. "You couldn't get them out, could you? That's okay."

KT let out a very long slow breath as the mask left her face, blinking like someone watching an unexpected sunrise. She looked over at him. "Hey, Oz."

"Hey."

"We gonna live?"

"Maybe."

Aquino watched Ichikawa gulping in air despite the pain the breaths were clearly bringing her.

How long did they sit there, waiting as the oxygen masks rotated among the Marines and the left behinds? Aquino saw the worried looks the rescuers were exchanging and knew those masks must be nearly depleted.

The lights came on.

The exploration and research ship *Darwin* seemed to shudder as every piece of equipment aboard powered up, the welcome hum of the fans filling the air.

Every fan except, ironically, the two he'd modified. But the other fans possessed more than enough power to compensate, life support automatically ramping everything up to full as it sensed how bad the air inside the ship was.

"Congratulations, Horatius."

Aquino looked over at KT and managed a smile despite his headache. "Thanks. But the bridge still needs work." He tried to rise, sagging back as dizziness struck. Raising his voice, he called to the rescuers, "This Marine lying in front of me. She has internal injuries and broken ribs and a couple of breaks in that arm. We need to get her to medical."

"Get a stretcher!" someone ordered.

Aquino thought she looked a bit familiar, finally realizing that it was one of the doctors he had seen in medical when they brought the body of Sergeant Antaeus there.

The doctor turned to Aquino. "Is anybody else hurt?"

"The other Marine, over there, has a broken leg."

"I'm fine," Obonsawin called. "Take care of Malice!"

"We will." The doctor spoke to one of the other rescuers, who raced out of the compartment.

"What shape are you in?" the doctor murmured, squatting to look into Aquino's eyes.

"My head feels like it's about to explode," Aquino said. "Dr…"

"Vance. Gayle Vance. You're…"

"Ensign Osiris Aquino."

"Oz," KT added.

"Okay, Oz. You're not great at the moment, but you seem mostly okay. A bad headache is a common side effect of hypoxemia, which is what we call low levels of oxygen in the blood. How's your heart?"

"A little fast, maybe."

"No confusion? Good. What happened to the badly injured woman?"

Aquino had to take a moment as he tried to come up with a simple explanation. "There was a large trap using tensioned metal struts as hammers. She got a glancing blow from two of those."

The doctor hesitated, looking as if she was reconsidering her earlier "no confusion" statement, but then her expression cleared. "Oh. Something to do with those squonks? I'm going to check on that Marine and then others in the room while we wait for the stretcher."

As the doctor went around the room, Aquino switched his attention to two people approaching him on unsteady feet. Third Officer Ergenian and Fourth Officer Nijmeh. "How are you guys?"

"Alive," Nijmeh said.

"Yeah," Ergenian said. "Alive. Thanks to you."

"Thanks to the Marines," Aquino said.

"How many…" Nijmeh hesitated. "Some got hurt."

"One died," Aquino said. "Three others hurt, a couple very badly. We were really lucky."

"We really appreciate it," Ergenian said. "We just wanted to say it as soon as possible. Whatever we can do for you guys, just name it."

Aquino smiled. "It's always good to have a friend working in supply."

"You said it! Anything you guys want. Just tell me."

"We need to get back to the others," Nijmeh said, gesturing to the crew members still gathered together. "But, yeah, whatever a fourth officer in operations can do for you, just let me know."

He watched them go, wondering if this nightmare was finally over.

No. Not yet. Not until he knew how Smith was doing and knew Ichikawa was getting the care she needed.

One of the automated stretchers had been activated now that power was restored, the device rolling almost silently into the auditorium after its treads "stepped" over the bottom of the hatch. Dr. Vance directed it to stop by Ichikawa, then bent to speak to her. "Hi, Malice. Is that your name?"

"Alice," Ichikawa muttered. "Name… Alice."

"Ah. Okay. I'm Dr. Vance. I'm checking your medical data chip. All right. Got it. Alice Ichikawa. I'm applying an anesthetic pump to your good arm. It will give you exactly what you need and no more, and alert me if any problems start developing. In a couple of seconds, you're going to feel great, but sleepy. Please don't try to move. We'll get you on the stretcher and to medical where we can fix you up. Who did this work on your arm?"

"Nurse Sastrinata," Aquino said. "It was the best she could do with what we had."

"She set the bones without anesthetic?"

"We didn't have any."

The doctor bit her lip and clearly decided not to comment on that. "How are you feeling now, Alice?"

"Not bad at all," Ichikawa said, smiling.

"Lift her," the doctor directed the stretcher. It lowered, the platform on top extending to slide under Ichikawa, then gently lift her and retracting to place her firmly on top. "Wings" extended to enfold her in a gentle but secure grasp.

"I'm coming," Aquino said, struggling to his feet.

"That's not necessary," Dr. Vance said. "She'll be fine."

"She's one of mine," Aquino said. "And I need to check on Smith. He's already in medical. What?" The doctor was eyeing him with hesitation.

Aquino realized that he was still wearing body armor, and still had his pistol holstered at his side. "Don't worry," he said. "I'm not dangerous."

"Take it easy," Dr. Vance advised. "You might still be feeling that hypoxemia more than you realize."

"I'll come along," KT said, getting to her feet.

"Private Obonsawin," Aquino called, "keep an eye on our equipment."

They followed the stretcher out of the auditorium, where Aquino came to a halt, momentarily startled by how different the passageway looked and felt with full lighting and moving air and other crew members and even a few researchers walking through it.

He didn't really notice much on the way to medical, his mind reeling through the impacts of too little sleep, the endurance pills wearing off, and the low levels of oxygen he'd been exposed to. The headache didn't help.

KT didn't say anything as she walked, occasionally wincing as loud noises hit them. Her headache must be bad as well.

Medical, brightly lit and crowded, felt even more alien. Most of those present had suffered injuries when the shuttles made their emergency lifts, resulting in a lot of sprains and bruises.

By staying right behind Dr. Vance, who was right behind the stretcher, Aquino and KT made their way through the crowd without being hindered.

The stretcher transferred Ichikawa to a bed where bots immediately began scanning her body to assess the injuries. Assured that Ichikawa would be okay, he went looking for the other Marines.

They were two rooms over, crowded in along with another doctor and some nurses, as well as medical bots. Private Smith lay on the bed, limp, his chest slowly rising and falling to show he still lived.

Sergeant Rodriguez greeted Aquino with a weary salute. "They say Smith is stabilized, sir. Nothing beyond that, though."

"How are you doing?" Aquino asked, moving his gaze to indicate the question was aimed at not only Rodriguez but also Kenyatta and Lachman, who were leaning against one wall trying to stay out of the way.

"Kinda beat, sir," Lachman said.

Kenyatta nodded. "It's been a long few days."

"We got a bit worried," Lachman added, "when we were having trouble breathing. But Rowdy said you'd make sure the shuttles got back in time."

Rodriguez might have more confidence in him than he did in himself, Aquino thought. "There isn't any sense in you three hanging around here. Go back to the auditorium to collect our gear and get it back to the barracks and the armory. I'm going to make sure Obonsawin isn't overlooked by the medical personnel."

"It's going to take more than one trip for the three of us to get all of that junk back," Kenyatta observed. "What about the other junk? The portable tools and everything?"

"I'll notify the ship's officers that those things need to be collected," Aquino said, thinking about the messes around the ship that would require cleaning up. The dead in engineering and elsewhere, bullets embedded in various walls, grenade damage, and two squonk bodies that had been very thoroughly killed. Not to mention the two traps, which were both sprung but still in place. He'd probably be hearing about all of that as the crew tallied up the damage.

Lachman looked pained. "How come everybody talks about how great winning is, but nobody ever talks about how much you got to clean up afterwards?"

"I think the losers are supposed to do the cleaning up," Kenyatta said.

"That so?" Lachman scoffed. "Cleaning up what's left of those squonks is going to be the worst part."

"That's a bio-hazard," Aquino said. "There are special teams from the crew that will handle that. Once you guys get our stuff out of the auditorium and into our area again, get some rest."

After the Marines left, he and KT leaned against the wall, watching the work on Smith, not understanding it but heartened by the smooth professionalism of the medical team.

Eventually, the doctor came over to him. "I guess you're this guy's manager?"

"I am his commanding officer," Aquino said. "Is Private Smith going to be okay?"

"He'll live," the doctor said. "I can't tell you more than that until a lot more tests have been run. But he's not in danger of dying any more."

"Thanks, Doc."

Aquino and KT walked out into the still crowded main room of medical, just in time to see another stretcher rolling in with a snoring Private Obonsawin on it. Relieved that was taken care of, he tried to focus on the next task. "I'd better…" Why couldn't he complete the thought?

KT studied his face. "You're a walking disaster, Oz. Get some rest."

"Not until…"

"I can barely function, and I haven't been pushed nearly as hard as you. Come on."

There were a lot of things he should be taking care of, but he couldn't center his thoughts on any of them, so he let KT lead him back to the Marine area. He didn't really remember getting to his room, pulling off the body armor, and collapsing into the bed.

FIFTEEN

HIS alarm went off.

Aquino woke up from the depths of a dark dream, gradually grasping that he was in his bunk, in his room, and was gazing up at an overhead that he had not known if he would ever look at again.

For a moment, he wondered if the events of the last few days had also been a dream.

That only lasted until he moved, and his stiff muscles protested. His discarded body armor lay in a pile on the deck, along with his holstered pistol. Which was still loaded. How many regulations had he broken by leaving that lying there?

He sat up with a groan, trying to decide whether he should keep trying to move or just give up and lie back down.

Except lying down would hurt, too. And he needed to check on his Marines, and the other weapons, and a lot of other things.

Aquino got cleaned up, wondering just how bad he had smelled. Based on the state of the uniform he'd been wearing, not very good at all. Putting on a new uniform made him feel almost halfway able to function.

Another alarm sounded. Aquino checked it. Morning quarters. He should be there. Picking up the pistol, he headed that way.

Walking wasn't too hard as long as he was careful.

Sergeant Rodriguez, looking astoundingly fresh, her uniform crisp, saluted as he approached. "Good morning, sir."

"Good morning, Sergeant."

They both turned to face Private Kenyatta and Private Lachman, who were standing shoulder to shoulder at attention.

Rodriguez called out as loudly as if they were in a big room crowded with people, "Private Kenyatta."

"Here."

"Private Lachman."

"Yo."

"Private Lachman!"

"Here!"

Sergeant Rodriguez turned to Aquino and saluted. "Privates Ichikawa, Obonsawin, and Smith are in medical. All assigned personnel present or accounted for, sir."

"Thank you, Sergeant." Aquino returned the salute before facing Kenyatta and Lachman again. "At ease." Kenyatta and Lachman relaxed, no longer standing at attention. "You've done very well the last few days. I promise you that is going to be officially reported. I was told… yesterday? I was told that both Private Ichikawa and Private Smith were out of danger and would recover. Today, though, we need to continue getting things in order. Are all weapons accounted for and back in the armory, Sergeant?"

"All weapons except for one pistol, sir," Rodriguez said.

Aquino handed her the pistol he was carrying. "Sorry."

"I wasn't worried, sir."

"Some of the carbines saw a lot of use."

"Yes, sir," Rodriguez said. "I going to have them all inspected and given full cleaning and any necessary repairs. The capacitors that were drawn down are recharging. Except for the two you used in the ventilation ducts."

"I'll have to get those back," Aquino said. "I'll talk to someone in the crew about it. What about everything else? The rations and all?"

"We need to report what was expended," Rodriguez said. "Ammunition, grenades, Q-7 explosives, and detonators. Lachman will inventory the rations and Kenyatta will handle the ammo and other munitions. I plan on reporting both field medical kits as expended. Maybe that will get us a higher priority for replacements."

"Do that," Aquino said. What else was there to worry about? "I want to focus on must-do items for the next week, at least. If you think of anything we haven't addressed, bring it up. Any questions?"

"Sir?" Lachman said. "Is Rowdy going to stay a sergeant?"

"Worried?" Rodriguez asked him.

"Yeah, a bit. She's already drunk with power, sir!"

Aquino smiled. "I'm afraid I have bad news for you. Yes, Rodriguez's promotion to sergeant is official. I need to fill out some paperwork, but it will date from the moment I gave her the battlefield promotion." And it wasn't like the personnel system wouldn't be grateful to have a replacement sergeant already here, instead of having to find one somewhere else.

"Any *other* questions?" Aquino said. "No? In that case, after carrying out the necessary tasks today, I want all of you to enjoy a rope yarn day."

All three Marines looked back at him with blank expressions. "A what day, sir?" Rodriguez asked.

"Rope yarn. Don't Marines have rope yarn?"

"Not to my knowledge, sir."

"It's a Navy term! It means you get to rest, run personal errands, do anything you want!" He paused. "Anything legal."

Lachman grinned. "The Navy has a special word for letting enlisted types laze around? Cool!"

"The Marines don't," Kenyatta noted in a dry voice.

"That's because it never comes up," Rodriguez said. "But, you heard Ensign Aquino. In keeping with the spirit of his order, I'll limit your tasks today to those absolutely necessary to be done. And we've already laid those out."

"I'm going to medical after this to check on our other three Marines," Aquino said. "Have fun. *Don't* get into trouble."

"Is it all right if I accompany you?" Rodriguez asked.

"Certainly." In truth, he welcomed having her along, not knowing what kind of reception he would get in the passageways from the crew and the researchers.

"I'll put this in the armory," Rodriguez said, hefting the pistol, "and be right back. You two get to work. Dismissed."

Lachman headed back into the barracks with unusual enthusiasm, doubtless because he knew once he got his work done, he could relax.

Aquino called out as Kenyatta moved to follow him.

"Oh, Private Kenyatta?"

"Sir?" She turned and walked back to him.

"I just wanted to let you know," Aquino said, "that even though the ship's security force has been gutted and Captain Jardyce is dead, which will probably upend any ongoing investigations, I don't want any more booze to disappear from the ship's stocks."

"Sir?" Kenyatta repeated in the tones of someone who doesn't understand.

"I know you know nothing about it. I'm just letting you know my expectations, and how… disappointed I will be if that doesn't stop."

"Yes, sir." To his surprise, Kenyatta actually smiled. "I'll keep that in mind."

She went into the barracks room as Rodriguez was coming out.

Aquino and the sergeant started off, leaving the small Marine area and entering passageways thronged with other people.

"It feels sort of weird, doesn't it?" Rodriguez said. "All of these people. The lights on."

Aquino nodded. "No squonks lurking in ambush."

"Good morning!"

Accustomed to being mostly ignored when he walked through the ship, Aquino was startled by the greeting. "Good morning," he replied to the smiling researcher.

His bafflement grew as nearly everyone they passed called out to him and Rodriguez. "Talk about weird," he muttered to the sergeant during a brief pause in responding to the greetings.

"I'm more used to being looked at like an animal that escaped from its pen," Rodriguez said. "How long do you think this will last?"

"No telling. Let's enjoy it while we can, I guess."

"Are you Ensign Aquino?"

He turned toward the voice, readied for another thanks, but instead saw an officious-looking man in the uniform of a ship's officer, displaying official-looking forms on an official data pad. "You have to sign these forms."

"Forms? What forms?"

"If you would sign them, please."

Aquino pushed the data pad away. "Not until I know what this is about."

The officer appeared aggravated at having to explain. "To acknowledge damage to ship's equipment and unauthorized appropriation of materials."

Aquino, momentarily unable to speak, glanced at Sergeant Rodriguez.

"This is only a preliminary accounting," the officer continued. "The final financial compensation requirements will undoubtedly be higher."

"Materials?" Aquino finally said. "Are you talking about the tools and traps we used to try to kill the squonks? Damage? What damage?"

The officer, with obvious irritation, checked his data pad. "Two ventilation fans that require repair to power and control lines and removal of unauthorized modifications, extensive harm done to equipment in various parts of the ship, primarily engineering—"

"Hold on," Aquino said. "The vent fans? The fans that were given temporary power so that the members of the ship's crew left behind during the evacuation, and researchers also left behind, could get enough oxygen to stay alive?"

"I'm not aware—"

"Damage to equipment? That was all done by the squonks, not my Marines. And we had nothing to do with the squonks being brought aboard this ship in the first place."

"Those determinations are outside the scope of my office's work," the officer insisted.

"And signing that is outside the scope of my responsibilities and authority," Aquino said. "Feel free to submit your claims to the government through normal channels."

"You are the government's representative on this ship!"

"And you are—" Aquino managed to avoid saying it. "Let me save you a lot of time. The fans were modified under emergency field conditions to guard against impending loss of life. The spare materials were requisitioned under emergency field conditions to help kill the squonks, without which everyone left on the ship, and all of you people on the surface, would have died. I suggest you see how Captain Lopez feels about your forms before you pursue this any further."

"Ensign Aquino, I must insist—"

That did it. "I don't need any thanks for saving your life, but there is no way in hell I am going to *pay* you for saving your life."

The official still hesitated.

"Hey, buddy," Sergeant Rodriguez said. Her voice didn't seem to have changed much, but something about her eyes and the way she held herself conveyed a message of imminent danger. "Go away."

The officer retreated hastily, leaving room for more smiling faces and cheerful greetings from others in the passageway who were unaware of the drama which had just taken place.

"I don't believe it," Aquino muttered. Then he sighed. "Yeah, I do believe it."

"What are you going to do?" Rodriguez asked.

"Just what I said. Talk to Captain Lopez. She seems to have a good head on her shoulders."

"She still works for a civilian company, though."

“Yeah. I guess we’ll see.”

Medical wasn’t as crowded as before, though still busy. Aquino came to a halt, looking over the line, and trying to decide whether he should just bypass the whole thing.

The last few days had been very long ones. Bypassing sounded good.

He led Rodriguez past the line, headed for the room where he had seen Smith last night.

The receptionist’s arm snaked out to block his movement. “One does not simply walk into medical,” she said. “You have to—”

Her eyes left her screen to look at him, and widened. “Oh! I’m sorry!”

“That’s all right,” Aquino said. “I want to visit the wounded Marines.”

“Of course! I’ll let the doctors know you’re here. They’re all in room six.”

“Thank you.”

“Let me know if you need anything else!” the receptionist said, her words accompanied by a dazzling smile.

As they walked to room six, Sergeant Rodriguez chuckled. “If your girl dumps you, I think that receptionist would be interested.”

“Not funny,” Aquino said. He didn’t want to say that every time he’d thought of KT this morning, he wondered how she would feel. The terrible dangers they faced had drawn them much closer. How would KT see him with things back to normal? It wasn’t hard to imagine her putting the brakes on something that had accelerated a lot faster than he expected.

Room six held three beds, each occupied by a Marine. Smith was still out, his body mostly encased in a healing and monitoring shell, but both Ichikawa and Obonsawin were awake.

Rodriguez checked the readout next to Obonsawin’s bed. “Huh. It says here you’re responding well and should be discharged this afternoon.”

"On light duty," Obonsawin hastily added. "I'll have a cast on for a few weeks."

"There's a lot of work you can do even with a cast on," Rodriguez observed. "Unless you're thinking of messing around with the medical records system on this ship."

"Ah, Rowdy, that's a low blow."

Aquino came close enough to clap Obonsawin on the shoulder. "I'm going to be putting you in for a medal just as I promised. Your hacking saved a lot of lives."

"A medal?" Obonsawin grinned. "That beats a court-martial any day. Did I already say that?"

"I'm not sure. Maybe. Some of my memories are a bit hazy." Turning to Ichikawa, Aquino smiled at her. "How are you doing?"

Her face still bore lines of strain, but Ichikawa smiled. "Any day I don't have to get out of bed can't be too bad."

"Are they taking good care of you?"

"Oh, yes, sir. I'm going to be here a little while though, because of the ribs and what they told me is internal bruising."

"Your guts got bruised?" Rodriguez asked.

"Yeah," Ichikawa said. "By my own trap! You killed the squonk responsible for that, right?"

"It was very, very dead," Rodriguez said.

"Thanks, Rowdy."

Dr. Vance came in, her glance sweeping across the other Marines and coming to rest on Smith. "I imagine you want an update on him. He's lucky to be alive."

"You don't know how lucky," Aquino said. "How long will he remain sedated?"

"We've got some deep healing going on to deal with the concussion's impact on his brain," Vance said. "Maybe two or three more days, then we'll want him awake and interacting as much possible. Having one of your people here to talk to him and keep him engaged would be very helpful for his recovery."

"We'll set that up," Aquino said with a glance at Rodriguez. "Just let me know when we should start. What's the long-term look like for him?"

Dr. Vance sighed. "In an earlier time, his injuries would've been too severe. Today, we can heal them. Mostly. But there will be a need for rehabilitation, and…" She looked troubled. "I'd say there's a high probability of minor long-term physical impairment."

"How bad is minor?" Aquino asked.

"He'll likely be able to function in normal life, but strenuous tasks requiring endurance and coordination will be difficult, I think. That's all preliminary, you understand."

"I understand," Aquino said. "Thank you, and thank the other medical staff on behalf of all of us, please."

"You did save a lot of lives," Dr. Vance said. "Consider it a partial payback."

Aquino didn't say anything, his mind filled with memories of the dead. Captain Jardyce, the chief engineer, those three junior researchers, other crew members.

He hadn't saved them.

Aquino stood just outside of medical, thinking.

Rodriguez shook her head in amazement. "Whoever or whatever runs the universe must like Smith a whole lot. I never would've guessed that."

"He was extremely lucky," Aquino said.

"Which means we've got a problem, sir. Smith is a genuine hero now. You're going to put him in for a medal, too, right? But he's also still Smith. If he stays a Marine, he'll screw up again. And because he's a hero, that screw up will attract a lot of notice."

"And then he's back to square one," Aquino said. "I think we may have an answer to that. I'd like your opinion on how Smith would take it. I'm thinking of putting him in for medical discharge under honorable conditions."

Rodriguez looked startled, then nodded. "From what the doc said, Smith will qualify for a medical, won't he? And that's practically the only way to get out of this assignment early. Let him go home a hero, and anything he messes up there they'll figure is because of the long-term injuries."

"Do you think Smith will be okay with it?" Aquino asked. "He really thinks you guys regard him as a part of the unit."

She hesitated, frowning in thought. "Yes, sir, he'll be okay. I mean, we can ask once he's awake again. But Smith was never happy with being a screw up. He knows he makes more work for the rest of us. I imagine he'll be relieved to know his friends don't have to cover for him any more."

"Good. I'll plan to run with that, then." Aquino glanced at her. "Speaking of long-term solutions, are you thinking of trying to hold onto those sergeant stripes this time?"

"Me?" Rodriguez grinned. "I'll give it my best shot."

"If you really do," Aquino said, "I have no doubt you'll do very well. I…" His next words caught in his throat. "When I first got here and read the records for all of you, I thought I was totally screwed. But you all stepped up. Even Smith."

"Facing imminent death is a great motivator," Rodriguez said. "Sir? There's something I want to say." She grimaced as if embarrassed. "Thanks."

"For what?" Aquino said.

"You're blaming yourself, aren't you? For everyone who died? Even the ones who died before anyone knew there was a problem?"

He nodded slowly. "I'll be thinking about them probably for the rest of my life. Wishing that I could have somehow…"

"But what if you hadn't been here?" Rodriguez asked. "What if Sergeant Antaeus had still been in charge, and he'd been the one who got the call that the squonks were loose?"

Aquino thought about that, imagining what would have happened. "He would have done exactly what he did, go in after the squonks without any preparations."

"And he probably would have brought us all with him to do the actual hunting for the squonks while he supervised," Rodriguez said. "No body armor, no weapons, just find the 'dogs' and collect them. We all would've died just like he did. Then the squonks would have started killing people outside of engineering, and there would've been panic as the ship evacuated, and a lot more people would've died. Give yourself credit, sir. It would have been a lot worse without you in charge."

"Why are you telling me this, Sergeant?"

"Because I think you're weighing yourself down, feeling guilty, because some people were killed, and three Marines are in medical."

"I'm in charge. It's my responsibility to keep those people safe," Aquino said.

"Yes, sir. And I'm telling you, we would've lost a lot more people if you hadn't been in charge. And those wounded Marines would be dead. Me, too." Rodriguez waved a hand to encompass the whole ship. "Maybe try to focus on the lives you saved, sir."

"I'll try." But he knew one would never balance the other. "Having a very good sergeant made a huge difference, too. You stepped in and held everything together. I should be thanking you."

"I just did my job, sir, making sure everyone did their jobs. Hey, after this, do you think they'll send us a full complement of Marines so we'll be up to strength?"

Aquino thought about that, and how nice it would've been to have twelve Marines at his disposal instead of six. "Maybe. Unless someone decides this proves they only need six Marines and cuts our numbers to save money."

Rodriguez nodded. "That's as likely as not. It's none of my business, but, um, what are you going to say about Sergeant Antaeus?"

What would he say? The blunt truth, that Antaeus caused his own death through arrogance and refusal to obey orders from his commanding officer, wouldn't fix anything. And such a harsh assessment felt like spitting on the grave of a dead Marine. What might make a difference? "I think I'll say that he exercised poor judgment in trying to deal with the situation single-handedly and without taking time to prepare, but… died valiantly… attempting to resolve a dangerous situation before others were harmed."

"That's more than fair, sir," Rodriguez said. "Are you coming back to the barracks?"

"No. I need to find Captain Lopez."

"About that expenses thing?"

"That and some other stuff," Aquino said. "I'll see you back there."

On the way to see Lopez, he passed the ship's cat, Judy, sauntering down a passageway on her daily patrol, just as if nothing had happened. "How are you, Judy?" Aquino asked, stooping to pet her.

Judy endured the affection, but gave him a look that made it clear he'd have to re-earn her trust.

Could he put Judy in for a medal? Or at least a commendation?

He found Captain Lopez in the First Officer's stateroom. "Do you have time for me, Captain?"

She nodded, looking tired. "Sit down, please. What can I do for you?"

"There are a couple of things I need to ask you about," Aquino said, taking a seat. Lopez's stateroom wasn't nearly as big as the captain's, her desk not quite as large. Although, it wasn't difficult to understand why she hadn't yet moved into Captain Jardyce's former quarters filled with memorabilia and other reminders of the former captain.

"Of course. Are the injured Marines being well looked after?"

"Absolutely," Aquino said. "No complaints there. I'm grateful to your medical staff for the care they've provided."

Lopez smiled slightly. "The company will be billing the government for that medical care, so don't feel too grateful."

"That's one of the things I needed to speak to you about," Aquino said. "I had a run-in this morning with a ship's officer who wanted me to sign forms taking responsibility for damage and repairs to the ship."

"What?" Lopez's reaction made it obvious she hadn't been aware that was happening. "Damage and repairs?" She checked something on her desk display. "I'm seeing the list of items identified so far. What specifically were you asked to sign for?"

"A couple of vent fans I rigged with batteries to keep oxygen levels good enough for longer in the compartment we were in," Aquino said. "As well as other things like damage to engineering, none of which was caused by the Marines."

Lopez sat back, rubbing her forehead, looking pained. "They can't charge the dead squonks or the equally dead Janusians for the damage, so they're reaching out to the government. Of course. Someone in accounting is doing things by the book."

"Well, I'm not going to sign anything obligating me to pay for what we had to do to deal with the squonks and keep everyone alive," Aquino said.

"I understand. Don't worry. I'll take care of this. We'll end up billing the government, but that can go to offices that aren't directly related to you. I'll have someone from accounting get in touch to let you know that legally and officially."

"Not that guy I met this morning," Aquino said. "How about Fifth Officer Craig?"

"You know Fifth Officer Craig? Oh, he was one of those left on the ship."

"Yes," Aquino said. "He helped with handling people."

"Good." Lopez paused, her eyes hooded. "I understand some of the crew gave you problems during that time."

"It wasn't anything that Third Officer Ergenian and Fourth Officer Nijmeh and Craig couldn't deal with." It was a lot easier to blow off those problems this morning than it had been at the time. Aquino gestured toward the area of the ship outside of the stateroom. "Other members of the crew, such as Steward Haycock, rendered a lot of help."

"Haycock?" Lopez made a note on her display. "I wanted to ask a favor of you. There's going to be a memorial service for Captain Jardyce tomorrow. I'll understand if you don't want to attend, but it would be a nice gesture."

Aquino nodded, remembering his first two encounters with Jardyce, his mind once again flashing the memory of finding her body in engineering. He took a deep breath to calm the reaction that generated. "Everyone says she was a real professional who knew her job. And we did have some good interactions the day before… she died."

"The crew looked up to her," Captain Lopez said. "I have some big shoes to fill. Oh, that reminds me. There's an open criminal investigation that I intend closing."

Aquino tried to look innocent. "Is there?"

"Yes. It involves missing inventory among the ship's liquor supply. I don't think we need to pursue that."

"I agree," Aquino said. "Will there also be memorial services for Security Officer Corba and the other security officers who died?"

"Yes." Lopez gave him a sidelong look. "Do you want to be informed of that?"

"Yes. I want to attend that as well," Aquino said. "Corba, and the others, died doing their duty, trying to protect the ship and those aboard it. I respect that."

"That's good to hear. Is there anything else? I have a *lot* to deal with."

"I understand," Aquino said. "But I have to ask you about something that I *don't* understand. You knew, and Captain Jardyce knew, that a good number of people would be left on the ship in an evacuation because there wasn't enough room in the shuttles."

Lopez grimaced. "Yes. As I told you before I left the ship. It's impossible for me to adequately express my gratitude to you for keeping them safe and protected."

"Thank you," Aquino said. "But, why did I have to do some of the things I did? If we hadn't had supplies meant for the Marines, it would have been much more difficult. There wasn't anything done to prepare for those people being left aboard. No food, no portable medical kits, no emergency equipment of any kind. The ship's officers left aboard had no training and no guidance, and no specialized skills to help them look after the other members of the crew and the junior researchers."

To his shock, Lopez simply nodded. "That's right."

"I don't understand. Why? Why weren't any preparations made?"

Lopez took several seconds before answering, her expression troubled. "Ensign Aquino, I will deny saying what I'm about to tell you. Don't try to quote me. But if anyone deserves to know the truth, it's you. I told you the reason why those people were left on the ship during the evacuation. The number of people on this ship has been increased over the years, until it exceeded the capacity of the two large shuttles we carry.

"Modifying the ship to add a third shuttle dock, and purchasing a third shuttle, would require a lot of money," Lopez continued. "Instead, as I told you, the company sought and received waivers."

"Which I didn't understand then and don't now," Aquino said. "How could the company operating *Darwin* get waivers for something like that? Waivers for not having enough life boat capacity?"

Lopez met his questioning gaze with a level look. "The basis for the waivers, the justification used to approve them, is that due to the reliability of a ship such as *Darwin*, and the lack of any recent requirements to evacuate a ship such as *Darwin*, there was no significant chance the ship would *ever* need to be evacuated."

Aquino shook his head. "That's… all right. That was the justification. Which I think is very wrong-headed. Except, what does that have to do with not preparing to provide for those people who couldn't be evacuated from the ship?"

"Don't you see?" Lopez looked away, her mouth working as if she were ill. "If *any* preparations were made to help those not evacuated, anything at all, it would mean the company *did* anticipate that the ship might someday need to be evacuated. The company's entire legal defense was based on the premise that this wouldn't happen. Any preparations to deal with it if it *did* happen would completely undercut that defense.

"Captain Jardyce fought against that. I swear that's true. She didn't believe it would ever happen, but she also thought some basic preparations would be wise. She was ordered not to do anything along those lines. And, no, you will not find copies of those orders anywhere. The company's lawyers are too smart for that."

Lopez made a face again. "Now… now the company will probably blame Captain Jardyce for the lack of preparations, while still denying there was any reason to prepare. Because there will be lawsuits, Ensign Aquino. I've spoken with some of those left on the ship who cannot wait until we reach a safe port again so they can contact lawyers and try to collect large sums for pain and suffering."

Aquino stayed silent for a few moments. "Then it was all about saving money and legal defenses. So what if a bunch of people died?"

"That's right." Lopez looked at him again, her eyes reflecting the hard-earned wisdom from a couple of decades serving as an officer. "Some lawyers and some bean-counters are comfortable with making decisions that will cost lives. So are some of the people who make big decisions. If you didn't already know that, you should learn it."

"I already knew it," Aquino said, thinking of how his unit on the *Darwin* had been at half-strength, and poorly-equipped, and given a Navy ensign as a commander instead of a Marine lieutenant. His force hadn't been prepared for what transpired, because of decisions made by other officers who could be certain they would never personally face the consequences of their actions.

Had they wrestled with those decisions, hating to make them, as he had with sending Private Smith out? Or was their sleep undisturbed because they wanted to make their bosses happy, and because they saw only profits and spreadsheets and fine points of law, and not those who paid the true price?

He could try to pin blame on Captain Jardyce. Maybe she should have done more, threatened to resign and blow the whistle on unsafe practices. Maybe. Or maybe she, like him, had been stuck with situations created by others and merely tried her best.

Aquino didn't feel right sitting in judgment on Jardyce, who died doing her job. "I'm going to be writing an after-action report with lessons-learned. If I can't quote you, I'll just say that the lack of preparations created some significant problems, and future waivers like that should be conditioned on ensuring everyone would be looked after."

"That's fair," Lopez said. "I can't dictate what's in your report. I ask that you don't paint Captain Jardyce too harshly. She was a good captain."

"I will not try to assign blame to Jardyce," Aquino said. "I will emphasize that she was worried about the squonks, or rather about the unanswered questions on Janus Five. I wasn't able to find the answers we needed in time to prevent the deaths."

"Could anyone have found those answers in time for that?"

"No one did," Aquino said.

"Maybe no one could have," Captain Lopez said. "The critical thing, for everyone on *Darwin*, was that you found the answers we needed before it was too late."

"I couldn't have done it alone. The most credit should go to the Marines." Was that ironic? That everyone aboard had been saved by six Marines that no one wanted?

"I won't forget that," Lopez promised.

Aquino wondered whether he should seek out KT. It was getting close to lunch time, though, so he headed that way, passing through the meal line with most of the servers smiling at him and urging him to take more. He sat down at the usual table, eating slowly.

"Hey!" Hakim Marvin sat down as well, a heaping plate of food before him. "How are you doing?"

"Okay," Aquino said. "Thanks for your help."

"I got to play hero," Hakim said with a dismissive wave of one hand. "You guys really did it, though. I guess you won't be hearing any questions about what you do for a while."

"Hopefully. Have you seen KT?"

"Not yet. She's probably still crashing. I heard what Dr. Trinh figured out about the squonks. Crazy, huh? Humans do some stupid things, but nothing that stupid."

"Maybe someday we'll find an intelligent alien species that is more rational than us or the Janusians," Aquino said.

Hakim surprised him by shaking his head. "I don't think so. Mind you, I'm just a chemistry guy. But I think at least a degree of irrationality is necessary the more intelligent any creature gets. Think about it. We know we're going to die. But we still take risks. We still do things. Why? We're going to be dead! We have kids, who we know will also die. Why? There's no rational reason to do anything or care about anything.

"You've got to be irrational when it comes to that, acting like you're immortal even though we all know we're not. Developing close relationships with other people, with pets, even though we know they're going to die, too, and how much that'll hurt." Hakim shrugged. "If that isn't crazy, what is? But how else do you cope with mortality?"

"I guess that's one reason we have faith," Aquino said. "To help stave off that fear, that knowledge. Though I see your point. Faith is unprovable, and I guess irrational in its own way."

"That's why we need doubt," Hakim said, pausing in his eating. "Too much faith is dangerous. Like the Janusians. You just know they had a lot of faith in what they knew, and too little doubt about the limits of their knowledge."

"But too much doubt is also a problem."

"Sure it is! Too much of anything is a problem!" Hakim said. "I'm a chemist. There are all kinds of things the human body needs to stay healthy and alive. And every one of those things will turn toxic or cause other problems if you ingest too much of them. Even water.

You can die from drinking too much water. So, sure, moderation in all things, like they say." He took another big bite.

"Except in eating?" Aquino asked, smiling.

"I'll moderate my eating tomorrow," Hakim said. "Today, I am making up for lost meals."

Aquino headed back to his room when he was done, thinking he should get to work on the report and the medal recommendations for all of the Marines and a dozen other things. Except his thoughts kept straying to KT. Was she rethinking things? Avoiding him?

That last question was answered when he saw KT standing by the door to his room, her expression solemn. Did that mean she'd rethought things?

"Um, hey," he said to KT.

KT nodded to him. "Hey. Can we go inside to talk?"

"Sure." Aquino led the way into his room, standing by the desk as KT went to stand by the bunk before facing him.

"Oz—" she started to say.

"It's okay."

That earned him an exasperated look. "What's okay?"

"I understand," he said. "People shouldn't be held to things said during a life-threatening crisis. You never promised me anything."

"What the hell are you talking about, Oz?"

"You… aren't you here to tell me the 'this was moving too fast and we need to put the brakes on but we can still be friends' thing?"

"That's what you think?" KT glared at him. "Listen to me, Oz. I just endured a very difficult few days. Do you know what really helped keep me going? It was knowing that you were in charge of dealing with those squonks. Watching you putting everything into saving the rest of us, trying again and again, refusing to give up. You're an idiot, do you know that, Oz?"

"I've been told that before," he said.

"Because anyone with any brains would have realized we faced an impossible situation. But not you! You kept trying. And I'm an idiot, too, because that's one of the reasons I love you!"

"Really?"

"You said you love me. Did you mean it, Oz?"

He could only stare at her, trying to find the right words. "I did mean it. I was thinking that surviving the events of the last several days was the greatest thing that had ever happened to me, was the greatest thing that would ever happen to me. And, because of you, I realized that I was very wrong about that. This is the greatest thing. You are. Yes, I love you."

She stared at him for several seconds before a smile finally formed. "Not bad, Oz. That wasn't bad at all. That's how you feel?"

"That's how I feel. You kept me going, too."

"What's going to happen to you, Oz?" KT asked. "Are they going to blame you for the deaths, or are they going to call you a hero? I'm with you, either way."

He shrugged. "Probably the hero thing, because we beat the squonks. Trying to pin the deaths on me would bring out too many things about how badly this unit was prepared to deal with a real emergency. The people in charge won't want that to happen. So, they'll pin medals on all of us and try to brush under the rug anything that could make them look bad."

"Will you stay on this ship?"

He smiled at her. "If I have any say in it. But I shouldn't get any chance to leave. It's a two-year assignment. And these Marines need me."

"These Marines? That's why you want to stay?"

"There's another reason. Are you going to be aboard for a while?"

"Probably another year. At least. I can ask for that to be extended. I think I will." KT canted her head. "Hey, that door over there."

"What about it?" Aquino asked, looking at the door to his room.

"Does it lock?"

"Yeah. Of course it does."

"Are you going to lock it?"

"Uh… yes. Yes, I am." He closed and locked the door, turning back to see KT sitting on the bunk, smiling and patting the spot next to her.

How about that? The worst possible assignment, and he had not only survived something that should have killed him and lot of other people, had not only saved the lives of the Marines depending on him, but it also led to the best thing he could have hoped for.

When people are counting on you, you have to do your job.

Maybe whoever or whatever ran the universe was setting him up for a bigger fall. But, at the moment, he felt as incredibly lucky as Private Smith surely would when he regained consciousness.

ACKNOWLEDGMENTS

I remain indebted to my agent, Joshua Bilmes, for his ever-inspired suggestions and assistance. Thanks also to Robert Chase, Carolyn Ives Gilman, Simcha Kuritzky, Michael LaViolette, Mary Thompson, Constance A. Warner, and the spirits of Aly Parsons and J.G. (Huck) Huckenpohler for their suggestions, comments and recommendations.